A Trace of Revenge | Lyle Howard

For Riva, the love of my life, this one is for you.

*And to my loyal readers who have
brought me this far, I love you all.*

A Trace of Revenge
Lyle Howard

Contact: lylehoward1@aol.com
ISBN 9781726723442

A TRACE OF REVENGE

LYLE HOWARD

Our destiny rules over us, even when we are not yet aware of it...

- Friedrich Nietzsche

Psychometry *noun*

psy·chom·e·try | \ sī-ˈkä-mə-trē \

Definition of *psychometry*

1   : The ability or art of divining information about people or events associated with an object solely by touching or being near to it.

PROLOGUE

Coral Gables, Florida
10:45 P.M.

Nearly four hours had crept by, and Anthony Magnetti was getting antsy. Waiting was always the hardest part. He had passed the time with a leisurely dinner of tuna steak and hash browns, but the restaurant had been nearly empty at that late hour, and his meal had only taken forty-five minutes to consume. The waitress had been flirtatious, annoyingly so, continually questioning him as to why someone who was so good looking would be dining alone. Ordinarily, he would have seized the opportunity to charm her and leave her derriere imprint on his hotel sheets, but tonight he was preoccupied, and the waitress, much to her disappointment, would have to settle for a large tip instead.

It was late, but he had another hour to kill. He could have gone back to his room, but that might have relaxed him too much. The mere sight of a comfortable bed after a full meal and with the sound of the heavy rain pounding on the hotel window would have been disastrous. He was in a rental car, and the tank was full, so he decided to drive.

He hadn't gone far before he pulled into a deserted parking lot beside a supermarket. The car screeched to a stop, the wheels begging for more traction on the rain-soaked asphalt. Flipping on the Porsche's interior lamp, Magnetti skimmed through some of the information the rental agency had given him. He read the brief paragraph describing this little suburb of Coral Gables that was situated just west of the city of Miami. Folding the pamphlet closed, he smiled, finding something he thought might pass some more time. If the directions were correct, he would head south toward US 1 and pass right by the University of Miami campus.

Out of a sense of nostalgia more than anything else, he turned in to the private college and drove past a few of the fraternity houses on San Amaro Drive, decked out in the school colors of orange and green. A few were already decorated with their holiday displays. A handful of Kappa Delta Epsilon brothers stood under the awning of their patio and waved admiringly with their upraised beer cans as the Porsche glided past them in the downpour. The sight of the students took Magnetti back to his own college days in New Jersey. What a strong baseball team the Miami Hurricanes always managed to field! In his senior year at Seton Hall, he remembered going three for four against the Canes and still losing the game in twelve innings. It was funny, the things that stuck in the mind.

As he drove the campus perimeter, he saw the infamous Mark Light Baseball Stadium looming darkly through the rain off to his left. If it had been any other night, he might have stopped and taken a piss on their field, just for old time's sake. If he hadn't been in Miami for another reason, he probably would have stopped off for a couple of frosty beers and then spray-painted the home team dugout in Seton Hall colors with all the delight of his lost youth.

But with thirty minutes to go, he turned onto US 1 heading north, leaving the contemptible campus to fade away in his rearview mirror. Half an hour would give him plenty of time to spare. Crooning a heartfelt rendition of Born to Run along with the radio, he turned right off US 1 and quickly found Old Cutler Road, which wound its way through the densely thicketed streets of Coconut Grove. The rain still showed no signs of slackening, especially through the thick canopy of trees that made the narrow old roadway feel almost claustrophobic. Traffic was light at this time of the morning, and according to the GPS, his final destination lay less than fifteen minutes due south.

As was his usual procedure upon arriving at his destination, he drove around the neighborhood over and over again until he felt like he had lived there his entire life. No chance of that though; the manicured lawns of Gables by the Sea were a far cry from the low-rent housing sandlots he had grown up in on the Jersey shore. Tree-lined and usually serene, these lush avenues had taken on a sinister pall as the thundershowers made the streetlights seem to glow with an eerie incandescence. Across the facades of these million-dollar homes, ornately manicured hedges and bushes cast menacing shadows that danced ominously over their protective walls.

He didn't need to recheck his watch to know that he was on schedule. Although he was always primed and ready for action, he preferred to wait for a break in the weather. Another vehicle cruised by the Porsche as it remained parked between two other cars, down the street from the Walker's house, to avoid any suspicion. The passing vehicle sprayed a sheet of water onto the hood and windshield of the sports car, but Magnetti, who reclined out of sight in the driver's seat, was oblivious to the incoming tidal wave, choosing instead to tread that transcendental line between sleep and consciousness.

Maybe he should read the dossier one more time, the cautious part of him whispered in the back of his mind. Like a "stay-put" signal from a third base coach, he shrugged off the advice. There was no need to read. He had committed all of the critical information to memory. He could picture their faces like they were his own family. He knew more about them than they knew themselves. To prove himself right, he ran down the dossiers in his mind...

PRIMARY OBJECTIVE: *(This was hand-stamped in bold letters)*

Name: Franklin Irwin Walker

Born: November 30, 1965, in St. Petersburg, Florida

(Well, happy birthday to you, Mr. Walker!)

Attended College: Florida State University

Graduated: 1985.

Degree: Finance

Past Employment: Commodities Broker 1987-2001 Smith, Grayson, and Fitch.

Current Employer: Mason International 2002-Present. Started 2002 in acquisitions. Transferred to Finance and Accounting Department in June of 2004. Named Department head in July 2005. Promoted to Vice-President of Finance in March of this year.

In his mind, he flipped the page to the attached photo and studied his quarry's face before continuing...

SECONDARY OBJECTIVE:
(This one spells b-o-n-u-s! Cha-ching!)

Marital Status: Married August 30, 1990, to Elizabeth Hartnett-Walker

NOT A FACTOR:

Children: One child. Matthew Barton Walker. Born March 15, 1996. Attends The Whitehall Academy, a private boarding school outside of Orlando.

(What more was there to know? The kid was away until December, so what was the worry? The house had an antiquated alarm system from the sixties that had never been updated. Snip and bypass a few wires on the box mounted outside of the home, and he was inside. A piece of cake! Ten minutes...tops!)

The high-beams of an approaching car flooded the interior of the Porsche, stirring Magnetti back into reality. The rain sounded like it was finally beginning to subside, so he raised himself to an upright position and wiped away the condensation that had accumulated on the inside of the windshield from his steady breathing. Everything was as he had hoped. The neighborhood was quiet except for the sloshing sounds of the occasional passing vehicle. Reaching over to the passenger seat, Magnetti grabbed for the brown paper bag that contained his ski mask. Pulling the dark knit cap over his head, he checked himself in the rear-view mirror, tucking away the last few stray curls that hung out in the back. White eyes stared back at him in the mirror like pearls on black velvet. With a tug on each finger, he tightened his leather gloves before opening the door and stepping out into the drizzle. *Showtime!*

The night air was crisp and moist, and through the mouth hole of his mask, a vaporous plume of smoke erupted with every breath Magnetti took. As he walked around to the rear of the car, he patted his back pocket to make sure he had the lock-picking set and wires for the alarm box. With silent precision, he quickly popped the trunk. A dim light partially illuminated the only item in the compartment, a black rectangular carrying case. Without a second thought, he reached up and shattered the bulb with one of his keys, making a mental note to report the light as broken to the rental agency. With all the care of a father handling his newborn child, he lovingly pulled the slim case towards him.

Every ballplayer, at one time or another in their career, has a favorite bat. Perhaps it is just a silly superstition, or maybe it is just the confidence that a particular piece of ash or maple can instill in a hitter when it feels just right in their hands. Some of these bats are well-made enough to last an entire career without ever splintering. These staffs of lore usually end up on display, exhibited as a part of their owner's memorabilia in Cooperstown, New York.

"Sweet Amy" was Anthony Magnetti's pride and joy. Thirty-nine ounces of raw thunder was how he described her. He called her "Sweet Amy," although no woman in his life had offered him such loyalty. She was nestled in her felt-lined box, tan, streaked by fine grain, lying like a calendar girl posing amid the soft red material.

"Sweet Amy" felt more than "just right" in Magnetti's hands; she was an extension of his arms and his soul. She was a slave to him—gratefully willing, and honor bound to do his bidding. Whether she was pooching a soft bunt that would trickle down the third base line and miraculously manage to stay fair, or when she was launching a four hundred and sixty-foot moon-shot into the waiting glove of some young fan behind the big green wall in a straight-away left field, "Sweet Amy" could do it all.

Tonight, he would call on her once more.

11:45 P.M.

The hibiscus hedges that lined the street offered him full camouflage as he worked his way down the block. Moving covertly but with a determined gait, Magnetti covered the quarter mile to the wrought iron gate that barricaded the Walkers' driveway in less than five minutes. A control box was positioned to the left side of the entrance, low enough that the driver of a vehicle could reach through their window and punch in the correct four numbers. From memory, Magnetti keyed in 1-1-3-0, and the light on the box flickered from red to green. *Didn't anyone ever use a code besides their birth date?* With all the speed of a tired plow horse, the gate opened, allowing Magnetti to sprint the last hundred yards up to the house. In less than two minutes, the alarm had been disabled.

The Walker residence was 11,500 square feet of creature comfort. It sat on a three-acre crest of land that leveled off behind the house to where the property line met Biscayne Bay. Post-modern in architecture, the concrete and glass-bricked edifice was an impressive landmark for the curious onlookers who periodically cruised by on their boats. During better weather conditions, it had been photographed for countless magazines and television shows; but now, in the early morning drizzle, the house stood gray and somber, water dripping from the rain gutters, puddles gathering in great pools on the front lawn.

Magnetti knew the floor plan as though it were his own home. There were fifteen total rooms. *Well, except for the fourteen extra rooms, it might have been.* The estate included five bedrooms, three bathrooms, one den, a sewing room, dining room, living room, kitchen, billiards room, and, of course, a study. *Who doesn't need a special place just to study in?* No live-in servants to account for, and only one sentry supplied by a security company who made rounds through the neighborhood every two hours like clockwork.

With Sweet Amy propped over his shoulder like he was waiting on deck, Magnetti pulled out a pass card and slipped it into the electronic lock in the front door. With a barely audible click, the deadbolt slid open. Silently, he slipped inside, holding his finger over the bolt so it would shut without that incriminating sound. Seconds later, he was standing in the foyer of the majestic home, marveling at his exquisite surroundings. Cathedral ceilings, teakwood floors... he wondered how many seasons he would have to play to afford this kind of place. *A wistful dream that assumed he ever possessed the discretion to bank away part of his salary.*

Even bathed in the pale glow that filtered in through the skylights, Magnetti could discern fine art when he saw it. He figured that just one of the paintings that hung on the walls, or one of the sculptures that graced the living area, could have easily paid his mortgage for three years. You didn't have to be some snooty art maven to tell that these were the genuine goods, not some reproduced lithographs or ceramic counterfeits. Just one of these pieces would have probably satisfied even the most discriminating of collectors.

Pulling a penlight out of his pocket, he made his way across the living room. Pausing for a brief moment, his eyes narrowed with speculation. He wondered if, in the aftermath, anyone would even notice if one of the smaller pieces had somehow vanished from the inventory. As he silently moved across the house, he shook off the wishful thinking like a bad sign from his third base coach, tapping the business-end of Sweet Amy against the side of his head for even letting himself entertain such a preposterous notion. He had to stay focused; fantasies of his own dingy pad enhanced by one of these exquisite objects d'art were not the reason he was here....

12:15 A.M.

Matthew Walker had dreams like any other nine-year-old boy. In the sanctuary of his own darkened bedroom, his eyelids fluttered as he shifted the pillow under his head. In the shallows of his restless sleep, a blur of festive colors filled his mind's eye. Streamers and balloons, confetti and horns; all the things that would make a birthday party seem so wondrous to a young child.

Even though the bed he tossed and turned on was fashioned after an Indy race car, there would be no dreams of taking the checkered flag this evening. Tonight, all of his thoughts were caught up in the excitement of his father's upcoming birthday celebration.

It was strictly to be a family affair, organized by his mother and attended only by the immediate family and a few of their closest friends. His father wasn't aware that he had flown in a day early for the party; his bedtime was long before his father came home from the office. His mother wanted it to be a surprise. His dad tended to work long hours and travel a lot, but when his father woke up in the morning and saw Matthew, it would be his best birthday gift ever!

His mother had it all planned out. She'd phoned the school administrators telling them that there had been a death in the family, having tipped Matthew off to her scheme beforehand. The school was pretty strict about allowing kids to leave right before midterm exams, and you needed a perfect excuse. Although he tried to look sad as per her instructions, he never was a terrific liar. In retrospect, he probably shouldn't have waved and giggled back at the Dean of Boys who'd suspiciously watched Matthew scurry down the boarding ramp that lead to his waiting flight.

But every silver lining has a cloud, and for Matthew, it was leaving his friends and classmates back at the Whitehall Academy. Even though he knew it would only be for the weekend, he would still pine for Hope Jannick. Over the past few months, Matthew had suddenly grown very popular with the girls, and although he wouldn't admit it—even if you gave him an Indian burn to his wrists—he kind of enjoyed all the attention. It might have been his tight blonde curls or his emerald green eyes that were unexpectedly stimulating the blossoming hormones of the opposite sex, but it wasn't like that with Hope. He just cared about her more than the rest of the girls. Maybe it was because he had known her the longest, since their fathers both worked for the same company. Whatever the reason was, he just knew he *liked* her better, and that was all he would ever say about that.

Matthew rolled onto his side in a fruitless effort to get comfortable. Nothing seemed to be working. This mattress was much softer than the one he had grown accustomed to at school, and it felt all squishy beneath his legs. He rolled over to the other side, facing the entrance to his room, his tired eyes little more than protesting slits through which he could just make out the locked door across the expanse of his pitch-black room. In what his mother always referred to as his over-active imagination in high gear, he thought he glimpsed a flash of soft yellow light sweep past the crack beneath his door. With his heart thumping so loud he could almost hear it, his eyes snapped shut. And then, slowly, apprehensively, he opened them again, only to find that the ghostly light had vanished as quickly as it had appeared. Taking a deep breath, he scolded himself for acting like such a baby.

Ghosts and robbers, how childish could he be? He was nine

years old! There was no fire-breathing dragon out there patrolling the hallway! No masked killer hiding beneath the stairs! He was nine years old, he kept telling himself. His father always referred to Matthew as his "little man," and there was no reason to doubt him now. He was nine years old, and that was too old to be terrified by such silliness!

Matthew lifted himself onto his elbows, trying to focus on the Florida Marlins clock that hung on the wall across the room over his writing desk. As his eyes struggled to adjust to the pitch darkness, the sad truth revealed itself. There were seven more, long, solitary hours to go until Spiderman would be spinning his cartoon webs across their big screen television downstairs. Still too immature to put this quality time to constructive use, Matthew just laid there in the morbid stillness of his room, listening to the rain spatter against his window, trying futilely to keep his mind from straying into that haunted place where the monsters roamed free.

For a nine-year-old, lying in a quiet bedroom produces much the same anxiety that sitting in a doctor's waiting room does for an adult. You'd rather be anywhere else but there. Maybe a glass of milk might do the trick, Matthew thought. After all, he was far too old to go climbing into bed with his parents, he assured himself. Yeah, a trip downstairs to the kitchen might be just the ticket. Maybe, if he could discover where his mother had hidden them, he could sneak a few of the chocolate chip cookies she had baked for the party. Milk and cookies! Boy, he could never get that after midnight back at Whitehall! He licked his lips with the wicked anticipation of a child who knew he was up to no good. Matthew realized he would be disobeying his mother's instructions, but it was the middle of the night, and they were fast asleep across the house in their bedroom. It was too late for second thoughts about the monsters in the hallway, and his mouth was already starting to salivate. It would be like a game of spy with the cookies as the goal and not getting caught by the enemy as the object of the mission.

Throwing his legs over the edge of the bed, he wiped the sleep from the corners of his eyes. Not wanting to push his luck, just in case there might be some truth to his fears, he sat for a moment and reached both arms toward the ceiling, surprised to hear the young bones in his shoulders express their objection. As his eyes adjusted to the darkness, he studied the familiar sports posters that covered nearly every square inch of wall space. Seeing all of his favorite football and baseball heroes frozen in action seemed to help allay his anxiety. His mother was always threatening to redecorate, but suddenly, he was happy she had never gotten around to it.

He was stepping over his opened duffel bag when he thought he heard a noise. He stood still, cocked his head to one side and listened. Visions of chocolate chip cookies that were as big as his fist suddenly crumbled into thin air. If it was his father, it was game over, and his mother would kill him for blowing their secret.

The wood floor was cold beneath his feet, so he reached into his bag and felt around for a pair of socks. He loved the way socks allowed him to slide around on the freshly sealed surface. Sometimes, when his over-protective mother wasn't there to see him, he would run full tilt across the house and down the long hallway that lead to his parent's bedroom, then hit the brakes and slide the last twenty feet. It was the closest thing to surfing the Banzai Pipeline for a child with a vivid imagination.

Sitting cross-legged on the floor next to his suitcase, Matthew tugged his athletic socks up around his ankles and pulled his pajama legs down over them. There was still no sign of that eerie light creeping in beneath his door, but he was confident he had just heard the faint creaking of floorboards coming from the hallway across the house.

An inquisitive look fell over Matthew's face as his ears zeroed in on the suspicious sound. The thought of an intruder never crossed his mind, since the alarm system his parents had installed was so elaborate. He couldn't even begin to count how many times he had tripped the system by accidentally knocking a glass of water off his nightstand. It was that sensitive.

There it was again...

And now, the unmistakable sound of a door squeaking on its hinge. The noise was distant but instantly identifiable to him. His parent's bedroom door was being opened like it was stuck in the mud...and then closed at the same sluggish pace.

Matthew stood transfixed in the impenetrable darkness of his room with his young hand wrapped around the doorknob. He listened for the footsteps that would surely have to follow...but they never came.

Putting one hand up to the seam between the door and its frame, Matthew cracked the door cautiously just in case it was his mother coming to check on him. The door was opened just enough to allow him a thin sliver of viewing space. The hallway was better illuminated than his bedroom, the walls shaded a soft gray color by the dim light pouring in through the overhead skylights.

From his room, he had a clear view of the house, but the living room was empty! How could that be? He was positive he had just heard their bedroom door open and close! Where did they disappear to? They must have come out. Had one of them changed their minds and decided to go back to bed?

Or worse... what if a monster had slipped inside their room? It could be in there with them right now!

Don't think like that! You're nine years old! Act like it!

What if it was standing at the foot of their bed? Its hideous fangs and razor-sharp talons dripping with blood! Its orange eyes on fire with vicious intensity! What if it was going to kill them while they slept? Then it would probably eat them both, leaving nothing on their sheets but guts and bones!

Suddenly, Matthew felt like he had to pee, but he had to fight the urge. He didn't dare leave the safe haven of his bedroom!

A nervous sweat ran down the boy's back, soaking his Miami

Heat pajama top. With the side of his hand, the youngster wiped his parched and pasty lips. What if the monster was saving him for dessert? It was common knowledge that creatures always kept the little boys and girls for last, using them to wash down the main course! Shivering with fright and with his knees squeezed tightly together to hold back the flood, Matthew continued to wait...and watch...and listen...

A cloud drifted across the night sky, throwing the living room into complete darkness. The seconds crawled by like hours. To a small boy caught up in his own world of macabre images, every branch that brushed against a windowpane was another creature that wanted in. Every tire that splashed through a pothole was the footfall of some prehistoric animal that hadn't eaten since the Ice Age. Every spark of lightning that momentarily lit the house, and each clap of thunder that shook the roof, took on ever more danger in the boy's young mind. Then he heard it...

It was loud and fast. A muffled noise coming from across the house! There was no denying it this time. There was definitely a monster in there!

Something inside told him to hide. It said, *Find a corner in your closet and stay there until the morning!* But that wasn't what his father's "little man" would do. What if he called the police? The inner voice affirmed his fear that they'd never get here in time. Now it warned him to *run*, but if he did, there would be no one else to save his parents! He had to help them!

Leaving the door still cracked, Matthew felt along his bedroom wall until he reached his desk. His small hands groped around in the darkness until he found what he was looking for. The pencil cup next to the stapler would contain everything Matt would need to defend his mother and father from those things that went bump in the night. He had sharpened pencils, *(they were made of wood, just in case this was some kind of vampire)* and a pair of scissors *(even if they **were** safety scissors, they still might be able to do some damage* *to soft tissue).*

Matthew grabbed a handful of pencils in one hand and took the scissors in the other, holding the shears safely by the blades just like his mother had always shown him. The last thing he wanted to do was to accidentally poke his own eye out.

This was a moment Matthew was sure he would remember for the rest of his life. From somewhere deep within his youthful spirit, he had somehow managed to summon up all the courage and strength of a young King Arthur. The pencil cup had been his mystical stone, the scissors his Excalibur. Chest heaving and confidence rallied, he was ready to slay the dragon!

Having no hands free, Matthew wedged his left foot into the crack and pried open his bedroom door. As he stood framed by the portal armed to the hilt, his eyes were fixed down the staircase into what now seemed like a massive expanse of living area leading to the corridor and his parents' bedroom. With his eyes tearing up in terror, every shadow that flashed across the floor, each dark silhouette that flickered up the walls, chipped away at his make imaginary fortitude. He swallowed hard, his hands gripping tighter around his weapons. Take it one step at a time, he cautioned himself...

Down each stair he descended, one stride at a time, each foot barely making a sound. A bolt of lightning seemed to hit somewhere in the backyard, illuminating the living room for a split second, its dark ambiance suddenly aglow in the bright white light.

Halfway into the living room, as he stood next to his father's favorite recliner, he heard it—a shriek so blood-curdling in its tenor that his bladder was terrified into release. A scream so shrill in its urgency, that it made the pencils clatter to the floor. Matthew Walker stood frozen in place, trembling, protected only by a pair of scissors that, even when new, weren't capable of cutting through more than one piece of construction paper at a time.

It was his mother! The plaintive wail came twice more before it was abruptly cut off mid-scream. Safety scissors upraised, stocking feet begging for traction, Matthew raced for his parents' bedroom door.

He yanked open the door...

He was right! The monster was there, standing on the other side of his parents' bed! Backlit against the meager light that filtered into their bedroom through the window curtains, the ogre seemed to have no specific profile. It was a common shape, and it was holding something over its head...what was that? He couldn't make it out.

The monster gradually turned his head in the boy's direction. His worst nightmare was coming true...it had no face! There was nothing above its neck, but a pair of bright white eyes that burned with an incendiary fury that Matthew knew couldn't be human!

Out of the merciless night sky, a bolt of lightning followed by a deafening clap of thunder shook the house. Illuminated by the momentary brightness, Matthew could see that it was a baseball bat that the creature held, and it was dripping with a dark liquid and some unnamable stuff that dripped off it in grisly-looking chunks.

He had to warn his parents!

When the boy turned his attention to the head of the bed, he realized that he was too late! What he had feared most in his fantasies had somehow become a gruesome reality. In his impressionable young mind, the "little man's" cowardly procrastination had cost his parents their lives.

Blood was everywhere! It clung to the wall like an abstract painting, crimson rivulets splattered outward across the stucco. The headboard was streaked with gore, patches of scalp, and clumps of hair that hung off the elaborate piece of furniture like air plants stuck to a piece of driftwood. There was nothing left of their skulls; they were unrecognizable. Their ears protruded from the mush at odd angles, like broken wings. Across most of their comforter covers, a nauseating red stain was already starting to spread and turn brown.

The monster turned his gaze to Matthew, and for an interminable instant, they just stared at each other, both caught off guard by each other's unexpected presence in the room. It was an awkward situation that might have almost looked comedic had there been a live studio audience to witness it. The creature was stunned, the boy was petrified, and neither seemed to be sure of their next move. But that hesitation didn't last long...

The crazed beast charged around the foot of the bed, grunting like a rogue elephant, his guttural outburst muffled by his mask. The youngster reacted out of unbridled hysteria and with a rush of adrenaline pumping through his veins. Without warning, the wooden cudgel came down in a sweeping arc that narrowly missed the back of Matthew's head as he turned to run.

12:30 A.M.

The boy wasn't supposed to be home, Magnetti snarled to himself! Someone was going to have the shit kicked out of them for screwing this up! Killing a child wasn't on his bucket list, but young or old, male or female...there were two rules he always lived by: Never leave men on base, and never leave any witnesses!

Matthew timed his slide perfectly, reaching out with his right hand and grabbing onto the hallway wall for support without losing a step. The storm outside had returned with a vengeance, pelting the windows and skylights with a shroud of rain so dense that it blocked out any chance of outdoor light illuminating the interior of the house. This gave Matthew the home-field advantage of knowing the exact position of each stick of furniture and every piece of artwork located in the living room. Fifty steps to the front door, and Matthew knew each one of them by heart.

But Anthony Magnetti was also in excellent physical condition. He was in the well-toned shape that only an entire 162 game season of running down fly balls could provide. He knew where the boy was heading, and there was no way in hell he was going to let him reach the door. He had no time to consider the heinous task that lay ahead for him; he was operating on pure gut instinct.

Matthew weaved his way through the minefield of bulky furniture, just as another quake of thunder rocked the house. The youngster's socks may have served their purpose while skidding for fun across a freshly waxed floor, but as for supplying him the needed traction to escape the clutches of a rampaging monster, they were fatally inadequate. He had just reached the couch when, even over the racket of the pounding rain, he could hear the steady breathing of the faceless creature as it closed in for the kill. Matthew began to dodge as he ran, running between the tables and chairs, trying to make himself as poor a target for the monster as possible. He could actually feel the hair on the back of his head rustle in the draft caused by each errant roundhouse swing of the bat.

The living room was turned into an obstacle course, with Magnetti repeatedly blocking any means of Matthew's escape. The boy was cagey and quick, but the murderer was just as smart, mimicking every juke, avoiding every object the youngster hurled in his direction. Through the living room and into the kitchen Matthew ran without the time or notion to throw on a light switch. Every time he thought he had managed to gain some ground, the creature would take longer strides and close the gap. A distance of fewer than four feet now separated the two, and Matthew could sense that the monster was about to swoop in and finish him. As they ran past the eating nook, a blinding flash of lightning lit up the kitchen momentarily stunning Magnetti. But the boy never faltered, sprinting past the refrigerator with the dazed creature in hot pursuit. Unaware of where the idea came from, but frightfully aware that the monster was right behind him, Matthew reached up and threw open the freezer door catching the raging ghoul square in the face. The freezer door slammed shut and then popped open again on its hinges, flooding half of the room with harsh white light. Magnetti screamed in agony as his nose was cleanly broken beneath his mask.

Sweet Amy clattered to the tiled floor as the killer ripped the ski mask off his head. Blood streamed from both his nostrils. He tried to use the knit cap to blot the gushing wound, but the crimson flood was uncontrollable.

Matthew never stopped running, and the guiding voice in his head was back again, urging him that he had a chance to make it now, pushing him to run faster than he had ever run before—but there is only one motivation stronger than a nine-year-old's fear, and that is his curiosity...

His legs stopped pumping...

His body turned back toward the light...

His eyes discovered the truth...

This wasn't some hideous demon from another dimension, it was just an ordinary man! A man whose face, even half-hidden in the shadows, was still visible. A man whose countenance would be the last memory chiseled into the granite of young Matthew's brain. Magnetti bent over and picked up Sweet Amy, still holding the knit cap firmly against his mangled face. "You broke my nose, kid!" He grunted.

Matthew's expression turned dour. "You killed my parents!"

The enraged killer pointed the business end of the bat in the boy's direction. "And I promise they died quicker than you're gonna!"

Matthew refused to be intimidated. Summoning up all the courage he could muster, he glared steely-eyed at Magnetti...then stuck out his tongue and ran!

Matthew bolted out of the kitchen and turned the corner. With fifty feet to the foyer, there was nothing between him and deliverance but the front door. His little heart pounded in his chest as he raced for freedom. Twenty more feet and he would be outside running across the lawn and screaming for help as loud as he could!

Magnetti was given the steal sign. With the imaginary crowd standing on its feet, the pitch was thrown, and he darted for a second... keep your head low, focus on the bag...the throw from home would be close, but his head first slide would make him a hero...

The killer dove the length of the foyer, gliding across the slick floor like it was Georgia red clay, catching the door just as the boy was opening it. The brute force of his shoulder caught the massive oak door flush, smashing it closed with a ground-shaking "*boom*" that would have made the storm clouds outside envious.

"You're not goin' anywhere, kid," Magnetti sniffled, as he rolled to his feet and tried futilely to blot his bloody nose on his sleeve, "'cept the morgue!"

Then Matthew did something unexpected...the last thing the killer would have ever anticipated... he smiled!

Magnetti just stood there, his mind suddenly void of any quick witticisms. Even though this job had gone sideways, this little guy had moxie. He actually admired that. Now he would have to stay and clean up all of his own blood before he could leave. *Can you believe it...a freakin' nine-year-old kid is going to blow this thing?*

Both his hands caressed the tape around Sweet Amy's handle. The kid knew what he had coming, and he was willing to take it like a man.

The assassin reared back with the bat, and that's when Matthew made his move.

Before Magnetti could react, the boy reached up to the security control panel next to the door and pressed the blue panic button... but nothing happened! Matthew jabbed at it twice more and still no alarm.

The bat stopped short and came to rest on Magnetti's shoulder. "Sorry kid," he apologized, "your folks should have invested in a newer system. Nice try though."

With freedom just out of his grasp, young Matthew Walker closed his eyes, hung his head, and began to sob as Sweet Amy, at long last, finished her work. The sudden pain was all-consuming. In the split-second that followed, Matthew thought he saw fragments of his skull fly past his eyes, as the bat connected with the back of his head. In that last instant of awareness, he heard his own scream choked off in his throat, like it was all taking place in a nightmare. He screamed so loud, in fact, that his prepubescent vocal chords actually gave out.

Matthew staggered for a moment and then stumbled backward, colliding against the foyer wall, a deep red splotch discoloring the floral wallpaper behind his head. His limp body slid down the wall in degrees, leaving a repulsive crimson smear that traced his collapse.

Then there was nothing...

No sight...

No sound...

And the darkness enveloped him.

1

Intensive Care Unit
Children's Memorial Hospital

The waiting room was an overcrowded gathering area for total strangers who suddenly found themselves thrown together under the most agonizing of circumstances. A cheerless place, even though the walls were covered with smiling cartoon figures that a child of any age would recognize. It was a place of nightmares, where the mere appearance of anyone in the doorway wearing hospital scrubs could cause the whole group to hold their breath in tremulous anticipation. It was hard to believe that so much anguish could be packed into such a confined space.

Each family member or friend who sat here on pins and needles had a loved one whose fragile life hung in the balance behind the two hissing metal doors that lead to the operating suites. Each caring smile they exchanged, and every sympathetic nod that was reciprocated, camouflaged the real dread and anxiety of knowing that, sooner or later, it would be their own turn to be on the opposite side of those sinister silver doors.

Magazines dating back to the dawn of man were strewn across the red plastic table in the center of the tiny room. Toy building blocks were scattered on the carpeting, itself worn threadbare in places, no doubt from the miles of overwrought pacing it had to endure. The television in the corner appeared to work, but the volume was kept so low that it was nearly impossible to hear the morning newscast. The complimentary coffee was cold, and only the bravest of souls dared to dip into the jar of powdered creamer that had been sitting open all night. Against the far wall, a young man waiting on word of his son's bypass surgery had succumbed to the strain and had fallen asleep with the sports section spread across his chest. Periodically, the fearful moment would arrive when an attending physician would enter the waiting room and, in a God-like manner, survey the occupants as though they were looking for some family resemblance before calling out the patient's name. It was an arrogant practice that only served to augment a doctor's already inflated ego and demean the families who were not called.

It was a harrowing experience to watch an entire family stand up in unison and step out into the hallway for their dreaded consultation. They would shuffle out of the room, clutching hands, slump-shouldered, as though walking their last mile, while the families left behind were compelled to crane their necks like nosey eavesdroppers, watching anxiously through the window for the telltale reaction which was sure to follow. This time around, the tidings were good, and even the most hardened member of the Gonzalez family—a brawny longshoreman who had worked the loading cranes at the Port of Miami for over twenty-two years— broke down with uncontrollable tears of happiness upon hearing the good news of his daughter's imminent recovery.

As David and Barbara Walker sat huddled together near the television, they were finding it hard to imagine the relief and exhilaration that the Gonzalez clan was experiencing. The elderly couple smiled halfheartedly and squeezed each other's hands at the family's victory over the Grim Reaper, but it was a feeble attempt at a false front. Deep inside, they had both been as mortally wounded as their son and daughter-in-law. It was never right when any parent outlived their offspring, and now, the last fragile link the elder Walkers held to their own son was battling for his life behind those ominous steel doors.

Matthew's grandparents had been notified too late to see the boy before he had been raced into surgery, and that was a good thing. Jacksonville was usually six hours away, but Matthew's grandparents made the trip in four, with Barbara Walker clutching the dashboard in terror the entire way. When grilled by the grandfather in the emergency room, the trauma specialist had tried to sound as upbeat as possible about Matthew's prognosis, but the pensive look on the Doctor's face contradicted his words. One of the attending paramedics would later confide in the old man that he thought his team had pulled off a minor miracle just keeping his grandson breathing while racing the twenty miles to the hospital.

For Barbara Walker, the not knowing was the hardest part. It had been nearly seven hours since anyone had come into the waiting room with an update for them. All they had been told was that the head of Neurosurgery, a Doctor Roy Soto, had been called in, and that the trauma to Matthew's head was extensive. That morsel of news seemed like it had trickled in years ago, and at the time, that was all anyone would tell them.

"Do you want a mint?" she asked, elbowing her husband as she searched her handbag.

Dave Walker ran his fingers through his bushy head of unkempt gray hair. The craggy lines that years of toiling in the Florida sun had chiseled into his face had become more profound over the last eight hours. His wife of forty-two years lovingly called them his "laugh lines" because, from a distance, they always seemed to broaden his sincere smile. But this morning, in the pale fluorescent light of the Intensive Care waiting room, they served to do nothing more than to deepen his frown.

Matthew's grandfather held open his palm. "As long as it's not your last one."

She pinched a mint off the top of the roll and rested her weary head on his sturdy shoulder. "I've got plenty," she whispered.

He patted her hand gently. For a venerable old sports fisherman like Dave Walker, Barbara had been the catch of a lifetime. He seriously doubted that anyone else could have put up with his shenanigans for as long as she had, and never once complained. She retaliated, but never complained. Any man who'd had to sit behind his desk wearing skivvies that were so starched they'd give his ass paper cuts could testify to her belief in quid pro quo.

Barbara Walker was sixty-two years young, and to hear her husband tell it, she was still the blue-eyed dream girl he had escorted to the senior prom. Slim-waisted and fair-skinned, she had taken up this Zumba fad two years ago, and much to his delight, it had put a gleam back in her eyes and a bounce into her step that he hadn't seen since the night their only grandson had been born. Now that sparkle was threatening to vanish again.

"What could be taking them so long in there?"

Dave Walker shifted his weight in the uncomfortable chair. "I'm sure they know what they're doing, Barb."

"I just know he's going to be alright."

The old man pursed his lips. "From your mouth to God's ears."

She forced a smile. "Amen."

Matthew's grandfather nodded his head. "Well, I hope your knack for predicting things correctly holds true again."

Barbara Walker stared blankly up at the ceiling. "You know, I sometimes wonder..."

"Wonder what?"

"Well, if I had the choice," she pondered, morosely, "Whether I'd want it to happen to me in my sleep, or drawn out like this."

Dave Walker knew his wife was thinking about her only son, and her pain was palpable. There would be no consoling her, and in her own time, when she was alone, most likely in the middle of the night, probably in the darkened den that they had converted from Frank's childhood bedroom, she would come to the understanding that her son and his wife were facing eternity together. And in a tidal wave of cleansing tears, she would come to grips with the inspirational reality of their fate. That was her way.

He too had valiantly tried to bury the gruesome death of his son and daughter-in-law into some dark pit in the back of his mind, but the grave was far too shallow, and he was failing miserably. He continued to tell himself that all he needed to do was to concentrate on the welfare of his grandson, and that would see him through. There would be plenty of time for mourning and remembrance, but for right now, he had to focus on the glimmer of hope that Matthew might need to overcome this ordeal.

"That's not the kind of thoughts you should be thinking about right now," he whispered. "We need to stay positive...for Matt."

She shrugged in his arms. "I know, but we've never discussed..."

He held his finger over her mouth. "Shh...I don't want to have that conversation now."

As Dave Walker tried to soothe his wife by rubbing the back of her neck, he was suddenly distracted by the bold black letters that flashed onto the television screen above his head. With the subtlety of a train wreck, the local newscast was interrupted by the graphic... **LATE BREAKING NEWS!** ...superimposed across the anchorwoman's face. It wasn't so much the size of the letters that captured the old man's attention as it was the live feed from the crime scene over the anchor's shoulder, which made him sit bolt upright in his chair.

They had set up shop outside of his son's house, the residence surrounded by yellow crime tape, the local reporter garbed in a neon-orange rain slicker. He was talking and pointing through the drizzle at the open front door, where a steady stream of official-looking people and police officers filed in and out of the house like it was between show times at the neighborhood Cineplex.

Walker nudged his wife. "Are you seeing this, Barb?"

Matthew Walker's grandmother blinked a few times trying to clear the haze that had formed over her tired eyes. "Can you tell what they are saying?"

The sound was turned so low it was barely audible. Dave Walker shot a cursory glance around the room, and seeing that no one else seemed to be paying attention, lifted himself out of his chair, raised the volume on the television, and stood with his face nearly touching the screen.

It was the tail end of the piece, and the reporter was summing up what the police knew to this point. *Nothing.* The word hung in the air like a bad odor. *"The details at this time are sketchy, but it looks like just another home invasion gone wrong. Two dead. One child remaining in critical condition, given little chance of making it through the day."* It was like being wide awake during a nightmare! This guy was talking about their Frank, Liz, and Matthew with the indifference of a stranger; finish this story and then just move on.

"Unfortunately, this sort of thing is becoming much more prevalent in South Florida; what is so unusual this time is that it happened in such a normally quiet and affluent section of town. This is Doug Nolan reporting for Eyewitness News from Gables by the Sea. Now back to the studio..."

Suddenly, David Walker didn't care if anyone was watching the television or not. With a disgusted twist of his wrist, he shut off the set. Barbara Walker patted the chair next to her. "Come, David. Sit back down."

But Matthew's grandfather didn't feel much like sitting. He'd been driving all morning. The worn grooves in the carpeting seemed to fit his feet just fine as he followed the tracks back and forth across the room. "They're making a spectacle out of our tragedy!"

"Please sit down, Dave. You're riling yourself up over something that we don't have any control over! It's what the media does."

"Why do they have to broadcast it for the whole damned world to see?"

"Because it's news, and maybe someone who sees it might be able to help."

Dave Walker jabbed his finger in his wife's direction. "They're a bunch of callous vultures!"

A sudden expectant hush fell over the entire room as an unfamiliar face appeared in the doorway.

"Excuse me," the Doctor announced, his voice just above a whisper. "The Walker family?"

Barbara Walker rose unsteadily to her feet and let her husband put his arm around her. "It's gonna be alright, Barb. I've got you."

Dr. Roy Soto looked much younger than what they were expecting, but the concern and compassion in his eyes helped to ease their anxiety. Still wearing his pale blue, sweat-soaked operating scrubs and paper boots, they studied the doctor as he came across the room to greet them. There was a reassuring confidence to Soto's stride that instantly lifted the old couple's spirits.

"Mr. and Mrs. Walker?" the surgeon asked, holding out his hand.

David Walker shook the outstretched arm like it was the handle on a well pump. "How's our grandson?"

The doctor wiped away a few errant strands of dark brown hair that were matted against his forehead. He could have easily taken the time to clean himself up, but there was no use in putting off the inevitable. He had been briefed on the case history and decided that the family had already been through enough.

The doctor nodded politely. "I'm very sorry for the loss of your son and daughter-in-law."

The couple nodded and sighed.

Soto looked around the room and, discovering that he was suddenly the center of attention, ushered the elderly couple out into the hallway. "Perhaps we should find somewhere a bit more private where we can discuss this."

The Walkers allowed the doctor to lead them to a vacant office down the corridor. It was only after David Walker examined one of the numerous diplomas and certificates that adorned the walls that he realized that this was, in fact, Soto's private office.

Barbara Walker took a seat in front of the Doctor's impressive mahogany desk, but David Walker chose to remain standing. "Talk to us, Doc. Is our grandson dead or alive?"

His wife noticeably flinched in her seat.

Soto ran his fingers through his hair. "Your grandson is a fighter. He's alive."

David Walker slapped his hand on the chair behind his wife's head. "Yes. Thank God. Thank you, doctor. Thank you so much!"

Soto leaned back in his chair and rubbed his eyes. "Well, the good news is, your grandson is quite a scrappy young lad, and although his recovery will be lengthy, I see every indication that he's going to make it."

Barbara Walker reached up to her left shoulder, grabbed her husband's hand, and kissed it. Her optimistic prediction had come to fruition.

For the first time in eight hours, David Walker let a faint smile crease his lips. "We owe you a debt we'll never be able to repay, doctor."

Soto winked kindly, knowing full well he had one more shoe to drop. "Yeah, well, I guess that's what insurance is for."

"So when can we see him?" Matthew's grandmother asked, excitedly.

The doctor reached over to the corner of his desk and pulled a transparent model of a human brain towards him. "There is one thing that you both need to understand..."

Barbara Walker could hear her husband's hand grip the fabric of the chair. It was quivering in perfect synch with her lower lip.

Soto, who was usually renowned for his polished bedside manner, could not find a tactful way of delivering the unwelcome diagnosis. As delicately as if he were actually performing surgery, the Doctor removed the posterior section of the clear skull and turned the model so the elderly couple could see the exposed part of the brain. "Matthew is not going to be the same young man that came into the operating room." *That didn't come out sounding the way he meant it to.* The doctor cleared his throat. "I'm sorry, let me amend that statement..."

Suddenly, David Walker needed to sit down.

"Your grandson will be the same by all outward physical appearances, but you've got to understand that he suffered an incredible amount of trauma to this area," he clarified, by pointing a pencil to a spot on the model. "Technology in this field has come amazingly far in the past ten years, and because of these advances, we've been able to run some preliminary tests on Matthew while he was still under the effects of the anesthesia. We can say with a high degree of confidence that he has sustained severe nerve damage at the base of his skull...here," he said, aiming the blunt tip at a specific section on the transparent replica.

The elderly couple locked hands, and it was Barbara Walker that was the first to speak. "What sort of nerve damage, Doctor? Is our grandson going to be paralyzed or something?"

Soto turned the model so that the lateral, or side, of the head was now visible. "What the tests tell us is that Matthew has sustained sensory damage...here."

"Sensory damage?" David Walker asked.

With his makeshift pointer, Soto traced a gaggle of nerves that ran from the base of the skull and spread to both ears. "I can think of no way of saying this tactfully, so I'm just going to come out and say it. We believe that your grandson has lost the ability to hear."

David Walker could feel his wife wilting in the chair next to him.

"As of now," Soto continued, "we're not sure of any other effects the blow to the head has caused. There is significant swelling that we expect to subside over the next few days. This is normal. But your grandson has suffered a sensory-neural loss, which simply means that there was damage to the sensors, or nerve fibers, which connect the inner ear to the hearing center in the brain. Since these nerve fibers are incredibly delicate and do not regenerate or repair themselves like other parts of the body, I'm afraid the extent of the damage is permanent."

"What about...another operation when the swelling goes down?" Barbara Walker stammered.

The Doctor shook his head regretfully. "I only wish we had that option, Mrs. Walker. Unfortunately, at the present time, surgery cannot correct the hearing loss. There would normally be options like a hearing aid or even a cochlear implant to regain some hearing loss, but in this case, the nerve damage is far too severe."

The office became as silent as a mausoleum, with both grandparents suddenly turning introspective, and the doctor sitting across from them, wondering how these two elderly people would care for a young child with whom they could no longer communicate normally. Soto waited patiently for the deluge of questions he would typically expect, but to his surprise, there were none. Perhaps they just needed some time alone. He hesitated as he got up to leave. "If you have any questions later, or need any advice," he said, picking one of his business cards out of the holder on the desk and sliding it in the Walkers' direction, "this is where you can reach me. Please don't hesitate; I'm only a phone call away, and I know specialists that might be able to help you. Again," he added, with a caring hand on each of their shoulders, "I'm very sorry for your loss, but your grandson needs you now more than ever. Please feel free to use my office for as long as you need."

"God bless you, Doctor," David Walker said, without looking up. "We'll manage just fine."

Soto paused in the doorway and turned back to say something, but caught himself. As he mournfully observed the old couple quietly hugging each other and rocking back and forth to comfort one another, he knew that their lives would never be the same again.

2

Dodge Island, Port of Miami

The headquarters of Mason Cruise Lines sat on a small man-made promontory at the eastern edge of Dodge Island, far from the bustling activity on the small chain of islands that had long ago become the Port of Miami. The eight-story triangular glass building pointed eastward toward the horizon, greeting the sunrise each morning. While huge cranes and noisy derricks loaded and unloaded container ships from every corner of the earth, passenger terminals busily filled and emptied their human cargo to and from some of the grandest ocean liners to ever cruise the world's mighty oceans.

The Port of Miami was rated as the largest passenger seaport in the world, so it was only fitting that the Mason Corporation would set up their headquarters there, though there were also additional offices in Jacksonville that were becoming a greater focus of the company as it expanded its fleet.

A self-made billionaire, Peter Mason came from a sketchy background, to say the least. His father was one of the infamous Cocaine Cowboys who, in the nineteen-seventies, made millions smuggling the white powder from Colombia into the United States through Everglades City, a small fishing village on the southern tip of the Florida Peninsula. His father had been caught and jailed like so many others, but not before stashing most of his illegal windfall in an offshore account in the Cayman Islands. His father was one of the few men who actually profited from those years of hell-raising and living with impunity. The old man eventually died in a Federal prison in upstate Florida in nineteen eighty-two, but not without leaving a safety deposit key for his son to receive on his eighteenth birthday.

Seemingly overnight, Peter Mason went from being a Marine Architecture student on a partial-tuition baseball scholarship at the University of North Florida to a cruise line magnate. He did it by staying under the radar just like his father had. In the early nineties, he purchased and renovated three retired cruise ships and operated them for overnight gambling junkets to the Bahamas. With the Bahamian Islands the shortest distance from Miami to legal gambling, business was lucrative. It was less than ten years before he was able to have the Norwegians build his first brand new ship, the Tempest. Now he owned a fleet of five hundred-ton ships, sailing out of Miami and ports in Europe, but that would never be enough for him. His aspirations were much higher. He wanted to expand. He wanted to create something newer, something different, something better. He wanted to combine both of his life's passions— and now he was about to.

There were only two offices on the eighth floor of the MCL building. The larger, triangular room was the conference room, massive in size and lit brilliantly by the morning sun. The other office, while still large by any standard, was Peter Mason's private office. Mason meticulously signed the contract on his desk, closed the manila folder, and took a deep breath. The day he had been waiting for had finally arrived, and he wasn't going to let this opportunity slip through his fingers again. He stood up and walked over to the full-length mirror on the western wall. He stood an even six feet tall, and although there was nothing exceptional about his looks, he'd managed to keep up his physique by working out daily and watching his caloric intake. He was a role model for his employee, never afraid to help load a piece of luggage while touring the dock or jump into a forklift to move a pallet of perishables aboard one of his ships. He was well-liked by his workers and staff, but more importantly, he was respected.

He stood straight in the mirror and pressed down the lapels on his gray jacket. He jiggled the knot in his maroon tie and ran both hands through his salt and pepper hair. He was ready...

The mood in the conference room was subdued as he entered the meeting. He wasn't expecting a twenty-one gun salute, but the tension in the room seemed palpable. Each of the sixteen seats at the oblong mahogany table was filled by his executive board. From lawyers to engineers, financial professionals to human resource specialists, each had their own area of expertise. Neither sex nor culture nor ethnicity mattered to Mason, as long as the best person for the job was sitting in one of those chairs.

Along each of the glass walls, which merged into a point at the far end of the massive room, stood a large pedestal—each containing a scale model of Mason's vision of the future. Each podium was set far enough away from the wall that you could walk around the model to admire the attention to detail. On the northern wall, a model of the *Hydra* sat under a glass box lit by small spotlights on each side. Nearly ten feet in length, the model pointed east, out toward the sea. She was a fantastic ship, still under construction, but almost complete. She was like no other ship to cruise the oceans. She was a hydrofoil about half the size of an average cruise ship. While other cruise lines were going larger, Mason was thinking smarter. His logic seemed worth the gamble. A faster, more luxurious vessel for those elite passengers who enjoyed being on the ocean, but didn't want to be there eternally; for those who enjoyed the first class amenities that a cruise ship offered, but for much less time. He was going to cater to those people who wanted to reach their destinations in a reasonable time, without the cramped confines and hassles of present-day air travel.

A hydrofoil is, by definition, a ship that doesn't travel in the water insomuch as it moves above the water. Nothing of this magnitude had ever been attempted, and many of the naysayers had warned him that the size and tonnage of the ship alone made the physics impossible…but they were wrong.

The *Hydra* was being built with a catamaran—a dual style hull. Two hulls, each buoyed by seven independent double-skinned inflated tubes that, once inflated upon departure, lifted the ship ten feet out of the water. The importance of this design was a priority for Mason. He'd had an entire team of designers work out the worst scenarios should one of these tubes rupture while the ship was at full speed. The initial trials met with disaster, with the models pinwheeling and flipping in the experimental test tank. It took almost two years to develop the technology for the double-skinned flotation tubes. Now, if a tube should rupture, it would be instantaneously ejected, and the inner tube would inflate in its place. Long nights and ingenious thinking had finally developed a system that worked.

The next hurdle in the development of the *Hydra* was how to lift a sixty-ton ship ten feet out of the water. This innovation took the design team years of sleepless nights. The resulting amalgam of concepts from his team culminated in what the staff had, for lack of a better name, called the fanbines. Two rows of three turbine driven fans, each twenty-five feet across, pumped out the equivalent of a category five hurricane in a downward force that literally boiled the water surrounding the ship and lifted it to the required height. Behind the ship, two more fanbines provided momentum and steering. While the average modern cruise ship could sail at a top speed of around twenty-five knots, the *Hydra* would do seventy-five without breaking a sweat.

Another advantage the *Hydra* would have over the competition was comfort and luxury. An ordinary cruise liner might hold three thousand passengers, and some of the larger ones even more. The *Hydra* was limited to one thousand passengers and crew, maximum. This enabled Mason to focus on relaxation, service, and safety. The mere fact that it traveled over ten-foot seas instead of plowing through it would relieve motion sickness by an estimated ninety percent—a factor that, in a recent survey, was the number one reason people hesitated to sail.

As he circled the model, the only thing missing was a last minute addition. He wanted a clear, enclosed glass walkway on both sides of the ship. Unlike a regular cruise ship, where passengers were able to stroll leisurely around the deck, the *Hydra* would be traveling so fast that it would turn a simple walk into a life-threatening event. Hence the enclosed walkways, where a person would be shielded from the wind, but could literally walk above the water.

As impressive as the replica of the *Hydra* was, it wasn't his favorite model in the room. His staff turned their heads in unison as he walked around the head of the table silently to gaze at his most beloved achievement: a miniature representation of The Mason Cruise Lines Ballpark.

This was his greatest dream. There was only one thing that transcended his love of the ocean, and that was his love of America's greatest pastime. During Major League Baseball's last expansion, he lost out to a guy that ran a garbage collection and videotape rental empire. That was a tough pill to swallow. If that wasn't bad enough, Mason watched as the Florida Marlins grew in popularity in his own backyard and won not one but two World Series titles. While he shared the city's pride in the team's success, this was unacceptable to him. Now he would be getting the chance to actually own a major league team. His plan to purchase one of the least successful current franchises was on track. He would build the new ballpark in Jacksonville. Obviously, Jacksonville wasn't his first choice to locate the new team, but the city had already proven it could provide a strong fan base with the National Football League's Jaguars.

Jacksonville also boasted Jaxport, one of the newest and busiest seaports in the United States. While he had no intention of moving his corporate headquarters to Northeastern Florida, Jacksonville being the largest city in the state in population and by area would prove a first-class home port for the *Hydra*.

Mason looked up from behind the model of the domed stadium to see his entire staff staring at him.

"Is there something in my teeth?" He chuckled.

It was only then that he acknowledged the second empty chair. "Where's Frank Walker?"

His staff looked at each other uncomfortably.

"Why isn't Walker here? The deadline for the stadium vote is today!"

David Jannick, the Vice-President of Marketing, pushed himself back from the table and stood up. With his fingertips pressed downward on the table, he was barely able to utter the words. "Frank Walker is dead, Peter."

Mason looked around the room incredulously and shook his head. "What do you mean he's dead? How…when?"

Jannick took a deep breath to regain his composure. He was very close friends with Frank Walker. Their kids even attended the same private school in Orlando. "Don't you listen to the news, Peter?" He asked with his eyes welling up.

"Not today I haven't. What happened? Why didn't someone notify me before this?

Jannick rubbed his forehead. He couldn't speak anymore.

Jane Rutledge, the Head of Human Resources, spoke up without leaving her chair. She was relatively new to the firm, but Frank Walker was a stand-up guy and had quickly befriended her and made her feel welcome. He didn't have an enemy in the world as far as she knew. "It was a home invasion."

"The house was being robbed?" Mason asked. "I've been to their house. The security system is state of the art. How is that even possible?"

Jannick sat back down and bowed his head. "His wife was killed too…lying beside him as they slept."

Peter Mason strolled to the head of the table and took his seat. For more than a minute he stared to his left at the empty chair. "Weren't they supposed to be celebrating his birthday this weekend?"

"This world has gone insane," Jannick muttered under his breath. "Frank was one of the good ones. He'd give you the shirt off his back."

Peter Mason drummed his fingers on the table. "Frank Walker was an invaluable asset for the Mason Cruise Line organization. We have to do everything necessary to make sure that his family is taken care of. He has children, doesn't he?"

Jane Rutledge spoke up. "They have a son. He was beaten and left for dead too. They say he is in critical condition, but he'll probably survive."

Peter Mason stared across the table at her. "Their son was home too? Didn't you say that he attended school with your daughter in Orlando, David?"

Jannick nodded. "He had come in for the birthday party. Frank didn't know. It was supposed to be a surprise. The poor kid was in the wrong place at the wrong time."

Peter Mason put his hands together as if in prayer. "This is horrible, two lives gone, one young child hanging on by a thread. David," he said, pointing across the table at Jannick. "You take the lead on this. Anything the family needs—medically, financially—you make it happen."

Jannick nodded. "Under the circumstances, I think we should postpone this meeting. I think I can speak for all of us when I say we need to each take the time to grieve in our own way and pay respects to the family. I believe Frank's parents have come to town to look after Matthew."

Mason let out a heavy sigh but then shook his head. "I don't mean to sound disrespectful or callous, but this vote needs to happen, and it needs to happen today—now. I too plan on paying my personal respects to the family, but this company is greater than any individual board member. We've been discussing the benefits and the drawbacks to the ballpark proposal ad nauseam. The City of Jacksonville is expecting an answer from me, so whether you feel I'm morbid, discourteous, or any other adjective you want to describe me with, this vote must be taken."

The fifteen executives at the table exchanged skeptical glances, hoping one would speak up. Ronald Kim, the Vice-President of Engineering and Development, took it upon himself to break the silence. Disrespect for the dead was unheard of in his culture. "How are we supposed to vote without the entire board present?" He asked. "Doesn't every department need to be represented?"

"We have a quorum," Mason snapped back. "Let's just do this, people. The sooner we vote, the sooner we can adjourn and pay our respects to the family."

Kim shook his head in disgust. Not only would they be demeaning Frank Walker's significance, but everyone sitting at this table knew that he would have cast the deciding vote against the project. More than once, he had argued against the expenditure of capital funds for something so entirely out of the realm of the company's comfort zone. He had made it crystal clear that he thought this enterprise would be a huge risk, considering it could take ten years or more to come to fruition. There were so many hurdles to overcome: researching a suitable location, zoning, finding an existing franchise willing to relocate, city support, not to mention the actual cost of building a brand new stadium. This wouldn't happen overnight.

Gerald Banks, the corporation's Chief Financial Officer, who always sat on Mason's immediate right, spoke up. "So I guess now you're the deciding vote, Peter."

"Let's see a show of hands then." Mason requested. He tried his best to look melancholy as he counted the raised hands. He saved his own hand for last. "Then it's official. The new Mason Cruise Line Ballpark project in the City of Jacksonville is a go."

Man's mind, stretched to a new idea, never goes back to its original dimensions.

- Oliver Wendell Holmes

3

The University of North Florida
Behavioral Sciences Laboratory
Nine Years Later

Matt Walker nonchalantly studied each of the objects before placing them down on the table before him. They were various household items that you would find in any kitchen, bathroom, or garage. There was a screwdriver, a slotted spoon, a phone charging cord, and a bottle of some corrosive smelling dandruff shampoo. He wasn't sure that this test would prove anything. He moved them around on the desk, sorting them by size. He really didn't know what the doctor really wanted from him. If she thought this was something he could just do on cue, she was sadly mistaken. He had no mental control over it.

Dr. Wanda Albright sat on the other side of the partition and concentrated on the photos of the same four objects spread out before her. Although she was regarded as an authority in the paranormal study of Psychometry, the majority of the teaching staff at the college treated her like an eccentric outcast. To her fellow professors, the doctor was nothing more than a pot-smoking, sixties throwback that dealt in too much hocus-pocus and not enough perceptible science.

Pressing each photo against the purple tie-dyed headband that she always wore, Albright tried to psychically transmit some kind of out-of-body energy across the table to the eighteen-year-old. To the untrained eye, it looked as though the old woman was in agony. In actuality, she also believed that if the boy managed to decipher one of the objects correctly, it would be a minor miracle. This test wasn't the real reason that Matt's grandmother had brought him to her in the first place, but she had to make sure all of the bases were covered. This was a rudimentary experiment that had to be given, and the results needed to be documented.

Albright held up the picture of the screwdriver and focused all of her resolve upon it. Matt leaned back in his chair, closed his eyes, picked up the slotted spoon and set it back down. *Nothing. This whole process was really starting to get ridiculous. How long had they been at it? Two hours? Three?* Trying to stifle a yawn, he watched as a black ant meandered up a nearby wall of the cramped room. Then he held up the phone cord and wrapped it around his right hand. *Zilch.*

The Doctor stood up and leaned over the partition so that Matt could read her lips. "Just a few minutes more, Matt," she promised. "Just clear your mind and relax."

Matt rested his head in his hands and yawned again, waiting for the small green bulb to light up. This simple light system was something they had rigged up especially for him, to signal that she had chosen another object, although he could clearly see her over the low partition. He rummaged through the four random objects before him and gripped the screwdriver to examine it. It was about six inches long with a black and red handle. *Bupkis, and to think, he was missing going to a Jacksonville Jumbo Shrimps' minor league baseball playoff game for this garbage!* Albright's hand began to shake, the photo she was holding was the screwdriver. *Big freaking deal! She had a twenty-five percent chance of getting it right! What, now they had some kind of psychic connection? This was like the twentieth set of household objects she had placed before him! If someone saw all this junk, they were going to think she had robbed a Bed Bath and Beyond!*

Once again, she stood up and leaned forward over the wooden barrier. "Are you concentrating?" she mouthed.

Matt blew out a heavy sigh of exasperation. "I'm really sorry,

Wanda," he apologized, in his deaf speech. Matt hated using his voice. He always imagined that his off-kilter cadence must have made him sound like he was choking on a prune pit.

"So you're not focusing on your selection?" she repeated.

"No, not really. If you want me to, I'll try harder this time."

Albright adamantly shook her head, her long gray braids flailing side to side. "No ... no, please! If you haven't been concentrating, then please don't try!"

Matt scratched his short-cropped blond hair. "You don't *want* me to try and trace them anymore?"

"Tracing" was the quaint term Matt had come up with to give his temperamental ability a designation. It was his way of explaining that he "traced" the object's history in his head. Take the screwdriver, for example; if his quirky cortex thought it was show time, he would have been able to see everywhere the tool had been, and everyone who had touched it. From the present moment back to its manufacturing, its saga would dance merrily before his eyes. But it wasn't that simple. He had no control over when it would happen. *The Lord gives it, and the Lord yanks it away.*

The doctor walked around the table, her diaphanous multicolored tie-dye chemise flowing about her. "I want you to continue to do whatever you've been doing, Matthew. It just seems like you perform much better when you don't try so hard."

Matt's emerald eyes twinkled at her. "Whatever you say, Doc. I just want to get this stupid test over with already!"

Albright went back to her station and drew another picture from her tableau. The light flashed on. Matt stared at the objects before him and studied the screwdriver again. This time he really concentrated, on the plastic handle and then the metal shaft. *Not today, Doc.*

The doctor disappointedly wrote down her results. Her notepad was a jumble of pen ink that only she could decipher.

Matt was undergoing these tests at the insistence of his grandmother.

Barbara Walker, now a spry seventy-one years young, sat in the next room behind a one-way pane of glass and winced every time her grandson got another card wrong. Unlike her husband Dave, she was a true believer in the mystical power that seemed to flow through her grandson's hands.

Years before the first incident, she had an unsettling suspicion that there was something special about Matt. Not just the usual braggadocio a grandparent rambles on about their only grandchild, but something truly unique. She regarded Matt's power as an offering of atonement. It was as if the God Almighty was rectifying a tragic mistake. An eye for an eye, or a sense for a sense, in this case. But if there was more to it, a scientific explanation, then she had an answer for those naysayers as well.

Barbara Walker believed that she might have been favored from birth. She had been born with a caul—a veil of skin covering her face—which, before the advent of prenatal medicine, superstition suggested meant she might be psychically gifted.

She had always been a spiritual person, living her formative years in a strict rural community in the Midwest. But from the time of her youngest memories, she always seemed to see things *clearer* than the other children did. Her use of the term *"clearer"* was just her own rural rationalization of explaining away what she didn't really understand.

Like it was yesterday, she could remember the exact moment when she realized that she was different from everyone else. Barbara was seven, just about the same age Matt was when he had been attacked and left for dead. As was their usual weekly custom, the entire Davidson clan was gathered around the Sunday evening dinner table. Her father would say Grace, which was followed by the customary idle conversation covering current events and topics of family interest. But after the discussion was over, when everyone grew silent, busily filling up on her mother's buttermilk biscuits and homemade walnut stuffing, she would continue to hear their voices! No one's mouth was moving except to chew their food, but she swore she could listen to what they were thinking! The sounds came as plainly to her as someone whispering into her ear!

Not everything she overheard was kind, nor was some of the language appropriate for her young ears. Some of the things she heard made no sense to her. There were words, cruel words, especially from her father, that she had never heard him use before, and she didn't know what they meant. When she asked him about these harsh words, the old man abruptly dragged her away from the table and force-fed her an entire jar of mustard for using them in the family's presence. That Sunday dinner was the first and last time she ever made her ability public.

Were these voices that shared her mind indeed a blessing, or some cruel affliction? It took her an entire lifetime to finally come to terms with the ephemeral whispers in her head. Decade after decade of eavesdropping on other people's intimate thoughts was enough to drive even the most rational-thinking person over the edge! She had no jurisdiction over it, even though she tried desperately to control it. It never worked when she tried to invoke it. Her ability wasn't just mental, it was temperamental! Whenever she tried to summon it, even *strained* to have it perform on a cue, she would come away feeling nothing but frustration and exhaustion.

And so, seventy-one years seemed to pass in the blink of an eye, and during this time, she taught herself to ignore the transient voices. Eventually, these whispers became merely background noise to her, much like the nagging buzz of a fluorescent light bulb. It wasn't until she saw the same power—and so much more—in her young grandson that she sought out more information and help.

Dr. Wanda Albright had come highly recommended. With patience and understanding, the doctor tried to explain what they were dealing with, in simple terms she thought the Walkers could understand.

"In every human being," Albright revealed to her, during their first meeting over lunch, "only a fraction of the brain's potential is ever used. The brain, still being uncharted territory, has many untapped functions and perceptive abilities that we're still unaware of. There are just too many things that occur in our daily lives that we tend to shrug off as mere coincidences. For instance," she said while poking through her alfalfa sprout and garbanzo bean salad, "how many times have you picked up the telephone receiver, and the person you were planning on calling is on the line already? You say to them, *hey, I was just about to call you.* And they say, *did the phone ring? I didn't even hear it ring!* Or how many times have you made a comment to someone, and they say, *hey, I was just thinking that?* It has happened to every one of us, at one time or another."

During another one of their lengthy discussions, Barbara Walker had suggested to Dr. Albright that perhaps these special abilities skip generations, like a recessive twins' gene. Her son, Franklin was extraordinary in his own special way, but he had never showed any outward signs of being psychically gifted. Matt, on the other hand, may have always had this psychometric ability lying dormant in his brain, an ability that *she* had passed along to him genetically. Perhaps it was the trauma to his head that helped release it. Whatever the cause, it was obvious that her grandson possessed an extraordinary skill that couldn't be dismissed as mere happenstance. Barbara Walker knew this beyond the shadow of a doubt because he had proven it.

***

In the spring of 2012, all Matthew Walker wanted was to live his life like any typical, high-spirited sixteen-year-old boy. Seven long years had passed since the home invasion that had changed his life forever. He had moved to Jacksonville to live with his grandparents, but the pain of that night still plagued his dreams. Those haunting images manifested themselves into disciplinary problems at school, and

Matt was eventually expelled from the Florida School for the Deaf and Blind in St. Augustine, for what the administration described as "total disrespect of authority and disruptive behavior."

The idea to send Matt away to a specialized school to learn lip reading and sign language was his grandfather's idea. In truth, David Walker was having a tough time dealing with his grandson's inability to communicate normally. The elder Walker felt too old to learn a new way of communication ... or at least that's what he claimed. Barbara Walker knew her husband of nearly forty-nine years much better than that. She knew the real reason her husband was shunning the boy was that he was embarrassed by him. She could tell it when they would go anywhere with Matt. David Walker would stay two paces ahead of them, unlike when the couple would go out alone, when he would stroll lovingly arm in arm with her.

Whenever she had the opportunity, she would mention this fact to her husband, and in his usual perfunctory manner, he would deny his guilt. She knew she was right though. Whenever Matt would come home for a long weekend or semester break, the house would become as quiet and cold as a cemetery. Only one person living under the Walkers' roof was unable to hear, but they all may as well have been deaf.

Matt was expelled from the State School in the summer of 2011. After a year of pranks, fights, arguments, and rebellion, the school had seen enough. The straw that finally broke the Administration's back was when they caught Matt, now only fifteen, sneaking out of the girl's dormitory in the middle of the night. Without hesitation, they expelled him the next morning, but no matter what disciplinary action the Dean of Boys threatened the teenager with, he couldn't wipe the contented smile off Matt's young face.

Barbara and David Walker were at their wits' end with their grandson. Little did they know that the answers they sought lay less than half a mile from their home For the two weeks following the expulsion, Barbara Walker made a steady stream of phone calls, asked mountains of questions, and for all of her trouble, received an invaluable education in return.

All roads seemed to lead to one person ... an idealistic young Principal named Carol Farmer. Farmer was the driving force behind Southside High School, a very old public school which turned out to be three blocks from the Walker's house. A school which Barbara Walker had driven by nearly every morning for the past twenty years.

Farmer was an enthusiastic advocate of a learning approach called "inclusion." The intention behind the concept of inclusion was to let the Deaf student be mainstreamed into regular hearing classes with the aid of a certified interpreter. The hope for this extraordinary educating philosophy was that the deaf student would flourish in a typical learning environment, and perhaps even the hearing students who shared the classroom would gain a priceless lesson in deaf awareness. Farmer saw this program as a win-win proposition.

Inclusion was the key that unlocked Matt's future. Barbara Walker believed that feeling like an exile from society was the foundation of her grandson's defiant attitude, and she was right. Within two months, Matt calmed down, his grades skyrocketed, and he began to make friends with kids who genuinely *wanted* to learn—not *had* to learn—his manual language to communicate with him. Matt had finally found acceptance, and he had also found a girlfriend.

Simone Goodman was blossoming into a gorgeous young woman. With her dark flowing hair, expressive mocha eyes, and perpetually tan complexion, she could have easily been mistaken for a middle-eastern princess. Sadly, Simone's mother had contracted rubella during her pregnancy—a leading cause of deafness. Simone was born into the same silent world Matt had found himself thrust into during his seventh year. Regardless of the time frame, life had issued them both a daunting challenge that each one courageously accepted.

The same American Disabilities Act that required ramps for

wheelchair access to public buildings also mandated Sign Language Interpreters be appointed for students who were academically qualified to be mainstreamed. With budget restrictions being what they were, Simone and Matt shared the same Interpreter, a perpetually grumpy woman named Iris Porter, whose gray-shocked hair made her look much older than her forty years.

With their learning curriculums scheduled to coincide, Porter was assigned to follow the school's only two deaf students from class to class to interpret whatever lesson was being taught. Spending nearly every learning moment together, it was no wonder Matt and Simone had become so close, so fast.

Unfortunately, not everything at Southside High ran as smoothly as their Inclusion Program. In the waning days of the winter of 2013, there had been a mysterious rash of robberies at the school. Lockers were being broken into with no sign of forced entry. So far, nearly three thousand dollars' worth of cash and personal belongings had been stolen from students and faculty alike. Every day before school let out, Principal Farmer would make an announcement over the public address system to remind the students not to leave anything of value in their lockers overnight. But these were still teenagers, and it never ceased to amaze Farmer what her heedless students would leave behind. From video games to jewelry, wallets to backpacks, when the afternoon release bell rang, the last thing on a teen's mind was the contents of their locker. All the students cared about was leaving the campus as quickly as their expensive sneakers would take them.

Added security didn't seem to be the solution either. One temporary guard was all the school's tight budget could afford, but even a trained night watchman couldn't be everywhere at once. There was never a sign of forced entry, so whoever was responsible must have found a secluded place inside the building to hide until they felt the coast was clear. The thieves had planned on stealth and guile, but they never anticipated what Matt Walker was about to discover.

It was a crisp Monday morning, just chilly enough to allow the students that mingled outside the building to laugh at the visible plumes of breath that punctuated their conversations. Spring was due to begin with the next page torn off the calendar, and heavy down parkas had already been replaced by light sweaters and long-sleeved shirts. While the other students spent their last few minutes before the morning bell swapping stories about their weekend, Matt chose instead to wait for Simone at their usual rendezvous spot, a cluster of royal palm trees near the teacher's parking lot. Blowing into his hands to keep them warm, he watched as the Goodman's blue minivan made a left turn into the parking lot. Simone's mother waved to him through the windshield, and he politely returned the gesture.

Simone looked wonderful that morning. Dressed in a bright yellow outfit, with her raven hair tied back with a matching yellow scrunchy, she seemed to radiate sunshine. As Simone sprang from the passenger side of the van, she was already signing a mile a minute. She knew that she was running late, and there was so much she wanted to tell Matt about her exciting weekend.

As was their usual routine, Matt and Simone would visit their lockers first thing, and then stroll upstairs to their homeroom, where saggy-eyed Iris Porter would be waiting for them. Matt and Simone had a standing gag that the woman never showered, and the fact that she sometimes wore the same clothes for two or three consecutive days tended to validate their suspicions.

This morning, they decided to go to Matt's locker first. The hallway leading to the bank of lockers was packed with bustling students. The few brave members of the faculty that struggled to keep the chaos in check may as well have been trying to fight back the tide. Overcrowding had become a reality in the suburbs, and until the school board realized the merits of running split shifts, there would be no relief in sight. Matt shouldered his way through the crowd of youngsters, running interference for Simone. For the two of them, the bedlam wasn't nearly as irritating as it might have been to a hearing individual. To Matt, the sound of the crowd came across as a soft, indistinguishable undertone, much the same way a person would perceive the sound of the ocean if they were to hold a seashell up to their ear. As for Simone, the distraction was even less. For her, there was no sound at all...just the emptiness of silence.

Upon reaching his locker, Matt wedged his way in between two other students while Simone waited. Every locker in the school was equipped with a built-in combination lock. Three correct numbers, entered in alternating directions, would release the latch. Matt dialed in the first number as the girl standing to his right retrieved her books and slammed her locker shut. Matt smiled at her as she strode away, and dialed in the second number. Simone wiggled in beside him. "So, do you think Iris is wearing the same stupid outfit today?" she signed.

Matt's mouth curled into a smile. "I would not bet against it," he signed back.

Simone's face was so expressive, it conveyed volumes when she laughed.

Matt was just about to dial in the last number when suddenly, he jerked his hand away from the dial as though he had been scalded.

Simone grabbed him by the shoulder, her face communicating concern.

"Feel the lock," he gestured.

Simone looked back at him perplexed.

Matt scrutinized his fingers. There appeared to be no irritation or sign of injury.

"Are you okay?"

Matt looked scared. "I know I must be going crazy. It felt like it burned me. "Simone cocked a skeptical eyebrow at Matt and then carefully studied the lock. Cautiously, she tapped her index finger against the numbered wheel. Feeling only the cold metal dial, she rolled her eyes and shot him a suspicious look.

"I'm telling you," Matt signed feverishly, "it felt like the lock was burning my fingers!"

Simone tapped on her wristwatch impatiently. "Get your things. We don't have all day. We only have seven minutes to get my books before homeroom starts!"

Matt looked around to see if anyone else had seen his reaction. During the daily ritual of the last minute rush, everyone else was so preoccupied with avoiding detentions for tardiness, they were totally oblivious. Feeling like an idiot, he sheepishly entered the final number. The metal door creaked open on its rusted hinges to reveal everything as he had left it before the weekend break. He grabbed his math book, notebook, and two sharpened pencils before shutting the door and spinning the dial.

The mob of students was already starting to thin out as Matt and Simone turned the corner and hurried toward another wall of lockers. Unlike the sterility of the hallway where Matt's locker was, this main corridor was alive with color. A hand-painted mural on the wall to their left depicted the arrival of spring. In the commemorative painting, fluffy white clouds floated over a meadow of multicolored flowers. A handful of picnickers and a smattering of nondescript birds were thrown into the mix to add a touch of realism. Seeing how wonderfully Simone's bright yellow outfit blended in with the mural, he wondered to himself if she had worn that color on purpose.

Matt leaned against the wall and continued to admire the artwork while Simone attempted to open her locker. It seemed she always had trouble with her combination especially when she felt she rushed. Was it left first, or right? No matter which she tried, she could never get it to work. Combination locks were just not her forte. She drummed her foot impatiently and gritted her teeth. She had heard something about spinning the dial a few times first to clear the tumblers, but in which direction was she supposed to turn it?

Matt wiggled his fingers in front of her face to get her attention.

"Having trouble again?"

Her lips were knotted in frustration. "I don't know why I can never do this! Why does this always happen to me?"

Matt politely nudged her out of the way and took hold of the dial. "Let me try...."

No sooner had Matt touched the handle than his head began to twitch like a thousand volts of electricity were being conducted through the muscles in his neck. At first, Simone thought he was just joking around with her, until she saw his eyes roll back into his head. Trying to control her mounting fear, she grabbed Matt by the shoulders and tried to pull him free of the metal cabinet, but his hand remained frozen on the black dial! Placing both her hands on his face, Simone attempted to hold his head steady, but it was no use; the convulsions continued to grow in their intensity! She tried to pry his fingers off the dial, but his hand had become rigid as steel, and just as steadfast.

She had to get help, but where? The hallway had already emptied out, and she didn't dare leave Matt alone! Matt was seizing like an epileptic, but somehow, he felt strangely at ease. It was a cruel twist of fate that had stolen his hearing ... and now it was that same providence that was intervening in his life once again.

He was no longer aware of the world around him. The colorful mural he had been staring at only seconds earlier had ceased to exist. It was the same sensation one would get sitting in a darkened theater waiting for a movie to begin—only Matt could no longer go to the movies.

A voice in his head whispered to him...a kind voice ... a haunting voice that sounded so familiar! It assured him that he could control the seizures if he would only try. As clearly, and as intelligibly as though he had never been struck down, Matt could actually hear himself answering the disembodied voice. He told it that he was too afraid.

There was a long pause, and then in a calm resonance that

instantly shushed all of his fears, the ethereal voice guaranteed him, *there was nothing to be afraid of. There wasn't anything in life that deserved to be feared.* It implored him to *try! To gather up all of his courage, and to just trust his intuition!*

Simone was bordering on the brink of hysteria. She wanted to yell for help, but the interpretation of screaming for a deaf person isn't the same as it is for someone who can hear their own voice. For a person who has never listened to the actual sound of the word "help," or has never had to form the word with their own lips, the guttural wail that can emanate from their throat can be a chilling sound. Thankfully, Simone never had to make an effort. As quickly as it had begun, Matt's seizure suddenly stopped.

The voice was gone, and the mesmerizing slide show was just beginning...

Colorless images flashed before his eyes in a dizzying collage. Faces of children he did not know passed through his line of sight in rapid-fire succession. One after another the unrecognizable young faces flew by, none remaining for more than an instant. Like the wooden horses on a carousel, the nameless children seemed to whirl around in his head without any apparent rhyme or reason.

The only distinctions Matt could perceive about the young faces was the steady modernization of the children's hairstyles. It was like peering into a barber's time capsule. Where the boys had started off with short-cropped hair, the blur of male faces continued to evolve through the generations of styles and fads. Crewcuts ... slicked-back hair ... long hair ... tight Afro curls ... medium length ... fade cuts ... all flashing by in a matter of milliseconds.

The same held true for the girls he saw too. Bobbed hair ... long hair with paisley headbands ... tight Afro curls ... the return of long hair ... then another face with short hair again, but this time dyed in punk shades of blue, orange and green! It was a whirlwind tour of hair fashion, but they were all blending together and moving so fast, he could feel his stomach turning in protest. Then ... without warning, it stopped! Like driving two hundred miles an hour, and hitting a brick wall, it just stopped!

Why was this happening to him? Was this what death was supposed to feel like? He had so many things he wanted to do in his life ... so many questions he wanted answered. Shrouded in shadows, encased in silence, all he could feel was the steady beating of his heart inside his chest. He was so scared, but he remembered what the voice had told him ... *no fear!* He hung on to that reassuring phrase like a lifeline.

The instant he concentrated on those two small words, the curtain of darkness parted, and Simone was all that he could see ... but there was something different about her. As she came toward him, she wasn't walking under her own power, but as if she was floating out of the light, and she was no longer wearing the yellow outfit he had admired only minutes earlier. As she approached him, her clothes kept changing ... from black slacks, to a green dress, to white pants, then to blue jeans, back to her yellow outfit ... they all merged into an endless kaleidoscope of style and fabric! But something was happening now ... the closer she advanced, the slower her pace became, and in turn, the less frantic the clothing transformations. When she was almost within arm's length, she stopped abruptly as two ominous shadows passed across her face! A bloodcurdling shiver shot down Matt's spine, as though one of his classmates had slipped an ice cube down the back of his shirt! There was someone else here ... someone bad! Other presences standing just beyond his view! He knew they were there ... he sensed them! He could feel their hearts beating ... hear their syncopated breathing!

No fear, he repeated to himself ... *there is nothing in life that should be feared!*

As Matt looked on in uncontrollable horror, a geyser of blood sprayed out of the back of Simone's head! Helpless in his vision, he was forced to watch as her face contorted into a mask of anguish. He wanted to close his eyes ... needed to blot out the terrifying image ...

"no fear," the voice repeated again.

Something wasn't right about this. Matt didn't know why, but he felt that things were getting all mixed up. Lines were getting crossed. What he was seeing wasn't real! His imagination was going berserk. Simone was fine ... she was standing right beside him ... he knew she was there! He could feel her there! *No fear!*

Suddenly, like a fog being lifted by the warmth of the sun, it all became so apparent to him! Like someone had kindled a clarifying beacon to lead him out of the darkness, he thought he finally understood what was happening!

There was no fear!

With newfound confidence, Matt turned his focus to the pair of visages lurking in the shadows. Only one was visible to him, and he took that to mean something too. Matt recognized the man, not by name, but because of all of the chance encounters they had shared. That had to be the explanation as to why he remained obscured by the darkness! In real-life, he worked in the background! The more Matt relaxed, the more he understood that everything he was visualizing in this trance was there for a specific purpose! He knew now that the endless procession of children he had witnessed had been every child that had shared this same locker for over forty years. He could feel their company as clearly as if they were actually standing right in front of him! Forty-two years' worth of students had led him right back here to the present ... and to Simone! And what's more, he now knew who was burglarizing all the lockers! The revelation hit him like a backhand across his face.

Simone didn't know what else to do ... she struck him so hard, the palm of her hand left a bright red imprint on his cheek. In a torrent of light and color, Matt's surroundings returned. Without hesitation, he reached for Simone and tugged her close, feeling her body trembling against his. She wrapped her arms around him, and together, they found contentment beyond their years.

Simone pulled back and began signing mere inches from his face.

"I was so worried about you! What happened? Are you okay now?"

Trying to be nonchalant about his actions, Matt casually brushed his hand across the back of Simone's scalp. There were no words to relate the relief he felt when he found everything intact. "I'm alright."

"You had me very scared!"

Matt tried to comfort her with a reassuring smile. "How long did I space out?"

Simone shrugged. "Just a few seconds, but you were shaking and twitching! Are you sure you are feeling okay now?"

Matt gnawed on his lower lip. "I don't think we should tell anyone what just happened."

Simone's gestures were frenzied. "What *did* just happen?"

Matt grasped her hands to silence her. "Everything is fine, I swear. I promise I will explain it all to you, but first, I need to know something."

Simone stroked her index finger across her palm, the sign for "what?"

Matt signed his words slowly and deliberately. "Did you leave anything valuable in your locker over the weekend?"

Without a moments' pause, Simone nodded in the affirmative. "I had a Doctor's appointment on Friday, and I forgot my backpack because I left school an hour early."

"What was in the backpack?"

Simone frowned. "Not my cell phone, I don't keep it in my pack, but my allowance was in there. My father gives me twenty dollars every Thursday night."

"That's it? Twenty dollars?"

She shook her head. "No, I had a watch and some jewelry that I always take off before P.E. I went directly from the track to the Doctor's office Friday afternoon."

Matt tried not to come off as too judgmental, but being deaf, he believed they both had to be even more observant of the world around them. "Didn't they warn us about leaving important stuff like that in our lockers over the weekend?"

Simone's demeanor turned defensive. "My mother was running late! Besides, there are over five hundred lockers in this school! Why would I think mine would get singled out?" Matt gestured with his thumb toward the locker. "Open it."

"Why don't you?"

Matt shied away. "There is no way you can get me to touch that lock again!"

After two unsuccessful tries, Simone finally manipulated the right combination and swung the metal door open. To her shock and dismay, the contents of her backpack were gone! She yanked out the bag and frantically rummaged through it again. "My parents are going to kill me!"

Matt waited for Simone to calm down and fill her backpack with books and then steered her toward the front of the building. "We've got to tell someone in the office about this."

As they passed the cafeteria, the malodorous smells that wafted through the hallway seemed to warn them of the impending Salisbury steak lunch. "How did you know my things had been taken?"

Matt was walking so fast, Simone was having a hard time keeping up with him. "I don't just know your things are gone ... I also think I know who took them!"

Simone grabbed him by the elbow as they turned the corner into the school's entrance hall. "How is that possible?"

Reaching the administrative offices, Matt grabbed the backpack from Simone's arm and held the swinging doors open for her. "I'll explain it later. Right now, we've got to try to get your things back," he signed.

Carmen Trujillo's official title was Registrar's Assistant, but when she wasn't filling out forms, or arranging class schedules, she stood behind the counter and ran interference for the administrators from the litany of student crises that wandered into the front office. Trujillo was a young woman, not particularly attractive to the eye, but with a disarming smile that always had a way of calming even the school's most unruly children.

She had always held a special place in her heart for Simone and Matt, and she was delighted whenever they came into the office. "Aren't you two supposed to be in class?" she asked, her mouth moving with a magnified pronunciation for their benefit. "Where is Ms. Porter?"

Matt hated to use his voice, unsure of what he sounded like nowadays, but since the interpreter wasn't around to help.. "Hello, Miss Trujillo. We need to see Mrs. Farmer."

Trujillo lowered her half-glasses onto her nose and studied both children. It was the same dubious stare a parent would give a child when they were trying to figure out what mischief their youngster had gotten themselves into. "And why, may I ask, do both of you need to interrupt Mrs. Farmer? Our Principal is very busy."

"She wants to know why" Matt signed to Simone.

Simone's gestures were all facial, but he knew she was urging him to tell the truth.

"I really need to speak to her. It's critical. I think I know who is stealing from the student lockers."

All heads turned as the Assistant Principal, a tall, lanky black man named Clarence Ward, came storming out of his office. "What's going on out here? What is all of this commotion about?" As petrified as Trujillo was by the massive man's sudden appearance, she could only imagine how terrified the children must have been. "I'm sorry, Mr. Ward. These students are insisting on speaking with Mrs. Farmer. I'll send them to homeroom right away!"

Out of an intuitive sense of self-preservation, Simone stepped behind Matt. She had always thought that with his shaven head and goatee beard, Ward reminded her more of a grizzled death-row inmate than a school administrator. As far as she was concerned, the man's only saving grace was that she needed no interpreter to translate what he was saying. His brusque body language and scowling facial expressions were more than adequate to convey his message. "Why is it that you two aren't on your way to class already?"

It was hard enough not to be distracted by the Assistant Principal's burning gaze, but even worse, Matt hated having to read the lips of someone who wore a beard. The hair rimming the mouth tended to hide or distort the natural motion of the person's lips.

"It's critical that we speak with Mrs. Farmer."

"I told the boy that Mrs. Farmer is very busy." Trujillo insisted.

Ward held up his hand to muzzle Trujillo. "Page Iris Porter to come down here."

Matt smiled in appreciation. "Thank you, Mr. Ward."

Ward leaned his imposing frame onto the counter. "It's not every day my two favorite students pay our office a visit." Simone peeked over Matt's shoulder and saw something she had never witnessed before. Clarence Ward was smiling. A happy, make-you-feel-at-home kind of smile. Maybe all of the horror stories she had heard about him were really unfounded? "Mrs. Farmer has a hectic schedule today. Why don't we go into my office and talk?"

Ward lifted the hinged section of the countertop and ushered Matt and Simone into his office. Inside the crowded room was an entire wall filled with diplomas and certificates of merit that would have impressed even the most cynical parent of Ward's experience.

The three of them sat quietly until Iris Porter arrived. "Why wasn't either of you in homeroom?" she signed to both of them angrily.

"We needed to see Mrs. Farmer," Matt replied, thankful that he didn't have to speak anymore.

"They say they need to see the Principal," Porter reiterated to Ward.

"What is so earthshaking that you couldn't see her in your free time?" Ward demanded to know.

Matt looked over at Simone who urged him on. "I think I know who is breaking into the lockers."

Iris Porter paused in mid-interpretation.

"What did he say?"

She did not quite believe what her eyes were seeing. "Matt says, he thinks he knows who's been stealing from the lockers."

Ward leaned forward in his chair. "Who?"

Matt was signing fast and furious. "I don't know his name, but he's one of the custodians. He's kind of young with dark hair. I would know him if I saw him!"

The Assistant Principal combed his fingers through his beard. "How does he know all this?"

Porter waited expectantly for Matt's answer.

"I can't tell you."

Ward leaned back, the disappointment was evident on his face. "You can't tell me?"

Matt looked over at Simone who wouldn't return his gaze. "I'm very sorry. I would really like to tell you how I know, but I just can't."

The Assistant Principal rocked gently in his chair, his meaty fingers flexed into a steeple under his chin. "If you can't tell me how you know, then how am I supposed to believe you?" He waited for Iris Porter to finish interpreting before he continued. "Do you want me to accuse someone of stealing just because Matthew Walker says so?"

Matt stared down at his feet.

"Don't look away from me!"

Iris Porter waved to get Matt's attention.

"Just what kind of proof do you have, that one of the janitors is steal...?" As if he had lost his train of thought, Ward abruptly stopped his diatribe. Something was bothering him about what the boy had just suggested. Why was a photograph he thought he'd seen months earlier, suddenly sticking out in his mind?

There was a picture he needed to find, but where had he seen it? Last year's class yearbook? No, they don't include the maintenance staff in the school annual. Was it one of the pictures from the faculty Christmas party? No, that wasn't it... What was nagging at

Ward the most was the fact that none of the lockers had shown any signs of forced entry. The custodial crew had always been at the top of his list of suspects, but because they were hired directly by the County, and not by the individual schools, delving into each worker's background was a nearly impossible chore because of all of the bureaucratic red tape that was involved. Besides, if it had been one of the janitors, as the boy claimed, the custodian would have needed the combinations ahead of time, and that information was only available to a restricted few on the office staff.

"Are you all right, Mr. Ward?" Iris Porter asked.

The Assistant Principal was staring into thin air, drumming his fingers on the desk to a tune only he could hear. Where had he seen the damned thing? *It couldn't have been outside the school grounds ... it must have been ... Yes! That was it!*

Ward jumped out of his seat and ran over to a bookshelf where he kept a stack of old school newspapers. Matt slid his chair out of his way as the Assistant Principal continued rifling through the pile of papers. A third of the way through the stack, Ward grabbed one of the papers and held it above his head victoriously.

"What is it, Mr. Ward?" Porter asked. "What do you have there?"

The Southside Source was a monthly student-produced newspaper covering a variety of topics such as school happenings, varsity sports, PTA socials, special fund-raising events, and other school matters of interest. Occasionally, when one of these special fund-raising events—such as a faculty basketball game—included local celebrities, the Jacksonville Daily News would send out a photographer to cover the event for their local section. With their kind permission, sometimes a few of these pictures were reproduced in the monthly student paper. Ward took the newspaper and folded one of the pages into thirds. What he left showing was only part of a surprisingly sharp photograph of a man sitting in the stands at one of these charity fund-raisers. He held out the picture for Matt to look at.

Matt's eyes opened wide. He sprang out of his chair and began shouting and signing excitedly. "That's him! I'm positive!" He poked his finger at the paper over and over.

"How do you know it was him?" Ward asked, seriously.

Matt shook his head without answering.

The Assistant Principal pulled back the newsletter so only Iris Porter could see the rest of the photograph. It was definitely a picture of one of the custodial staff, a young dark-haired man named Enrique Sandoval. In the photo, Sandoval appeared to have the friendliest smile on his face, Ward thought. Perhaps it was just because he was enjoying watching all the celebrities make fools of themselves on the basketball court ... or could it have been the fact that Sandoval had his arm wrapped around his new fiancé... Carmen Trujillo?

Later that afternoon, the Broward County Sheriff's Department arrested Enrique Sandoval on twelve counts of robbery after a cache of the stolen goods was recovered from a hidden compartment in a bedroom closet of the couple's new home. Carmen Trujillo was charged as an accessory in the thefts for disclosing the confidential locker combinations. Upon further investigation, it was discovered that Sandoval's brother owned a pawn shop where the couple, who were living far beyond their means, was fencing the stolen property. Trujillo and Sandoval plea-bargained their sentences down to two years, and each ended up serving less than nine months. The Sandovals never ended up getting married, and both promptly left the State of Florida. Matt was repeatedly questioned about how he knew that the janitor and registrar were the culprits. He never divulged his secret to anyone except Simone—and, of course, his grandmother.

4

Time had passed quickly since the locker incident, and Barbara Walker had grown more concerned about her grandson. There weren't any physical changes for her to worry about, but she had an insight into his psyche that no one else had. She knew that he doubted himself. This wasn't the standard coming-of-age sort of reservations—more of the "edge of sanity" type. This was why she wanted him tested: for his peace of mind...and hers.

"I think that is enough for now," Dr. Albright said, as she gathered up the objects from Matt's side of the desk and placed them in a plastic tub with all the rest of the household menagerie.

Matt pushed himself away from the table and arched his back, trying to work out the kinks he'd gotten from sitting for over two hours of testing without ever shifting positions. "So, what did all of this tell you, Doc?" He voiced gutturally.

Albright put her hand on Matt's cheek and smiled compassionately. "This test is only one step on a long journey of examination, my dear boy. Surely you can't expect me to be able to tell you anything from just a few tests?"

Matt winced. "So how long is this journey supposed to take, Doc? If it takes much longer, I'm going to make you pull over and let me out to throw up!"

Albright lowered her hand to Matt's shoulder and laughed. "Aw, come on now! It hasn't been that bad, has it?"

Matt was polite enough not to answer.

The doctor pointed at her own lips. "Matt, have you noticed that your speech has improved since the frequency of these events has increased?"

In turn, Matt touched his index finger to his ear and then to his mouth, the sign language gesture for 'deaf.'

Albright shook her head. "It just seems to me that your spoken language has greatly improved since the first time we met. I would imagine that the speech of a person who has lost their hearing would usually deteriorate over time ...but yours appears to be doing quite the opposite."

Matt waved his grandmother into the room through the one-way mirror. "You're kidding me, right?"

Albright looked surprised. She hadn't realized the young man was so sensitive about his voice. "I'm absolutely serious!"

Barbara Walker strolled into the room and gave her grandson a peck on the top of his head. Matt wrinkled his face and rubbed his hair.

"I was just complimenting your grandson on his improved speech," Albright remarked. "Have you noticed it too, or is it just because I don't see him as often?"

Barbara Walker put her hand on her grandson's shoulder. "Of course I know about it. It doesn't surprise me."

Albright was taken aback. "It doesn't?"

"No, why should it?"

The doctor sat on the edge of the desk and began rifling through the set of more than fifty photos. "I don't purport to be an expert in the field of deafness, but it's only logical to assume that someone who can no longer hear the spoken word would lose their tonal fluency in the spoken language."

Barbara Walker looked at Wanda Albright quizzically. "Who ever said that Matt couldn't hear?"

Caught totally off guard, the deck of photos dropped out of the doctor's hands as if she was starting a game of fifty-two pick up. "Excuse me?"

Matt stood up to collect the pictures off the floor.

"I never told you that Matt couldn't hear," Barbara Walker said.

"I'm confused," Albright admitted. "Matt *is* reading my lips when I speak to him, am I correct?"

Matt's grandmother laughed. "Of course he is! I didn't mean that he could hear you or me."

The doctor closed one eye skeptically. "I'm at a loss. Then who can he hear?"

"He hears the voice in his head!"

"The voice in his head?" Albright couldn't help but repeat skeptically.

"Sure! He hears a voice as plain as you're hearing me now."

Albright nodded. "Ah…"

Barbara Walker put her fists defiantly on her hips. "How else would you explain it?"

Matt was down on his knees trying to get the last card that had slipped under the desk when the doctor tapped him on the shoulder. He grabbed the card to complete the deck and handed them back to Albright. She made sure they had eye contact. "Your grandmother tells me you hear voices in your head!"

Matt turned to his grandmother with a menacing glare. *They were visions, not voices. Why couldn't she grasp that basic concept?* "She doesn't know what she's talking about."

Albright glanced over at Barbara Walker and then back at Matt. There was apparently some underlying tension there. It was clear that this line of questioning would have to wait until Matt was ready to confide in her. She rubbed her hand over her heart signing one of the few words she knew. "I'm sorry, Matthew. Sometimes I feel like I need an interpreter myself," she said, as apologetically as possible. "I must have misunderstood her."

Matt no longer wanted to be here. He walked over to the door and waited.

"I've really hit a nerve, haven't I?" Albright sighed.

Barbara Walker put a compassionate hand on the doctor's wrist. "I'm the one who's let him down."

The doctor shook her head. "No need to feel guilty about what you've told me, Barbara. It's going to take a while for Matt to trust me enough to open up to me. Don't worry. Just let it happen naturally."

Matt's grandmother looked over at him standing agitatedly by the door. "Oh, this isn't going to be a pleasant drive home!"

Albright chuckled, and set the deck of cards down on the desk. "I'm sure everything will be fine. Just keep strong, and listen to what your grandson has to say. I like to consider myself a pretty good judge of people, and I think Matt is hiding an extraordinary ability that none of us can even *begin* to fully comprehend yet!"

Barbara Walker joined Matt by the door and ruffled his hair. "He *is* an extraordinary young man, isn't he?"

The doctor smiled. "Absolutely!"

Barbara Walker opened the door to leave. "Well, have a good day, doctor. We'll see you again."

Wanda Albright waved to get Matt's attention. "I'll see you soon, right Matt?"

But the teenager never answered her. Little did Matt know that that would be the last time he would be seeing the doctor.

Take chances, make mistakes. That's how you grow. Pain nourishes your courage. You have to fail in order to practice being brave.

- Mary Tyler Moore

5

Suite 1807, Jax Tower
Jacksonville, Florida
After regular business hours...

A *number cruncher. A bean counter. The company doormat.* Those were the most merciful epithets she had berated him with during today's latest bombing run. *That's all he would ever amount to,* she had shrieked at him before hanging up on him. *Unless he finally found the balls to demand the recognition that someone with over twenty years in the family business deserved!*

She was an alcoholic shrew who couldn't see beyond her six martinis at the Meadhaven Country Club to realize that ninety-nine percent of the middle-aged women on the planet would kill for the lifestyle that she seemed to loathe so much.

When had it all gone sour? He wondered as he stared out the window at the busy thoroughfare below. Maybe the clock on his desk held all the answers. It was nearly six thirty. The office staff had cleared out well over an hour ago, and he was still in his office. He sat in the same chair that he always sat in, behind in his paperwork, sifting through the same folders he always sifted through, oblivious to the same people he had always been oblivious to.

How could she be so selfish? Didn't she understand that he was doing it all for them? What was so terrible about their life? They lived in the lap of luxury. He knew the move north wasn't an easy decision, but it had to be done. So what if he spent a little extra time at the office, what did he have to come home to? Couldn't she realize that no one was indispensable, and there was an entire swarm of summa cum laude, know-it-all college graduates ready and willing to do his job for a tenth of his salary? Where did she think the money came from to pay for all of that booze?

Of course, he never discussed this anxiety with her; it was his predicament, and he would deal with it as he knew best...with hard work and long hours! That was his way! He had to make himself indispensable to the company!

Through his panoramic window, the setting sun was igniting the concrete skyline in a blaze of orange and pink hues. In the distance, across the shimmering waters of the Saint John's River, the nocturnal colors of the city of Jacksonville were coming to life. But it wasn't that far away kaleidoscope of neon luminescence that was capturing his attention. There was a closer temptation. Bright lights down on the street that had teased him for years; and for just as long, he had denied his curiosity. Perhaps, after twenty years, tonight would be the night that he would finally escape the bonds of monotony, and venture across the street to the flashing colors and energetic music that pulsed through the doors of the One Eleven Club. Why not? It was exactly what he deserved.

He switched off his computer, closed the files on his desk, and carried them over to the wall safe where he stored most of the company's significant financial documents. Giving a cavalier glance into the mirror that hung behind his door, he ran his fingertips over his graying hair like a brush, trying desperately to accentuate the dwindling number of dark hairs that had managed to outlast his tumultuous marriage. For a long moment, he fidgeted with the knot in his tie, contemplating whether or not to leave it perfect like it was or to loosen it and go for the casual, less anal-retentive look. He modeled it for himself both ways, turning from side to side and casting out flirtatious pick-up lines into empty waters. Wearing it loose made him feel awkward and vulnerable, so he decided to leave it knotted. Now he was ready! Now he was dressed to kill!

6

The One-Eleven Club—or the Three Aces, as it was known in organized crime circles, was like a vine-ripened tomato: an enticing outside concealing an incredibly seedy interior. At the core of this corruption was Nicholas Coltello—or, since Coltello was the Italian word for "Knife," Nicky the Knife. Although no one who was still breathing ever dared call him Nicky the Knife to his face.

Coltello was a fourth generation Messinian, but somewhere along the line his family tree had branched off toward Havana, and for this reason—and the fact that he was fluent in all three languages—he was given absolute reign of the family's interests in Florida.

Gambling, drugs, prostitution, gun-running...if it was done anywhere in the Sunshine State, Nicky the Knife either had a hand in it, or knew about it...and if he knew about it, and didn't have a hand in it...it didn't prosper for long.

Standing an impressive six and a half feet tall in his hand-crafted Italian loafers, Nick Coltello was a piranha in an angelfish's clothing. Although Coltello himself would be the first to admit he had been dealt a runt hand when it came to his looks, he never lacked the two qualities it took to interest his concept of the ideal woman: money and power. He had no doubt that it was these two features that had made him so irresistible to his wife, Mary; but then, life had a whimsical way of balancing the scales. Married for nearly ten years, he had never been faithful to her for more than ten days at a stretch (including his honeymoon).

Clean shaven, and with his jet-black hair tied back in a small ponytail, this living scarecrow was the walking embodiment of the club that his New Jersey family had established. Coltello governed his underworld empire from his lushly-appointed office suite at the rear of The Three Aces. Some of his opulent conveniences included a full bathroom with a shower, and a walk-in closet containing a complete wardrobe of imported European suits, shirts, and neckwear. Then there was his most valued amenity: a garish bedroom hideaway that sported mirrors covering every square inch of available wall or ceiling space. To say that Nicky the Knife never lacked for any of his creature comforts would be putting it mildly. As a precaution, and because he was not particularly known for his passive demeanor, Coltello had also had the outer walls of the suite double-insulated with soundproofing to keep some of the more disillusioning aspects of his business within the confines of his private domain.

Appearance was Nicky the Knife's calling card, and he was a master at plying his trade. To his adoring community, he was a dapper enigma, who unselfishly bought up overgrown, weed-infested tracts of land and converted them into neighborhood parks where inner-city children could have a secure environment in which to play. He was a gangly savior, who single-handedly subsidized these safe havens where kids of all ages and backgrounds could participate in organized sports and learn that there was more to life than just street gangs and drive-by shootings. That was how the public perceived Nicholas Coltello. But the public was dead wrong.

It was customary for Nicky the Knife to his hold daily council between five and seven o'clock in his office in the back of the club. No one knew how or when this tradition had started; it was just the way it had always been. After the day's business had been handled, Coltello would sit behind his desk and wait for his Lieutenants to arrive. Sometimes he would uncork a bottle of imported Chianti and listen attentively to what his underlings had to report. Other times, such as today, the Knife was too agitated to enjoy what he considered one of life's simple pleasures.

Estefan Padron, an oafish-looking brute with short-cropped

black hair, tramped into Coltello's elegant office on this evening to find the lanky kingpin pacing around the room, trying to decide the appropriate place to hang a few new pictures of his wife and himself, taken at yet another charity function. Padron, who was one of the few people who could stand nose to nose with his boss, cheerfully offered to help.

Coltello slipped a couple of threepenny nails between his lips and held one of the pictures against one of the walls to judge the right placement. "What? You don't think I can hang a couple of freaking pictures all by myself?" He grunted, in his crude Jersey accent.

Padron managed a fractured smile, which coordinated well with his boxed-in nose. "Of course not, Nick."

"You think that I need to hire a carpenter to hang a frame?" Coltello asked, the unpolished inflection of his words making him sound even more menacing.

Padron, who revealed the only slightest trace of his Cuban ancestry through his accent, grew increasingly jittery with each passing moment. "I...I didn't say that, Boss. I just offered to help."

"Well, that's what you were thinking, am I right?"

Tipping the scales at a hefty three hundred twenty pounds, Padron was not a person that was easily intimidated by anyone, but Nicky the Knife scared the shit out of him. Whenever Nick got into one of these psychotic moods, there was only one thing to do...clear out!

"Maybe I should come back later, Boss?" The burly henchman stammered.

Coltello was getting more and more annoyed with his picture arrangement dilemma.

Padron took a few steps back. "I mean, when you're not so busy?"

Nick shook his head, disgusted at not finding just the right spot for the photos. "Park your ass in one of those chairs, Jumbo. We need to talk."

Padron took a seat in front of the desk and watched uneasily as his employer began to stride around the office, brandishing the claw hammer in one hand, the nails clenched tightly in his other.

The big man tried but failed valiantly to cross his legs, but they were the size of tree trunks and just as flexible. "So, what's so important that we need to talk in private, Nick?"

Coltello stretched his neck to one side until he heard a comforting "crack" of the vertebrae. All this tension was wreaking havoc on his alignment. "Being alone with me bothers you?"

Padron's fingernails dug deep into the arms of the black leather chair. "Well... yeah...I mean...you've got the other guys waiting outside watching the dancing boobies, when we usually all meet together. I do something wrong, Boss?"

Nick toyed with the hammer in his hand. The weight felt just about right. "How long we known each other, Estefan?"

The big man looked up at the ceiling. "Jeez, I don't know...ten years maybe?"

Nicky The Knife shrugged indifferently. "Yeah, that's just about how long I got it figured for too."

Padron continued to stare up at the acoustic tiles above his head, trying to be more precise, but he wasn't very sharp when it came to adding and subtracting. "Maybe it could be eleven."

Coltello exhaled onto a garish diamond ring that dressed up one of the fingers holding the nails, and then rubbed the stone against his lapel to polish it. "And I been good to you for all that time haven't I?"

Padron's fleshy jowls flapped like a turkey's wattle as he nodded in agreement. "Definitely, Boss...definitely. You have been good to my family and me! Why just the other night Teresa and I were..."

Coltello shot Padron an armor-piercing glare. "I'm not done talking."

Padron waved one of his fingers in front of his mouth as if to warn himself to keep quiet.

"You know that over the years, whenever I've had a delicate matter that needed to be dealt with, I've always counted on you."

Padron's chest puffed up proudly. "Because you can count on me to always do the job right the first time, Boss!"

Coltello examined the pronged end of the hammer by holding it up and twisting it in his hand. "And you've never second-guessed any of my orders..."

Padron shook his head. "Never, Boss! Not even once!"

"And you've always been on the up and up with me..."

The big man squirmed in the chair and placed his hand over his heart. "Always, Boss!"

"So last week when I asked you to handle that Guatemalan punk who thought he could deal *his* rocks on *my* streets, you took care of him, right?"

Padron gazed up at the clock hanging on the wall behind Coltello's desk. Only five minutes had passed since he had first entered the office, but this unexpected interrogation was making it seem like a lifetime. "What's left of him is planted in the concrete field, Boss! Just like I always do!"

Coltello could feel his anger boiling up inside of him. "So tell me, how the hell did you find the kid?"

"You know, Boss...the usual way...one of our guys on the street told me where his crib was."

Taking up a position behind Padron's chair, Nicky the Knife rolled his eyes. *Crib*...he hated that ghetto slang bullshit!

"So you did it in his *house*..." Coltello confirmed, making sure to emphasize the word he preferred.

"Yeah," Padron giggled, "right there in his living room while he was watching a Seinfeld rerun."

Coltello undid the rubber band that was holding his ponytail together. His hair fell limply to his shoulders. "Messy?"

Padron could still visualize himself pulling the trigger, and then, the scattered flecks of batting as they floated to the ground, passing lazily through a shaft of sunlight that had suddenly appeared in the back of the couch. The memory was so vivid he could still almost feel the sensation of walking around to the front of the couch and seeing the Guatemalan impaled on that same brilliant spike of light. He just stood there, transfixed by the repulsively surreal sight, marveling at how the shimmering spear protruded from the bloody opening in the dead guy's chest. "Well, I don't think anybody's gonna be entertaining on that sofa 'till they get it reupholstered!" the big man chortled.

"And then you searched the place and found his stuff?"

"Sure did, Boss! I handed over nearly five kilos of it to Jimmy D. on Friday afternoon!"

Nicky's right hand noticeably tightened around the handle of the tool. "And the money?"

The single black eyebrow that stretched above Padron's eyes began to twitch involuntarily. "Money?"

Where his complexion would typically flush with indignation at the mere thought of an employee's duplicity, now Coltello's face had grown red as a match tip, and nearly twice as combustible. "Am I suddenly not talking English here?" he snarled, with his voice intensifying. *"Did I fucking stutter you pezzo de mirda? The Cash! Dinero! Lira! Which one of these terms do I gotta use, to help you better understand a three-word question?"*

"I don't know what money you're talking about, Boss!"

Nicky The Knife tapped the head of the hammer against the back of Padron's skull. *"Two hundred and thirty large, you fat prick! That's what I'm talking about!"*

Padron lifted his bulk out of the chair and held up his hands defensively. "I...I don't know nothing about no two hundred-thirty grand, Boss," he stammered. "I sw... swear to you!"

Even though Coltello looked anorexic compared to the barrel-chested killer, the claw hammer tended to equalize the weight advantage. Nick grabbed Padron by the necktie and pulled his petrified eyes inches from his own. Spittle flew from the corner of Coltello's mouth as he foamed like a rabid mongrel in Padron's face.

"Are you gonna stand here and lie right to my face, you overstuffed bag of shit?"

If strong bladders hadn't run in his family, Estefan Padron would have peed in his pants. "I...I..."

Coltello swung the hammer with all of his might, burying the prongs deep into Padron's forehead. The big man collapsed to his knees, his vacant eyes rolling up as if staring at the prongs protruding just above them. Over and over again, Coltello mercilessly pounded the hardened claws into soft flesh and brittle bone and then ripped them back out. The big man's body flailed as his brain short-circuited. Continuing headlong into the muddled realm of derangement, Nicky the Knife would accentuate each sickening blow with one word per stroke.

"No...one...ever...steals...from...me...and...lives!"

When they burst into the office, it took three of Coltello's men to pull him off the writhing body. Rock music from the nightclub flooded into the room as Jimmy Diaz, Coltello's right-hand man, grabbed the hammer at the apex of its arc and pried the bloodied tool out of his employers' maniacal grip.

"Let go, Nicky! That's enough. He's more than dead."

Coltello was a frenzied mess. *"The fat fuck was stealing from me!"*

Diaz, a thin, but deceptively strong man, let the hammer topple to the blood-stained carpet. "You swore to me that all you were gonna do was talk to him!" he reprimanded, trying not to look down at the mangled corpse lying at his feet. "Sweet Jesus," he said, shaking his head disgustedly. "Why didn't you just shove a lit stick of dynamite up his ass? It would have been a hell of a lot cleaner!"

Coltello wiped the hair out of his face with a blood-soaked hand. "Because you can't hang pictures with dynamite," he growled.

Diaz surveyed the room. "Look at this fucking place! This is *your* damned office, Nicky! How do you suggest we get rid of this dead whale? Drag him through the fucking nightclub?"

With the front of his two thousand dollar suit drenched in blood, Coltello took a step back and tried to regain his self-control. "That son-of-a-bitch was stealing from me. I could see it in his eyes!"

No matter how many times Diaz's men had witnessed Coltello jump the rails like this, it always managed to scare the hell out of them.

"You're out of control, Nick!" Diaz urged. "You need to calm down, or you're gonna give yourself a stroke!"

Coltello wiped the back of his clenched fist across his cheek. He stared at the blood for a long moment, and then, with a cat-like movement that caught the other two henchmen by surprise, he spun around and pointed one of his gore-spattered fingers at them. *"And I'll do the same thing to you if I ever catch one of you mamalukes trying to steal what belongs to me!"*

Diaz, a lifelong friend of Coltello, was one of the few people who possessed the backbone to stand up to the raging crime lord. "Leave them out of this, Nicky!"

Ever the quintessential clothes horse, Coltello adjusted his blood-soaked jacket back to its appropriate position on his shoulders and felt to make sure the buckle on his belt hadn't slipped too much out of alignment. *"Shut the fuck up, or I swear I'll..."*

Diaz stepped back from the tide of blood that was spreading across the plush beige carpeting toward his shoes. *"I'm not gonna shut up, Nicky. This bullshit has got to stop! You're out of control again!"*

Coltello snapped his fingers at Diaz's men and pointed down to the inanimate hulk stretched out in front of his desk. "Bury this bastard out in the concrete field, and then I want every strand of this carpeting replaced by tomorrow morning!"

Diaz grabbed Coltello by the sleeve. *"Are you listening to me, Nick?"*

But he got no response. Diaz had seen this all too often. One minute Coltello was seething with venom and fury, and then, without warning, he would merely turn oblivious to the world around him. It was like someone had flipped a switch inside of his head. Nicky The Knife would just check himself out of the Hotel Reality, and withdraw into a nearly catatonic state of apathy.

After each of his sadistic rampages—which were becoming more and more frequent—the mobster's brain would just short-circuit, as though overloaded by the violence he had just committed. And just like now, his face would become void of all expression, and his eyes would glaze over with an all too familiar, deer-in-the-headlights stare. It was a chilling scenario, played out time and time again, that had to be seen to be believed. Diaz wasn't a shrink, but it didn't take one to understand that if Nicky didn't get some help soon, these reoccurring episodes would eventually trash everything they had worked so hard to accomplish.

Diaz and his men stood speechless as Coltello, still in his stupor, abruptly began to peel off his clothes in the middle of the office and drop them haphazardly on the floor. "I got to take a shower now," he said, dreamily. "Make sure you burn the suit."

"Nicky!" Diaz pleaded.

He was already down to his underwear and socks and heading for the cold shower that always managed to snap him out of his delusion.

Diaz's men stared at their second-in-command with a mixture of dread and wide-eyed bewilderment. "Just do what he says, guys," he shrugged back at them, doubtfully. "I'm running out of answers. I just don't know how to handle this anymore."

With the drone of the shower coming from the adjoining bath-room, there was a collective pause taken for reflection and prayer as all three men huddled over their colleague's mutilated cadaver. After the somber moment had passed, the taller of the two henchmen was the first to break the memorial silence. "Jeez Jimmy," he whispered out of the corner of his mouth, "You really think Padron would've pinched the Guatemalan's bankroll?"

Diaz gazed down at what was left of Estefan Padron's pitifully contorted face and crossed himself in respect. "Not in a million years!"

7

A fish out of water...a sore thumb...a fifth wheel...how many other tired clichés could he think of to describe how he was feeling right now? As he patiently waited in the line for his turn to fork over the One Eleven Club's exorbitant fifty-dollar cover charge, he became acutely aware that he was the only person dressed in a business suit. Amid the flamboyant and boisterous crowd, he suddenly felt as gray as his suit. After ten minutes of creeping along the wall, he finally reached the entrance, paid his admission, and had the back of his hand stamped. "No chance of you wanting to check my identification, eh?" He ribbed the no-necked bouncer. His weak attempt at humor was greeted with a vacant stare and an order to go in or fuck off.

With a gracious smile, he held the door open for a leather-clad woman, whom he could have sworn was smoking a joint. When she failed to acknowledge his act of chivalry, he just chalked it up to the country's declining moral values. Perhaps he had set his expectations a bit too high, but he decided he should look upon this little adventure as a journey of enlightenment and discovery... kind of like Neil Armstrong first landing on the moon. His instincts would prove accurate, for indeed, it was like stepping foot on another world.

The throbbing bass that reverberated throughout the nightclub bludgeoned his body like a jackhammer. As he hunted for a square foot of clear floor space, he was confident that at any moment, his eardrums were going to rupture. The harsh tribal chanting they tried to pass off as harmony was a far cry from the soothing melodies served up by his country club's thirty piece orchestra at last year's Christmas Gala. But it only took a quick visual survey of the club's customers to confirm his suspicions that an appreciation of fine music wasn't what most of these people came here for.

As he pardoned and shouldered his way through the crowd toward the bar, he chuckled to himself when he realized that he probably owned socks that were older than most of the One Eleven Club's clientele. It was an uphill battle snaking through the mob, and when someone bumped into him, he would instinctively check for his wallet. *Was he that paranoid? Did it show?*

When he eventually made it to the bar, he was swallowed by a wall of humanity three deep and screaming out their choice of alcohol at the top of their collective lungs. Six bartenders raced around behind the counter in a whirlwind of activity, filling drink orders and collecting payment. Every time one of the mixologists received a tip that was worthy of the tribute, they would dart to the far end of the bar and ring a ship's bell. Judging from the regularity of the bell's pealing, either they poured very generous drinks here, or church had just let out.

A quick study when it came to grasping a sense of the crowd's character, he suspected that there would be no vodka gimlets served here, only drinks that needed to be washed down with beer chasers, or mixed with cherry flavored Jell-O and slurped out of someone's navel.

Trying not to jar anyone's glass, he carefully managed to wriggle his hand through the teeming herd and called out his order. While he waited for his drink, he scanned the crowd, taking a quick tally of all the garish tattoos being flaunted in plain sight. It was almost like a game to him. Whenever he felt uneasy, he counted. He loved to add; he was compulsive about it. He did it for a living, he did it for fun. When his watered-down gin and tonic finally arrived, he smiled casually at the bartender and handed over a twenty dollar bill expecting change. To his regret, the bell rang instead.

As he backed away from the bar, he was fascinated to add two more roses and an ornate cross to his aggregate of twenty-three verified tattoos. That was twenty-three more than he guessed he'd ever see at the country club. Tattoos, he mused, as he decided to take in the rest of the nightclub at a leisurely pace; every generation had them. What would some of these people think when they were in their nineties, standing naked and wrinkled in front of their full-length mirrors, wearing nothing but the liver-spotted skin God had cursed them with, and a faded tattoo of barbed wire indelibly etched around their sagging biceps? He squeezed the twist of lime into his drink, took another sip, and laughed at himself for being so cynical.

Still trying to spy any body art that might add to his total, he made his way toward the dance floor. The forbidden territory. It was an open display of eroticism, where sweat-soaked bodies writhed to the profane lyrics oozing from the enormous loudspeakers. An upright orgy bathed in swirling red, green, and yellow strobe lights, where public fondling wasn't frowned upon; it was the norm. He was starting to think that maybe drowning his sorrows here wasn't such a brilliant idea after all.

She careened into him, spilling his drink down the front of his jacket, and leaving the lime dangling from his breast pocket. "Oh, I'm so sorry," she apologized. "This damned place is so crowded, you can't take two steps without trampling over somebody."

His throat went dry, his words trying to form through parched and trembling lips. "It's not your fault," he said wiping down his jacket with the cocktail napkin, "really, it's okay."

"Look at this," she pointed. "I'm afraid I've made a terrible mess of your suit."

The first thing he noticed was the enticing aroma of her perfume. Even through the noxious cloud of tobacco fumes, she seemed to possess her own fresh smelling atmosphere. "No, I insist on paying for the cleaning."

She looked up at him with toffee-brown eyes framed by a face that was as timeless as a classic work of art. Her soft cranberry lips were parted in a gentle smile that revealed an inner kindness that his life had been sorely missing as of late. She was dressed conservatively in a floral print, not spray painted in leather and spandex like most of the women who patronized this place. She was a lighthouse shining for him in the darkness.

"The least I can do is buy you another drink," she pleaded, reaching up and pulling out the slice of lime that had landed in his pocket. "Something with a twist of lime, no doubt?"

He blushed for the first time in what seemed like a hundred years. "Look... you don't have to..."

She grabbed him by the hand, sending a jolt of electrified excitement coursing through every fiber of his being. "Nonsense. I won't take no for an answer!"

He hesitantly let her guide him back through the horde of partying customers. "Oh, please...not the bar again! You'll never..."

She cupped her hands around her mouth so she could be heard clearly over the thumping music. "Don't worry about it," she winked. "I've got clout! One of the bartenders is an old friend of mine!"

As they weaved their way toward the bar, he found himself no longer seeking out tattoos, but instead scanning the crowd for familiar faces, in the unlikely event that someone of consequence was to spot him in the company of this woman who was half his age. A roomful of skin-tight leather, ventilated mini-skirts, and multi-colored hair eventually calmed his unwarranted apprehension.

"What are you wearing...I mean, drinking?" she razzed him.

"Gin and tonic, but really...you don't have to..."

A few seconds later, she was handing him his drink, and he found himself staring at her, wondering who she was to deserve such preferential treatment. "How did you do that?" he asked, tipping his glass courteously.

"It pays to know all the right people!" She said loud enough to be heard over the thumping music.

He nodded with admiration.

"I'm sorry, I never introduced myself. My name is Rain," she said, holding out her hand.

He looked taken aback. "Excuse me?"

She scratched her finger over her heart. "I swear...that's my name!"

"Rain," he said, thoughtfully, "that's quite original."

She waved to someone that called out to her, but she was considerate enough not to respond in a way that could have made him feel like an outsider. "Care to guess the weather on the night I was born?"

He laughed heartily. "Well, I guess it was a good thing that it wasn't cold out that night too, otherwise your friends might be calling you frigid!"

She rolled her eyes. "Wow, and just when I thought I'd heard them all!"

Was he really smiling like the cat that had just chowed down on the canary? It felt like the corners of his mouth were touching his earlobes. "I'm just messing with you. It's actually quite a beautiful name."

Rain generously offered her extraordinary smile once again. "That's very nice of you to say, but now I suddenly find myself at a disadvantage."

He apologized for his bad manners and offered his name.

She looked at him suspiciously. "No. That wouldn't have even been my second guess."

Who was this young woman, and how was she managing to lift the entire weight of his troubled marriage off of his shoulders? One thing was for certain: he had to learn more about her! "So what would have been your first guess?" he asked her.

Her delicate eyebrows furrowed as she studied his well-worn facial features. "I think maybe Edward would have been my first choice, but the more that I look at you..." she theorized, shriveling her nose, "you're not really the Edward type. Yep, I guess your name fits you pretty well."

The blaring music that he had found so annoying only a few moments ago had suddenly taken a backseat to an entirely new set of emotions. "I'm so relieved you're okay with it," he said, pressing his hand to his chest in mock relief. "Now I can call my parents and tell them they were right!"

She batted her eyelashes and cooed over the rim of her glass. "You would do that for me?"

He grinned like a shy seventeen-year-old. "For you? Anything!"

She wound her arm around his. "Anything? Then how about a dance?"

Oh, if only his golfing buddies could see him now! "You can't be serious!"

She began dragging him toward the center of the club. "Why not?"

"I can't dance to this stuff," he protested.

She took the glass from his hand and set it down on a table beside the bustling dance floor. "Sure you can! It's easy! Come on!"

Of course, with a smile like that, she made him feel like he could do just about anything. "Maybe we should wait for something just a little bit slower," he shouted after her.

She had him by both hands now and was pulling him into the congregation of bouncing bodies. "Just go with it!" She yelled back to him. "You'll never know what you're missing until you try!"

Disoriented entirely by the arrhythmic beat of the music, he began shuffling from side to side like he had rocks in his shoes.

She gave him the "thumbs up" signal. "What were you so afraid of? You're a natural!"

They had been swallowed whole by the gyrating multitude that thrived beneath the spinning colored floodlights. It was a world within itself where nothing was taboo. With a total lack of propriety, a young woman wearing an indecently short dress crafted from what appeared to be aluminum foil shimmied past them. If her outfit wasn't bizarre enough, she had three safety pins skewering one of her eyebrows. He winced at the thought of surgical steel pins piercing the flesh anywhere near his eyes. Rain was laughing hysterically at his reaction, but he was only able to manage a half-hearted smile to disguise his revulsion. He interrupted his inept dancing just long enough to cup his hands around his mouth, "Is it just me, or is the whole world cracking up?"

Rain moved closer to hear him better. "The Three Aces attracts all kinds, doesn't it?'

He shivered as though someone had just poured a bucket of ice water down his back. "I'll say!"

She had come close enough for him to smell her perfume again. It was intoxicating. "This is obviously your first time here?"

He let her sweet scent fill his lungs. "Does it show?"

"Believe me, I would have noticed you if you had come in here before!"

Aw, man! Nothing puts lead in your pencil better than a woman who says all the right things! "That's very kind of you to say!"

She ran her fingers inside of his lapel. "I really mean it."

Was it suddenly getting warmer in here? "I...I don't know...what to...."

They were living proof that Copernicus and Galileo were wrong. The sun wasn't the center of the universe; it was the two of them. No longer in motion, everything and everyone else was revolving around them. As she gazed up into his face, time took a much-needed vacation. She made him feel twenty again, with a size thirty-two waist and no corrective reading glasses. "This isn't right."

Her tongue moistened her lips seductively. "What isn't right?"

As she pulled him even closer, his heart was beating so loud, he never noticed that the music had mellowed into a soft, romantic ballad. "Is this better?"

He could feel her ample breasts pressing against his chest. "I've never done this before."

Her mouth curled devilishly. "What? You've never slow danced before?"

"That's not what I..."

She put her finger over his mouth. "Just relax and enjoy yourself.

Life is too short!"

Life wasn't fair either. At a time when he should have been basking in the glow of expectation, his mind was ambushing him with the complexities of following through on such an illicit tryst. *First, there would be the phone calls to the office from...who? How about, Ms. Johansen from First National Bank? His secretary wasn't an idiot! Then, there was the place...a hotel? A motel? Behind the dumpster in an alley somewhere? What about evidence? No receipts! That was important! He would have to pay cash for everything!*

She snapped his fingers in his face. "Are you alright? I thought I lost you for a minute."

He looked down at her. "Of course I am, there's no place I'd rather be."

"Well, I've got my ear pressed against your chest, and your heart is doing a drum solo!"

Edgar Allen Poe...the telltale heart! "I'm just a little nervous. It's been awhile since I've held such a beautiful woman in my arms!"

She playfully slipped her hand inside his jacket. "Now I'm the one that's embarrassed!"

"Maybe..."

Rain tilted her head until her lips were inches from his. "Maybe what?"

"I don't know. I was going to suggest that we go somewhere a bit quieter..."

She lifted an eyebrow flirtatiously. "A bit quieter, eh? Like where? A library?"

He could feel himself blushing. "You'll have to excuse me, but I'm new at this."

"Don't worry, I know the perfect place," she said, with an impish wink. "Just wait here while I go to the bathroom and make a quick phone call to see if it's available."

He didn't want to let go. "Are you sure?"

Rain kissed the tip of her finger and pressed it against his lips.

"Just count to three hundred and wait right here, so I'll know where to find you."

The ear to ear smile was back. "I'm glued to this spot!"

The woman of his dreams waved once and then melted into the crowd.

So much stuff was running through his mind! *Safe sex. What had he heard about it? He tried to remember! Condoms! He hadn't needed one since the eighties! Would she let him stop off at the drug store? Was that too tacky? Could he buy just one? Did women carry them nowadays?* His head was spinning so fast, he was starting to feel the onset of a migraine!

The music had renewed its thunderous amplitude, but all of a sudden, he was oblivious to its ear-numbing effect. The thrill of anticipation was insulating him like a cone of silence. He was alone in a mob, unconscious to the tumult around him, luxuriating in the excitement of the moment. *What would it be like, to let his fingers trace her exquisite form? To kiss the nape of her neck? To have her roll off of him sweaty and spent, with a satisfied smile that he could only compare to his own?*

He pulled back his sleeve and glanced at the luminous dial on his watch. Five minutes had turned into ten. He craned his neck to see over the crowded dance floor, but the room was too dark and the busy lights too distracting. He didn't want to seem desperate by chasing after her. That might make him look too anxious or too possessive. He would just have to be patient and give her another few minutes.

8

The scene in the One Eleven Club was becoming more crowded and wilder by the minute. The toxic stench from the alcohol, tobacco, and marijuana made it nearly impossible for an amateur to breathe.

Ten minutes had turned into fifteen...

He hoped something hadn't happened to her. How long did she say she'd be? Maybe he *should* check on her? She would understand his concern. He didn't want to give her the impression that he was coming on too strong. He felt ridiculous just standing on the same spot, tapping his foot to music so loud that it made his chest throb. He grabbed the attention of a passing waitress. "Excuse me, could you tell me where the bathrooms are located?"

She bent over and picked up an empty glass off a nearby table and gave the surface a quick wipe with a bar towel she kept in her apron. "Over there."

"Over where?"

She pointed over his shoulder. "Back there...in the corner."

Never one to let a favor go unappreciated, he reached into his jacket for his wallet to tip her for her kindness, but his hand came out empty! *No! It couldn't be!* He began frisking himself, frantically patting every pocket in search of his billfold. Nothing! No cash, no credit cards, no identification! She had taken it all! **"God damn it!"**

The waitress spun around. "Hey, what's your problem, pal?"

He grabbed her by the shoulders. "Did you see the young woman that was here with me? She was wearing..."

The waitress broke loose of his grip. "Let go of me, mister! You're hurting me!"

"But she stole my wallet!"

Holding her tray in front of her like a shield, the waitress backed away. "I don't know anything about your mystery woman, mister! You got a problem? You should take it up with the owner or the cops!"

How could he have let this happen? How could he have been so stupid? It was all so clear to him now. He remembered how she blotted his jacket earlier in the evening. She was setting him up! How could he have been so blind to think she was really interested in him? That's what happens when you let yourself be dragged around by your Johnson! If he ever got his hands on her again, death would be the easy way out!

He cut through the crowd like a tornado, pushing people out of his way regardless of their size or gender. "Did you see a woman come in here?" he asked a girl standing outside the women's restroom. "She was wearing this dress with pastel flowers all over it!"

The girl took a long drag off her cigarette and exhaled a long plume of smoke into his face. "Do I look like a fucking hall monitor? Fuck off!"

Sweat was running down his face as he held open the door to the restroom. "Rain!" he yelled inside.

Another woman wearing stiletto heels strolled out, squeezing her nostrils and sniffling like she was having an allergy attack. "No rain in here stud. But if you're into golden showers..."

He had no idea of what she was talking about, but it didn't sound inviting. "Which way's the office?"

The woman squeezed her nostrils again, tilted her head back and shivered. "Does it look like I work here?"

His panic was growing exponentially. *He never should have come here! Now God was punishing him for his depraved transgression!* He reached out to yet another passerby. "Do you know where the office is?"

This time, he latched onto a disheveled punk who reeked from the foulest case of body odor he ever had the displeasure of inhaling. "The what?"

What was going on here? Had a bus from a carnival sideshow broken down outside this place? "**The...office!**" He made sure he spoke slowly and succinctly. "**Where...is...the...office?**"

The malodorous teenager almost lost his balance as he turned and pointed toward the far corner of the building. "Jeez, Pops, do you think it might be over by that big neon sign...," he burped, "... that says 'office'?"

He pushed the obnoxious teen away with enough force to send him sprawling onto his back and into the women's restroom. *Enough of this garbage! He had to get his wallet back! Forget the cash, what if she started charging things to his credit card? She had all of his identification! She'd know his address! What if she showed up at his front door demanding more? What if she did her research and found out how much he was really worth? It wouldn't take her very long to realize that she had just plucked the golden egg from the proverbial fucking goose! Oh, this was trouble! This was all the ammunition his wife needed! She was just itching for an excuse like this to dump his ass and suck his bank account dry!*

He muscled his way back through the nightclub toward the glowing orange sign that indicated the office. Two colossal bodyguard types stood post on the door. "I want to see the manager!"

The behemoth on the left remained stone-faced, while the one on the right let a slight grin crease his lips. "The manager isn't seeing anyone right now!" he grunted.

He studied them both standing as stationary as the statues on Easter Island. "You don't understand! I've been robbed right in the middle of *your* club! A woman lifted my wallet!"

The one on the left pouted contemptuously but remained silent.

"Don't 'ya just hate when that happens?" the one on the right chuckled.

He couldn't let these two bruisers intimidate him. Not now. Not with his entire financial future on the line! "I demand to see your boss about it!"

The silent one tried to stifle a laugh, as the talkative one jabbed an elbow into his ribs. "This guy's *demanding* to see the boss!"

With every warning bell going off in his head, he had no idea how he was managing to stand his ground. "Yes, I am! Doesn't Nick Coltello own this club?"

Both of their faces turned hard. Their eyebrows meeting in the middle. "You a friend of Mr. Coltello?

A chink in the armor! "No, but I have a feeling he wouldn't want me calling the police to investigate this problem."

That's the last thing he wanted either! A police investigation meant questions, a paper trail, calls to his house...his wife would toss him out for sure! "I'd be willing to bet Mr. Coltello wouldn't want them questioning all of your customers..." *Keep it going, you've got their attention now!* "Who knows what else they might find once they started looking? Are you aware of what's going on in those bathrooms?" *How was he finding the nerve to talk to them like this?*

The two goons stared at each other uncertainly. "Wait here a second," the one on the right grunted.

Two minutes later, he returned with another tall, sophisticated looking man.

"You're not Nick Coltello!"

Jimmy Diaz smiled politely. "No sir, I'm not." He said as he held out his hand courteously. "My name's James Diaz, and I am the manager of the One Eleven Club. Mr. Coltello is the owner, but he isn't available right now."

Something about this guy made him think of earthworms. Slippery, slimy, living deep down in the soil kind of worms. "No disrespect to your position, Mr. Diaz, but I'd still prefer to speak to your boss! This matter is of the utmost urgency."

Diaz's smile never faltered. "Mr. Coltello is feeling a bit under the weather right now, but rest assured, my associates here," he said, wrapping his arms around the two bodyguards, "have briefed me on your problem, and I promise I will do everything within my power to retrieve your wallet. But I must tell you, I fear the chances of recovery are very slim. These people are professionals. They prey on innocent people for a living. Unfortunately, they found you an easy mark."

This wasn't the first time someone tried to screw him over. Working in accounting and collections, he had been bullshitted by the best! "So, that's it?"

Diaz stepped down a step from between the two guards. "Excuse me?"

He stepped forward and leaned toward the manager. "Do you think you can just blow me off, and everything will be coming up daisies? I'm not part of your cocaine snorting riff-raff out there! I know she's a God damned criminal! She set me up!"

"Just what are you implying?" Diaz asked.

He pointed a finger at the manager's chest, but he was mindful not to make actual contact. "I'm not *implying* anything! What I'm *telling* you, is that I know this woman was a regular here. She called herself Rain, although I doubt that's her real name. She knew one of the bartenders, and some of your customers as well. She has to be a regular here!"

Diaz stared down at the encroaching finger and bit his lower lip to control his rising indignation. "And what would you suggest we do? Run a background check on all of our customers? Maybe install a metal detector at the door? Do you think that would help?"

He took a deep breath and sighed. *This flunky wasn't getting him anywhere. It was like beating his head against a brick wall.* "Well, it's obvious to me, that you don't know the first thing about what goes on in your own nightclub, Mr. Diaz!", he said as he started to walk away. "I guess you leave me no choice, but to call in the police! Perhaps *they* can help me find this Rain character!"

Diaz turned and glanced back ominously at the office door.

"Sir…please wait!"

He stopped dead in his tracks, making sure the manager didn't see the satisfied smile that brightened his face. "Having a change of heart?"

Diaz waved him back like a used car salesman afraid to lose a prospective buyer. "Why don't you give me her description and I'll talk to my bartenders. You said she knew one of them, right?"

"She said she did."

Suddenly, Diaz was treating him like a long-lost brother, patting him on the back and putting his arm around him. It was too touchy-feely for his own liking. "Why don't we walk on over to the bar together and see what we can find out, okay?"

He wriggled out from the manager's clinging embrace. "Why don't you go and I'll just wait for you in the office?

Diaz shook his head.

"Why not?"

Diaz's men instinctively closed ranks to defend the door.

"Because we're in the middle of having new carpet installed and the office is a mess! For liability purposes, we can't let you inside." He pointed to a vacant table just behind a brass railing that separated the office hallway from the rest of the club. "Why don't you take a seat over there, and one of my men will get you something to drink. Anything you want! It's on the house!"

He crossed his arms over his chest. "Really? A drink? You think that's going to make this all better?"

Diaz escorted him to the table. "Just give me five minutes, and hopefully, I'll have some good news for you!" He snapped his fingers, and the silent one guarding the door stepped forward. "Jorge, get our friend here a drink, or maybe something to eat. You hungry?"

He shook his head in disbelief. "No, I'm not hungry! Just find the woman who took my wallet, and I swear, I'll never step foot in your club again!"

Diaz excused himself and vanished into the crowd. It was nearly eight o'clock now, and time was quickly running out. If he didn't find the billfold soon, he was going to have to come up with something that would explain its disappearance. *A mugging? Possibly. Just misplaced it? His wife would never believe that. She knew him better than he knew himself sometimes. He didn't get to be this successful by losing his wallet. If he didn't get it back, he was a dead man!*

He peered through the railing at the two gorillas guarding the office door. The more he studied them, the more he came to realize that *guarding* was too loose a description. *It seemed more like they were defending the office...like it held the gold deposits from the Federal Reserve or something! And then there was Diaz's suspicious reaction at his suggestion of waiting inside...what was that all about?*

In desperate situations, the mind can become one's worst enemy. It plays tricks with your ability to reason rationally, turning the absurd into reality. As he sat at the table, drumming his fingers idly on the black Formica surface, ideas that would generally seem far-fetched suddenly didn't strike him as being so preposterous. *What if this club was just a front? Maybe this entire place was riddled with professional crooks!* He looked around suspiciously. To his unhinged mind, everyone suddenly looked guilty to him. *Other people seemed to know her. What if they were all part of some clandestine organization of thieves? Maybe Coltello was running this whole operation!* He read the newspapers, he listened to the radio and watched the news on television. *He knew Coltello wasn't the saint some of the media made him out to be! He was aware of the stories that connected the owner of the One Eleven Club to organized crime!*

No one could comprehend the chain of disastrous events that losing his billfold would start into motion. His wife would hire the most cutthroat lawyers his money could buy! His impeccable reputation would be in ruins! It would mean starting all over from scratch! He'd never be able to find a commensurate position at his age! This was no ordinary corporation he worked for! The head of the business was his brother-in-law, and no matter how much of a drunk his wife was, she was and would always be the little sister.

Now, the irrational thoughts were whizzing through his head. *What if Rain was still in the building? That had to be it! She was probably lying low in the office...and that's why they didn't want him in there! That meant...he still had a chance at salvation!*

"Hey fellas," he shouted up to two guards as he rose from his chair. "Would you mind if I made a quick phone call? My cellphone's dead."

The guards looked at each other skeptically as he jaunted up the steps towards them.

"It's getting late, and the wife's gonna really start worrying if she doesn't hear from me. You know how it is, right? Women, what can I say?"

Their faces remained expressionless, their posture, stiff as granite.

"Hey," he gestured at the office door, "it'll only take me a second. One quick call."

The chatty one, Jorge, reached into his breast pocket and pulled out his phone. "Here...take it...talk all you want...be my guest!"

He looked down at the phone and hoped his frustration wasn't apparent. This temporary setback only served to stoke fuel on the wildfire that was running amok in his brain. Now more than ever, he believed that the con artist whose despicable act had threatened his very existence was holed up behind that door!

He pretended to dial a number and waited, smiled at them, tapped his foot impatiently, rolled his eyes, smiled again...anything that might lull them into a false sense of security.

Did he still remember what his high school football coach had taught him? Hit 'em low, and hit 'em hard! He counted the seconds down in his mind.

Three...*Remember, the wallet is all that matters! No pressing charges, no big scene. Just get the billfold and go!*

Two...*Everyone can just forget that this evening ever happened! He'd never breathe a word of it to anyone...ever!*

One...*Our Father, who art in heaven, hallowed be thy name...*

Fortified by his faith in a benevolent God, he spun around and lowered his shoulder all in one flawless, aggressive movement. Jorge and his silent partner were outsmarted by the sudden gambit. He was like an unstoppable train thundering toward them! When he slammed into the door, he heard an earsplitting *crack*! He only prayed that it was the lock giving way, and not his vertebrae. Completely off balance, he went reeling into the office, just to end up tripping over a carelessly placed bolt of carpeting. Stunned and sore, he found himself sprawled out on a cold, barren, concrete floor.

"What the fuck is going on here? Who is this prick?"

Even dressed in a bathrobe and with his hair sopping wet, Nicky the Knife was still one of the most recognizable figures in Florida.

Jorge grabbed the intruder by the scruff of his jacket and brusquely yanked him to his feet. "I'm sorry, Boss. He's crazy. He busted right past us!"

Standing beside his desk, Coltello reached into the top drawer and withdrew a keen-edged pair of scissors. After wiping off some excess moisture from his forehead onto the sleeve of his robe, he flipped open the humidor on the corner of the desk and pulled out a hand-rolled Dominican Corona. Before cutting off the tip, and lighting it, he savored the sweetness of the tobacco by running the cigar under his nose. "Did he break my fucking door?"

Jorge walked over to the door, checked the lock, and scowled.

The words shot out of Coltello's mouth like bullets from a machine gun. **"Hey, dickhead! You broke my fucking door!"**

Instinctively, although probably more out of self-preservation than anything else, he shied away, tumbling backward over the large spool of floor covering again. When he collided with the roll this time, the bolt uncoiled just enough to expose what appeared to be a human foot!

At that same inopportune moment, Jimmy Diaz came sprinting into the room, breathless. "Oh, Jeez!"

Nicky the Knife took two puffs from his Corona and sent a set of smoke rings floating lazily toward the ceiling. "Nice of you to join us, Jimmy! Now, would you like to tell me **just what the *fuck* is going on?**"

The second in command bent down and tucked Padron's wayward limb back into the carpeting. With his back to Coltello, Diaz gave the innocent businessman, who was still on his hands and knees, a doleful look that seemed to say, "*Now you've done it. You should have waited for me!*"

"Is somebody gonna tell me who this asshole is, and why he's laid out on my floor?"

Although his hands were spotless, Diaz found himself rubbing them briskly as though he were trying to cleanse a stain only he could see. "This guy," he said, pointing his chin at the accountant, "says, that another customer stole his wallet."

Coltello leaned back on his desk and rolled the cigar between his lips. "So when did my office suddenly become the lost and found department?"

Diaz scratched his forehead. He wondered if the businessman realized that his life hinged on whatever happened in the next few seconds. "I was handling the situation, Mr. Coltello," Diaz said, formally for the businessman's benefit.

"But then he threatened to go to the police." One of the bodyguards chimed in, trying to rescue his own reputation.

Diaz's head snapped around in the guard's direction, and he immediately shut up.

"The police, eh?"

Diaz held up his hands defensively. "Would have never happened, Mr. Coltello. I had the entire situation under control."

Nicky the Knife spun the scissors around his finger and watched as the hypnotizing blade glistened in the light. "This would be a really inopportune time for the police to show up!"

Diaz felt like an eyewitness to an impending train wreck. He could sense that sickening knot building up in the pit of his stomach, as he helplessly watched the two engines heading towards each other. No matter what he did, no matter what he said, nothing could avert the looming catastrophe. "Look at the poor guy, Nick! He's harmless!"

Coltello wiped a few strands of wet hair off his face. "Harmless?" Diaz rested his foot on the roll of carpeting. "Like a gnat!"

Nicky the Knife walked over to the businessman, and grabbing a handful of his hair, lifted him to his feet and jerked his head back until they were staring eyeball to eyeball. Then he spoke softly. "Are you harmless as a gnat?"

The businessman's Adam's apple bobbed up and down in his exposed throat. "I'm…harmless," he managed to stammer. Coltello's lips peeled back into a wicked smile. He leaned forward and whispered into the man's ear. "*I don't think so...*"

9

Jimmy Diaz leaned against his bosses' desk and stared down at the floor. The only thought going through his head was where he was going to get another bolt of carpeting at this time of night. With his arms crossed over his chest, he could feel a headache coming on. Nicky was out of control. Diaz knew that if he actually owned a dog with his boss' temperament, he would have put him down years ago. But then, one doesn't bite the hand that feeds them, and Jimmy Diaz was paid very well indeed.

While one of the guards fumbled with the knob and lock on the office door, the other stared hesitantly up at the ceiling. Neither wanted to watch what was about to happen next.

A speck of blood dripped down the tip of the scissors as the blades pricked just below the stranger's exposed throat.

"You don't want to do this, Nicky," the interloper said uneasily.

"What the fuck did you just call me?" Coltello growled.

"I'm sorry, I meant Mr. Coltello," the stranger faltered.

"Do I know you, pal? Are we suddenly best friends?"

Diaz let out a long sigh of air as he shook his head in exasperation. *This didn't have to end like this. I tried, I tried, I tried. He actually seems to be enjoying this. It's like watching a cat corner a lizard and play with it for awhile before he finally kills it and then walks away like it never happened. Someone else would always come by and scoop up the remains. The cat only makes the mess and never considers the aftermath.*

Then something happened that took Jimmy Diaz by surprise. He looked up from the floor and noticed that the customer was almost smiling as he spoke. The stranger suddenly sounded aggressive. *This was different.*

"Mr. Coltello," the customer pleaded. "You don't want to do this." Nicky the Knife smiled. "Of course I do. I do it all the time."

The stranger moved his head slightly back and forth feeling the tip of the scissors scratch his neck. "You need me," he said, bluntly.

Nicky pressed the scissors harder against the customer's throat making him raise his head a few inches and rise on his toes. "Need you? I don't even know who the *fuck* you are! You come busting into my place of business like some kind of superhero and expect me to believe anything that comes out of your fucking mouth? Are you fucking kidding me?" Coltello looked to his left at Diaz who just shrugged. "If I broke into your office would you trust me?"

It wasn't comfortable speaking with your chin pointed at the roof, but the stranger managed to mumble what he needed to say. "Who does your books?" He asked, trying desperately not to lower his head.

"Who does my books?" Coltello asked. "Is that what you're asking me? Who does my *fucking books*? What are you, an accountant looking for work?" Coltello wiped a strand of wet hair out of his eyes. "Are you sure you want 'who does your books' to be your very last words?"

"I'm not here for a job interview, Mr. Coltello," pleaded the customer. "Trust me. I'm trying to save my life."

Nicky Coltello tilted his head from side to side, not sure what to make out of this intruder. So, like the cat and lizard, Nicky decided to play with his prey for a while longer. "I already got a whole team of accountants that do my books. I ain't in the market."

The customer shook his head slowly. "No, I mean your *books*. Not the ones that the government audits…your *real* books."

Coltello's eyes narrowed. "I don't know what *the fuck* you're talking about, pal. We only got one set of books here. This is a legitimate business. I'm just a bighearted entrepreneur who runs a trendy nightclub, pays every penny of taxes he owes and tries to do right by his fellow man, period. End of story."

The stranger didn't know where he got the guts from, but he very slowly and cautiously raised his right hand and put it on Coltello's left wrist easing the blade downward, away from his neck. "I can tell your heart is huge, Mr. Coltello," he said softly, not wanting to pull the trigger of the half-cocked gun standing before him. "But let's just say hypothetically there *were* another set of ledgers somewhere. And that these notebooks or computer records revealed other income that you would rather not have the government pry into. Who do you have keeping track of those transactions?"

Nicky the knife smiled and took a step back. He looked at the customer like he was some sort of oddity that he had never come across before. "I gotta admire your balls, mister. They must be gigantic. For you to come into my workplace and *hypothetically* accuse me of running an illegal enterprise out of this nightclub," he chuckled. "You don't fear death at all, do you?"

The customer could feel a drop of blood dribble down to his collar, but he dared not make any sudden movement to wipe it away. "It's obvious I have nothing to lose by asking, Mr. Coltello, so I'll ask you again. Who cooks your books?"

Diaz took a step forward from the desk, either in anticipation of interfering, or catching the body, he wasn't quite sure yet.

"Do you believe this mamaluke?" Coltello asked no one in particular, as he tightened the knot in his robe while still grasping the business end of the scissors. "Okay, I'll play along just for shits and giggles. I got a whole team of very knowledgeable accountants who oversee my business affairs. They are highly competent, and I trust them implicitly to keep all my transactions on the up and up should the government ever decide that they want to *subpoena*…I mean, *request* to examine them. *Hypothetically*."

Diaz spoke up. "Nicky, I think you need to stop talking."

Coltello held up his hand to stop him. "My associate over here thinks we should discontinue our conversation and I am inclined to agree with him. I think I might have inadvertently stepped over an acceptable boundary of familiarity with you." He snipped the scissor blades twice in the air.

"I'm better than all of them combined," the stranger blurted out. "I have been hiding assets and laundering money for one of the largest corporations in the State of Florida for the last twenty years. I know every loophole in the U.S. Tax Code, and I can double your profits through specialized investments that make any dirty currency sparkling clean. I'm like Mr. Clean."

Coltello looked over at Diaz and then back at the accountant and smirked. "You're Mr. Clean, eh? You don't look nothing like him."

The customer held out his hand and spoke slowly and precisely. "If I had my wallet, I would gladly give you one of my business cards, but I told you, I was pick-pocketed by a woman out there."

Coltello spoke to Diaz while keeping shark-like eye contact with the accountant. "Is Veronica working our joint again?"

"Probably," Diaz admitted.

The accountant interrupted. "Excuse me, but she called herself Rain, not Veronica."

"Rain," Coltello chucked. "That's fucking rich. Find Veronica and bring me the wallet," he ordered.

Jimmy Diaz signaled one of the guards to track down the missing wallet. He knew Veronica would still be in the club hunting another easy mark. She was a two-bit hustler that no one in the office thought about twice. Diaz knew she carried a change of wigs in her purse to dodge guys like this. He had seen her change her hair color and clothing more than once in the evening. It was quite a clever scam actually. *Hell, everyone had a right to make a living.*

"And make sure everything in the wallet is intact," Coltello yelled, as the door shut.

"What do we do now?" The accountant asked trying desperately to ignore the corpse encased in a bolt of rug lying a few feet away from him.

Coltello untied the knot in his robe and let it fall to the floor. Walking naked across the office, he reached into a dresser and slipped into a pair of navy blue trousers sans underwear. From another drawer, he pulled out an orange v-neck t-shirt and pulled it over his head.

Okay, that was incredibly normal and uncomfortable, the accountant thought. *At least he put down the scissors for now. That's a good sign.*

Coltello walked over to Diaz and whispered something into his ear. The customer thought he heard the word "concrete," but he wouldn't bet his life on it. And then he wondered if that was exactly what he was doing.

Ten minutes later the office door opened and the guard returned with Rain in front of him.

"Is this her?" Coltello asked aloud, never taking his eyes off the girl.

The accountant nodded.

"I can't hear you shaking your fucking head, jerk-off. Yes or no, is this Rain?"

"Yes," he said.

Coltello smiled sweetly. "You've been very busy tonight, Veronica. Do you have something that belongs to this gentleman?"

The young woman was trembling. "Mr. Coltello, if I had known that..."

Nicky held up his hand again. It was his universal signal for silence. "Do you still have this property?"

"Excuse me?"

"The wallet, do you still have this man's wallet?" He demanded impatiently.

"Oh yes, sir," she replied meekly, as she reached her quivering fingers into her purse. She pulled out the billfold and held it up. It was at the same instant that she noticed the roll of carpet on the floor.

Coltello looked at the rug and then back at her. He shook his head remorsefully. "It's okay, Veronica, there's nothing to worry about. There's nothing to see here. We're just doing a little redecorating. You returned the merchandise you took, and that's all that matters to me." Nicky nodded to the guard standing behind her. "Take Veronica and get her a drink on me. Get her whatever she wants. Are you hungry, Veronica? We've got some pretty good pasta dishes here. The sauce is a Coltello family secret. I'd tell you what was in it, but then I'd have to kill you," he snickered.

The young pickpocket's eyes started to tear up. "Thank you Mr. Coltello, for your generosity, but I'm not very hungry. I'd just like to leave now, and I promise I'll never come back to the Three Aces again." She swept her finger across her heart.

Nicky the Knife smiled warmly. "Oh, I assumed that was a given."

He shrugged his head at the beefy guard standing next to her. "Escort Veronica out and take care of her."

The guard grabbed her by the elbow and pulled her toward the door. There was a long moment of unbroken eye contact between her and the accountant as she was being led away that spoke volumes. Neither of them wanted to admit it, but they both assumed that before this night was over, they would end up together anyway.

10

Nicky Coltello opened up the wallet and pulled out the Florida driver's license from behind a transparent window built into the leather. He looked at the name and the picture and confirmed that the wallet did indeed belong to Mr. Clean.

"Gerald Banks, that's you?" He asked, handing the license to Jimmy Diaz.

"Yes sir," Banks confirmed. "That's my billfold. Now if I could just have it back, I would really appreciate it."

Jimmy Diaz walked around Coltello's desk and removed a laptop computer from one of the desk drawers. In less than a minute, he had searched the name "Gerald Banks" and begun reading any information he could find on the alleged accountant.

"You'll get your wallet back when I'm good and ready to give it to you," Coltello grunted. "What's it say on there, J.D.? Is this guy who he says he is?"

Diaz ran his finger across the screen. It was a bad habit he had attained as a slow reader back in parochial school. He held up another finger while he continued to read to himself. "Just give me another second, Nicky, I'm almost through."

Coltello stood silently and waited. He never took his eyes off the man he now knew as Gerald Banks. What was it about this guy that made Costello uneasy? The mobster considered himself a good judge of character and his intuition was usually on point. There was just something about the way this guy handled himself that intrigued him. "I'm growing impatient, Jimmy. What did you find out?"

Diaz looked up from the monitor. "You work across the street?" Diaz asked.

The customer nodded. "Yes, sir."

"On the eighteenth floor?"

"Sixteenth through eighteenth actually."

Coltello felt like a third wheel in the conversation. Something he was never used to. "Does anyone want to clue me in here? Is this guy who he says he is, or isn't he?"

Diaz stood up and closed the lid on the laptop. He walked around to the front of the desk, hitched up the knees of his slacks and took a seat. "Mr. Banks works for Mason Cruise Lines, boss. Peter Mason is the new mover and shaker in town."

Coltello grimaced. "I know who Peter Mason is. I know everything that happens in this burg. So you're Peter Mason's accountant?"

Banks nodded. "And his brother-in-law."

The owner of the Three Aces took a step back. "Whoa, his brother-in-law? Then why were you over here chasing a piece of ass? The old lady cut you off?"

Banks rubbed the back of his neck. "It's a long personal story that I would rather not get into if you didn't mind. So now you have something on me. Happy?"

Coltello looked over at Diaz. "Get on the blower right now and call Tiny off the girl. We may need her if something goes sideways here."

Diaz pulled out his cell phone and dialed. "Yeah it's me," he said into the phone. "Don't touch the girl. Put her somewhere safe for the minute." Then there was a pause. "No," he continued. "Stay away from the field for now. Bring her back if you need to. We need you and Jumbo to clean up this mess and get some new flooring in by tomorrow. Yeah, just come back."

"You know what I want?" Coltello announced. "I want a tour of your office. Can you take me there now?"

Banks nodded. "Sure, but why?"

Coltello shrugged. "I want to see how a classy guy like Peter Mason decorates his place. I've never really been in a big corporate office before. Maybe I can get some ideas for this shit hole. You got a problem with that?"

Banks looked over at Diaz who raised his hands. "Let's take a walk."

Coltello smiled as he tied his hair back into a ponytail. "Yeah, let's take a walk, and we can talk on the way about what you think you can do for me. Worse comes to worst," he chuckled, "we can always take you up to the roof and toss your ass off!"

The accountant smiled. Coltello didn't return the gesture.

With Banks walking between them, the trio left the office and made their way through the chaos of the One Eleven Club. People pointed at Nicky the Knife as he sliced through the throng of humanity. Seeing him in person was like spotting a great white shark. You knew they were out there, but you rarely came face to face with one—and really didn't want to.

When they reached the sidewalk, Coltello looked up at the skyscraper across the street. The wind was brisk, and a line of customers was still huddled against the wall of his club waiting to get inside. There were only a few random offices lit up as cleaning crews went about their business. "I remember when they built that fucking monstrosity," he bemoaned. "It ruined the skyline. What a damned shame!"

Banks tucked his hands into his jacket pockets as they stepped off the curb. "I wouldn't know. We only moved into these offices last year. Most of corporate are still in Miami."

"Like Mason himself?" Coltello asked as he waited for a car to slow down so he could cross.

"He comes and goes. I think he'll be starting to spend more time here in the future. He's got big plans for his financial interests in the city of Jacksonville."

Jimmy Diaz was the first to reach the entrance to the Jax Building lobby, and he held open the door for Coltello and Banks. The interior was austere and cold. A local bank had a branch office in the on the ground floor which was closed now, but otherwise, there was just a security desk and a few pieces of non-descript art adorning the marble walls.

"Mr. Banks, you're back?" The security guard sitting behind the desk called out.

The three men stepped up to the desk. "Yeah, I need to get something from my office. No problem, right?"

"Of course, Mr. Banks. No problem. I'm just going to need you to sign in," he reminded him, as he placed a clipboard with an entry log on the desk.

"Sure, Freddie. Thank you," Banks said, signing his name.

The guard exchanged smiles with the other two men. "You fellows don't need to sign in as long as you're with Mr. Banks.

"They're with me, Freddie." Banks confirmed.

"Yes sir, Mr. Banks. I'll turn on elevator three. Shouldn't be too long."

The three men arrived at the wall of elevators just as the door to number three slid open. Banks waved to the guard who was still watching them.

Once in the elevator, the floors seemed to take forever to click by.

"So, in my office you implied that Peter Mason had some shady dealings. Did I hear you right?" Coltello asked as he stared at the numbers ascending.

Banks stepped out into an empty foyer when the elevator finally stopped. "You're kidding me, right? Do you know how the Mason fortune was created?"

Diaz interrupted. "His father was a drug runner in the eighties."

Coltello sounded perturbed. "I know that. Everyone fucking knows that."

They turned the corner and Banks pulled open one of the glass doors with the Mason Cruise Line logos etched into it. Nicky the

Knife ran his hand over the insignia. "Nice."

The offices of The Mason Cruise Line Corporation had quickly overtaken the top three floors of the Jax Tower. Marketing filled the sixteenth floor; Operations occupied the seventeenth floor; and Administration and Accounting filled the Penthouse suites.

"This is some freakin' operation going on here," Coltello conceded. "Sweet...very sweet."

A photograph, lithograph, sketch, or watercolor of one of the company's vessels decked out each wall along the hallway to the conference room. "I'm glad I'm wearing comfortable shoes." Coltello blurted out. "This is quite the fucking hike."

"I thought we would be more comfortable talking in the conference room." Banks said. "I'm afraid my office would be kind of cramped."

"Cramped." Coltello laughed. "I'll bet your office is bigger than the Three Aces."

The trio of men turned yet another corner. "Not even close." Banks admitted.

Nicky tapped Diaz on the back. "You know, the irony of an accountant named Banks hasn't been lost on me. Did you wonder about that, Jimmy?"

Diaz shook his head. He was too busy being impressed by what some illegal drug money had grown into in less than a generation. "No, Nicky, I didn't. That's clever."

Coltello smiled. "Really fucking ironic!"

The hallway emptied into the spacious and luxurious conference room. Taking up a quarter of the entire eighteenth floor, the room had an almost identical arrangement to the conference room in the Miami Headquarters. Teleconference screens filled the far wall, while the opposite wall revealed an absolutely jaw-dropping vista of Jacksonville at night. The same models of the *Hydra* and Mason Ballpark stood guard on each of the other walls.

Coltello stood by the window nearly speechless. "Are you seeing this, Jimmy? Top of the world, Ma…top of the world!"

Banks sat down at the head of the table. The position felt awkward, but good…very good. "Would you gentlemen like to sit down so we can discuss our business?" he asked.

Jimmy Diaz pulled out a chair a few seats away, but Nicky the Knife was mesmerized in place at the window. In the distance, even though it was miles away, he could see airplanes taking off and landing at Jacksonville International. Ships of all sizes traversed the Saint Johns River turning the dark water into a light display that was breathtaking. There weren't many things in this world that Nicholas Coltello was envious of, but this view suddenly skyrocketed to the top of his list.

"I'm good from here," Coltello said. "So tell me, Mr. Banks. Other than the threat of loss of life, I have pretty good instincts, and I get the distinct impression that there might be more to your motivation here than just your offer to keep my enterprises looking legitimate."

Banks looked at him quizzically. "More than a swan dive from the roof? Seriously?"

"I am an excellent judge of people, Mr. Banks, and I can read you like People Magazine. Big conference room, a tiny office, sitting at the head of the table when no one else is around. Banished to lowly Jacksonville instead of bikini hunting on South Beach." Coltello looked over his shoulder at the accountant. "Sounds like a man who thinks he's been done wrong."

Banks shook his head. "You don't know me. You don't know what motivates me."

"Greed motivates you, Mr. Banks. Greed motivates everyone."

Banks shook his head. He would never permit himself to be jealous of his brother-in-law. But he knew where all of the skeletons were hid. He knew where all the money was really coming from. He saw it every day. It was his job to cover it up. He was Mr. Clean.

"Fucking family," Nicky the Knife sighed. "You know being the black sheep isn't so bad, Gerald. Take it from me, the black sheep don't show as much dirt. Am I right?"

Banks looked over at Diaz who was leaning back in his chair staring at the scale model of the *Hydra*. "Your boss is quite the philosopher."

Diaz nodded. "One of his most endearing traits."

Coltello rubbed his chin as he gazed down upon the roof of his nightclub far below. "This isn't about opening the family vault and letting the secrets out. I don't give a damn how Mason makes his money. But you have the look of a man who thinks he deserves more. A man who wants more." He waggled his finger. "Trust me. It's in your eyes…they don't lie. Just the fact that you showed up at my club alone tonight tells me as much. All of this opulence and you're resigned to working in a broom closet? A member of the family? Fuck that shit. You're tired of Peter Mason walking all over you, taking credit for the job you do, raking in the big bucks while you stay up in this tower working your ass off until thirteen o'clock every fucking night. Go ahead. Tell me I'm wrong."

Banks pounded his fist on the table. "You're wrong."

Nicky the Knife smiled with success. "Don't sweat it, Gerald. I was no different from you. I had an older brother that got all the love from our family. I was the thorn on the rosebush, and he was the flower. He couldn't do nothing wrong."

The accountant never looked up. "So what happened?"

Coltello shrugged matter-of-factly. "I killed him, what did you think I did?"

Banks let out an audible gasp. "Excuse me?"

Coltello laughed heartily. "Nah, I'm just fucking with you."

Banks took a deep breath. "Phew, for a moment there…"

Nicky the Knife's face tightened. "No seriously, I killed him. Put a gun to his head and blew his brains out on his twentieth birthday. I hated him like cancer. He was the first body I ever buried in the field."

Banks looked over at Diaz to see if Coltello was actually telling the truth. Diaz shrugged. "Wouldn't have been my first option," Diaz supposed.

Without skipping a beat, Nicky the Knife strode over to the model of the *Hydra.* "So tell me about this thing. It looks pretty cool."

Banks felt like he was going to throw up. He just realized he was in the presence of an authentic homicidal psychopath. What had he gotten himself into? He slowly rose to his feet and with trembling legs walked over to the model ship. He put his hand on top of the glass case that protected the replica. "This...this is the *Hydra,*" he stammered. "She's the flagship of our new hydrofoil fleet. She will sail from Jaxport to Bermuda and the Bahamas. She's been out on trial runs and is proving to be everything Mason says about her."

Coltello bent over and pointed beneath the ship. "What's going on down here?"

Banks tried to maintain his composure in front of the deranged gangster. "Those are turbine-driven fans that raise the ship out of the water and carry it above the waves. They allow the ship unheard of speed and mobility."

Coltello tapped on the glass. "J.D., you should come here and take a look at this thing. It's fucking amazing!"

Diaz spun in his chair. "I read about it in the news, Nicky. It's been all that they talk about."

"Yeah? Maybe I heard something about it," he admitted. "I only read the news when it's about me."

Coltello nodded his head in approval and walked abruptly to the other side of the conference room. Banks trailed behind him. "And this is the new ballpark, I suppose."

"Yes, that's Mason Cruise Lines Field. We're expecting to break ground in the next few weeks."

Diaz spoke up. "Really? Have they reached a decision on a location? I thought the city commission was still deliberating."

Banks shook his head as he watched Coltello study every aspect of the model. "The commissioners are just putting on a show for the press and the city. Peter Mason already knows where the ballpark is going to be built, and it's none of the sites that the commissioners are considering. He's using them as a distraction while he works out the arrangements for the parcel of land he really wants."

Jimmy Diaz leaned forward in his chair.

"So are you going to give us some insider information here, as a sign of good faith on your behalf? If we know ahead of time where he's buying the land, then maybe we can make a last minute real estate investment and get in on a piece of the action."

Banks didn't care. The public was going to find out next week anyway. Maybe this would score some points with the lunatic. "Take a look out the window, and I'll show you."

Coltello gestured for Diaz to get up and join them. The lights of the city glistened like it was the winter holidays even though it was only mid-July. "You see that stadium over there," Banks pointed.

"Yeah, that's the Baseball Grounds where the minor league Jumbo Shrimp play ball. God, I hate that stupid name," Coltello complained. "What was the problem with calling them the Jacksonville Suns? What the hell is a jumbo shrimp anyway? That name is an oxymoron, am I right? How can you have jumbo shrimp?"

"Anyway." Banks continued. "Just to the east of the Baseball Grounds is EverBank Field, where the Jaguars play. Mason wants to make this area a showcase for sports."

Diaz pointed at the baseball field. "So he's going to raze the Baseball Grounds and build the ballpark on the old field's footprint?"

Banks shook his head. "No. The Baseball Grounds have been there since two thousand and two. They knocked down the old Wolfson Park Stadium that was built in the nineteen fifties to replace it. That's historic ground in Jacksonville. We can't touch it. One of our minor league teams will probably move in there."

Jimmy Diaz studied the glistening lights of the city and tried to imagine where the proposed stadium would fit. "So where else is there room down there?"

Gerald Banks slowly moved his finger across the window to a dark patch of land that was hiding like a shadow amongst the lights. "Peter Mason is buying that tract of land over there. Just east of the Hart Bridge Expressway, between Bryan Street and the Saint John's River."

Nicky the Knife and Jimmy Diaz stared at each other in stunned disbelief as Banks continued to unveil the plans. "There are some old concrete plants over there now. Mason is paying each of those companies more than enough to relocate north of the city. The new ballpark will be the new gem of Jacksonville, perched right on the edge of the city with the Saint John's River flowing just over the wall in dead centerfield. We're getting the land for chump change. It's like the companies are glad to be moving." Banks confessed.

Nicky the Knife pulled his accomplice off to the side and, in a barely audible whisper, expressed his urgent concern. "First thing in the morning I want to meet with Artie Beckworth."

"Beckworth—the City Commissioner?"

Coltello seethed. "He's *my* commissioner, God damn it. I need to make sure that he understands the importance of this matter to our partnership. If this vote goes through, we all go down...including him."

Diaz stared out the window at the dark patch of land and wondered about the actual number of bodies buried beneath it. "Consider it done, boss."

Coltello turned back to Banks with his eyes filled with rage and the veins bulging in his neck. It was plain to see that he was about to lose his shit again. "I have a message for your employer that I want you to deliver personally," he fumed as he grabbed Banks and pulled him close by the necktie. "Tell Mr. Peter Mason that if he should opt to build his fucking ballpark anywhere near those concrete plants, he'll never live to see the first pitch."

11

Summer vacation had come to Florida, and everyone in Jacksonville welcomed it like a long-lost relative. The sky was alive with slowly moving clouds, and a warm breeze rustled between the cars in the school parking lot. You could sense the change in attitude coming on this last day of school. Matt opened the door of his Sentra for Simone and held it open until she climbed in. She unbuttoned the top few buttons of her tennis shirt before pulling the seatbelt over her shoulder. She didn't care for the heat and hated the way it made her clothes cling to her body.

"Turn on the air to cool it off in here." She signed as Matt slid in next to her.

Driving down a side street, caught behind a line of yellow buses, they saw an ice cream truck parked off to the side of the road with young children from the nearby elementary school gathering around it. Matt and Simone smiled at each other, but Matt began to feel sad. The happy sounds coming from the truck were something from his childhood he could still remember. She was oblivious to how he was feeling, never having heard the jingling rhythm. It was a simple thing, the old familiar sound of that truck coming down your street every afternoon. It was the simple things like that that ripped him up inside.

The Pizza Palace was the neighborhood hangout, since it was located so close to the school. The pizza tasted like matzo with tomato sauce, but the students paid no attention. It was the hangout where everyone went.

Matt pulled into the second space from the entrance. The first space was reserved for handicapped parking, which he refused to use. His friends might, but Matt wouldn't. He held the restaurant door open for Simone as she walked through. Fellow students paused from their eating, leaving strings of mozzarella dangling from their chins. Most waved; some who had decided to take the American Sign Language class the school offered signed to him. He returned the conversations politely and even corrected a few of their faulty signs. He appreciated the extra effort, and knew they were making the deaf kids feel as integral to the student body as every other student. No more, no less.

Matt finished his greetings and pointed to a booth way in the back. When they reached the table, the red and white plastic checkered tablecloth looked like it hadn't been washed in weeks. There was a small round stain on it by Simone's elbow. They swore it was a pepperoni that had disintegrated over a week or two of just lying there. Matt handed Simone a sauce-stained menu. He didn't look at his. The waitress came over, and she ordered for both of them by pointing at the items they wanted on the menu. The waitress walked away and returned shortly with the order. Simone figured the pie had to have been made in advance and was just reheated. She took a slice and placed it on Matt's dish and took a slice for herself. She gestured for Matt to start eating, but he wasn't paying attention. He was just staring out the window. She touched his hand to get his interest. "You did well back there," she signed trying to make small talk. There was something obviously bothering him. "You could have just waved to those kids, but you helped them out. That's very cool, but what's bothering you now? You're giving me the silent treatment. No pun intended."

"It happened again," Matt admitted uncomfortably.

"It?"

"It." He emphasized with his facial expression.

"Like when you touched my locker?" she signed. "Give me all the details."

"I was fortunate that I didn't completely pass out." He signed to her. "It was over really quick. A minor incident, but it seems to be happening to me with more frequency lately, small stuff."

Matt turned to look at her, no longer paying attention to the traffic on Baymeadows Road. "I was leaving Hope's house the other night."

Simone didn't like discussing Hope Jannick. She had even created a very nasty name sign for her whenever Matt wasn't around.

"Her father was going away on a short business trip, and she invited me over for some dessert. Her father and mine used to work together, remember?"

"Yes, I remember. So, how did it go?"

"We had a fight."

Simone was secretly delighted and sat forward in the grimy booth.

"It was silly, really. I don't even remember what it was about. I was driving home really pissed at her, and I was gripping the steering wheel much too hard. The next thing I knew, I was watching my car being built and rolling off the assembly line! Luckily, I instinctively hit the brakes and let go of the wheel, which must have broken the connection."

Simone realized that he was driving at the time and he could have been killed. "Matt, we have to get you to someone who can teach you to control this power. You could really hurt yourself, or, God forbid, someone else if you're not careful!"

He stared at her with disdain at the suggestion. "And what? Be a lab rat for the rest of my life? No thanks! It's bad enough that my grandmother is having me tested. I thank God every day that the press has finally left me alone. Can we drop this conversation now? Let's just finish the pizza and get out of here." Matt knew she meant well, but there was no way she could comprehend this feeling. He recalled the time he had been in a department store buying a bottle of perfume for his grandmother; he'd taken a delightful tour of Paris before the salesgirl snapped him out of it. There were times the trace could prove enlightening, but more often than not, it was a curse.

"Have you decided if you're coming next Saturday?" Simone signed.

Matt looked up from his third slice quizzically. What had he forgotten? He cut another slice of pizza for himself. It broke in half before it reached his plate. "Where are we going?"

Simone finished her slice and wiped the corner of her mouth. "To the ballgame," she signed. "You do remember that my father invited you and your grandfather to see the game, don't you?"

Matt took a sip from his glass of water. "Sorry, I forgot."

"You still want to go, don't you? It's the biggest event to hit the town since the Jaguars' inaugural football game! The Commissioner of Baseball wants to see how large the attendance will be. If there's enough interest, they might consider letting Peter Mason build his new stadium and relocate a team here. This might be the opportunity the city has been waiting for. It's between Charlotte and us. Everyone who loves baseball will be there. My father's had the tickets for weeks."

Matt looked at the check and pulled out his wallet. "Sure, it should be fun. I've only been to the Baseball Grounds a few times. Even when I lived in Miami, I never got to see the Marlins play. My dad was always too busy to take me." He attempted to shake some coagulated grated cheese onto his last slice, but the shaker was having none of it. "I'm not sure if my grandfather will go. He doesn't want anything to do with me."

Simone was well aware of Matt's home life; his grandfather would never change. She asked if she could leave the tip as they finished up. Matt said no.

"Try and convince your grandfather to go. We'll pick you up at eleven, and the game starts at one. If your grandfather gives you an argument, tell him we'll drop you both back home right after the game. It might be a good thing for the two of you."

Matt shrugged indifferently. "I can try, I guess. He might go along with it if he knows your father is going too. At least he'll have someone to talk to."

Matt seemed mesmerized by the traffic out on Baymeadows Road again. He had a strange feeling, but it wasn't one of his visions. It was difficult to describe—a sense that something wasn't right. It was ominous, and not like anything he had ever felt before. Maybe going to the ballgame and being out in the fresh air would do him some good and help shake off the sensation of impending trouble.

They both finished their lunches in silence as a pair of speakers on the far wall played music for everyone else but them.

Treachery has existed as long as there's been warfare, and there's always been a few people that you couldn't trust.

- **General James Mattis**

12

USCG Station Mayport
Jacksonville, Florida

The specially modified Coast Guard cutter *Harry S. Truman* sat calmly in her berth as Captain Roy Sowell came onboard. The rising tide slapped a mist of pale green salt spray onto the side of the ship. In the distance, commercial fishing trawlers from Mayport Village were getting an early start on the day's catch. They puttered out to sea, the men on deck preparing their nets for the day's bounty.

The sun was just peeking over the horizon now, and it cast the eastern sky in a fiery pink glow. Two seamen standing watch outside an open loading compartment saluted as he walked past with his clipboard. "All quiet, men?"

They stood at attention, their eyes tired from the all-night vigil. "All quiet, sir," came the unanimous response.

This was so much more exciting than sitting behind a desk, shuffling papers and pushing pencils. Sowell could feel his anticipation growing inside. He was proud and a little bitter to have been chosen by the Vice Admiral himself for his final mission. Slowly and deliberately, he walked the two hundred-foot length of the ship and checked off every item on his list to ensure readiness. The Truman reminded him of the naval base itself. Everything was so serene and peaceful on the exterior, but deep inside the heart of both was a hive of activity. A chill ran through him as he stood on the fantail of the ship. The early morning air blowing in off the sea was more cooling than he had expected this early in the summer. It seemed like he was always feeling cold nowadays.

Sowell walked back past the two seamen on post and entered the mid-ship hatch of the cutter. A cup of dark, hot coffee was what he needed most now, so the galley would be his first stop. Once inside the ship, Sowell had a hard time recognizing anything. The last time he was on the Truman was a month ago, before any of the modifications had been made. She looked completely different.

The Truman had a long and storied history. The ship's most publicized rescue had occurred during January 1986, when the Truman was one of the first to arrive in response to the space shuttle *Challenger* disaster. In November of 1995, the Truman had helped rescue 578 migrants from a grossly overloaded seventy-five-foot coastal freighter, the most significant number of migrants rescued from a single vessel in Coast Guard history. Now, she was being gutted, retrofitted, and prepared for her last operation... just like he was.

Technicians scrambled past Sowell, making last minute adjustments to their equipment. He had to be careful where he stepped, as the deck was a mass of electrical equipment and cables. Computer consoles were installed where the sonar equipment had been. The tiny green and red lights of their panels blinking on and off like the nighttime sky on some alien world. What had they done to his ship? It didn't really matter how she looked inside, as long as she did the job they modified her to do. If this test was successful, he knew the Truman was going to be decommissioned and a brand new cutter outfitted to the new Department of Defense standards would take her place. There would be none of this exposed wiring. *Why use something twice, when you can spend the taxpayer's money and build a new one?* It wasn't the fact that he had grown so attached to the Truman that bothered him; it was that he was also a taxpayer.

The galley was still intact and abandoned when he entered it. A coffee maker with a full pot and all the condiments sat against the far bulkhead. Sowell poured himself a cup of the warming liquid and headed up a level to the bridge. Checking his watch, he knew the cargo would be arriving any minute. By this evening they would be underway. Once out to sea, he would let the crew in on how they would be spending their next twenty-four hours.

The bridge was quiet, aside from the usual noises. The radar screen beeped monotonously as the antenna atop the superstructure spun around in its endless orbit. He had time to do some heavy thinking while alone on the bridge. He leaned against the starboard window and contemplated his mission. Even though it was a worthy send-off for his ship, it was less so for him. Sowell was being forced into early retirement after the operation. He was part of the old guard, and like his decomposing ship, he was being sent to dry dock.

The importance of the operation was apparent. The United States Department of Defense had to prove this technology worked. If the North Koreans could detect the Truman, it might just escalate events past the point of no return. He shook off that horrible thought and picked up the intercom to muster his officers.

The Truman would carry a total of thirty-eight men and seven women. That was less than two-thirds of his usual complement of seventy-five, but half had been replaced by scientists and technicians. Somewhere in that count, there had to be one or two intelligence people skulking amongst them as well, Sowell figured.

The cutter would be underway with the least amount of crew available to operate the ship safely. Sowell's actual Coast Guard personnel consisted of eighteen hand-picked men and women of various rank and skills. Many of them had served under Sowell before. They had jumped at the opportunity to serve with the Captain, knowing it would be their last chance. Being only a few years older than most of them, they considered him part of "their" group.

A career navy man, Sowell rose quickly through the ranks, reaching his present position at the age of thirty-five. Now, thirteen years later, he was sick and being put into mothballs because of his illness. Sowell had won many a battle during his life, but the one against the disease that was eating him from the inside out would be his last. His features had turned gaunt, and he wasn't moving as fast as he used to, but he could still hold his own with his crew. His thick brown hair had begun to fall out in great clumps from the rounds of chemotherapy, and his once steely blue eyes now sat pale and recessed in their sockets. It just wasn't right the way they were easing their consciences by throwing him this last bone to send him off in style. It wasn't dignified—but there was a job to do.

He shook off his depression and reached for the squawk box microphone. "This is the Captain," his voice boomed, "I need all officers to meet me in the galley for your briefing in one hour.... that's one hour!"

13

Standing outside the bridge with his binoculars held to his eyes, the Captain called out star coordinates to his second in command. Even though there was a low cloud ceiling tonight, Sowell was an experienced sailor and knew his positions. Ensign Terry Hale would stop writing every few seconds to blow warm air onto his hands. The temperature on deck was only seventy-five degrees, but with the Truman running at top speed, the wind made it feel like the fifties. The Ensign thought what they were doing was ridiculous. With all the navigational equipment onboard, there was no reason to use the stars. Stars rarely malfunctioned, Sowell had told him in jest.

The southern Atlantic Ocean off the coast of Florida had a natural warm water river running through it known as the Gulf Stream. That swift Atlantic ocean current originated in the Gulf of Mexico and stretched to the southern tip of Florida, and flowed northward along the eastern coastline of the United States and Newfoundland before crossing the Atlantic Ocean. The Truman crossed the Gulf Stream approximately seventy-five miles off the coast. Over the centuries, the current had become the burial ground for many ships and Spanish Galleons blown off course during the time of Ponce de Leon and the discovery of the New World. There would always be room for one more ship in its indigo depths.

Sowell shouted over the churning Gulf Stream as it was sliced open by the bow of the Truman, calling out another coordinate. "Did you get those last numbers, Ensign?"

"Uh, yes sir. I did."

The Captain let the binoculars hang loosely around his neck. The fur of his parka collar bristled against the wind. "You've lived your entire life in Florida, son?"

"How can you tell, sir?" The young man answered, a shiver running up his back.

"The bluish tint of your skin is a definite tip-off. Why don't you go below and get a pair of gloves or a heavier jacket? I can't stand to watch you shaking like this."

"Thank you, sir. I'll be right back." The Ensign excused himself and headed below deck.

The seas were getting rougher. The Truman was cruising in large circles, simulating a search pattern. If the simulated enemy radar spotted them, it was meant to look routine. Sowell knew the ship's rendezvous point and the designated time. Getting it there in rough seas and with this dense cloud cover hadn't been an easy task.

Bundled up in an oversized parka, the Ensign made his way back up to the bridge. Coming out of the commotion below decks, the serenity outside was a welcome pleasure. The only sounds he could hear were the hypnotizing hum of the Truman's engines and the constant slapping of the ocean against the hull of the ship. Closing and securing the hatch behind him, he walked over to the railing. The stillness outside was almost threatening. A hand on his shoulder shook him from his trance. Sowell was standing beside him. "Sorry, Ensign. Let's go back down. We'll be on sight in a few more minutes. Get ready to prepare the crew."

Placing his clipboard between his legs, Hale reopened the hatch. The Captain stepped through first. Hale was about to close the hatch when he heard an unfamiliar sound over the noise of the engines. He paused and stepped back out to the railing.

"Are you coming, Ensign?" Sowell called from the bottom of the stairway.

"One second, sir," Hale said cocking his head from side to side. It sounded like...fans? That couldn't be! The sound might as well have been the sirens from ancient mythology: impossible. His imagination must have been running away with him. He turned and followed the Captain to the control room below.

The contrast between above and below decks was as startling as night and day. The control room was full of activity as crew and technicians moved about the cabin, bathed in red light. The red glow of the compartment took a few seconds to get oriented to before the two men could move around freely again.

The sounds of electronic machinery coming to life surrounded them as they made their way to the chart table in the middle of the room. A digital map of the entire area was displayed on the table. Sowell and his officers huddled around the chart and talked in whispers, not wanting to bother any of the technicians making their final preparations for the test. "This is it, lady and gentlemen," he said, pointing a shaky finger at a mark on the diagram. "There is no margin for error. We'll only get one shot at this. It has to be on target. If this test fails, it's because we've let her get out of position, is that understood?"

The crew all nodded in the affirmative. The Chief Petty Officer at the far end of the chart chimed in. "Pardon me, Captain, I was wondering—if we maintain radio silence after the test and all the way back into port, what if something goes wrong? We could be stranded out here!" Sowell smiled at the woman and tried to show patience in his voice. The rest of the crew listened attentively; they all had the same question on their minds. "C.P.O., if we go off radio silence at any time out here, we'll be sitting ducks. The North Koreans would have their patrol boats on us like flies on shit. They would have a squadron airborne before Kim Jong-un could get himself off the toilet."

"I understand that, Captain, but then, aren't we sitting ducks out here anyway? Jacksonville wouldn't know that we were missing until morning."

Sowell hung his head in frustration. His demeanor and patience were beginning to crack, and he couldn't let that happen. There was too much at stake. He took a deep breath to regain his composure. "Once the sun comes up, and we're not back in port, they'll send support after us. I guarantee it. We're only a few hours away from the base. The rescue ships would probably cut that time in half. Now if you'll excuse me, I'm going back to the bridge." He had to get away; he couldn't look into their fresh faces a minute longer. The Ensign took over. "Okay, people; let's get her ready for knockdown in... seven minutes," he said, checking his watch. "I'll be on deck with the Captain if you need us. You're dismissed!"

The crew dispersed quickly and went about their assigned duties. Sowell found it an effort to push the hatch to the bridge open. The Truman had slowed considerably, and the tranquility of the open sea made him feel more relaxed. He took a deep breath and let the fresh salt air wash away his conscience. He turned to find the Ensign staring at him. "What's the problem, Ensign?"

"Are you alright, sir? The crew's worried about you."

"I'm sorry, son. I guess I'm just a little edgy tonight. Tell Boyd I'm sorry for snapping at her like that. It was a fair question."

The Ensign noticed that Sowell had forgotten to put his parka back on. "Cold, sir? Can I get your jacket for you?"

The Captain shook his head. "Don't worry, I'm fine. Is everything at ready stations?"

"The weather desk says there's a fog bank rolling in from the east. Heavy fog's pretty unusual this far out here, don't you think?"

Sowell stared at the eastern horizon through his binoculars. "It shouldn't affect us until after the test. I wouldn't be surprised if it drifted right over us with the winds blowing this way."

The Ensign paused. "Do you hear that sound, sir?"

The Captain quickly changed the subject. "We should be coming to our destination, Ensign. Tell the technicians to prepare the laser."

The Ensign saluted, still listening to the strange sound emanating from deep within the mysterious fog bank to the east. "Will we be able to watch the test, Captain?"

"You can't see the laser, son. You will be able to hear it, though." Sowell said as he disappeared back down into the ship leaving Hale alone on deck.

The Ensign looked through his binoculars at the fog bank which remained stationary off the port side of the Truman. He could never recall seeing fog that thick, not this far out to sea.

Below deck, the crew stood behind the technicians as they monitored their equipment. A large digital clock on the rear bulkhead counted down the last thirty seconds. Up on deck, a small hatch, the size of a hubcap, opened in the stern. While all the heavy electronics were below decks, the only part of the laser turret visible above was a glass tube about a foot long, pointed up at the heavens.

In its sights was the twenty-year-old malfunctioning N.O.A.A. weather satellite. In the past few weeks, its orbit had been decaying by itself. Now, it was expendable. The targeting system was programmed into the laser circuitry back in Houston. This kept the target a secret, restricted to only those with enough clearance to be in the know. If the North Koreans, the Russians, or even the Chinese were alerted to something going on with the weather satellite, they might just monitor it themselves. They might not know what was happening, but they would be able to tell that the satellite was brought down by something other than gravity.

Hale kept his binoculars focused on the fog bank. The wind had shifted direction, and the fog would surround the Truman in about five minutes. He was watching it intently as the laser began to sing out. It sounded like a chorus of angels, starting at a low pitch, then gradually building to a high-range climax that he could no longer hear. All this happened in a matter of seconds. He looked at his watch and then back to the fog bank. It was three minutes away.

In the control room, the Captain was monitoring the time too. The digital clock on the bulkhead clicked to zero, and the compartment erupted with applause. Everyone stood and hugged each other. Only the men monitoring the path of the target stayed eyeing their terminals. They tracked the satellite as it began to wobble wildly, then plummet and burn up s it re-entered the earth's atmosphere. Technicians came by and slapped the Captain on the back and thanked him for a job well done. Climbing the stairs again, he opened the outside hatch and let the Ensign know that the test was a success, but the Ensign was preoccupied with something else.

"Sir, the fog is closing in. Shall I get us underway?"

Sowell patted Hale on the shoulder. "Five more minutes son, then its full speed back to the base. If you need me, I'll be in my cabin."

"That's an affirmative, sir."

Sowell stepped carefully down the companionway and hurried through the control room, past the technicians and crew who were still celebrating. He looked at his watch again in the pale red light of the passageway. In two more minutes, the gas would be surrounding the Truman. He had to get to his cabin and put on the only gas mask aboard.

14

Pacing back and forth outside the bridge, Ensign Hale was the first to feel the effects of the gas. As it slowly rolled over the bow and began engulfing the Truman, his fingers started to go numb. Unaware of what was happening to him, the clipboard fell from his hands as he futilely grasped for the handrail in front of him. He tried stamping his feet on the deck to relieve the loss of sensation in his shoes. As he lost consciousness, he thought that the Truman had started spinning in a vast whirlpool of ocean current, but to the contrary, the ship was quite still. Finding it impossible to walk, he had to turn his head to prevent falling flat on his face when he collapsed on the cold steel deck. It was an agonizing five minutes before he completely blacked out.

The decision to use this type of gas was made because it was odorless. The drawback was the excruciatingly long time it took to work. Hale, and any other breathing organisms onboard, would be immobilized for the next three to four hours. The fog poured over the Truman and slipped lazily through the air intake vents. Within minutes, the entire crew was immobile. Technicians that had been busily calculating the probability of an accurate knockdown were now nothing more than bodies slumped over computer keyboards. The control room of the Truman, which had minutes earlier been filled with the sounds of joyous celebration and laughter, was turned into a wax museum cast in an eerie shade of red light, like the core of a volcano.

Sowell looked around for the last time at the quarters he had for so long called home. He picked up the parka off his desk and used a tissue to clear the condensation that had collected on the outside of his mask. He tried to open the door to his cabin, but it wouldn't budge. A technician returning from the galley had collapsed in the corridor and fallen against the Captain's hatch. The man's white coat stained with black coffee he had spilled. Sowell wasn't sure he still had the strength to force the hatch open. Fortunately, the technician was lying on his side, and Sowell was able to push the door open wide enough to squeeze through sideways.

Stepping over four more crew members on the way to the control room, he realized that no one had been spared. His subordinates were lying limply draped over the chart table, the dim white light from below casting evil shadows across their contorted faces.

Making his way up on deck, he found Ensign Hale curled up in the fetal position at the top of the stairway, his expression the same as the crewmen and technical staff below. He was checking his wristwatch when, out of the corner of his eye, he spotted it.

It emerged out of the fog like a one-eyed leviathan. It was the *Hydra*, and not a moment too soon. The only running light was the one large spotlight above the helm. He could tell that the beam wasn't on full power; it was just being used for navigation to prevent a collision with the Truman.

They had better work fast, Sowell thought. If the gas burned off, they might be spotted by a commercial ship.

The *Hydra* surprised Sowell with its stillness. Nearly twice as long as the Truman and undoubtedly faster, the *Hydra* smoothly pulled alongside the cutter, the huge rear fans dispersing the gas in immense whirlwinds that dissipated nearly a hundred yards behind the massive hydrofoil. The *Hydra* came about, turning its stern toward the Truman. Now the colossal rear fans were blowing directly at the Captain. At first, he thought the *Hydra* was turning to leave, but he soon caught on to the logic. He quickly braced himself for the onslaught of hurricane force winds, wrapping his elbows around the handrail.

The *Hydra's* fanbines were increased in power as the air brakes were applied at the hydrofoil's bow. The result was monsoon force winds, which cleared any lingering gas from the deck of the Truman in a matter of seconds. The gas blew off to the west, carried by the trade winds far out into the ocean to eventually dissolve. It would be gone by sunrise.

Sowell struggled to keep his footing on the slippery deck. He walked cautiously to the starboard side of his ship to help the boarding party from the *Hydra*. Within an hour he would be gone, and the crew would recover a few hours after that. In two weeks, he would have enough money to live out the few remaining months he had in a style he'd never even imagined. He owed it to himself; he was just a number to the Department of Homeland Security. When they found out about his cancer, they gave him two weeks leave. Now, he would leave them something to remember him by.

Sowell moved to the railing and helped tie the two ships together. When the vessels were finally secured, a ramp emerged from the side of the *Hydra*. Sowell aided the *Hydra* crewmen in attaching the gangway to the Truman. Six men boarded the cutter and walked right past the Captain. None bothered with pleasantries; it was as if he didn't exist. The men moved directly to the stern of the ship and their mission of removing all of the laser equipment.

The two ships drifted silently in the water, bobbing up and down in the gentle swells. In the dim light, Sowell could just barely make out a figure on the bridge of the *Hydra* signaling him to come aboard. He stopped halfway across the gangway and tossed his gas mask into the water. It sank slowly and swayed methodically in the dark Atlantic until it settled onto the sandy silt nearly one hundred fifty feet below.

"Welcome aboard the *Hydra*, Captain. Did everything go well?" Peter Mason asked as he swiveled the captain's chair to face Sowell as he entered the control room.

Captain Roy Sowell was rarely caught off guard, but Peter Mason himself at the helm of the *Hydra* had actually startled him.

"I can see from your expression that you are surprised to see me running one of my own ships," he smiled. "Not to worry. I've hired an entire staff of Norwegians to pilot my fleet of ships, but on special occasions such as this evening, I like to take them out for a spin personally."

Sowell toured slowly around the room, having never seen such sophisticated equipment. He had spent two tours of duty aboard a Trident submarine before accepting a promotion and switching branches of the service, but this technology was insane. "I don't know if the test was a complete success, but the gas worked perfectly."

"We have all the confidence in the world that the test went off without a hitch; otherwise we would have left you out there with your crew."

"You don't have to worry."

"I know I don't," Mason said, relaxing into the Captain's chair. "Once the laser is secured, we'll be on our way. We should be in Cockburn Town way before the sun comes up."

Sowell sounded shocked. "You can make it to the Turks and Caicos Islands by sunrise? That's nearly nine hundred miles! Are you kidding me?"

"Just watch this baby move once we hit top speed. With the seas as calm as they are tonight, we should be there with an hour to spare. The *Hydra* is the flagship of my hydrofoil fleet. She can fly like the wind and turn on a dime."

"This is truly an amazing vessel. Will you be selling any to the military?"

Mason shook his head bitterly. "I wouldn't sell anything to the Department of the Navy or any other department of the United States Government. The DEA threw the book at my father to set an example, while other families who were just as guilty walked away scot-free. Yeah, you could say I've got a bone to pick with our government, and tonight is just a small token of my loyalty."

Sowell stood over a piece of digital navigation equipment that used a three-dimensional display. "The Navy would pay a pretty penny for this new technology. I'm curious that they haven't made an attempt to steal or seize it."

"Spoken like an honest military officer. Those are hard to come by." Mason admitted. "No, this is strictly a passenger ship, privately owned. I won't let anyone inspect her except for her monthly safety checks. This bridge is off limits. You are my honored guest here."

"Really remarkable," Sowell said with the utmost reverence, as he peered out at the Truman. "You have every reason to sound like a proud papa."

Through the bridge window, Sowell spotted Ensign Hale's body lying on the deck softly shrouded in the pale moonlight. The Truman looked like a ghost ship now, but by tomorrow afternoon, she would be back at the base, and the crew would be debriefed. They wouldn't remember a thing. The Truman would be safe, but a little lighter and a little less expensive. By tomorrow night, once they realized he was missing, every government agency would have Sowell's picture tacked on their bulletin boards, but he knew he'd be long dead before they ever caught up with him.

A blinking semaphore signal coming from the deck of the Truman let Mason know that the transfer was completed.

Sowell tried not to look at his old ship, but it was difficult not to. He was sorry for the pain and suffering he had put the technicians and the crew through, but by morning they would all be a bit queasy but otherwise healthy. The Ensign would be fully capable of getting the Truman back to port in Jacksonville. They might even think Sowell was lost at sea…for a while at least.

Mason walked over and put his hand on Sowell's shoulder to comfort him. The hand was cold and sent a chill through the Captain. "Are you ready to get underway?"

Sowell nodded sadly without turning around. Mason picked up the microphone and let everyone aboard know that the Hydra was preparing to make way. The two ships were untied, and the Truman began to drift away aimlessly.

Sowell couldn't take his eyes off his Ensign lying prone on the deck as the *Hydra* backed off. He thought he saw the young man's arm begin to move as the Truman floated further away. The hydrofoil turned slowly to port, and the fanbines started to spin faster. Sowell couldn't believe how smooth the ride was. In an instant, there was over a mile between her and the Truman. Deciding to sit in the engineer's seat, he was just starting to enjoy the trip when the ship began to slow down. The fanbines crept to a halt, and the *Hydra* started a slow turn to port. Now, Sowell could only make out the silhouette of the Truman from her running lights. They glowed like stars low on the horizon.

Sowell looked over at Mason to see if something was wrong. Mason never returned the stare; he was too busy holding a conversation with one of the crewmen below by radio. "And the depth beneath her is still seventeen hundred?"

"Yes sir, but she's drifting with the current," came the response.

Sowell assumed they were talking about the *Hydra*, but he would soon find out most horrifically that he was mistaken.

The Truman sat alone on the sea like an orphaned child. She would return to port in shame. The Ensign's career would probably be ruined.

The next words Mason spoke would echo through Sowell's mind for the rest of the time he had left in this life. He never expected to hear...

"Do it now then!"

Sowell looked on in terror as the explosion lifted the Truman out of the water amidships. The flames blossomed out of her side like a fiery orchid against the dark horizon. Shrapnel was blown out for hundreds of yards. It came down in an orange cascade of burning fuel. The Captain turned and looked at Mason with hatred in his eyes. "You never said anything about scuttling my ship! There were nearly fifty crew members aboard the Truman! That was mass murder!"

Mason scratched the side of his face without the slightest hint of remorse or compunction. "No, Captain," he began. "I'm just a businessman living in uncertain times who has to raise enough capital to build a baseball park bearing his family's name. My motives are just that simple. As we speak, there are more than a dozen countries down on their knees bidding to make that dream a reality."

Sowell gritted his teeth. "So now you can add treason to your resume?"

Peter Mason shrugged. "I guess you can take the pirate out of the family, but you can't take the family out of the pirate."

Sowell fumed as he imagined Ensign Hale lying on the deck, starting to regain consciousness. Now, he was only a part of the molten mass of twisted metal sinking to the bottom of the Atlantic.

It would probably be a day or two before the search and rescue teams were back to scour over the wreckage. It might be even longer before they would discover that the laser had been stolen and that the explosion aboard the Coast Guard Cutter Truman was more than just a horrific accident.

That would be all the time that Roy Sowell would need.

15

As the sunrise painted the horizon in shades of yellow and orange, the Cyclone class cutter *Intrepid* glided through smooth seas at almost thirty knots. Unlike the Truman, this ship was built for speed. It was usually called upon to help in Coast Guard efforts to stop smugglers in the waters off the southeastern seaboard. The *Intrepid* was stripped of any unnecessary equipment which would hinder its ability to pursue the new ships being built for smuggling.

Captain Richard Fitzpatrick paced on the foredeck as the crisp morning air rushed through his thick brown hair and beard. He gazed out at the emptiness of the ocean. In ten minutes, the *Intrepid* would be over the test site, and there was still no sign of the Truman. He picked up the intercom and called down for any radar contacts.

"There's nothing in the vicinity except for commercial traffic, Captain," came the response. "Do you want us to run sonar?"

Fitzpatrick hung his head. He knew what running the sonar check meant; besides, there were so many shipwrecks in this part of the ocean they could be chasing their tails for weeks. "Belay the sonar for now. Wait until we're over the last known coordinates."

"That's affirmative, Captain. We should be over the last position in approximately eight minutes."

"Very good, let me know when we're close. I've got all eyes peeled for oil slicks and wreckage just in case."

Fitzpatrick could see a chain of reefs off to port where the water turned lighter and was more disturbed by the coral outcroppings. He prayed that the Truman had run aground, but the further out they traveled, the less likely those chances were. Just before leaving the base, Captain Fitzpatrick had been semi-briefed on the Truman's situation. It had been nearly twenty-eight hours since the ship had sailed from port. His commanding officer had been very cryptic on the secrecy of Truman's actual mission, but revealed that all of her communication equipment had been disabled or removed so she couldn't be monitored by any foreign power. Inevitably, the Truman would have been spotted by reconnaissance aircraft at daybreak if they had hit a reef and run aground. He was surprised to find out that no such aircraft had been dispatched yet. The high command wanted to maintain secrecy as long as possible, and launching a conspicuous airborne search and rescue mission was not an option at this time. The investigation was still in its infancy, and there was a lot of ocean to explore.

While he didn't know Captain Roy Sowell personally, Fitzpatrick was aware of his distinguished reputation and had to assume that he was too good of a sailor to allow his two hundred foot cutter to misguidedly strike a reef and sink.

The color of the water changed from light green where it was shallow to sapphire blue where it ran to its darkest depths. The Captain shielded his eyes from the bright sun, which was rapidly rising on the eastern horizon. He turned and looked up behind him at the railing of the bridge. He could just make out a pair of orange Coast Guard issue binoculars peering out at the ocean. "See anything, Ensign?" Fitzpatrick shouted above the wind.

"Negative, Captain," the Ensign replied, looking down over the railing. "We're the only ones alive out here, sir." The Ensign would have given his right eye not to have said what he did.

"Mind your mouth, Ensign! When I want an editorial, I'll watch the six o'clock news!" "I'm sorry, Captain, wrong choice of words."

Fitzpatrick turned back and watched the waves break across the bow. The last time he'd made a new wreck dive was an event he would never forget. A Navy cruiser was on a routine trip out of Norfolk when an engine fire caused an explosion at her stern. The blast ripped a hole in the hull the size of a small Toyota. The ship went down in two hundred feet of water in twelve minutes. Many of the crew members were caught below decks, still sleeping.

When he had reached the wreck eight hours later, everything inside the ship had turned upside down like in the movie The Poseidon Adventure. Anything that wasn't battened down was floating on the ceiling—including sailors. He had almost thrown up into his regulator when he first arrived at the wreck. To get in, he and another diver had had to use acetylene torches to cut open a waterproof hatch that had sealed itself automatically after the explosion. While the outside was secured, the compartment inside had still flooded: the inner bulkhead had been breached by the massive concussion of the blast.

When they had finally managed to release the outside hatch, a grim procession of dead humanity floated through to the surface above. The sailors had been trying to get out when they drowned. There were nine of them, and they drifted out of the hatch in single file, one after another. It was a memory Fitzpatrick could never erase, and the sight of those men became more vivid the closer they got to the test site.

The water surrounding the *Intrepid* began to turn a darker shade of blue as the bottom slowly began to slip away from the surface. "We're almost there, Captain!" A voice came over the loudspeaker, as the cutter began to noticeably slow its forward progress. Fitzpatrick leaned over the bow railing and noticed that the water was becoming slick and oily. "Commence your scan, sonar." He ordered.

Less than a minute later, another voice boomed out of the squawk box above the Captain's head. "This is Sonar, Captain. We have a large contact on the bottom, Sir!"

He picked up the microphone and spoke down to the engineer.

"All stop! Keep her right here." The Captain looked up at the Ensign who was still scanning the area. "Do you see any signs of survivors or wreckage?"

The Ensign cast his gaze off to the east and then slowly back to the west. "Nothing, sir. Wait...hold on. Two o'clock, sir. It looks like a body! It's definitely a floater, sir. It's wearing a uniform!"

Fitzpatrick reached down into a small storage hold and pulled out an identical set of binoculars. He tried to locate what the Ensign had spotted. The waves were pitching back and forth which was making it difficult to focus on one specific point in the dark water. Then he saw him, floating face up. He was off to port, about fifty yards. The body looked charred, the uniform shredded.

A handful of the *Intrepid*'s rescue divers gathered out on deck to spot the body. The only sign of identification Fitzpatrick could recognize through the gently rolling swells was the officer's insignia of rank. The crew of the *Intrepid* had recovered Ensign Hale.

16

A bright yellow inflatable was carefully lowered over the port side of the *Intrepid* to help with the rescue. Two seamen clad in fluorescent orange life vests climbed down a rope ladder to the tiny boat, where they attached a five-horsepower outboard motor securely to its stern. The little boat was tossed about by the swells bouncing off the cutter as she rolled gently in the dark, oily water.

Fitzpatrick was almost ready, fully dressed in his bright yellow and black wetsuit when he heard the outboard engine kick to life. He stood up and awkwardly walked over to the railing with his flippers slapping the deck. Fitzpatrick was going to wait to slip on his fins until the body was brought on board. He called down to the two crewmembers that were pushing away from the *Intrepid*.

"Look for any flotsam while you're out there! Any scrap of wreckage that's floating and you think you can handle, I want it brought back aboard!" The seamen acknowledged with waves of their hands. The Captain sat down on the deck and secured his diving knife around his right ankle. He looked over at his diving partner, who was checking out a high powered halogen light. They would need the most reliable light possible to see through all the oil in the water.

Chief Petty Officer Gary Parker had volunteered for the dive. He was experienced in underwater photography and was the only man aboard to dive a real wreck besides the Captain. "How deep is she, Captain?" Parker asked as he spit into his mask to clear it.

"She's resting at one hundred feet, straight beneath our bow. That depth is pushing the maximum you and I can dive without being crushed by the water pressure, so we need to stay together—no wandering off. Sonar says most of her bow is hanging off the edge of a pretty precarious shelf. Ten more feet to the south or a shift in her ballast and she would have been gone for good in over fifteen hundred feet."

"How is the bottom? I mean...is it firm?" Parker asked.

Fitzpatrick could sense the concern in the young C.P.O.'s mind.

"I know what you're thinking, Chief. I don't know the stability of the shelf or whether the Truman is just resting there for the time being. Just keep one thing in mind: we've been ordered to head for the stern of the vessel and assess the damage."

"Are we looking for anything in particular, Captain?"

Fitzpatrick spit into his mask as he shook his head. "I'd like to tell you, Chief, but then I'd have to kill you."

"I understand, Captain." Parker nodded, as he went back to checking his regulator and tanks.

One hundred yards to port, the inflatable was making its way over to the body floating with the current. After nearly twenty-eight hours, the Captain was surprised that the remains hadn't drifted farther from the wreck. Many of the other deceased still might have.

As Fitzpatrick grabbed a hose and wet himself down, he hoped that the Ensign's body might shed some light on what happened aboard the Truman. He could feel his wetsuit beginning to constrict in the morning sun. The cold water felt good on his face and hair. Parker came up alongside the Captain and handed him a pair of binoculars. "I thought you might want these to see when they pulled him into the inflatable."

"Thanks. I hope he hasn't been in the water too long. I can only see the top half of his body from here. He could be shark food from the bottom down, by now." Fitzpatrick focused in on the inflatable as the sailors pulled the body aboard. As the Ensign was lifted out of the water, he could see that the lower portion of his torso was crimson in color against the yellow boat. It was as the Captain feared; the *Intrepid* wasn't the first to reach the body. He put down the glasses and slammed his fist on the railing. "Damn!"

"What is it, Captain?"

"Now the whole area is probably teeming with them now. Damned sharks! You can handle yourself down there, can't you Parker?"

"No problem, sir," he boasted, patting the knife on his ankle. "I haven't met a fish I couldn't whoop yet!"

"Well, can you 'whoop' five or ten of them, Chief?" The Captain said in all seriousness.

Parker's attitude abruptly changed. There was no more excitement in his eyes, no more thrill in his voice. The water suddenly looked much darker and ominous to him.

"I'm not trying to scare you, Parker. I just want you to know what we might be up against if that man's injuries were caused by sharks. You cover my ass, and I'll cover yours. Have we got a deal?"

Parker reached out and shook his Captain's hand; the grip was firm and reassuring.

As the inflatable pulled back alongside the *Intrepid*, a port side hatch was opened. Fitzpatrick quickly ran below deck to meet the boat. He ordered that only the medical staff that needed to be there remain.

"Get the doctor over here on the double! Everyone else make like ghosts!" Fitzpatrick shouted.

The medic pushed his way through the dispersing crowd and helped lift the body aboard. He was slipping on a pair of latex examining gloves when the *Intrepid* hit a large swell and he nearly fell through the open hatch. The Captain made a one-armed lunge and pulled the doctor back inside.

"Get a thermal blanket and some fresh water over here!" The medic screamed.

Fitzpatrick leaned over the body and picked a piece of seaweed off the Ensign's nameplate. Hale's face was bloated and distorted. There was no telling how much sea water he had swallowed. The doctor opened the buckle to the Ensign's trousers and pulled them down below his thighs. The few remaining members of the medical team quickly turned away from what they saw. There was a hunk of metal the size of a dinner plate jutting out of Hale's hip. The blood had coagulated around the wound but had loosened when he was pulled aboard. An inky substance trickled down from the Ensign's wounds onto the deck.

"What's the verdict, doc? Did he die in an explosion?"

The medic held up a finger to silence his commanding officer as he pulled the stethoscope from his ears. "You're not going to believe this, but he's still breathing. It's very shallow and weak. It sounds like his lungs are barely functioning."

"You're kidding me!" Fitzpatrick muttered. "How is that possible after all this time?"

"His lungs are probably burned to a crisp," the doctor confirmed. "There had to have been a fire. I'd give him oxygen, but it would only exacerbate his condition." He looked over at the Captain. "This isn't good, sir. We need to airlift him out of here right away if he is going to have any chance at all. There is nothing I can do for him here. If we can't get a chopper here within the hour, he doesn't stand a chance. I'm sure he'll never make it back to port," the medic added as he covered the Ensign's inert torso with a thermal blanket.

The doctor put his ear to the badly burned Ensign's mouth to check on the amount of air he was pushing out. "I honestly don't know how this man is still alive...wait, hold on a minute. He's trying to say something!"

"Move over, doc. I've got to hear this." Fitzpatrick ordered as he pushed the medic out of the way, almost knocking him over in the process. The Captain leaned over and put his ear over the Ensign's mouth. "Just whisper, Hale. Come on man, tell me what happened to you."

Fitzpatrick had his right ear nearly pressed against the Ensign's mouth, and he could hear what could only describe as a baby's breath. With his face staring down Hale's torso, he couldn't help cringing at the chunk of metal protruding from the body like an enormous fin.

"Soul," was the single word Fitzpatrick was able to make out of the Ensign's garbled murmuring.

"Come on Ensign, what are you trying to tell me?" The Captain couldn't feel any more warm air on his cheek. He lifted his ear as Hale's head slumped to the side. A huge gush of bloody water poured from the Ensign's mouth. Fitzpatrick backed off and let the medic take over. His wetsuit felt warmer than it ever had before. He stood up and leaned against the open hatchway, the cool air tingled on his wet face. He turned back to see the doctor fully draping Hale's body with the blanket. The Captain took a deep breath and spit into the ocean. "What do you think he was trying to tell us, doc?"

The medic, who was a very devout Catholic and who willingly served double duty as the ship's chaplain, knew immediately what the Ensign was trying to say to them. It was a dying man's last request. He stood next to the Captain and looked out on the vast emptiness of the ocean.

"I believe Ensign Hale wanted us to pray for his eternal soul."

Fitzpatrick nodded his head. "So you think he was a religious man, Doc?"

The medic spread his opened hands across the watery expanse before him. "Yes, I'd like to believe that. You look at this magnificent ocean and tell me, who wouldn't believe in the Almighty's existence?"

The Captain, who couldn't remember the last time he had crossed the threshold of a house of worship, nodded mainly to mollify the doctor. "Amen, Doc. So what are you going to do with his remains?"

"Well, I'd like to find out the extent of his lung damage. That would tell us a lot. An autopsy is in order, and any family will have to be notified. This was a classified mission, so I don't know which will come first. The guys with all the stars on their caps will have to make that decision."

"Are you going to do the procedure?" The Captain asked rubbing his wet beard.

"I can't do an autopsy onboard," the doctor admitted. "They are going to want people who are better trained in determining the actual cause of the Ensign's death. When we get back to the port, they'll most likely ship the body off to the Jacksonville Police Department. They have one hell of a forensics unit there. It's one of the best in the southeast."

Fitzpatrick looked surprised. "Really? I never knew that."

The medic snapped off his gloves. "I've heard cases from all over the country are referred there. They do great work."

Fitzpatrick stared down at the oily water. "Take care of Hale's body until we get back to port, Doc, he deserves first-rate treatment. And have this hatch secured once the inflatable is aboard."

The doctor nodded. "I'll take care of it, Captain."

Fitzpatrick made his way up on deck where Ensign Parker was waiting for him. "Are you okay, Captain? Is the ensign dead?"

The captain pulled on his neoprene hood. "Yes, he died onboard. He tried to tell me something before he succumbed. Some people believe it was a miracle that he lasted this long. I just can't stop thinking about his last word. I think he said 'Soul.' What does that even mean? What was he trying to tell me? The doctor thinks he wanted us to pray for him. He may be right, but it still bothers me."

Parker leaned against the railing and pulled on his first flipper. "Maybe he was talking about Captain Sowell of the Truman."

Fitzpatrick turned to Parker. "What?"

The Ensign wasn't sure what he had suddenly done wrong. "You said Sowell, sir. I just assumed you meant Captain Sowell of the Truman."

Fitzpatrick's eyes widened. "God damn it, Parker! That's got to be it! I didn't even make the connection!"

Parker shrugged innocently. "It... just came to me, sir."

Fitzpatrick smiled. "Good job, son. You just keep on guessing. You're good at it."

The Captain tucked his hair under the stretchy yellow and black diving hood. If he didn't get into the water soon, this mystery was going to drive him crazy. When they got back to the surface, he would have to do some critical research on the commander of the Cutter Truman, Captain Roy Sowell.

17

Fitzpatrick gave the thumbs up signal to Parker as he checked the communicator in his face mask. The Ensign climbed down a rope ladder to the wooden dive platform attached to the stern of the *Intrepid*. Fitzpatrick followed him, but his left flipper caught in the last rung of the ladder and he fell backward onto the deck.

"Are you okay, Skipper?" The Ensign's voice echoed in his mask.

"Yeah, I'm fine. Just a little clumsy and embarrassed, that's all. How is the reception, still loud and clear?"

"You're breaking up a bit, Captain. You may have damaged the transmitter in the fall. Do you want me to replace it for you?"

"Negative, we can't waste any more time. As long as you can understand me, we'll be okay."

Parker returned the thumbs up signal.

"Now remember, you follow me," Fitzpatrick said. "Once we get down to fifty feet or so, we're going to have to follow the guide line we dropped down there. Don't let go of it until we reach the Truman. The water is going to be especially tough to see through because of all the oil. Keep your light pointed toward the bottom like I do. Don't lose the air bubble trail I leave behind."

Parker nodded affirmatively. "No problem, sir. The lights are working perfectly. They should help us once we get down to the ship."

"I hope so. Just remember that we go to the stern first."

The Ensign's voice came a bit too loudly inside his mask, so Fitzpatrick adjusted the volume control by his right ear. "It would be helpful if you could tell me what we're supposed to be looking for, Skipper."

The Captain waggled his finger. "Just keep sweeping your light once we're inside the stern of the Truman. I'll know it when I see it."

"I'm ready to go then, sir."

"After I search the interior of the stern, we can move forward toward the bow and investigate the extent of the total damage. And Parker, most of all, stay away from the shelf. It's a sheer drop over that ledge. We don't want any surprises down there."

"No problem, Skipper. I don't intend to go anywhere near it. I'll be on your six the entire dive."

Fitzpatrick smiled behind his foggy mask. Once he hit the water, he knew it would clear. The two divers looked up one last time at their ship and the bright, blue sky arching above them. They turned toward each other and covered their facemasks with their free hands. Holding onto their lights, they fell back into the murky water.

At fifty feet, Fitzpatrick was the first to reach the line dropped over the port side of the Truman. He pulled himself along with the Ensign trailing a few feet behind. At seventy-five feet they lost all light from the surface and turned on their halogen lamps. The water was still plenty viscous from the oil and fuel leaking from the wreck below.

Every few seconds a shadow or shadows would skirt along the periphery of their lights. Bull sharks. Not what either man wanted to see. They were probably curious about the sudden intrusion of light into their murky realm; but as for attacking them, the divers were morbidly composed, figuring that the shark's hunger had already been satisfied by the feast waiting below.

As they continued to pull themselves downward, the silhouette of the Truman grew from shadow to muted color as the two divers approached. *She looks so serene*, Parker thought.

The cutter was resting with four feet of her bow buried in the silt. A diverse community of sea creatures had already claimed the ship as their own. The sea life was a multitude of bright colors and odd shapes that darted and swam lazily in and out of the mangled wreckage.

The Truman looked to Fitzpatrick to be listing about twenty degrees to starboard. While the right side of the ship looked like someone had reached in and ripped out her guts, she appeared to have very little structural damage on her port side.

"I know I told you to stay close, Ensign, but I need to go into the stern alone. Either you stay here, or go up to the bow and work your way back toward me. Either way, I want you waiting out here for me in five minutes. Understood?"

"Aye, Aye, Captain," Parker said as he began kicking furiously against the current. A handful of brightly colored angelfish darted through his light. There was no way he was going to tread water for five minutes while there was exploring to do.

Parker swam the full length of the Truman's port side, pausing every few seconds to shine his light into an open hatch or glass porthole. There were no signs of life that he could see from the outside. Even through the hull, Parker could hear the dull pounding of cargo shifting around as he swam by the cargo hold. Twenty feet below him, he didn't notice a small metallic object attached to the side of the Truman. The disc-shaped explosive was half buried in the sand. His ears did not pick up the rhythmical ticking of a second set of detonators that had failed to explode halfway up on the Truman's port side.

Parker made his way over the bow railing and swam toward the bridge. The windows had been blown outward, and glass was scattered all over the deck. What he saw inside, through his bright beam of light, he could only describe as the first course of a very ravenous group of diners. Two seamen were floating against the overhead bulkhead with very little of their flesh intact. Parker had seen enough. His five-minute limit must have been close to over. He began kicking as hard as his fins would allow and did a double-timed tour of the starboard side of the ship from its bridge back to the stern.

"How are you doing, Captain?" The Ensign asked as a curious

jellyfish swam through his light. "Any sign of sharks?"

Fitzpatrick's words came through garbled with static. Parker could only make out a few words. "I'm...searching stern ...pack ...gone ...calling surf..."

The Ensign waited until the Captain was finished and pressed his microphone. "Did you catch that, on the surface? The Captain is breaking up in my ear. How are you receiving him?"

A radioman on the surface that was monitoring and recording all of their transmissions spoke up. "He's coming in clear as glass up here Mr. Parker. You can't make him out?"

"No, the problem may be on my end. You're sounding okay, but not perfect. Did you get the Captain's message?"

"He said, he was searching the stern, and the package was missing." The Ensign stopped kicking his feet to remain in place; he wasn't sure what to do now. What package was the Captain talking about? He tried to clear his thoughts. The Truman's mission was clearly above his pay grade, but whatever the package contained, it had to be mighty important. What were the chances that the Truman had been sunk deliberately? It was a shame that the state of affairs in the modern world made him think of terrorism first and foremost. Now, he had to look for signs of sabotage.

"Captain, I'm taking another lap around the ship. I will be back in a few minutes. Do you copy me?"

Fitzpatrick's voice came in clearly now. "Are you outside of the stern?"

"Aye, Captain. I've witnessed that the starboard side is breached in multiple locations, but the port side appears to have taken no damage. Do you copy on the surface?"

The radioman piped in. "We're recording every word, sir."

Fitzpatrick's voice was commanding. "I want you to stay put, Ensign. I have one more place to look, and then we're going to take a lap together to survey the damage. Then it's topside. Do you copy?"

Parker frowned inside his facemask. Moving laterally along the side of the ship, his beam illuminated only thirty feet in front of him. He thought there would be more bodies in plain sight, but if the crewmen on the bridge were merely the appetizers, he was okay without spotting any others. Parker watched as the railing above him became bathed in soft white light. Fitzpatrick had swum out of one of the hatches and was coming over the top of the stern to join him. The Captain gave Parker the "thumbs down" sign as he swam up to him. The Ensign acknowledged the gesture.

"Did you see the holes in the starboard?" Fitzpatrick asked.

"Aye, Captain. There are two holes the size of compact cars below the waterline. The metal is bent inward, which means the blast was caused by an explosive charge placed on the outside of her hull."

Parker shook his head in agreement. "Are you getting all this on the surface, *Intrepid*?" "Affirmative, sir," came the reply from above.

The Ensign pointed towards the deck of the Truman. "We've got to go inside, sir. We're down here anyway. We have plenty left in our tanks. Let's try the forward compartments. We've got to take a look, sir. There are Coast Guard seamen in there."

Fitzpatrick took a deep breath which Parker and the surface both heard clearly. "Fine, but I don't want to stay down here too much longer. We can make another dive after a few more ships arrive."

The two divers rose slowly over the side of the ship and swam slowly toward the bow of the Truman. Reaching the small round hatch, Parker set his light down on the deck. The light showered the two men with a cloudy brightness. A large grouper, puzzled by the trespassers, swam just out of arm's length and watched them with natural curiosity.

Parker waved to the fish, which was nearly five feet long. "Don't worry, Captain, he's as nosy as we are."

Once above the ship, the Ensign struggled to release one of the forward hatches, but it wouldn't budge. Fitzpatrick reached down to his ankle and removed his knife from its sheath. He wedged it between the spokes of the handle and used it as a lever to loosen it. The deep-rooted vision of those bloated corpses floating to the surface in a single line of death made him take a momentary breather.

Parker noticed that the Captain had paused. "Do you want me to do it, Captain?"

Fitzpatrick didn't answer, so the Ensign grabbed the knife and began twisting the wheel.

"Is everything okay down there?" questioned the familiar voice from the surface. "Everything's good," Parker replied.

Fitzpatrick instinctively backed away as the hatch was lifted open. Huge air bubbles gushed toward the surface as the pressure inside and outside the Truman equalized. Parker found it hard to see until the bubbles slowly subsided. The pale glow of the halogen light slowly began turning a pinkish hue. Both men instinctively took a few strokes back as soon as they realized that blood was flowing freely through the opened hatch. Gallon after gallon of blood poured from the opening, blending with the salty water.

"Shut it!" Fitzpatrick screamed, almost damaging Parker's eardrums.

"Okay Captain, she's closed. Are you going to be all right?"

The Captain could feel the cold sweat dripping inside his wetsuit. "Let's leave her interior for another team that's more qualified to deal with those men. I want to examine the starboard side again to examine the damage to her hull. It might give some clue as to the exact cause."

Parker nodded, but he knew what the Captain meant. He wanted to check for evidence of explosives. "Aye aye, Captain. I copy. I'm going to finish checking out the port side. Maybe there was some damage below the waterline that I didn't notice the first time around." Parker was trying to sound steady, but he wasn't too thrilled about whatever awaited either of them. There were hundreds of effective ways of sinking a ship the size of the Truman. Perhaps they would find something that could narrow it down to a few.

Parker swam slowly around to the port side of the ship. He floated a few feet above the soft, sandy bottom, nearly walking on it with the tip of his fins. There was no debris on this side of the ship. The pattern that formed on the bottom was as expected. It had settled in waves of decreasing size the further it was from the vessel. Soon, the underwater current would wash away any signs of the initial impact, and order beneath the sea would be restored.

As Parker moved slowly past midship, something half buried in the silt a few feet away caught his light. It was very close to the bow, which hung dangerously over the ledge of the shelf where the Truman had come to rest. It glistened like a piece of glass, but there was no other material like it anywhere nearby. Parker glided away from the Truman towards the object. Even directly over it, he wasn't sure what he was looking at.

"Captain, do you copy? I may have found something over here. Do you copy?"

Fitzpatrick's voice was garbled again, but Parker could make out that he was on his way.

The Ensign directed his light directly on it. Two-thirds of the object was buried beneath the sandy bottom. He reached down and pulled out the trusty knife strapped to his ankle. As he dug around the fringe of the object, he tried to clear away the sand by waving his hand above it. As the thing revealed itself, Parker stared at the gas mask for a full minute before realizing the significance of his find. Why was there a Navy issue gas mask just lying here? They weren't standard issue in the Coast Guard. Pulling a plastic inflatable pouch from his weight belt, the Ensign slipped the mask inside. He was about to fill the bag with air from his regulator and let it float to the surface when Fitzpatrick's voice came through his receiver.

"What are you doing out there? I told you to stick close to the ship."

The Ensign could see the Captain's light coming down the side of the ship. He was moving over the railing and swimming toward the bottom, casting an eerie shadow against the hull. Fitzpatrick was halfway down the hull when he suddenly started kicking downward to slow his descent.

"Parker, get over here. I think I found another live one!" The Ensign swam quickly over to the hull of the ship to see what his Captain had found. Parker tapped his transmitter; he thought he heard things. The faint ticking sound was definitely coming from the saucer-shaped object attached to the hull of the Truman. Parker was sure it had to be a dud, or it would have exploded with the other ones. Before Fitzpatrick could stop him, he reached out and touched it ever so lightly with his metal knife. He never could have guessed that it was a proximity mine explicitly placed for anyone who got close enough to investigate the wreckage.

The crewman monitoring them on the surface ripped the earphones off his head. The Captain and Ensign were dead before they felt the actual energy of the detonation. The entire structure of the Truman trembled and let out a mournful cry as the shelf beneath her keel collapsed.

On the surface, the radioman instinctively reached over and slammed his fist down on the button which sounded the general quarters alert. The piercing alarm was drowned out by the sound of the explosion and the deluge of water that erupted just off the port side. It was as if the *Intrepid* was under attack. It was only a split second before the surface water surrounding the cutter began to churn wildly. The majority of the crew had no time to secure themselves for the blast. A few that were near the railing were thrown overboard into the turbulent water. They were the lucky ones. The remainder of the crew was tossed around on deck, crashing against steel bulkheads or exposed pipes. One seaman recruit that was scrubbing the mast tumbled from his scaffold and was impaled on the radio antenna, knocking it out of commission.

Far beneath the *Intrepid*, Parker and Fitzpatrick's bodies were quickly crushed by the water pressure in the whirlpool caused by the Truman descending over the ledge. It took less than two minutes for the cutter to split apart as it impacted with the rocky sea floor some seventeen hundred feet below. At this depth, the wreckage would only be accessible by a submersible, and that would take months.

But yet, there was a proper epitaph yet to be written for the cataclysmic events of that day. A bright yellow pouch had pierced the surface of the water and bobbed gently in the swells, just waiting to be spotted and retrieved.

18

Vice Admiral Theodore "Teddy" Baer stood on the warm concrete dock and tapped his left foot impatiently. He looked down at his watch, and then out to the inlet as the *Truman* limped back into port. He had just got off the phone with Washington, and they were eager to learn what had happened. Only his closest advisors and medical personnel had security clearance to come to the pier to await the arrival. Three other officers, who all held the rank of Lieutenant Commander or greater, stood by his side. The three other officers didn't have the combined years of service that Baer had himself. He was in his fortieth year in the Navy and had won almost every conceivable commendation awarded. All of the fruit salad on his chest didn't mean a hill of beans to him now. If this mess weren't straightened out soon, all of his accolades wouldn't buy him a rum punch on Jacksonville Beach.

The afternoon humidity was on the rise. To hell with protocol, he thought as he removed his tie and took off his coat.

"There she is!" Someone called out.

Baer grabbed a pair of binoculars and searched the horizon until he caught his first glimpse of the disabled ship. "I need to find out what happened to their communications. I know that no cell phones were allowed on board because of the mission's secrecy, but it sounded like all hell had broken loose when their scrambled radio signal went dead."

Captain Gene Wells, who was in charge of the air reconnaissance group, spoke up. "From what Recon One reported on his first pass, the ship looked like she had been through a hurricane. A crewman signaled our plane with a white flag that everything was under control."

Baer began pacing while waves of hot air rose off the surface of the concrete dock. "I hope that seaman was right. Washington is all over me about this, and they want answers yesterday! We don't even know if the equipment is still intact on the *Intrepid*! I'm sure that Captain Fitzpatrick will be able to fill us in on what he saw first-hand."

The base had fallen into an unusual silence for this time of day. No traffic was allowed in or out of the gates until the crew of the *Intrepid* had been debriefed. Baer looked up at the few clouds that dotted the light blue sky; they hung, motionless, like cotton balls. The large brown pelicans which would typically be pestering the men for scraps of food sat idly by, perched on the wooden pillars of the dock.

As the *Intrepid* slowly made her way back into her berth, Petty Officer Second Class Scott Simms walked the deck surveying the damage. Onboard there had been only one casualty, but there were at least another thirteen men receiving treatment in the sick bay for broken bones and/or concussions. The loss of Captain Fitzpatrick and Ensign Parker made the trip back seem eternal. Even he had taken a nasty gash above his right eye.

The *Intrepid* was running on only one engine; the other was shut down as a result of an oil leak caused by the ship being slammed around. Simms had never experienced anything like that in his life. The explosion directly under the vessel had been deafening. When the *Intrepid* had started spinning in the whirlpool caused by the blast, he didn't think the cutter was going to withstand the metal stress. He had hung onto the railing like he was on an amusement ride. He watched in terror as many of his fellow seamen were tossed around on the deck like dressing on a salad. He had no idea where the socket wrench came from that hit him above his eye. He considered himself lucky that it hadn't caught him an inch lower. If it had, he would be wearing a patch right now.

Simms was highest in rank after Ensign Parker. He had reluctantly taken command and circled the *Intrepid* for nearly an hour, picking dazed and injured crewmen out of the oily water. Simm knew that Air Sector Jacksonville would be sending out a recon flight as soon as the ship's transmitter went silent. He had been the one to signal the plane using his handkerchief. The aircraft had dipped its wing in response before turning back. He watched it become a tiny speck off in the distance, and wondered what the pilot was going to report.

The *Intrepid* performed like she was built to. She cut through the calm seas like a wounded warrior returning from a victorious battle. As the ship bounced and slid through the gentle swells, Simms walked down to the foredeck and stared at the broken men and women that were once a vital, well-disciplined crew.

The ship's medic had set up cots and blankets on the deck. There were too many injured seamen to treat in the sick bay and not nearly enough space. Simms strolled amongst the crew and asked how each was feeling. One cot lying against the portside railing had a sheet entirely over its occupant. It was a clean white sheet with one red stain that had spread over the chest area. It was Seaman Recruit George Todd, who had fallen off the scaffolding and onto the radio mast. Simms didn't know him that well, but he knew he had a family with children.

A Seaman Apprentice who was manning the bridge called down to Simms and mercifully ended his morbid train of thought. "The base is in sight!"

Simms didn't answer; he just acknowledged the message with a wave of his hand. The broken and battered crew each acknowledged Simms' presence as he walked amongst them. They knew who was in charge now; Seaman First Class Scott Simms had become their leader this day.

The neon yellow pouch containing the gas mask was still lying on the deck by the ladder. One of the crewmen on the stern had spotted it while circling for survivors after the explosion. No one bothered opening the pouch until now. Simms saw it lying on the deck and out of curiosity picked it up. At first, he thought that it was just something that a crewman had left sitting there by mistake. Gas masks weren't standard equipment on Coast Guard cutters, and it didn't take long for him to ask around as to where the pouch had been found. Once he learned that it had been recovered adrift, he began to wonder why.

Simms was there when Ensign Hale of the *Intrepid* was pulled onboard. Simms was an avid detective novel reader and prided himself on being able to figure out the "whodunit" before the protagonist did. If he hadn't gone into the Coast Guard, he would have almost certainly been an investigator of some kind. He was determined now more than ever to find out what was going on. He had to find out what happened aboard the Truman—and if Seaman Todd had died in vain. He owed it to Todd's family.

Simms paced the deck, waiting for the *Intrepid* to dock. It was taking too long for the ship to get back into its berth. Sure, they would have questions for him, but right now he had some issues of his own. The mooring cables were tossed over the side and tied to the large metal cleats on the dock. Simms could see Vice Admiral Baer and three other Captains waiting impatiently for the ship to come to rest. One of the other officers waved up at Simms, but he ignored the gesture.

The Vice Admiral and the three other officers surveyed the injured as they were helped off the ship. The last two stretchers carried off were completely covered. They carried the bodies of Seaman Todd and Ensign Hale. The tallest of the three officers motioned for Simms to come over. Simms disregarded him and helped lift Hale's body into the back of a waiting Jeep. The ships' medic climbed into the rear of the vehicle next to the body and strapped it in.

"When you get to the infirmary," Simms instructed him. "Tell the doctor I want to talk to him later, okay? Tell him I'll be there in half an hour."

The medic frowned at Simms and then looked back at the Vice Admiral. "Do you honestly think he'll be through with you in half an hour?"

Simms nodded. "I'll make sure he is. Just tell the Doctor, I'm on my way."

The jeep pulled away with the white sheet covering Hale's body flapping in the wind. Simms turned and gave a distasteful look at his commanding officers. If he was going to pull this off, he was going to have to make them believe he meant business. He didn't move, so the officers had to walk over to him.

Vice Admiral Baer stared at Simms but was taken aback when the Petty Officer Second Class didn't salute him or stand at attention. It appeared that proper military protocol had been abandoned out at sea.

"Where is your commanding officer, Simms? Is he still onboard?"

"My commanding officer sir? All my commanding officers are dead, sir!" Simms snarled, overemphasizing the word "dead."

The Admiral and the officers exchanged shocked glances. It was Simms's turn to play his aces.

"What's the matter, Admiral? Cat got your tongue?" Simms tried unsuccessfully to control his anger. The bandage above his eye was slipping, so he reached up and tightened the knot.

"Come inside Simms, and we'll talk," Baer said as he reached around to put his arm on Simms's shoulder.

The Petty Officer shrugged the hand away. "We'll talk now, Admiral. Right here and right now or you won't get any answers from me. Go ahead and lock me up for insubordination if you want, but I need to know what my commanding officers died for. I want to know what was so damned important about the Truman that everyone aboard died for. I want to know why my crewmembers were injured and maimed. This is the United States for God's sake, not the middle east!"

The three officers stared at each other in disbelief. How could this enlisted man dare to speak to a commanding officer with that tone? The beefiest of the three officers, Commander Troy Johnson, rushed up and grabbed Simms by the collar. With the Commander's bulldog face inches from his own, Simms quickly rethought his strategy.

"Do you know who you're speaking to P.O. Simms? I'll have you scaling fish in the brig for fifteen years for not showing the Admiral the respect he deserves!"

Simms swallowed audibly but returned the threat with glaring contempt.

"You cocky son-of-a-bitch!" Johnson screamed as he pulled back his fist.

"COMMANDER JOHNSON," Baer yelled. "AT EASE!"

Johnson grudgingly released his grip and Simms straightened his uniform. The Vice Admiral pulled the officers aside and began whispering to them. Simms looked over at the *Intrepid* and the ocean beyond her bow. He wondered if he would ever be allowed out to sea again. After today it didn't much matter to him anymore.

Baer walked over to Simms and gave him a reassuring smile. "Okay Petty Officer Simms, you win. You have me over the proverbial barrel here. I have to get you the proper security clearance first, but then I want answers."

"Yes, sir. Thank you, sir, but one more request."

Baer raised one eyebrow in incredulity. "Are you sure about that son? I might think twice before you flip that switch a second time."

Simms stood at attention as was the proper indication of respect. "Sir, I request that I accompany Ensign Hale's body to the Jacksonville police, sir."

"What gave you the idea that we would be sending his body to a non-military location?" Simms looked around and realized he and the Admiral were suddenly alone on the dock. The injured had all been taken to the infirmary, and the three officers had headed back to the command center to start the paperwork for Simms's security clearance.

"May I speak freely, sir?"

Baer nodded. "Talk to me, son."

"Our medic said there was something strange about the way the Ensign died, sir. It wasn't the shrapnel that killed him. He is requesting that an autopsy is performed to examine the Ensign's lungs. The doctor claims that the Jacksonville Police Forensics Team is the best-equipped unit to do the procedure properly. I just figured that you would want the results kept confidential. I could act as a Coast Guard liaison to expedite the autopsy and make sure that any results were kept under wraps. I would bring the report directly back to you. No one would know the results until you opened them."

Baer looked deep into Simms's eyes. He saw something familiar in those two brown mirrors. Even though he was staring at a hot mess, he saw himself standing there thirty years younger. Something instinctively told him that Simms could be trusted. "Okay, Petty Officer Simms, I will draw up the orders to transfer the Ensign's body to the J.S.O. Forensics Lab, and I'll allow you to accompany him, as long as I have your assurance that I'm the only person besides yourself who will read the findings."

Simms raised an eyebrow. "What makes you think I would disobey a direct order and read the content?"

Bear smiled. "Because I would have done the same thing thirty years ago. It'll take a while to make a few phone calls and get the paperwork in order, so go catch a shower and be in my office in two hours for your debriefing."

"Yes sir, Admiral!" Simms said as he saluted.

Back at his base apartment, Simms let the warm shower wash away his discomfort and anxiety. Had he really spoken to a commanding officer, no, the highest ranking commanding officer on the base, in that manner? What the hell was he thinking? He loved the Coast

Guard and could see himself making a career out of it. Why the hell would he jeopardize it like that?

Two hours later he was ushered into a conference room in the base administration building. Vice Admiral Baer was sitting alone at the oblong table, scribbling notes into a binder and holding a tele-conference with a monitor mounted on the far wall. Simms imme-diately recognized the Secretary of Defense, Retired Rear Admiral William Ford. He no longer wore a uniform, but the dark blue suit and familiar rounded eyeglasses made him just as formidable a fig-ure.

"Petty Officer Simms," the Secretary greeted him from the screen as he entered the room. "Take a seat. Vice Admiral Baer and I were just discussing your demands."

Simms froze behind one of the high-backed chairs. He was speechless. "I...I..." Secretary Ford waved his hand in jest. "We're just yanking your chain, son. Please, have a seat. You've had a pretty rough forty-eight hours."

Simms could feel his legs trembling as he sat down. The Secretary of Defense of the United States just made a joke at his expense. He was so thankful that he had emptied his bladder in the shower.

"Before we start your debriefing," The SecNav continued, "I would just like it entered into the official record that Petty Officer Second Class Scott Simms personifies the high standards of excellence that the Coast Guard of the United States stands for. He was thrown into a chaotic situation and proved himself a worthy leader by bringing his ship safely back to port and earning the respect of his entire crew. He is to be commended."

Simms couldn't find words for the second time in less than a minute. "Thank you, Mr. Secretary," he stammered.

"Take your time and try to relax Petty Officer," Baer instructed him from across the table. "This is not a courtroom, simply an official inquiry, but we want you to know that this conversation is being recorded. We need a permanent record of your account of the events that transpired aboard the *Intrepid*. We've already indicated the official date and time, so you don't have to worry about those minor details. To the best of your recollection, tell us what happened. We will try not to interrupt you."

Simms was going to tell the Secretary and Admiral everything that they wanted to know. But the gas mask? Simms thought he would keep that ace up his sleeve until he heard what the pathologists at the forensics lab had to say. It would merely chalk it up as an omission in his testimony that he would recall at a later time.

Simms sat forward in the plush leather seat and reached over to a nearby pitcher and poured himself a glass of ice cold water. The chrome pitcher left a ring on the table, so the P.O. wiped it away with his palm. He let the liquid act like axle grease to lubricate his tongue and throat. He had a lot to say.

Simms revealed everything that he could remember…almost. It took nearly two hours to describe the shocking details. In return, the Admiral asked the Secretary for permission to explain about the defensive weapon that was at the core of all the destruction and death. "He deserves to know why so many men and women perished, Mr. Secretary."

As long as the P.O. swore under oath, the Secretary agreed to divulge the truth behind the Truman's covert mission and the *Intrepid*'s search and rescue operation. "Anyone who possesses the technology aboard the Truman controls the negation of the world's nuclear capability. You watch the news, son. Some nations are poised to strike their neighbors and have even threatened the United States itself with nuclear weaponry."

Simms sat, mesmerized by what he was being made privy to.

"We've exhausted our air to air missile defense technology," the Secretary admitted. "It's just not precise enough to ensure we can take down an enemy's first strike. Now we have the most reliable defense weapon ever developed. A laser with pinpoint accuracy and tracking capabilities second to none. It can identify and take down a rocket launch anywhere in the world within seconds of detection—and according to the late Captain Fitzpatrick's message from inside the Truman, it's gone missing. We would prefer to assume that the laser was taken by force at sea and that the Truman was scuttled to cover the hijacker's tracks. There have been other, more nefarious scenarios bandied about by the Intelligence Branch, but we dare not tarnish the late Commander Sowell's unimpeachable reputation and advance any sort of conspiracy theories until all other possibilities have been excluded."

Simms had to do whatever he could to help recover the missing laser. He sat silently as the Secretary and Admiral discussed a plan of action. Something was bothering him. This was the first time he learned that the Commander of the Truman's last name was Sowell. He was part of the group hovering over Captain Fitzpatrick and the medic listening to Ensign Hale's final request.

The Petty Officer remembered back to his childhood and his insatiable love of jigsaw puzzles. The more complicated the pieces were, the better. He loved to dump out the entire box and scatter all the bits and turn them over one at a time. There was an image concealed in all those fragments, but just like this real-life brainteaser, it would eventually link together and reveal the entire picture. The laser and the gas mask were both pieces scattered before him. He just had to figure out how to fit them together.

The Admiral signed off from the SecNav and turned to Simms. "Let me give you a name," he said, jotting on the back of one of his business cards. He slid it across the desk. "When you get to the police department tomorrow, ask for Toby Bilston, the Head of the Forensics Department. I've already called him, and he is making this case a priority. "

"Tomorrow, sir?"

"Unfortunately, as I with speaking with Toby, he received an emergency that would be taking him out of the lab for rest the day. He promised that he would meet with you first thing in the morning. He's a man of his word. The two of us go way back."

Simms frowned, but maybe he could use this extra down time to piece together a few more parts to the puzzle. "Yes sir," he said standing up to shake the Admiral's outstretched hand. " I'll be there first thing in the morning."

"And remember, even though Toby will try his best to pry it out of you, don't give him any details you don't have to. He's still a civilian with zero security clearance."

"Of course, Admiral. I understand completely."

The Admiral closed the binder in front of him. "If anyone can tell you what killed Ensign Hale, Toby Bilston can."

Simms slipped the card into his chest pocket. "He's that good?" The Petty Officer asked.

"He's the best there is!" The Admiral's replied.

Revenge is an act of passion; vengeance an act of justice. Injuries are revenged; crimes are avenged.

-Samuel Johnson

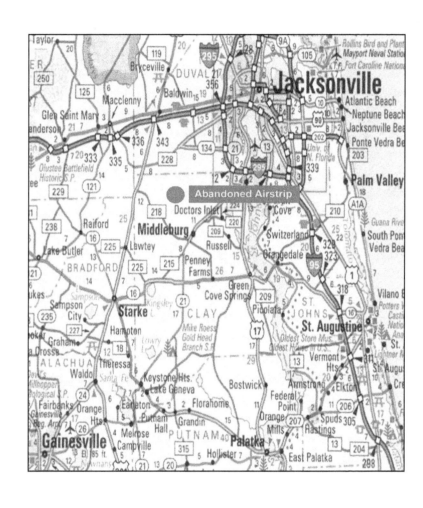

19

An Abandoned Airstrip
45 Miles Southwest of
Jacksonville, Florida

No one knew an exact time of death yet, but now man-made machines had replaced the buzzards that circled the desolate and overgrown runway. Prohibited from flying within a half mile of the cordoned-off airstrip, news helicopters loaded with ravenous reporters hovered around the perimeter of the crime scene, just like their carnivorous predecessors. A pair of blue and yellow police helicopters made sure the press kept their distance by flying perilously close whenever one would breach the invisible boundary.

Fearless cameramen dangled precariously out of open hatches, braving buffeting winds in the slim hope of catching the best perspective of the significant events unfolding on the tarmac some five hundred feet below.

Two days of speculation had passed since the ranking City Commissioner of Jacksonville, Arthur Beckworth, had disappeared. He had excused himself in the middle of an exclusive dinner held for the entire City Commission at Peter Mason's Star Island Mansion in Miami. It had been a lavish affair with entertainment, dancing, and plenty of pressing of the flesh. The board of seven commissioners and their spouses had been invited to the dinner to discuss Mason's upcoming redevelopment of the riverfront, including the new Mason Cruise Line Ballpark.

Beckworth, being the lone bachelor at the gathering, had slipped away after excusing himself from the dinner table and then just vanished. Throughout the City of Jacksonville, the lead story on every newscast, the headline on every front page, the argument around every office water cooler, all centered on his disappearance.

Supporters and critics alike seized any public opportunity for heated debate on Beckworth's virtues or motivations. The local political pundits were having a field day. From beneath every overturned rock, the talking heads on the cable news networks spread their innuendos and proffered up their libelous allegations about the Commissioner's alleged mob ties and bribery schemes. They would say just about anything in the hopes of extending their fleeting fifteen minutes of fame.

The media had been whipped into a furor by these zealots. One renowned newspaper reported that, through an undisclosed source, they had learned that the once-esteemed Commissioner had absconded with city funds and was heading for the French Riviera. On the same day, one of the television tabloid shows had him checking into the Betty Ford Clinic under the pseudonym of Paul Welsh. After further investigation, the patient in question turned out to be just another washed-up corporate executive—who was neither pleased nor flattered by his sudden notoriety.

But now, after forty-eight hours and all the whispered hearsay and media rumination, the story was about to be laid to rest. Commissioner Arthur Beckworth had been found.

The corpse was first spotted by a student pilot in a small, two-seater, single-engine Cessna. The eighteen-year-old had been practicing figure eights and stalls using a nearby row of high-tension towers for reference points, when he noticed the obscured airstrip for the first time. Figuring it would be the perfect spot to practice his touch and go landing drills, he lowered the plane's nose for his first trial landing—but quickly realized, much to his alarm, why the airfield was abandoned. The weed-infested, fractured concrete runway was in no condition to be used.

Barely managing to pull out of his steep descent in time, the inexperienced pilot spotted what he thought at first glance was just a flock of hungry buzzards tearing at the carcass of a dead alligator on one of the two adjacent taxiways. Although the sight sickened him, there was nothing unusual about seeing something like that in this swampy region of the state. Out here, the only law was Nature's Law...survival of the fittest.

As soon as he had cleared the looming wall of sawgrass at the far end of the field, he banked the small plane to the north. It wasn't until that moment, when the pilot's side of the cockpit dipped toward the ground, that he was able to clearly see what the birds were actually fighting over. It was horrifying! Just lying there...not more than a hundred yards in front of the old ...they were chomping and gnawing on the torn garments and grisly skeleton of a human being!

That was less than two hours ago.

It took the first airborne unit on the scene some ten to fifteen minutes just to repel the pesky buzzards. This was no easy task, because this particular flock of birds had taken to guarding the decomposing body like it was their last supper. The repugnant black birds looked up at the intruders, squawking and screeching. They had no intention of giving up the hearty remains of the meal that had been so graciously set before them. It wasn't until one of the quick-thinking officers decided to shoot one of the pesky birds that the rest of the flocks' cannibalistic appetite shifted toward the fresher bird meat.

That was when the feeding frenzy really started...

The position of the body had already been photographed from every conceivable angle and outlined on the pavement. The chalk silhouette raggedly following the normal contours of the corpse until it reached the area above the shoulders. There the sketch abruptly became oblong above the neck, marking a spillway for a dark brown flood of dried blood and an amalgam of brain matter, hair, bone, and tissue.

Numbered evidence cards had been placed as identification markers on questionable locations in the general vicinity of the body, including the victim's wallet, which was conspicuously lying open next to the corpse. These tiny yellow pyramids were scattered across the tarmac by the first set of criminalists that had arrived on the scene. These trained professionals were merely evidence "finders," not evidence "interpreters." They knew exactly what to look for in cases such as this, and they placed a marker on anything and everything that looked like it didn't belong in the natural environment. Ferreting out clues was all they did, and they were meticulous in their responsibility. They photographed the area down to the smallest detail without disturbing the body. Analysis of their findings would be left up to the lead detective assigned to the case, and to the Forensic Pathologist—and the City of Jacksonville had two of the very best.

Another blue and white police helicopter came swooping out of the sun like it was on a bombing run. The pilot, who had been warned ahead of time by one of his passengers that he hated to fly, thought he would take this opportunity to have a little fun at the passenger's expense. They were old friends, and it was a sitcom that had been played out time and time again for over fifteen years.

When the helicopter's skids finally embraced terra firma, Toby Bilston, the head of the City of Jacksonville's Forensic Lab, stumbled out of the hatch, set his evidence collection kit on the ground, and fell to his knees. His thick salt and pepper beard surrounded a mouth that always seemed to be frozen in a perpetual smile...except for now. A descendant of English ancestry, at this moment, with the green tinge to his face, Toby could have easily passed for Irish. His eyes were a soft brown, and the lines that had sprouted around them like grins with the passing years seemed to accentuate his unusually optimistic demeanor.

Toby Bilston was a short, rotund man forever locked in a battle with his waistline. Never a candidate for the centerfold of Health and Fitness Magazine, Toby liked to describe his hairline as "receding," but his wife Harriet always lovingly described her husband of thirty years as simply being "follically challenged." Together, they had raised two beautiful daughters and an extraordinary son. Tanya and Bonnie were both off at school in Gainesville at the University of Florida, with Bess studying physical therapy and Tanya two years behind her older sister, still undecided about her prospects. Tanya's vacillation was okay with Toby and Harriet since she was still young, and they knew she would come around in time, as her sister had.

It wasn't as straightforward with their only son Benjamin. While Ben's dreams and ambitions far exceeded those of his sister Bonnie, his future was far more uncertain than Tanya's. During his last year of middle school, Ben had been diagnosed with Multiple Sclerosis. Less than a year later, he was confined to a wheelchair. Life was a daily battle for Toby's son, and with new drugs and treatment, his future was looking brighter now than ever. Young Benjamin still had dreams of becoming a criminal attorney, and nothing would give Toby more pleasure than to one day have the opportunity to be raked over the coals in a courtroom by his offspring. It was his faith in that vision that made the concept of life and death so meaningful to Bilston. It was his son's hope that made him such a doting father in his home life, and it was his indignation over his son's disease that made him so tenacious at his work.

"Dear God Toby, it was only a half-hour flight!"

He could barely hear her voice over the *whapping* of the rotor blades. Lauren King was standing over him, one hand on his back, the other trying to hold the hem of her navy blazer from flapping in the prop wash. "Are you going to be alright?"

Bilston was still on all fours as he shot an angry look over at the cockpit. The pilot was pointing at him and laughing hysterically. Toby waggled a finger of warning at his supposed friend and pilot, Chuck Wingate. Both men knew Toby's revenge would come Sunday night as they faced each other across the table at their weekly poker game. "You just wait!" Toby mouthed.

Because of Wingate's headgear and visor, only his mouth was visible, but the return grin was ear to ear.

"That son-of-a-bitch knows how afraid I am of heights, and every time he flies me somewhere, he pulls that aerobatic shit!" Toby snarled, as the helicopter lifted off.

King shook her head like a teacher scolding a misbehaving student. "It's hard to believe you two can stop sniping at each other long enough to play a single hand of cards, much less share a pair of season tickets for all those Jaguars games! Aren't you two ever going to grow up?"

Toby rose to his feet, dusted off the knees of his trousers and picked up his kit. Squinting against the sun, he watched as the helicopter banked to the east and vanished over the horizon.

"Sometimes I wonder what possessed me to make that idiot my son's Godfather."

Now that Toby was back on his feet and the correct hue was returning to his cheeks, Lauren King was no longer interested in small talk. Tall and shapely, she was the maverick of the Jacksonville Police Department's Detective Squad, choosing to wear faded jeans, snakeskin boots, and a plain blue coat instead of the standard monotonous business suit. She didn't dress down to flaunt her individuality, as much as to play down her distracting good looks. Her long red mane was tied behind her head with a simple elastic band, and her jade green eyes were almost cat-like in the way they darted about the airstrip, drinking in her surroundings.

The daughter of wealthy—but not particularly nurturing—parents, Lauren was born with a remarkably keen sense of intuition. Starting at an early age, while her neighborhood playmates were preoccupied with playing doctor and throwing tea parties, young Lauren found her entertainment in tracking down such things as a missing socket wrench that her father had absent-mindedly lent to another neighbor some six months earlier. It took her two long days, plenty of intense interrogation, and miles of legwork to finally reunite her father and the tool, but the sleuth bug had taken its incurable bite.

After receiving her degree in Criminal Justice from Florida State University, Lauren's meteoric rise to the position of Homicide Detective was unprecedented in the history of the C.J.P.D. She graduated top of her class from the state-sponsored police academy, becoming proficient in weapons and tactics, as well as earning special recognition from her supervisors for the uncanny deductive skills she displayed during her training.

She served the minimum three years in uniform and was promptly tested for reassignment to the Detective's Division. To her commanding officer's delight, Lauren passed the rigorous examination with the highest possible marks. After less than a week in her new surroundings, she came to realize that she had finally found the missing piece in her life. This work gave her purpose, and King quickly earned the confidence and respect of her fellow investigators. Less than a year later, she was on the street and working Homicide. Lauren thrived on the adrenalin rush of the hunt. It was her drug of choice...and she was a junkie.

This wasn't the first time Lauren and Toby were teamed together, but this case was high profile, so it went without saying that the Chief of D's would personally request them both. They worked well together, complementing each other's abilities and respecting each other's boundaries. Lauren was the bloodhound, and Toby deciphered her findings. They knew each other's limitations and demanded nothing less than excellence from each other.

Toby reminded Lauren very much of her late father. Not in the physical sense, but emotionally and sentimentally. Early on in their working relationship, Toby realized he was filling a crucial void in her life, and never minded being placed in that surrogate role.

In fact, the entire Bilston clan gladly welcomed her into their lives whenever Lauren needed somewhere to turn or someone to talk to. She held a particular fondness for Benjamin, and would quite often drop by just to keep the wheelchair-bound boy company. Sometimes they would talk for hours, and other times, King would push the teenager around the block, and they might never speak a word. It was these times she appreciated the most. The silence was truly golden, and each of them was wealthier for sharing in it.

"What have you got?" Toby asked, noticing the intense glare that soured her face whenever her senses were on the prowl.

"Not much access to this place," she said, pointing at the wall of grass surrounding the field. "Runway's all shot to hell. Notice any roads on our way in?"

Toby wiped his forehead with the back of his hand. "You're kidding, me, right? Do you really think I ever took one look out the window?"

Lauren shrugged. "Well, I didn't see any. Flora and fauna are reclaiming this place. No access roads anymore."

Less than three minutes on the ground and already Toby was beginning to sweat. He was a habitual sweater, and he did it profusely. If he could have done it for a living, he would have retired years ago as a wealthy man. He reached into his inside coat pocket and pulled out a spiral notebook, flipping it open to the first page.

"Just like you figured, the first unit on the scene couldn't make it here by patrol car. The turnoff from the main road was overgrown with heavy brush. They were the ones to call in the choppers."

Lauren toyed with her lower lip thoughtfully. "Then there are only two other ways in, I would imagine. The runway is too broken up for a small plane to land, so I figure the two ways in by chopper and possibly by airboat."

Toby thought he had finally one-upped her. "Or possibly by foot!"

Lauren studied the tall grass as it gently swayed in the meager breeze. "Only if you don't plan on making it back to civilization alive! Lions and tigers and bears...oh my!"

Toby wrinkled his nose. She was probably right. "Not to mention the alligators and panthers."

Lauren never took her eyes off the dense wall of foliage. "So where is the helicopter then?"

The thunderous roar of an engine caught both their attention as the flat bow of a park ranger's airboat burst through the bulwark of grass less than a hundred yards to their left. A distressed ranger quickly shut off the engine, jumped out of the elevated steering chair, and pulled the nose of the boat onto the concrete until he judged it wasn't going to slide back into the underbrush.

Within seconds, two uniformed officers were leading the ranger away against his will. The ranger's protests that the airstrip was situated on State Park property had apparently fallen on deaf ears.

"You see that?"

Toby nodded. "He was just trying to do his job."

Lauren wasn't referring to the ranger. "I'm not talking about the ranger; I'm referring to the airboat!"

Toby looked over at the flat-bottom. Everyone who lived in the State of Florida knew what an airboat was, and he saw nothing unusual about this one, but then again, he didn't see it through Lauren's disciplined lenses. "What am I missing?"

She started walking toward the boat, her pace picking up, mimicking her excitement. "Look at the way the bow of the boat broke down the roots of the foliage!" She knelt on the edge of the runway, the murky water lapping at the toes of her boots. "You see this? The branches down here at the roots are very rigid! When the boat busted through, the heavy bow bent the roots outward and even snapped some of them off! Look here!"

Toby didn't plan on getting too close to the stagnant water without his rubber gloves on. The water smelled awful, and who knew what kind of vile bacteria was having sex in it. "Only you would catch something like this," he said, with a mixture of admiration and foreboding. "But don't you think we should examine the body before we start worrying about how it got here?"

Lauren stood up and pointed out the periphery of the cordoned area. Her intuitive radar was sweeping the entire area. There was only a single tarmac and a dilapidated hangar at the end of the runway. The airplane-sized shed had one door hanging off its hinges and was overgrown with Kudzu, a weed-like vine that had been spreading throughout the Southeastern United States for years now. The leafy vine could envelop anything stationary in a matter of months. It had quickly become problematic when it was first introduced from Japan as a ground cover for farmers. Now, native plants were dying, and old buildings like this were being swallowed whole as a result.

"I want to get someone to walk the perimeter of this entire airstrip to look for this same kind of new root damage. It might give us a lead on how the body got here."

Toby put his collection kit down, pulled a handkerchief out of his back pocket, and dabbed his face. He knew better than to argue with her whenever she got like this, but he could see where she was going and didn't want her rushing to conclusions just yet. "If you don't mind me playing the Devil's advocate for a few moments here," he proceeded delicately, "according to the reports, this place has a reputation for being a hideout for poachers and drug runners."

"So?"

Toby blotted the back of his neck with the monogrammed cloth. "Well, what happens to your theory, if some poachers or dope smugglers just happened to show up or maybe were already here when the Commissioner's helicopter shows up?"

The detective took a step back. "What leads you to believe he was brought here by helicopter?"

Toby's eyes widened. "You think he got here all the way from Miami by airboat?"

King pursed her lips dejectedly. "No, of course, I don't."

King pulled out a small spiral notepad from her breast pocket.

Nowadays all of her colleagues were using tablets to track their case notes, but she found the old-fashioned way much simpler.

"So if there is a mysterious helicopter somewhere between this hell hole and Jacksonville," Toby continued, "It's vanished too."

Bilston scratched at his beard. "This is ridiculous. How is someone supposed to check the flight records and manifests for all non-commercial air traffic that took off from any level surface in Miami and may have landed on any other level surface somewhere over the last two days? Freaking helicopters, they're like mosquitoes. Speaking of which," he protested, as he slapped the side of his face.

King jotted it all down.

Bilston did a three hundred sixty degree scan of the crime scene. "Okay, so let's assume for argument's sake that Arthur Beckworth left mid-party of his own volition or was somehow taken by force and loaded onto a helicopter that wound up landing here in the middle of bum-fucked Egypt. Then, something goes tits up for him, and he's just left lying here out in the open?"

King grimaced. "Not the exact phraseology I would have used, but it's one possible theory nonetheless."

Toby fluttered his fingers. "And then our magic helicopter just takes off and disappears into the night sky without a trace." He blew out a deep, frustrated breath. "This is the biggest bowl of spaghetti I've ever seen. Damn, it's humid out here!"

Toby pointed toward the body that was being guarded by a group of air patrolmen. "Well, I can tell you that from over here that I can plainly see that the body is still intact, so it certainly wasn't dropped from any great height. So the mystery helicopter had to have landed. And besides, look around here. If you were going to dump a person—dead or alive—out of an airplane or helicopter, how lousy would your aim have to be to miss the swamp? If someone would have dumped him out there," he pointed toward the dense forestation, "no one would have found him before the wildlife and natural exposure consumed his body." Toby waggled his finger. "No, someone wanted him to be found. Someone is sending a message."

Lauren tapped her foot impatiently. "But there's no record of Beckworth leaving by helicopter. The entire entourage was flown back and forth to Miami in Peter Mason's own private jet."

Toby shielded his eyes from the sun. "Only Beckworth wasn't on the return flight later that evening. We've got to go over every inch of this place with a fine-toothed comb. We need to come up with something more definitive before we leave. I need to check out the body while you do your thing."

Lauren wrote a few notes on her own thoughts. The list was growing longer by the minute. Engine problems, smugglers, payback, wrong time wrong place, they were all credible theories. She tapped her pen on the pad as she spoke. "Dope runners might have been out here when the helicopter developed engine problems," she proposed. "They might have killed Beckworth for the interruption of their work, overpowered the pilot or threatened him into flying them somewhere."

Toby shook his head. "But if this was a staging ground for drug smugglers, then why leave a body out in the open to draw attention to your ideal hideout? And for Pete's sake, how did our bad guys get to and from this place? Do you think they were stranded out here and prayed for random helicopters with leaky gaskets to show up and save them? This has nothing to do with smuggling or drugs. You need to do some of what you do best when it comes to the late Commissioner. Dig into his background. I'll bet you dollars to donuts this was a premeditated murder." Toby's eye's narrowed. "We can't leave any stone unturned out here. We need to see where the physical evidence takes us and leave the supposition for later. There are too many eyes watching us and waiting for our findings."

The two investigators walked over to the corpse like a father and daughter. Toby set his evidence kit on the ground and removed his jacket. His white shirt was nearly transparent with sweat. "Whoever did this didn't care whether or not we found the body; that's why they left his wallet out in the open. Otherwise, they could have chopped him up and tossed the pieces into the swamp. This was an act of revenge or meant to give notice to someone."

Toby gazed down upon the remains and then shifted his stare to the flock of vultures circling overhead. If the body *had* been here the majority of the time since the Commissioner first disappeared, it wasn't going to be a pleasant examination. The heat, the carnivorous birds...he shuddered to think what the corpse had gone through. No one deserved such a gruesome fate.

Lauren understood Toby's cynical attitude, and she learned from it. "So what do you think about my airboat theory? Do you think it's even worth investigating?"

There is a Japanese proverb that asserts *to teach is to learn*, and Toby Bilston was a true believer in such sage wisdom. "Well," he said, scratching his scalp thoughtfully, "if the perimeter *is* undisturbed, that would probably mean there were no airboats out here lately, and that alone would save us a heck of a lot of legwork checking out airboat registrations and rental places. So yeah," he said, with a congratulatory grin. "I think you should definitely have a few officers check it out!"

Lauren smiled appreciatively as Toby waved for Tom Hopkins, a Sergeant from the Uniform Division, to join them. She understood the vote of confidence her mentor had given her, and she loved him for it.

"So if we both agree the motive wasn't robbery, then this is quite a little conspiracy theory we're concocting here," she admitted.

"Let's just focus on the facts for now," Toby warned.

King asked Hopkins to have the perimeter searched, which he told her would be done immediately. She watched as he walked away and began recruiting uniformed officers to help check for any sawgrass that looked as though it had been disturbed recently.

Bilston walked around the remains and from a safe distance began studying the position of the corpse. Commissioner Arthur

Beckworth was a rather large African-American man, and somewhat on the hefty side. He had played on the offensive line for Jacksonville University in the late seventies and hadn't lost much of his bulk since his college football days.

Beckworth was lying on his back while most of the skin on his exposed face and hands had been picked clean by the birds. He was barely recognizable. There was a large puddle of coagulated blood and bone fragments beneath his head. If the brain was exposed underneath, then the birds had most likely eaten it too. Bilston was genuinely surprised that Beckworth's eyes were still intact, since those were usually the first thing the birds would go for. To the east, he spotted a trail of blood leading to the corpse that started near the overgrown hangar. It appeared that the commissioner had first been attacked over there and then dragged himself along the tarmac trying to escape his assailant. Any chance of discovering defensive wounds on his hands was pretty much a total loss by now, though.

While the airstrip itself was a beehive of activity, no one except the original pair of criminalists on the scene had gone anywhere near the body. Cross-contamination was the biggest hindrance to the successful completion of any investigation. One errant shoeprint could lead the detective team on a baseless tangent that could stymie the investigation for weeks.

Lauren stood quietly next to Toby as he squatted down to examine the remains from different angles. Not as flexible as he used to be, his knee joints protested loudly. He tipped his head from side to side trying to see the crime scene from every possible perspective. His gut instincts were like no one else's. After a few seconds, and not wanting to disturb him, Lauren whispered to Toby that she was going to check out the hangar. Toby heard her, but he was already in a Zen-like state and didn't acknowledge her either way.

As Lauren walked ponderingly toward the vine-covered structure, she was absorbing everything her five senses could glean from the surrounding area. Most laymen would think a person needed to put on blinders, literally blocking out everything else to focus on the complexities of her task. In actuality, it was just the opposite for Lauren. She gave her awareness free reign, taking in every sight, every sound, and every odor that others might merely take for granted. She followed the blood trail toward the hangar, careful not to step anywhere but on untainted concrete. She listened beyond the background bantering of her fellow officers, hearing the drone of the insects and the screeching of the occasional osprey. She wouldn't let her eyes focus on any single object. Instead, she took in the entire scene as a whole, imagining what it would have looked like without all of this commotion.

Toby Bilston understood that not everyone was cut out to deal with dead bodies. Especially one as decomposed as this. It was the nasty part of the job, but not a part everyone got used to. He had. Lauren hadn't. This was his area of expertise.

Toby backed away from the body to where he had neatly set down his coat, opened his collection kit, and removed a pair of paper booties. With very little finesse and even less dexterity, he struggled to tie the protective covers over his street shoes. This was easier said than done for a man whose idea of doing exercise was getting up for more potato chips during commercials.

Whatever slight breeze there was seemed to be blowing in from the east. At times the wind was enough to ruffle the tops of the sawgrass, but it was nowhere near the strength needed to rid the tarmac of the putrid stench wafting off the decomposing body. The closer Toby moved toward the remains, the worse the fetor became.

Hundreds of flies buzzed around the body. Some of these had laid eggs on the corpse. Eggs to maggots, maggots into flies…circle of life…a quantifiable circle of life. Toby carefully stepped around the face-up body, letting his eyes be the first and most important tool in his investigation.

Most of the flesh and muscle had already been stripped off the bones by the birds. Even parts of Beckworth's suit had been torn in spots by the buzzards trying to pick clean the carcass. He could plainly see where the coat and trousers had been clawed away by the buzzards' razor-sharp talons. Any internal organs that the carnivorous birds managed to harvest must have been yanked out through the ribs while the scavengers perched themselves on the Commissioner's chest. This was a hideous image that Toby had to consciously banish from his thoughts.

Beckworth's arms were bent at the elbows, the bones of his hands clenched into fists. This was a standard defensive pose found in a lot of homicides. The legs were not splayed awkwardly, but instead, they appeared as though they had been working in unison at the time of death. Viewing the corpse while standing behind the feet, Toby could almost imagine the Commissioner trying to crawl away from his assailant on his hands and knees, much the same way an infantry soldier would shimmy along the ground during battle. Beckworth had spent the last seconds of his life struggling valiantly to escape his attacker, but ended up dying slowly and horribly.

"Toby!"

Lauren was calling to him from inside the hangar.

Bilston glanced over his shoulder. His bones continued to crack in protest as he stood up. He pulled out his telephone and called her number directly. "I'm still working over here, and I need your help to roll the body over."

"But I think we've got more blood in here!"

"First things first," Toby replied. "I need you out here."

A minute later Bilston and King were turning the Commissioner's body onto his stomach. Lauren struggled for breath when she saw the back of Beckworth's head. "Oh sweet Lord," she gasped, covering her mouth. "What could cause that kind of damage?"

The entirety of the Commissioner's skull had been caved inward, and just as he had suspected, the birds had already finished their feast. Toby lifted the Commissioner's jacket as far up as it would go and commented that there were no entry wounds of any kind to be found. Beckworth had been neither shot nor knifed. He made that point to Lauren, who had turned her back but was still writing.

"Reach into my kit and get me a pair of tweezers, will you please?" Toby asked. Lauren reached down and handed him the instrument without looking at the body.

"Can you shine your penlight into the skull for me?"

Lauren swallowed hard. "Say what?"

Toby twisted an object close to his eyes. "It looks like a splinter of wood."

Lauren was confused. They were in the middle of a swamp and forest. "Is that supposed to tell us something? It's a splinter, big deal. You can't spit without hitting tree bark out here."

Toby smiled. "It's time for a refresher course in Dendrology."

"Dendrology?"

Toby continued to study the splinter up close. "Dendrology is the study of woody trees—unlike its cousin Botany, which is the study of plants in general."

"You're a font of knowledge," Lauren quipped.

"Listen carefully and learn wisely from the great guardian of the forest, my young apprentice. This wood looks to be ash."

"So what about it," Lauren asked. "It's ash, a common enough wood. Does that matter?"

"Ash doesn't grow anywhere around here. So how do you suppose this little sliver found itself embedded inside Arthur Beckworth's skull?"

Lauren thought for a second and then realized what Toby was proposing. "The killer brought the murder weapon with him?"

"Did you see any sort of tools in the hangar?"

"No, the place is barren, but I did find a small amount of blood evidence that I want you to look at."

Toby was trying to time travel. "I'll bet the confrontation started in the hangar, and the Commissioner, who is strong enough not to be overpowered easily, might have gotten in a few licks of his own.

Good for him."

"So what was the assassin doing here in the hangar? How did he get here?"

Toby thought for a second. "If we were to just assume for the moment that Beckworth was taken against his will from the dinner, then the killer was most likely already waiting for him on the helicopter, or could have been the one who actually kidnapped him."

Lauren paused her note taking. "And then our killer pulls out a stick made of ash and starts beating the Commissioner to a pulp as he tries to flee?"

"Not just any stick made of ash."

Lauren looked at him with astonishment. "Toby, don't tell me you figured out what the murder weapon was from a splinter."

"Just another theory, but the majority of baseball bats used in the United States are made from ash or metal alloy. Maple, hickory and even bamboo is used to make them too, but not nearly in the same quantities. So now that I'm certain that the Commissioner was bludgeoned to death, blunt force trauma will be my official cause of death," he announced, as he slowly rose to his feet.

"That's a great start," Lauren congratulated him.

"Aside from the official cause of death, everything else is still all speculation, but you know that striking someone repeatedly with that much force shows some deep-seated rage. This was the most brutal, primal form of assault. Whoever did this continued to pound away until long after Arthur Beckworth had stopped breathing. The fragment I found was lodged in the front of the skull which tells me that it splintered when the weapon contacted the concrete. Only when he hit the tarmac did the executioner stop swinging. Then he rolled the body over, perhaps to stare into Beckworth's dead eyes one last time."

"You said 'he.' Male?"

Toby nodded. "No offense, but this bloodbath was not committed by a woman unless it was Wonder Woman."

Lauren scrunched her nose at the grisly description. "You should really write greeting cards."

Toby smiled as he slipped the splinter into an evidence bag. "Benjamin Franklin once said, 'Either write something worth reading or do something worth writing.' I think I'll do the latter, thank you very much."

Toby walked with Lauren over to where the Commissioner's blood trail started. On the horizon, the sky was turning pink and amber as the sun began to set.

"We're gonna need to light this place up," Toby said.

Lauren pulled out her phone. "I'll get it done."

Contentious Vote Sends City's MLB Future to Voter Referendum

BY JARROD BLACK

JDN SPORTS EDITOR

BILLIONAIRE Peter Mason's dream of officially bringing a Major League Baseball Franchise to the City of Jacksonville has been put on hold for now.

After a divisive ten year battle, the cruise ship magnate's struggle to lure a team to the city will be put off until November, when it can be brought up for a citywide public vote.

In a vote early yesterday, after the untimely death of Commissioner Arthur Beckworth, a staunch opponent of riverfront expansion plans, the Commission voted in favor of passing the decision to the voters using a special referendum.

The recent events surrounding the mysterious death of Commissioner Beckworth remain a mystery, with the Jacksonville Police Department in charge of the investigation.

Beckworth's body was found at a deserted airstrip forty miles Southeast of Jacksonville by a student pilot two days ago. Details surrounding the Commissioner's death have yet to be disclosed, but a police spokesman has confirmed that homicide has not been ruled out.

Peter Mason was unavailable for comment, but sources close to the billionaire have said that he is deeply saddened by Beckworth's death and disappointed with the Commission's vote.

In the past, Mason has been quoted as sounding highly confident in his chances of bringing another professional team to the Jacksonville area. "If the state of Florida is able to support professional football in three cities and two other Major League Baseball franchises, it seems a natural fit to bring another rivalry to the state."

The last Major League expansion took place in 1998, with the addition of teams in Arizona in the National League and Tampa Bay to the American League.

Major League Baseball has been considering additional teams for the last few years, with Mexico City, Rhode Island, Las Vegas, and even Orlando as viable choices. The City of Jacksonville was always considered a dark horse, but once Mason sweetened the deal with a new privately-funded stadium, the Baseball Commissioner's selection committee vaulted Jacksonville to the top of potential candidates.

"While the spread of baseball internationally has always been the Commissioner's vision, the viability of a team playing in Mexico—considering the recent instability between the U.S. and its southern neighbor—has put any league expansion plans on hold for now," an MLB spokesman told the Daily News.

Peter Mason has quickly changed tactics and has been courting some of the more financially strapped current franchises to relocate to the state-of-the-art ballpark he is planning. None of the more than six struggling franchises have commented publically about being wooed by Mason, but it is believed that negotiations are being held daily, and that more than one of those teams contacted have expressed some interest.

Mason plans on having a public contest to name the new team should his plans eventually come to fruition, but these plans are now on hold until the public decides on the November third ballot.

The new stadium, if approved, will be built a mile east of the current Jacksonville Baseball Grounds, a 6000 seat stadium now the home to the Miami Marlin's AA franchise, the Jacksonville Jumbo Shrimp.

Mason has already signed a contract to purchase land on the site of a barren parcel of land known locally as "the concrete field," adjacent to the cluster of cement plants that line the west banks of the St. Johns. Part of the proposal is that those plants will be razed and relocated elsewhere to ensure a clear view of the river.

An exhibition game Saturday afternoon at the Baseball Grounds is still on schedule, although a moment of silence will be held in Commissioner Beckworth's honor before the first pitch.

For now, it's business as usual; but Peter Mason and the citizens of Jacksonville will now have to wait to learn the future of Baseball here until November.

20

Set on five acres of oceanfront property, with a secluded entry from Ponte Vedra Blvd, Nicky Coltello's distinctively modern beach house had become a landmark for pilots, boaters, and beach walkers. The main house—with its five bedrooms—and the guest house opened out to a spacious pool courtyard. It was no surprise the Architectural Record named it "House of the Year" in 2006.

The sun had been up for two hours now as Coltello sat out at his pool and dug a spoon into half a grapefruit. His hair was still wet and hung down like a soggy mop. His monogrammed robe was barely cinched at the waist, revealing a chest that was bald from frequent waxing. A naked woman was swimming laps in the pool. Her name was Bianca, or maybe Miranda; Coltello couldn't remember, and it didn't really matter anyway.

A seagull was perched on one of the chairs at the table. He had become a regular morning guest. Coltello had nicknamed him "Slick," and the bird, like the owner of the house was confident and unafraid. He sat on the top of the chair and waited patiently for Nicky to throw him a scrap of muffin or whatever other starch was on the morning's menu. Occasionally, another bird would try to encroach on Slick's territory and the bird would scream and flap his wings in a show of defiant ownership. Nicky loved that about the bird, and he would toss him an extra treat whenever he protected his position.

The sliding glass doors opened to one side, and Jimmy Diaz stepped out into the warm morning air. He was dressed in casual attire this morning: a pair of jeans and a long sleeve shirt with the cuffs rolled up just below the elbows. On his feet, he wore white rubber-soled running shoes, because his boss hated black scuff marks on the imported Italian tile. He adjusted the sunglasses on the bridge of his nose as he pulled the glass doors shut behind him. Walking up to the table, he grabbed a small vine of red grapes off a fruit platter and stared at the woman who continued her swim. Slick ignored Diaz and just picked fiercely at one of his wings.

"Nice," Diaz commented.

Coltello never looked up from his grapefruit. "If you say so."

"Nicky, she's gorgeous. Look at that body!"

Coltello glanced up and then continued to dig out pulp. "Feed her then send her packing."

Diaz popped a few grapes into his mouth as he watched the swimmer do a professional turn at the deep end of the pool. "You don't even know her name, do you?"

Coltello set down his spoon and paused. "Does it matter, J.D.? I told you to feed her and kick her to the curb. Call her an Uber if you need to, but I want her gone by the time I shower and shave."

Diaz pulled out a chair and took a seat. Slick still didn't move. The water on Ponte Vedra beach was unusually calm this morning. Usually, there was a light chop with whitecaps foaming a few hundred yards from the beach, but today the water looked as still as an oil painting. Occasionally a few beach joggers would run past the house and wave as if they expected some gesture of familiarity in return. They would continue past the house unfulfilled.

The woman finished her swim and began to climb the stone steps in the shallow end of the pool. She pulled herself out of the water in standard time, but it looked slow motion to Jimmy Diaz. Her body was flawless; she had all the curves that God had intended, and they were natural. Diaz held his breath as she bent over to retrieve a towel from one of the chaise lounges and began to dry her hair. Anyone on the beach would have seen her in her naked glory, but it was apparent she couldn't have cared less. With her hair draped in one towel, she wrapped a second one around her torso and tucked it in to cover her perfect breasts.

She waved at Diaz who wiggled his fingers in return. Coltello was too busy trying to hand feed Slick to pay her any attention.

"Is it okay if I take a shower, Nicky?"

Coltello held out a wedge of wheat toast, and Slick cautiously nipped away at the offering. He never answered her, so Diaz spoke up. "Use the one in the guest house. When you're done, just leave the towels in there. Are you going to need a ride?"

She bent her head forward and let her dark hair cascade out of the towel. "I'll just call a taxi."

Diaz smiled warmly at her. "I'll have a ride waiting for you at the front door in twenty minutes. Is that okay?"

The woman looked at Coltello who acted as though she were invisible. She wasn't sure whether she should feel offended or honored. "That will be perfect, thank you," she said, walking toward the adjacent guest house, "Thanks for the nice night, Nicky."

Coltello was too busy chuckling at Slick's antics to show her any interest.

"Damn," Diaz observed. "That's ice cold, Nick. Not even a parting meal?"

Coltello leaned back in his chair. "The food is sitting here if she wanted some. I didn't tell her not to eat."

"But you didn't exactly make her feel welcome at the table."

Nicky looked at his manager with sincere perplexity. Proper etiquette seemed to elude the mob boss. "What? I needed to send her an engraved invitation?"

Diaz shook his head as he took his phone and scheduled a Lyft driver to arrive in fifteen minutes. He would have to buzz him through the gate when the ride reached the outer gate.

Nicky pulled his wet hair into a ponytail and secured it with a rubber band from the pocket of his robe. He leaned his head back so that the early sun would bake his face and help dry his hair. "So what brings you to my house on this fine summer morning?"

Diaz laid the empty grapevine onto a paper napkin. "I want to talk about Arthur Beckworth."

Coltello's eyes were closed as he listened to the soothing sounds of the relentless surf sweeping up and down the beach. "Beckworth is dead. End of conversation."

Diaz leaned forward so that he didn't have to compete with the pounding waves. "No. I think it warrants a bit more discussion, Nicky."

Coltello wiped a fleck of sand off his cheek as he drew in a deep breath. "We paid him to sway the vote. The vote never took place because he died. Now the vote is delayed for another five months. Mission accomplished. What more is there to talk about?"

Diaz pulled off his sunglasses and placed them carefully on the table. "What did you do, Nicky?"

Coltello leaned his head to the right so that he could look directly at Diaz. "What makes you think I did something?"

"He was the Senior Commissioner on the City Council, Nicky. They're not going to let it slide. There's going to be a full-blown investigation into this. His carcass was nearly picked clean by wildlife, for Christ's sake!"

Coltello chuckled at the image. "I guess someone was trying to make a point."

"Someone?"

Coltello pushed his chair away from the table. "Good riddance, I say. The man was a fucking money pit. All we ever did was feed him cash and never got shit in return. I'm not worried about any damned investigation. The ends justified the means as far as I'm concerned. It couldn't have happened to a nicer guy."

Jimmy Diaz rubbed his temples as his boss stood up. He could feel a headache creeping up the back of his skull. "We've got to talk about this, Nicky. This wasn't just some barebone that you go after with the business end of a hammer."

Coltello shook his head. "Don't try to speak Italian, Jimmy. It fits you like a K Mart suit. I know he wasn't just some bum. Don't ever lecture me on how to run my business," he chastised his manager, as he loosened the knot on his robe. "The man was a cancerous tumor that's been eradicated from our lives. There is nothing more to say. Please don't bring this subject up in my presence again."

Diaz fell silent as his boss turned to enter the house.

"I'm going to take a shower and shave, and then we'll head downtown," Coltello announced, pulling open the glass doors and disappearing inside.

Jimmy Diaz sat quietly in the salty morning air. Slick remained on the chair across from him still scuffling with something beneath his wing. Diaz let out a sigh and slipped his sunglasses back onto his face. Slick decided it was finally time to leave as Diaz stood up to go inside. As he slid open the door, Diaz looked over his shoulder one last time at the enormity of the ocean behind him. He just couldn't shake the nagging feeling that nothing good awaited him over the horizon.

21

Gerald Banks sat behind his desk on the eighteenth floor and tried to keep his mind occupied with the tasks at hand. A tall stack of folders was piled high to his left, and it didn't seem to be shrinking. His severe lack of concentration was a definite factor in why very little work was getting done. Every few seconds he would spin in his chair to look down below at the One Eleven Club. At this time of day, the building was nondescript: no blinking lights, no bumper to bumper valet parking line, no procession of customers pressed up against the wall, waiting for their turns to get in.

The events of two nights ago were still haunting him like a bad dream. What he had uncovered was far worse than his brother-in-law's offshore accounts or bribery money having to be laundered. This wasn't while-collar minimum security with tennis courts and hot tubs, this was federal penitentiary stuff. The getting banged up the butt by your cellmate kind of stuff. Was it any wonder the same spreadsheet had sat on his desk for nearly three hours?

The keyboard sat quietly before him, the monitor having gone back to the sleep screen hours ago. He stared at the columns of numbers on the paper before him, but they were suddenly nonsensical, just meaningless numbers to a person who...

"Am I interrupting?"

Banks was shaken out of his reflection by a familiar but still unexpected voice. "Peter, what are you doing here?" He said, rising to his feet and holding out his hand.

Peter Mason walked into the office, accepted his brother-in-law's handshake, and stood in front of the desk.

"Please, take a seat," Banks offered.

Mason sat down and crossed his legs, running his fingers along the seam of his pants to make sure it stayed as it should.

"What brings you to Siberia?"

Mason chuckled to himself. "Is that what you call this place, Siberia?"

Banks leaned back in his chair. "You know what I mean."

Mason didn't react either way. "So how's my sister doing?"

"Pretty good, yes, I'd say pretty darned good."

Mason examined his fingernails. "Is that a euphemism for staggering blind drunk?"

Banks shook his head. "Not really. I think she's trying her best to adjust to this new situation here. This isn't quite the lifestyle she aspires to, but once she gets her head on straight, she'll start to come around."

Mason frowned. "It's been almost two years, how much time does it take to straighten one's head? She's always been a bit of a diva, but now I'm afraid her situation could really escalate. Do you think she needs professional help? An intervention, maybe some time in a rehab center?"

Banks squirmed uncomfortably. This was the worst ice-breaking conversation ever. He's been here less than five minutes, and there's already talk of committing his sister? Who talks like that? Mason sat there like he was discussing the weather, as ruthless and devoid of feeling as a shark. "Surely you didn't just fly up here to discuss your sister's well-being. I know you have more important things on your agenda."

Mason looked at Banks curiously. "What's more important than my sister?"

There was a long, awkward silence between the two men until Mason burst out laughing. "My sister's well-being, are you crazy? That's hysterical. Sherri can drink herself into oblivion for all I care. She became your problem the day you said 'I do.'"

Banks could literally feel the frigid lack of sympathy coming across his desk. It was as if a cold front had dropped the temperature in the office by thirty degrees.

"I'm here to discuss this weekend's events, along with what Arthur Beckworth's death might mean to the future of my ballpark."

Banks intertwined his fingers on the desk. "The remaining council members put the project up for a public referendum. But you knew that already."

"Yes," Mason lamented. "I've been watching the news. Not a setback I had anticipated. But on the bright side, it gives me more time for negotiation with the interested franchises, and the general contractors and vendors."

Banks leaned forward with interest. "So you've secured financing for the entire project?"

Mason shook his head as if he were scolding a small child. "I know you handle that end of the company, Gerry, but let me worry about the funds for the ballpark. I've made arrangements."

"But that's a huge sum of money. The company is already spread pretty thin with the launch of the hydrofoil line. It's going to take awhile to recoup that investment. I thought you were going to convince the city to help finance the park?"

Mason wiped a smudge off one of his fine Italian shoes. "Things change, Gerry."

"But as your Chief Financial Officer…."

Mason held up a finger for Banks to silence himself. "Gerry, I trust you implicitly when it comes to the day to day managing of the company's assets and capital, but there are just some decisions that are…let's say, to use a military term, above your pay grade. I am in the midst of securing enough financing to build two stadiums if I was so inclined. When that funding arrives, I will trust that you will use all of your financial skills and inventiveness to make sure the sudden influx of money is allocated so as not to be easily traced."

Banks leaned forward and rested his chin on his clenched fists.

"You mean business as usual."

Mason shrugged. "But on a much grander scale this time around. This might take some creative bookkeeping on your part, but that's why you're the man. I just stopped by to give you a personal heads up. We're family after all, and that's something you should never take for granted."

The threat was unspoken, but it hung in the air like noxious cigar smoke. Banks tapped his hands together. "I'll come up with something. I always do. No worries, Pete."

Mason smiled with a toothy grin that probably cost more than a year of Bank's salary. He pointed across the desk with both index fingers shaped into guns. "I don't worry about you Gerry; never have and never will."

Banks picked up a pen and jotted a quick note about what the accounting might entail. He used words that were in a code that only he understood. "So, before you get back to Miami, you said you wanted to discuss Arthur Beckworth and the game this weekend."

Mason looked puzzled. "I thought we already had talked about poor Arthur. While the man's death is a sad and horrifying affair, there is nothing more to say about it. Life goes on and all that. His untimely demise has caused a small glitch in my plans, but we'll work around it. Mason Cruise Lines Ballpark and the hydrofoil line will be an overwhelming success."

Banks thought carefully about his next question, or whether to even ask it at all. He really wanted to hear Mason's perspective. "You realize that you'll probably be questioned in the scope of the investigation into Beckworth's death. You were one of the last people to see him alive. Just for my own curiosity, what happened at dinner when Beckworth vanished?"

Mason grinned. "That's why I have an entire team of lawyers on my payroll, Gerry. So I don't have to answer questions from the police. We have worked out a written statement, and we'll see if that satisfies them. If push comes to shove, I will gladly answer whatever questions they may have for me."

Banks put his hand on his chest. "But you can tell me, we're family."

Mason suddenly felt put out, and made no attempt to hide his annoyance. "Go ahead, Gerry. You can ask me one question, but just one. And it's only because we're family and the fact that I feel true remorse that you have to have sex with my sister."

Another condescending slap in the face, but after years of Peter Mason's derision, Gerald Bank's cheeks had turned to leather. "What *really* happened to Arthur Beckworth?"

Mason stood up and walked over to the window. To the east, he could see the concrete plants that would soon be demolished to make way for his dream. The water in the Saint John's River beyond the dilapidated structures flowed north, one only of two rivers in the world, the other being the Nile. This ballpark would be *his* pyramid, the monument to *his* legacy. Nothing and nobody would stop him. "I'll tell you what I wrote in my statement for the authorities," he said, casually. "Arthur Beckworth excused himself from the middle of a delightful dinner with the rest of the Jacksonville City Commission and their spouses and never returned. I was just as shocked as anyone to hear of his grisly demise. How he ended up where he did is anyone's guess."

Bravo, Banks thought. "So not one guest questioned his suddenly vacant seat? No one asked, 'where'd he go'?"

Mason was still envisioning the crowded stadium sitting majestically on the empty field behind the concrete plants. "Everyone was having too enjoyable an evening, I guess. The steak au poivre was impeccable, and the conversation was, I must admit, quite fascinating all night."

Banks swiveled in his chair to look at Mason at the massive glass wall. "So nobody took a head count when they boarded the jet home? No one asked where the hell Beckworth went? That's the story you're sticking to?"

Mason had his right hand pressed upon the glass, trying to block out the unsightly concrete silos that stood in his way. "It's the truth. I didn't notice he hadn't returned, and as far as the other commissioners, they will tell the events of that evening from their own perspectives. I can only state what I know myself."

Banks had to press the subject further, well aware that any action Mason took unilaterally could have dire effects on the company. "But it's common knowledge that Beckworth was a leading opponent of the stadium project. So you're telling me there was no animosity during the dinner, and nothing happened or was said to make Beckworth suddenly leave his excellent steak au poivre behind?"

Mason turned and glared at his brother-in-law. "I don't think I appreciate your prosecutorial tone, Gerald. Please don't speak to me about this subject again. We have more important issues to discuss. I've come here to finalize plans for this weekend's exhibition game and the maiden launch of the *Hydra* next week, and I don't want this cloud hanging over us. Let my legal eagles deal with any queries the authorities may have. We have too much at stake. This game and the *Hydra*'s first passenger voyage to Bermuda need to run as smooth as a newborn's ass. There are going to be a lot of important dignitaries onboard, and the weather is perfect. Not a storm cloud in the forecast for the entire week."

Gerald Banks apologized if he had offended Mason with his line of questioning and the apology was grudgingly accepted. He turned back to his desk, picked up the phone and called for an immediate staff meeting. He smiled confidently at his brother-in-law. There was no cause for concern; everything would go as planned.

22

Petty Officer Scott Simms sat in the outer office of the City of Jacksonville's Forensics Lab and stared at the clock. The dial read nine-fifteen. That wasn't a problem. The problem was that Simms had been sitting and staring at the same clock for nearly two hours.

"Are you sure that I can't get you something to eat or drink, Mr. Simms?" the not-unattractive secretary asked.

"It's Petty Officer Simms, ma'am," Simms replied. "But thank you anyway."

The secretary smiled cordially. The Petty Officer had arrived half an hour before her shift started and was waiting patiently in the hallway until she unlocked the office. "You're here to see Toby Bilston, correct?" She asked.

"Yes, ma'am. I'm accompanying a body that the Coast Guard has turned over to this department for examination. It's critical that I..."

The office door swung open, and Toby Bilston trudged in. He had just enough time to run home, kiss Harriett and jump in a shower before heading into the office. Working on no sleep was taking its toll on his disposition and patience.

"Good morning, Toby," the secretary chirped.

Toby set his leather briefcase down on her desk and grunted totally unaware of the Petty Officer's presence behind him. "Mail?"

The secretary shook her head. "Not yet, but as soon as it arrives, I'll bring it into you."

Toby tapped his fingers impatiently on the handle of the briefcase. "Lauren King. Is she in yet?"

"I wouldn't know, Toby. Do you want me to call the Detective's

Squad room for you?

"Please. I want her here when we do the Beckworth autopsy. The body did arrive, correct?

The secretary hit a few keys on her computer and checked the screen. "Arrived at four o'clock this morning. Drawer twelve twenty-nine."

Toby nodded tiredly. "Good. I want to throw down a few cups of coffee and then get to work as soon as King arrives. Let me know when you track her down."

Petty Office Simms stood up and cleared his throat. Toby was surprised by the noise and flinched.

"This is Petty Officer Simms," the secretary was almost gun shy to announce. "He's here to see you."

Toby turned slowly and eyed Simms the way someone with no sleep in almost twenty-four hours would eye any annoyance. "You're Admiral Baer's man, correct?"

"Yes, sir. I'm here accompanying Ensign Hale's body. Admiral Baer speaks very highly of you."

Toby grabbed his briefcase and let the heft of it drag down his arm. "I might have forgotten that you were coming. It's been pretty hectic around here. We're in the middle of the investigation of one of our City Commissioners."

Simms nodded. "Yes, sir. I've been listening to the story on the television. I know you're a very busy man, but Ensign Hale's remains might hold the clues to why a United States Coast Guard cutter was destroyed along with the lives of nearly fifty seamen onboard."

"The Truman. What a terrible tragedy. Your Admiral was very vague when it came to the cause of the ship's sinking."

"Yes, sir. May I be perfectly candid with you, sir?"

Toby suddenly felt uncomfortable. "You don't need to keep calling me 'sir,' Petty Officer. Please just call me Toby or Dr. Bilston. Whichever makes you feel more comfortable? I get the whole military etiquette thing, but we're pretty casual here in my lab."

"Okay, Dr. Bilston, is there somewhere we can talk in private?"

Toby looked at his secretary and widened his eyes. "Sure, Petty Officer. We can talk in my office. Is 'Petty Officer' how you prefer to be addressed?"

"Today it is Doctor. Today I am here representing the deceased men and women of the Truman."

Toby held open the door to his office for Simms and glanced back at the secretary. "Coffee…now. Better make it a whole pot."

Simms took a seat in front of Toby's desk and waited while the doctor settled in. "It's been a crazy twenty-four hours, Petty Officer. I'm sorry if I seem a bit distracted. I want you to know that I am fully aware of the importance of your visit and that although I wish some days I were twins or even triplets, I will do my best to help answer any questions Ensign Hale's body proffers."

Simms couldn't help but be impressed by the number of diplomas adorning the office walls. Besides the degrees, there were pictures of the doctor posing with various dignitaries and celebrities, from World Champion Boxer Muhammad Ali to the former Prime Minister of England, Margaret Thatcher.

"You run with a pretty impressive crowd," Simms confessed.

Toby reached into his briefcase and pulled out an egg sandwich on an English muffin his wife had prepared him as he ran out of the house. "Do you mind if I eat in front of you?"

"Of course not," Simms said, "There's a lot of sheepskin on these walls."

Toby swallowed a bite of his sandwich and wondered what was taking his secretary so long with the coffee. "Lesson One, Petty Officer Simms. Never stop learning. You stop learning, and your brain dies a little more each day."

Simms smile. "I'll have to remember that."

Toby wiped a crumb away from the corner of his mouth. "See? Lesson learned."

The secretary walked into the office carrying a carafe of coffee and two mugs with Jacksonville Sheriff's Office logos. "Would you like a cup, Petty Officer Simms?"

Simms declined. "Never acquired a taste for it, ma'am."

Toby looked at his secretary and guffawed. "Ma'am. Wait until I start calling you 'ma'am.'"

She shot her boss a wicked stare and stormed out of the office. Toby poured himself a cup of coffee and savored every sip. "Elixir of the Gods," he sighed. "So what has you all hot and bothered, Petty Officer Simms? What is so crucial to this investigation that made you escort Ensign Hale personally to my facility?"

Simms straightened up in his chair. "May I be candid, Dr. Bilston?"

Toby balled up the aluminum foil wrapper from his sandwich and threw it into the trash basket in the corner. "Swish," he declared, before turning his attention back to his guest. "I already told you Petty Officer. You are among friends here. If you tell me something in confidence, it will stay that way unless I feel it breaches the law, military or civilian. Then the cat's out of the bag."

Simms nodded his understanding. "Of course, Doctor. I wouldn't expect otherwise."

"So then talk to me," Toby said.

The Petty Officer stared across the desk making sure he never lost eye contact or the Doctor's attention. "I don't believe Ensign Hale died from drowning."

Toby leaned back in his seat. "I really haven't read any of the incident reports yet, but wasn't the Ensign found floating in the ocean?"

"He was, but he managed to hang on until he was dragged onboard the *Intrepid*."

"Your ship?"

Simms nodded. "The Ensign was able to utter one word before he succumbed. I heard him say it as plain as day."

"And this single word holds some significance?"

Simms nodded. "I believe so."

Toby reached across his desk for a pen and prepared to write. "And that word?"

"I'd rather not say. It doesn't matter to the outcome of your autopsy, does it?"

Toby carefully placed the pen back on the desktop. "You put me in a very awkward position, Petty Officer. I thought we held a mutual respect for each other, yet you would withhold information that you feel might be significant to this case. I'm not sure I am comfortable with this arrangement."

Simms leaned forward and placed both hands on Toby's desk. "Look, Doctor, I understand that I'm cryptic here, and I apologize for my discretion, but I have only the very best of intentions. I need you to examine Ensign Hale and let me know if there might have been some other cause that led to his drowning."

Toby looked confused. "You're implying that someone drowned him?"

There was a knock on the office door, and Lauren King walked in. "You're looking chipper, this morning Toby."

Toby rolled his eyes and proceeded to do a quick introduction of the Petty Officer and Detective.

"Petty Officer Simms was just giving me some background on the Ensign they found floating in the Atlantic from the Cutter Truman."

Lauren took a seat on a couch that had more than once served as a makeshift bed for Toby when he had to work through the night. "I heard about it. Terrible, just terrible."

Simms looked at the detective and then back at Toby.

Toby smiled. "Anything you can say to me, you can say in front of the Detective. We work as a team. She's the brawn, and I'm the brains."

"Well someone has to be the brawn," Lauren chuckled.

It took a few seconds for Simms to grow comfortable with the idea of a second person being informed of his theory. But she was a detective, and if Doctor Bilston trusted her, then Simms figured she must know her stuff. "As I was saying, I think there was an additional cause to Ensign Hale's drowning, and it might be the same phenomenon for everyone onboard the Truman that perished. I would like to explain more, but I believe it would be easier if you examined the body first, and then we talked. If you come out of the autopsy and tell me that Ensign Hale simply died by water filling his lungs, I will gratefully shake your hand and be on my way back to the base. But if you find anything suspicious, I know you'll want to question me more, and I will be more than willing to let you in on my opinion."

Lauren King slapped her hands on her knees and stood up. "Then what are we waiting for? Let's do this."

23

Inside the City of Jacksonville's Forensics Lab was like a world unto itself. For all intents and purposes, it operated like a fully functional hospital. The only difference was, its patients no longer needed the services essential to sustaining life. J.F.L. patients no longer complained about the food, the unhurried nursing staff, or the lack of doctors' visits. Now they all patiently waited their turn, lying in their refrigerated compartments silently—but still filled with questions that needed answers.

The main examination room was stark and cold, with its silver chromed accessories and white-tiled walls and floor. In the center of the room was the main examination table, with three huge, round lights hanging above it to cast daylight on the subject of the investigation. A sterile table nearby held an assortment of surgical utensils, from a Stryker saw used to cut open the top of the skull to dissecting scissors and bone cutters.

Toby Bilston was in full surgical attire as he adjusted the tiny microphone in front of his mouth. Every procedure taken, each observation made, would be recorded for the official record, along with video taken by a camera that hung over the center axis of the table from the light stanchion above. Lauren King was also attired in medical scrubs, but they felt awkward to her, and she hated whenever she had to wear them. They always represented terrible memories.

"Just look at these lungs! Can you see these tiny perforations in the lining here?" Toby asked.

Lauren leaned over Ensign Hale's body and stared at the portion of his lung that had been cross-sectioned for examination. "They're definitely inflamed." She remarked. "What do you think caused this? That wouldn't be caused by salt water, would it?"

Toby reached for a pair of serrated scissors and excised a section of the Ensign's right lung. He held the tissue up to the light and studied it carefully. The detective took a step backward. This was the stuff she would never get used to. It almost made her want to turn into a vegetarian.

"In addition to the obvious seawater damage, the lungs have tiny perforations; we don't know if they were caused by a previously existing condition or another type of trauma. There are traces of a foreign residue on the sample taken, the origin of which has yet to be determined. The section will be tagged and sent to the toxicology lab for further screening," Toby said clearly into his microphone. He began describing the condition of the rest of the corpse for the permanent record. When it came to determining the cause of death, Toby reached up and shut off the microphone. He took a seat on an aluminum stool and crossed his arms over his chest.

Lauren stepped forward and stared into the lifeless chest cavity. Going against every belief she had ever cherished, she reached in and peeled back a layer of muscle which protected the right lung. Scraping her finger under the lung, King noted more pinholes in the tissue. When she pulled her finger out, her blue surgical glove was smudged with fine yellow fine particles which reminded her of pollen. "Is this the residue you were referring to, Toby?"

"Toby stood up and walked over to his computer. "Any thoughts on what it might be?"

Lauren held her fingers a safe distance from her nose and sniffed. "I might."

"Would you care to enlighten me?"

Lauren walked over and nudged Toby away from the keyboard and began typing. The subject line of her search was "Chemical derivatives of Fentanyl, Remifentanil, and Carfentanil."

Toby watched with admiration as her fingers darted across the keys. He was still more of a hunt and peck kind of typist.

Lauren waited while the medical search engine pulled up its results. "I think I may have found our culprit. Check this out..." she began to read aloud. "In 2002, Chechen terrorists took a large number of hostages in a Moscow theatre siege and threatened to blow up the entire theatre if any attempt was made to break the takeover. An incapacitating agent was used to disable the terrorists while the theatre was stormed by Special Forces. However, the incapacitating agent, unknown at that time, caused many of the hostages to die. The terrorists were rendered unconscious, but roughly fifteen percent of the eight hundred people exposed were killed by the gas. The situation was not helped by the fact that the Russian authorities kept the nature of the incapacitating agent secret from doctors trying to treat its victims. At the time, the gas was reported to be an unknown incapacitating agent called 'Kolokol-1.' The Russian Health Minister later stated that the incapacitating agent used was a Fentanyl derivative."

Toby was following along as she read the article. "How in the hell did you come up with this?"

"Date rape."

"Excuse me?"

Lauren sighed. "We see this sometimes in cases of date rape. The drug is introduced surreptitiously to the victim through an alcoholic drink or even in a cigarette or marijuana. It renders them unconscious for more than enough time for the assault to occur."

Toby smiled. "That's why we make such a great team. I'm too busy working with the deceased to realize that everyday life can be just as dreadful."

Lauren pointed at the screen. "Look here. The article goes on to say that when they examined the clothing and lungs of the victims of the Moscow theatre assault, they found remnants of the drug on their clothing and in their lungs. Unfortunately, the Ensign's clothes were probably washed clean while he floated in the ocean."

"So you hypothesize that the Ensign and his entire crew were roofied?"

Lauren shook her head. "Not likely. Even if the drug were introduced in pill form, not everyone on board would have been willing to take it. There had to be another form of a delivery method. I'm willing to bet that if you check the Ensign's uniform, you'll find more of this."

Toby sat back down on his stool. "Gas. You believe the crew was gassed then."

Lauren shrugged. "You don't think it's possible?"

Toby waved his hands. "I didn't say that. I'm just trying to figure out how an incapacitating agent like Fentanyl could have been dispersed in the middle of the Atlantic Ocean. To engulf a two hundred foot Coast Guard Cutter, the gas cloud would have to have been the size of a fog bank."

"When you put it that way, it does seem sort of far-fetched," the detective pouted.

Toby walked back over to the Ensign's body.

"Don't kid yourself, Lauren. These days, conspiracies are as common as red baseball caps. So what do you think the Coast Guard is trying to cover up?" Toby asked, as he removed his gloves and stepped on the pedal of the stainless steel trash receptacle. As the lid opened, he tossed the blood-soaked gloves away. "I'll close up the Ensign later. I want to talk to Petty Officer Simms first. I think you should be in on the conversation."

The detective peeled off her gloves as well. "I don't understand your logic, Toby. We must find out exactly what killed the crew of the Truman."

"No, Lauren," Toby insisted. "We must find out *who* killed this man. Listen to me carefully. I don't want you going all bad cop on the Petty Officer. He told us that the Ensign was barely alive when they found him. He also said that he had probably been bobbing in the water for hours. Did you forget about that piece of metal jutting out of his side? That's what killed him! How long do you think you could have survived with that thing in your thigh?"

The detective turned back to the table and saw the oddly shaped protrusion beneath the sheet covering the Ensign's lower extremities.

"Lauren, this man did not die because of exposure to gas. Hell, I'm surprised he lived as long as he did, considering what he must have gone through with that huge chunk of shrapnel in his leg. There might have been some sort of gas that knocked him and the crew out, but it was the explosion and blood loss from that shrapnel wound that killed him."

Lauren stood quietly and listened to her experienced mentor and friend.

"The most important thing right now," Toby said, "is to find out why the Petty Officer out there is being so secretive about the Ensign's death. He wants us to believe Hale drowned. At the same time, he wants us to disclose anything we uncover. Doesn't that seem a bit odd to you?"

Now they were about to enter the detective's realm of expertise, interrogation. "So, how should we handle this?" she asked.

Toby rubbed the back of his neck. "Well, I think we should go out there and give as little information as we can get away with. Don't mention anything about the gas unless I bring it up first. Let's see if we can find out whatever the Petty Officer doesn't want us to know."

Toby pressed a square silver button on the wall, and the doors to the operating room slid open with a hiss. "You know what I find really amazing about this job sometimes?"

"What?" Lauren asked.

"The fact that you can go for months without an interesting case, and then...wham! Two totally different cases drop into our laps at the same time!"

24

Petty Officer Simms was feeling a tad uncomfortable with his surroundings. The simple cement block walls were painted in an uninviting pale green tone, there was a single spotlight that hung over the plain wooden table, and the sizeable one-way mirror that filled nearly an entire wall made him squirm in his metal chair. The duffle bag he had brought with him from the base sat by his feet. "This is an interrogation room, right?" He asked. "Have I done something wrong? Am I in any sort of trouble?"

Toby was sitting across from him while Lauren had turned her chair around and was resting her arms on the back of the seat.

"Not at all, Petty Officer, not at all. Look, we just want some information that you seem to be stashing away from us, and we in no way think you are involved in any criminal activity. I really didn't want to hold this discussion in my office and get interrupted every other minute by my superiors about another case we're involved with. Rest assured that there are no recorders on in here and there is nobody on the other side of the glass. You are amongst friends here. We just want to talk. Is that okay?"

Simms eyed the both of them, and they seemed sincere. "Sure. Okay, we can talk."

Lauren leaned forward. "Petty Officer, can we skip all of the military and medical propriety and just use our first names? I'm Lauren, by the way, and you know the doctor is Toby."

Simms continued to study their body language to see if they were trying to scam him in some way. They appeared to be genuine, but he decided to remain leery a little longer. "Sure, why not? Call me Scott."

Toby clasped his hands on the desk. "That's great. Scott's a strong name."

Simms grinned. "Not fond of my initials lately, but what can you do? You play the hand you're dealt."

"That's pretty funny," Toby said. "These are crazy times we're living in. I'm sure as a member of the military, I don't have to tell you how much we appreciate your selfless dedication. I admire you for your service."

Simms nodded. "Thank you, that's nice to hear every once in a while."

Lauren sat back and watched a master at work. She knew that while Toby's words were truly heartfelt, he was like a talented baker kneading dough until it was pliable enough to create a delicious loaf of bread.

"So Scott," Toby began. "I'm guessing that within a few hours' time we're going to have the Feds crawling up our ass wanting to know what happened to Ensign Hale. I'm sure they're probably pouring over satellite imagery as we speak looking for clues as to what might have happened to the Truman. This is the top-secret kind of stuff that Lauren and I will never be allowed to see, so we kind of have to work with one arm tied behind our backs, so to speak."

Simms nodded. "I understand."

"So time is of the essence here," Lauren chimed in.

Toby leaned forward. "You told us that if we suspected anything out of the ordinary after Ensign Hale's autopsy, you would be forthcoming with more information."

Simms sat up straight in his chair feeling suddenly energized. "You found something, didn't you?"

Toby's eyes narrowed. "Let's do it this way: why don't you tell us what you think we found?"

Simms reached down into the duffle bag and withdrew the yellow waterproof pouch. He unzipped it quickly and set the gas mask on the table. "Does this connect to whatever you might have found during your examination?"

"Holy shit," Lauren exclaimed. "Where did you get that?"

"We found it floating on the surface just after the Truman exploded for the second time and slipped off the shelf it had been resting on. I lost my Captain and Chief in the explosion, but I'm assuming that one of them found this and sent it to the surface before the ridge collapsed."

Lauren looked at Toby and smiled. "You might as well tell him, Toby. I think he's earned it."

Toby nodded in agreement. "We did find trace elements of a type of gas that could have been used to debilitate the crew of the Truman. It wasn't lethal though."

Simms sat quietly for a moment while he let the news sink in. He had been right. "Okay, let me give you a hypothetical scenario. I know it's going to seem crazy, but there are a few more details I can let you in on that the public doesn't know about the Truman's mission. I don't even know most of the details, but I can tell you what I do know. Let me just throw out my theory and tell me what you think."

Lauren turned her chair around and moved closer to the table.

Simms took a deep breath. "I can tell you that in the days before she set sail, the Truman was being retrofitted."

"To modernize her?" Lauren asked.

Simms shook his head. "I don't think so. A lot of the equipment was high tech stuff and a new system that involved stealth technology. They're outfitting a lot of our ships with it to remain undetectable to drug smugglers for as long as possible. The Truman was the oldest Cutter in our fleet. She was due to be decommissioned after this last mission. Her Captain wasn't in good health and was due to retire as well. I heard that they were kind of throwing the Captain a bone just to send him off with a bang. Why would the Truman need to be outfitted with stealth technology on her last mission?"

Toby frowned. "Poor choice of words."

Simms apologized. "Sorry, but you know what I'm trying to say. But anyway, before the second explosion, my Captain, Captain Fitzgerald, radioed up from the wreck that 'the package was missing.'"

"Package?" Lauren asked.

The Petty Officer nodded. "'Package' was the exact word he used. There was something important, a piece of equipment or something, that was gone. My Captain must have been given specific orders to look for this 'package,' otherwise he never would have done the dive himself. We had divers who are far more qualified in underwater scavenging. Whatever the 'package' was, it was on a need to know basis and no one else aboard the *Intrepid* knew about it."

Toby drummed his fingers on the table. It was an old habit whenever his brain was working in overdrive. "I don't mean to interrupt you Scott, but are you implying that this was a heist?"

Simms reached across the table and held up the mask. "What I'm implying is that someone gassed the crew of the Truman to knock them out while the ship was boarded and this 'package' was removed. So yes, that would imply a theft. I believe that the Truman was scuttled after the 'package' was taken to cover the thief's tracks. I think whoever was responsible for the sinking of the Truman expected the ship to miss the shelf and sink into nearly two thousand feet of water where it would have been almost impossible to investigate. Whoever is responsible for the sinking of the Truman has a callous disregard for human life and needs to be brought to justice for this treasonous act."

"Are you suggesting this was an act of terrorism, Petty Officer?" Lauren asked seriously.

Simms was defiant. "No, Lauren, I don't, and let me tell you why. Before Ensign Hale finally succumbed on the deck of the *Intrepid*, he managed to say one word. Just one. Now, if you could only say one last word, wouldn't you try to name who you thought was responsible for your death?"

"And you think he did?" Toby asked.

"I heard it plain as day along with my Captain, Chief, and a few other essential personnel. Hale said 'Sowell.' At first, most of us thought he meant soul, s-o-u-l, as in pray for my soul, but I actually believe he was saying 'Sowell,' s-o-w-e-l-l—as in Captain Roy Sowell of the Truman. I think the Ensign was trying to name his killer."

The detective felt suddenly out of her element. The closest she ever had to a nautical experience was a rubber ducky in her tub when she was three years old. "So how do you think this gas was dispersed?"

"So you did find evidence of gas?" Simms asked eagerly.

Toby nodded. "We did, but I want to hear more of your thoughts."

"Okay," Simms continued, as he twisted the mask in his hand. "Masks like this aren't Coast Guard issue, which means that someone brought in onboard the Truman."

"And you think it was this Captain Sowell?" Lauren asked.

Simms shrugged. "I don't know. Possibly. All I know for sure is that someone knew ahead of time about the gas attack and was prepared for it. Was it the Captain? I would hate to think so, but any DNA you might have found on this thing was probably erased by sitting in the seawater for so long. For now, let's just move past that. Somehow this gas needed to be dispersed in a huge quantity for it to overcome the entire crew. At first, I considered airborne delivery of the chemical, but how would they have been able to remove the 'package' they were after? To me, it makes more sense for the hijacking to take place by sea, and the fact that the Truman was probably running in stealth mode means that whoever robbed the Truman knew precisely when and where she was going to be. And if they planned on scuttling her, they wanted the ship to go down in the deepest part of the ocean. So the more I think about it, Captain Sowell might have been involved. He would be the only person who could order a course change."

"So you think there was a second ship out there?" Toby asked.

"It would make perfect sense," Simms agreed. "Think about it: if there were a second ship, it would be on Sowell's orders to ignore it when it showed up on the radar. He could have identified it as a freighter or some other harmless vessel unaware of the Truman. Then the second ship disperses the gas somehow, ties up and boards the Truman, steals the 'package,' and slips off into the night—but not before setting off the explosion that kills nearly the entire crew."

"Nearly?" Lauren asked.

Simms became angry. "Well, someone was wearing this mask. I seriously doubt they went down with the ship."

Toby stood up and began pacing. "Wow Scott, you've really done some thinking about this, haven't you? You should consider joining the force after your stint in the service."

"No sir," Simms disagreed. "My father and his father before him were life-long military men, Air Force and Marines. It's in my blood—but I appreciate the job offer."

Toby tapped his foot as he considered his options. "I really need to get my hands on that satellite imagery."

The Petty Officer hated to sound negative. "Never going to happen. If this were a top-secret mission, which I think we can all assume it was, they would never release those pictures to you. I can guarantee it."

"Okay," Toby said deliberately, while still walking around and thinking. "Then we'll have to go at this from another direction. I'm going to see if I can track down large purchases of the toxin used to incapacitate the crew, and I also want to dig into Captain Roy Sowell's background. Maybe I'll turn something up there."

"And what can I do?" Simms asked.

"Petty Officer Simms, you have gone above and beyond your responsibilities in this case. I want you to go back to your base and put your ear to the ground. See if you can find anything else that might substantiate your theory. And please, please don't raise any suspicion. If the Admiral or anyone else finds out you're digging around, you could find yourself in big trouble, and I don't want that to happen. I'm sure by now there's a transfer request sitting on my desk for the Ensign's body, which means we have about a twenty-four hour lead on the Federal Government. They'll discover exactly what we did and start their own investigation, so don't be surprised when you get called in. Just tell them exactly what you told us. No need to lie. We're all on the same side."

"And me?" Lauren asked.

Toby reached out and shook the Petty Officer's hand. "Thank you for all of your help, Scott. You're everything our military strives for. You do honor to your family. I promise we'll be in touch."

Simms stood up and put the mask back in the yellow pouch. "I'm guessing the Feds will want this too."

"If you don't mind, can you leave it with us?" Toby asked, reaching out for the bag. "I want to run a few tests on it. I'll let you know what we find out, and if it fits into your theory. If the Feds question you, just give them answers. Don't ask any questions. Don't even let them think you know more than they do. Be careful."

Simms shook Lauren's hand, thanked her and left the room.

"He's a good man," Toby said.

"And his theory?"

"Occam's Razor, Lauren. The simplest answer is usually the correct one."

"So what do you want me to do?"

Toby sat down on the edge of the table which creaked grudgingly under his weight. "You're not going to like this, but I need you to focus on the Beckworth case. We can't run both these cases simultaneously. We're bound to miss something, and I don't want that happening. I need you to go into the archives and track down if there have been any other murders with the same M.O."

"You mean, with a baseball bat?"

"Specifically white ash baseball bats. I think I'm going to have my hands full dealing with the Feds on the Ensign's death, so I need you to fully invest yourself in the Beckworth case. I don't think the City of Jacksonville administration is going to wait too much longer for answers. I need you to do what you do best and nail this son of a bitch before he strikes again."

"Are you sure?"

Toby stood up and reached for the doorknob. "The forensic work is done on Beckworth. We need to divide our resources. These two cases seem totally unrelated, so we each need to focus on them separately. If you need me, you know where to find me. If I have a question for you, I'll give you a call. And please, for now, let's keep this all under wraps. See how much you can find out by yourself. I think the fewer people involved, the better." He blew her a kiss as he left the room.

Lauren stood alone in the interrogation room and scratched her head. As much as she hated deskwork, she knew it would pay off in the long run. She didn't need anyone's help. She had trained her entire life for just this sort of thing.

As she stepped out into the corridor, she had no inkling of what had just fallen into her lap—and the extraordinary young man she was about to meet.

25

Lauren King sat at her desk with her back to a windowless wall inside the Police Memorial Building on East Bay Street. Less than a block from the flowing Saint John's River, the main base of the Jacksonville Sheriff's Office was vertically challenged compared to the height of the surrounding pre-trial detention buildings, law libraries, and other state and Federal centers.

A half-eaten turkey sandwich on rye sat on the corner of the desk. Compared to many other workstations in the open expanse of the Detective's squad room, hers appeared to be the best organized. There were a few case folders and a very old picture of the parents that had adopted her at an early age. There was also a newer photo of her and Toby's clan standing in front of Cinderella's Castle at Disneyworld; a monitor, phone, and a two-inch cactus plant in a tiny clay pot; and that was it. The cactus, which was the only species of plant that could thrive in the sunless environment, was a present from the Chief of Detectives. She remembered what he told her the significance of the gift was; he'd said that the only difference between the cactus and his office was that the cactus had the pricks on the outside. That always made her chuckle.

King always believed that a person's clutter said a lot about them, even if it was just a façade. From what she could see, most of the other detectives must have lived by some other belief.

She had her elbows on her desk and rested her head on her right hand while her left fingers worked the keyboard. She had been at this for hours now, and if it weren't for the occasional self-induced slap to the face or a brisk walk around the busy squad room, she would have easily nodded off.

She knew the search on AFIS, the National Automated Fingerprint Identification System, would come up empty because Toby had found none at the airstrip or on Arthur Beckworth's body or clothing. So the one thing she did know about the killer was that he or she was meticulous and thorough. The additional fact that Arthur Beckworth was a relatively large man had her leaning toward a male suspect, but if the murder weapon was indeed a baseball bat, it could prove to be a great gender equalizer.

CODIS, the Combined DNA Index System, would be her next stop. This database tracked the DNA of anyone that had been arrested or even swabbed by any contributing police agency anywhere in the world. Over 190 public law enforcement laboratories participated in the system across the United States. Internationally, more than 90 law enforcement laboratories in over 50 countries used the CODIS software for their own database searches.

Matches made among profiles in CODIS could link crime scenes together, possibly identifying serial offenders. Based upon a match, police from multiple jurisdictions could coordinate their respective investigations and share the leads they developed independently.

Since the evidence suggested that Beckworth had been hit from behind and all the damage was done to the back of his skull, the killer may not have even had actual physical contact with the commissioner, who must have had his back to his attacker. There were just so many things that didn't make sense about this case. She kept going back to the established time of death. The last time he was seen, Beckworth was hobnobbing at a dinner party with a shipping mogul in Miami; and then, two hours later, he's clubbed to death in the middle of a swamp.

As the CODIS search continued on her monitor, something else crossed her mind. Something Toby had mentioned...Occam's razor, the idea which proposed that the simplest answer is most often correct. She minimized the ongoing database pursuit on her screen and pulled up the websites for both the Jacksonville Sun and Miami Herald newspapers. Perhaps something in their coverage would give her something to go on. Anything was worth a try.

The coverage in the Miami newspaper was sparse. There were a few mentions of Beckworth's disappearance and a few more about his body being found, but otherwise the focus of most of the articles was on Peter Mason and his new line of ships and his quest to bring another baseball team to Florida. King didn't really follow sports, having devoted most of her free time to reading procedural manuals and brushing up on the latest investigative techniques.

The Detective jotted down Peter Mason's name, being as familiar as everyone else recently was with his sudden influence in the city of Jacksonville. There was a definite link between the two men, but Mason was still entertaining the rest of the city council when Beckworth was being murdered.

Just to touch all of the bases—*pardon the pun*, she thought— she pulled up an online profile of the cruise line owner. She read about his father's dubious past, but there wasn't anything about the "Cocaine Cowboys" of the eighties that stood out to her. You didn't have to be a rocket scientist to connect the dots as to where Peter Mason got the start-up capital for his business. As far as she could tell, the son had probably laundered his father's hidden money through legal ventures and went on to live the American dream. If there were anything hinky there, the Feds would have been all over it by now. Peter Mason's finances weren't her problem.

The Jacksonville Sun's coverage of the Beckworth murder was a different story. There were hundreds of articles written over the past few weeks about Beckworth's contrary viewpoint on Peter Mason's development of a new ballpark on the waterfront. The detective leaned back in her chair and rubbed her chin thoughtfully as she began to read the voluminous text on the commissioner's objections to rezoning for the stadium. As the pages scrolled by, she couldn't help shake the feeling that something was hiding in this excess of information. Something was supposed to jump out and enlighten her with one of those rare "ah-ha" moments. She just couldn't see it yet.

At the bottom of her screen, the minimized icon for the CODIS program began to flash red. She clicked on the icon and began to read the results. Over the last twenty-five years, there were over sixty deaths with the same earmarks as Arthur Beckworth's. When she requested the program to chart the deaths, they dotted the American landscape like a bad case of pubescent acne. New York, Cincinnati, Houston, Los Angeles, Miami, Atlanta, Baltimore, Seattle, San Francisco were just a small sampling. The cities were as indiscriminate as they were disturbing. Much to her dismay, the randomness of the dots on the map revealed no pattern, nothing other than mere happenstance that all the deaths were caused by a wooden weapon. She stared at the screen for what seemed like hours. She was stumped, and she despised that feeling of helplessness.

Okay, she thought. *Let's take it one step further.* She typed in the word "unsolved." All but fourteen of the dots disappeared. Atlanta, Los Angeles, Baltimore, Houston, and a handful of other major cities including Miami remained. All densely populated, she figured. It also listed Jacksonville, which she assumed was Arthur Beckworth, because geographically, even though he was found outside of the city proper, it was still the largest metropolitan area nearby. No small towns, no rural areas except the airfield on the outskirts of her own city. Something was there, something she wasn't seeing.

King jotted down the date of the Miami incident. It was nearly twelve years ago, and the trail had grown cold. She hit the print button and sent the names and dates of the other thirteen unsolved murders to her printer. She would start with Miami.

Sitting upright in her chair, she laced her fingers together and bent them back until all the knuckles cracked. They were limber and ready for active duty. Thirty seconds later, she was linked into the City of Miami Police database. She tapped in all the information

it required to gain access to their files and then typed the date...
November thirtieth, two thousand and five. The curser spun while
she waited. Looking up at the clock she realized it was eight thirty in
the evening already. Her shift had ended at six. No rest or overtime
for the weary.

First, a case number revealed itself, and then a name, but not a
single name—two names: Franklin and Elizabeth Walker. She read
the background information intently. It looked like a burglary gone
wrong. They had been killed in their sleep. She pulled up one of the
crime scene photos but quickly clicked off it. The picture, as she had
imagined it would be, was gruesome and heartbreaking. According
to the report, there were no signs of a struggle in the bedroom, but
the living room was found in disarray. It made no sense to her until
she scrolled down to the last page of the report. There had been
a survivor of the attack! A seven-year-old boy had been found at
the scene. He had also been bludgeoned, but it appeared that the
assailant hadn't waited around to confirm the boy's death. She now
had a possible eyewitness!

Lauren dug through more of Miami P.D.'s database for follow-up
reports. There were no fingerprints found. The pathology reports
looked incredibly familiar. King's Spider-Sense was beginning to
tingle. She leaned back in her chair and closed her eyes trying to
visualize the events of that night. A burglar breaks into a house full
of people? That made no sense. If the killer is thorough enough not
to leave prints, he has to be smart enough to case the house first. She
skipped down to the property report. Nothing had been reported
stolen.

Burglary my ass, she muttered under her breath.

Of the two lead detectives listed on the case, only one was still
alive, but had retired out of state. She was going to need to have a
chat with him. Twelve years ago was a long time, but if he were a cop
worth his salt, he wouldn't forget an unsolved case that had stained
his record.

Lauren jotted down his name and the last known address. He was living in San Diego. There was a three-hour difference, so it was around dinner time in California. She pulled out her cell phone and dialed the number. After five rings, a man's voice answered.

"Is this Jack Harris," she asked "Detective Jack Harris?"

There was a pause on the line. "Holy crap, no one's called me Detective in over five years. Who is this?"

"I hate to bother you detective, but my name is Lauren King, and I'm a detective with the City of Jacksonville. I'm working a homicide that I believe has something in common with an old case of yours."

"First off Detective, call me Jack. And second, I should have you know that I've been diagnosed with the onset of Alzheimer's disease. I think if you had called me in a year from now, I probably would be trying to answer the microwave oven."

King shook her head. "I am so sorry to hear that, Jack. Perhaps I can give you one last shot at clearing your case. I'd really like to try if you're up to it."

Harris spoke to someone in the background. "I'm living with my son's family, and every time I answer the phone, they think I'm ordering a Sham-Wow."

Lauren chuckled. "That's funny, Jack. I remember those commercials."

Harris berated whoever was there with him. "God damn it, when I start to drool then you can take the phone away, but until then back the hell off!"

Lauren interrupted. "Is this a bad time? Do you want me to call back?"

"Hell no," he snapped. "I just wish my kids would read up on the disease or something. I'm coherent, aren't I? I just misplace stuff every once in a while."

"I lose stuff all the time too," Lauren admitted.

"Everyone does! I know they're watching my every move because they care about me, but God damn it, people! Give me some breathing room!"

Lauren wondered what Harris looked like, so as she spoke to him, she pulled up his retirement records. He was a good-looking guy. He had a rough looking face, surrounded by salt and pepper hair. His eyes were dark, almost black in the picture. He looked very no-nonsense, but there was compassion in his countenance. "I would like to talk to you about a twelve-year-old case of yours. Are you up to it?"

"Frank and Elizabeth Walker and their son Matthew...November thirtieth, two thousand five," he answered without missing a beat.

"I guess you are up to it then?"

"Definitely; that case haunts me to this day. Just let me just step outside where I can talk without being scrutinized by the local KGB."

Lauren could hear heavy footsteps followed by a screen door slamming. "That's better. Before you start asking me questions, I want you to understand that while my family and doctor may say I'm losing it, there are certain things I will take with me to the grave that are as clear as day. The Walker case is one of those things. There isn't a day that goes by that I don't wonder how that little boy is doing. Well, I guess he must be all grown up by now."

Lauren agreed. "I guess he would be nineteen or twenty now."

Harris eased himself into a chair on the front porch. The house was located in the Hillcrest area of town, just north of Balboa Park and the San Diego Zoo. It was a lovely location. He liked visiting the animals. "I'm going to tell you something, Detective, that I've never told anyone else. I was on the force for another seven years after the Walker double homicide, and for that entire time, I kept the case folder in the right-hand drawer of my desk. For seven years, I hoped for a lead. I wanted so badly to bring closure to that young boy."

Lauren smiled. "You know what Jack? I believe you. That just seems like someone as dedicated as you would do."

Harris let out a sigh. "So how is it that the Walker case landed in your lap? I thought for sure it would have been locked away with all the other cold cases."

"Actually," Lauren admitted. "Today was the first day I ever heard about your case. It turns out we had a homicide of a very prominent city official here in Jacksonville that might fit the same M.O."

"Are you kidding me?"

"I'm very serious: our victim was bludgeoned to death, and the forensics team believes that the weapon of choice might have been a baseball bat. It could be a coincidence, because I never read anything in your report suggesting the weapon was a bat, but CODIS thought it was close enough to suggest it might be a match."

"Where did you say you were calling from?"

Lauren repeated herself. "Jacksonville, Florida. I'm with the Jacksonville P.D."

"Holy crap," Harris exclaimed. "Before you do anything else, I want you to do me a favor."

"Excuse me?"

"Listen to me carefully, Detective. As soon as you hang up, I want you to go out and buy two lottery tickets, one for you and another for me. Pick whatever numbers you want."

"Why would I do that, Jack?"

Harris began to laugh joyously. "No, don't worry, it isn't the Alzheimer's kicking in. I say this in all clarity. You've got to be the absolute luckiest person on the face of God's green earth!"

"I am?"

Harris couldn't hold in his excitement. His blood hadn't circulated this fast in years. "Did you know that the boy's grandparents were granted custody of the boy? They live in Jacksonville! Can you freaking believe it? How cool is that! You need to find out if this family is still living in your area and see if you can track down the boy and talk to him. You need to find out if he remembers anything from that night."

Lauren began to write notes with her free hand. "Why didn't I read about this anywhere?"

"Why would you? The only reason I was never able to question the boy was that he was very young at the time and I know that he suffered some type of brain damage from the attack. That's not a very credible combination. The next thing I heard, the grandparents had taken him back to Jacksonville to live with them. I'm pretty sure they were the paternal grandparents, so the last name would be Walker as well. You've got to check it out and call me back, Detective. Promise me you will! I've got to know how Matthew is, and if he remembers anything!"

Lauren put down her pen. "I promise to let you know if I find him, Jack. Now, is there anything else that you can tell me that might not have made it into the case file?"

Harris closed his eyes shut and tried to remember. He could visualize every inch of the crime scene, only now it was like he was looking at it through a gauzy shroud. "Let me think…"

Lauren waited patiently and listen to the old man breathe. "Did I mention in my report that Franklin Walker worked for one of the cruise ship lines in Miami? He was like the C.F.O. or some other hot shot in the company. I don't know if that matters. That trail dried up real quick."

Lauren leaned forward in her chair. "Which cruise line, Jack?" She pressed, "Do you remember the name of the cruise line?"

There was another pause on the line as Lauren closed her eyes tightly in anticipation of the answer she prayed was coming. Her right hand was clenched into a fist.

"Mason, I think. Yes, that's the one…Mason Cruise Lines. Does that mean anything?"

Lauren King didn't realize that she was suddenly grinning from ear to ear as her fist pumped the air. Ah-ha.

26

The Coast Guard base known as Sector Jacksonville had been established when the Mayport Naval base was reorganized in 2005. Sector Jacksonville was located on six acres of land adjacent to the Naval Station Mayport, along the St. Johns River.

Turning onto the base, Toby found himself third in line at the guard gate. He checked his watch, even though his dashboard clock told him he had fifteen minutes to spare. Reaching over to the passenger seat, Toby pulled out his police and personal identification from his coat pocket. When he finally reached the guardhouse, he smiled and handed both to the Coast Guard Military Police Officer, who eyed him suspiciously.

"State your business, Doctor Bilston," the M.P. requested as he checked Toby's credentials.

Toby leaned his head out of the perpetually broken window of his 1972 Ford Gran Torino Sport and tried to sound nonchalant. "I have a nine o'clock appointment with Admiral Baer. I should be on the list."

"Yes sir," the guard replied as he swiped Toby's license through a scanner. "Do you know where the Admiral's office is, sir?"

Toby reached out to take his identification back. "I've never been here before. If you could point me in the right direction, I would really appreciate it."

The M.P. stepped out of the guardhouse and pointed to a cluster of buildings to the east. "The Admiral's office is in the main building. It'll be numbered 10426 over the doorway. Park in a visitor's spot, and when you go inside his office is at the far end of the main corridor. You can't miss it."

"Thank you, officer. I appreciate the directions and your service to our country."

The M.P. held up his hand for Toby not to leave quite yet. "Is this a seventy-three?"

"Seventy-two," Toby answered.

The M.P. took a quick stroll around the rust pitted car. "Nice! Are you in the middle of fixing her up? Looks like you've still got a lot of work ahead of you."

Toby let out a mournful sigh. A week didn't go by when someone didn't stop and ask him about his car. "Nope, not fixing her up, I'm the original owner," he said by rote. "I got it when I was in high school. It was a graduation present from my grandparents."

"Are you kidding me? You're the original owner? Why don't you get her fixed up? I bet she'd be worth a ton!"

Toby shook his head. "I like her fine just the way she is. She shows her age just like I do. Fixing her up would be like having plastic surgery on this magnificent specimen of male pulchritude you see before you. She's like a fine wine."

The M.P. leaned in through the window that had been stuck halfway down for the last two weeks. "The inside is still in pretty good shape. How many times have you spun the odometer?"

Toby looked over at the dashboard clock. He wasn't as early anymore. "I have over two hundred thousand miles on her."

"Wow, that's incredible!" The M.P. said, jealously. "This is an awesome ride. I hope the both of you make it another two hundred thousand."

The gate slowly began to open. "Thank you, officer, that's very kind of you to say."

"Well, have a great day, Doctor. And if you take care of your patients the way you take care of your car, they are some lucky folks."

Toby looked up at the M.P. and smiled. "All my patients are dead."

In the rearview mirror, Toby could still see the speechless look on the guard's face. Sometimes he really loved his job.

As he drove along the docks that were built on the Saint John's River, Toby could see that there were only three cutters in port, one being the *Intrepid*. He slowed down as he passed by the ship. It was up in dry dock and repairs were already underway. There were only a handful of recruits working on the exterior, but they appeared hard at work. As he approached the main building, Toby had his choice of parking spaces, of which he chose the closest. Even this early in the morning, the perspiration was beading up on his forehead. The air conditioner in the Gran Torino was aftermarket and very temperamental: it hated working when it was hot out. Just like its owner.

Admiral Theodore Baer's office was sparsely decorated. There was a female Ensign behind the desk in the outer office and she offered Toby a seat. "Can I get you anything, Doctor?"

Toby let himself sink into a faux leather sofa. "No, thank you. I'm fine."

"The Admiral is expecting you. He'll only be a minute."

Toby attempted to cross his legs but then thought better of it. He put the beige case folder down on the sofa next to him. There were a few small photos of various sized naval ships from the past to the present scattered on the walls. A few were in color, but most were in black and white. The Ensign seemed to be wearing a permanent smile, but Toby didn't mind it. She seemed sincere. The phone on her desk buzzed and she answered it.

"The Admiral is ready for you, Doctor. Just go in, no need to knock."

Toby struggled to lift himself out of the sofa. Just when he was getting comfortable; wasn't that always the way?

The Admiral rose to his feet as Toby entered his office. "Holy mackerel Toby, how long has it been, thirty or forty pounds ago?"

Toby winced and held out his hand. "I'm glad you only lost your hair and not your sense of humor, Teddy."

"Touché my friend. So really, how long has it been? How are Harriett and the kids? How is Benjamin doing?"

Toby took a seat in front of Baer's desk. Pictures of the Admiral with various politicians and other noteworthy people adorned his walls, along with a myriad of framed medals and certificates. "The family is good, Teddy. Thanks for asking. The girls are grown up and ignoring every word I say, Harriett is still the commanding officer of the Bilston crew, and Benjamin is still making me proud just to be his father."

The Admiral smiled as he sat down. "That's terrific. Send them my love."

"And how's your family?" Toby asked. "Ronnie and the kids okay?"

Baer nodded. "Everyone is fine. Veronica is running a little boutique in Southside, and Jesse and Tony are both attending Florida State on tennis scholarships. Full ride."

Toby struggled to find a comfortable position in the chair. It was apparently made for someone with a smaller caboose. "Tennis, very cool. I never had the stamina for tennis."

The Admiral shook his head. "We could never get you out of the library, Toby. You were always nose deep in some anatomy or biology textbook. But look at us now! A doctor and an Admiral. Who would have guessed?"

Toby smiled. "Good times."

Baer agreed. "So, enough with the trip down memory lane; what did you find out about Ensign Hale?"

Toby patted the envelope on his lap. "I have the results here Teddy, but the autopsy has raised more questions than it answered."

The Admiral leaned forward attentively. "Such as?"

Toby clasped his hands together. "Look, I know you aren't at liberty to reveal classified information to me, but I am well aware that you lost a ship, and more importantly, an entire crew. Before I tell you my findings, I need to ask you some questions that might clarify what I discovered about the Ensign."

The Admiral turned stern. "You and I go way back Toby, but we're not close enough for me to betray my country."

"I didn't ask you to do that," Toby disagreed.

Baer nodded. "I think that's what you were implying. I will gladly tell you what I can, but I won't reveal anything that's considered classified. Ain't gonna happen."

Toby put his fingers to his lips. "How about this, then: you let me ask you a few questions, and if the answers are off limits, let me know. How's that?"

"And then you'll tell me the results? You know I can just pick up this phone and have a couple of M.P.'s make you hand over the envelope. It is government property."

Toby lifted himself up and slid the envelope under his rear end. "Better make it four of them."

The Admiral smiled. "Ask your questions."

Toby smiled back. "Were there any satellite images of the Truman before she went down?"

Baer shook his head. "Without revealing the Truman's mission, I can tell you that there were no images because satellites are easily hacked."

Toby bit his lower lip. "Okay, that makes sense. Were there any other ships in the vicinity of the Truman when it went down?"

"None that we are aware of. Understand that the Truman's mission was classified and that they were ordered not to communicate to avoid detection. I can tell you that she was retrofitted with stealth technology so she would have been invisible to any ship's radar unless that ship just happened to cross her path. We went to extreme lengths to make sure that the Truman was nowhere near any commercial shipping lanes."

"So the Truman was a ghost ship."

"Pretty much. Where are you going with all of this, Toby?"

Toby cocked his head back and forth. He could feel a tension headache coming on. "Nothing adds up here."

The Admiral reached over and took his phone off the hook. "Let me tell you what I can, Toby, and then you tell me if any of it jives with your findings."

Toby pulled out a pen and a small spiral notepad.

"No notes," Baer warned. "This is between you and me. Not for public consumption. None of what I will tell you is classified, but it's not to be made public either. Don't forget, we have our own internal investigation going on."

Toby slipped the notepad back into his breast pocket. "Okay, I'm listening."

The Admiral leaned back in his chair. "This was to be the Truman's last trip to sea. She was due to be decommissioned after this mission. I can tell you, without revealing any details, that her mission was a success. We know she achieved her objective because there is physical proof. What happened after that is where our information dries up. Something catastrophic happened onboard the Truman, and Ensign Hale was the lone survivor. He died shortly after being rescued by the Cutter *Intrepid*."

"Which was sent to look for survivors and investigate the wreckage?"

The Admiral became tight-lipped. "I won't talk about the *Intrepid*'s assignment."

"But you lost two men on the *Intrepid* as well."

Baer's eyes narrowed. "I think I need to have a long talk with Petty Officer Simms."

Toby leaned forward in earnest. "Simms lost two of his commanding officers. He wants to know why."

"We all want to know why Toby. Now, quid pro quo. Tell me what the autopsy revealed."

"One last question."

The Admiral drew in a frustrated breath. "You are really pushing this friendship, Toby. One more question and then you start giving answers."

Toby put up his hands in surrender. "Fair enough. Tell me what you know about the Truman's Captain."

Baer looked skeptical. "Roy Sowell? Why are you asking about him? He was a fine officer who gave his life in the service of his country as did the rest of his crew."

"I heard he was very sick and that this mission was his sendoff."

You could plainly see the color of the Admiral's complexion turn beet red. "What the hell did Simms tell you?" He fumed, reaching over and slamming the phone receiver back in its cradle. "Sowell was retiring. This was to be his last assignment. He was passed over for promotion numerous times during his career because of his temperament. He was insubordinate at times, but he ran a tight ship. I can't speak to his health due to regulations, but he wasn't happy that he was being put out to pasture. What dedicated officer wouldn't be? It's all in his personnel file. Or did Simms already fill you in on all of this?"

Toby raised his voice which he never did. "Simms only told me what he was a witness to. He knows nothing about the Truman's mission. He was only trying to help me piece together what happened. He lost friends on the Truman, and he wants some closure."

Baer's teeth were clenched. His Ensign had crossed a line. "Enlighten me on what else Simms told you."

"Listen to me Admiral," Toby said, showing his college friend the utmost respect. "Simms is a good man. He only wants the truth. He brought me the only piece of evidence that matches my findings on Ensign Hale. He also told me that whatever was onboard the *Truman* was missing when his commanding officers dove down to the wreck to investigate. He was in the radio room when Captain Fitzpatrick radioed that 'the package' was missing. He also told me that Hale's last word was Sowell."

The Admiral crossed his arms over his expansive chest. "Hale could have meant anything by that. Is that all you've got, Toby? The nonsensical utterances of a dying officer?"

The two men stared at each other like a matador and a bull.

Neither one was flinching. Toby broke the extended silence. "I couldn't care less about 'the package' Teddy. I just want to be able to tell you what really happened to the crew of the *Truman*. Petty Officer Simms brought me a gas mask that they found floating above the wreck. It was inside of a flotation bag. He told me that this gas mask was not one customarily equipped onboard a cutter. One of the divers had to have sent it to the surface before the *Truman* exploded for the second time."

Baer ran his hand across his face in exasperation. "Is there anything Simms didn't tell you?"

Toby shook his head. "That doesn't even make sense. How would I know what he didn't tell me?"

The Admiral pounded his fists on the arms of his chair. "I think I'm having a stroke. You're a doctor, right?"

"And a brilliant one," Toby added. "I studied a lot of anatomy and biology."

Baer closed his eyes and counted silently to ten. "What does a gas mask have to do with the price of tea in China?"

"Relax Teddy," Toby advised, as he lifted himself up and placed the folder on the Admiral's desk. "The autopsy revealed that Ensign Hale was exposed to a form of non-lethal knock out gas before the *Truman* exploded. His lungs revealed evidence of the debilitating drug."

Baer undid the clasp on the envelope and began looking over the report as he spoke. "So you're suggesting that the crew was put to sleep before the *Truman* sunk?"

"Do you want to hear my theory of what might have happened?"

The Admiral looked up briefly from his reading. "I fear I have no choice."

Toby smiled. "You don't."

Baer went back to his reading as Toby continued.

"This wasn't an accident. The *Truman* was scuttled to hide the evidence of a heist," Toby said matter-of-factly.

"Is this just your speculation," the Admiral inquired, "or have you already posted your findings on social media?"

"None of this leaves your office," Toby promised. "I'm just doing my job. I would be remiss if I didn't carry my investigation to its ultimate conclusion."

"And we wouldn't want you to be remiss," Baer mocked.

Toby leaned forward and rested one of his elbows on the Admiral's desk. "This proposal only makes sense if there was a second ship out there. That's why I asked you about the satellite imagery. I believe there had to be another ship. Follow my logic…if this other ship was somehow capable of spreading a cloud of knock out gas, it follows that stealing 'the package' was their primary objective. I don't give a damn about the missing technology. The only thing that matters to me is that the *Truman* and its sleeping crew were then killed to hide the evidence of the robbery. This case isn't about espionage, this is mass murder!"

The Admiral dropped the paperwork onto the surface of his desk. "Okay, I'll play along. There's only one humongous hole in your terrorist plot. The *Truman* was running without lights, deliberately on a moonless night, and in stealth mode to avoid detection. How were they found?"

"I never said anything about terrorists," Toby insisted.

Baer shrugged. "Isn't that what you're implying?"

Toby didn't skip a beat. "Not even close. As we crime fighters like to say, they had someone on the inside. Someone who knew when and where they were going to be. Someone who knew enough to wear…"

"A gas mask!" Baer interrupted.

"So who onboard the *Truman* knew their location?" Toby asked.

The Admiral stared up at the ceiling while he considered the question. "Three or four technicians."

Toby wasn't having any of his friend's duplicity. "And one other person. The one prepared with a gas mask. The one Ensign Hale identified by name. The one holding a grudge against the Coast Guard. Captain Roy Sowell."

The Admiral didn't sound as skeptical anymore. "So you're alleging…"

Toby nodded. "I'm not alleging anything, Admiral. I'm going to prove that the *Truman's* Captain was complicit in stealing technology from the United States Government and he never went down with his ship. I'd be willing to bet the farm that the son-of-a-bitch is out there somewhere—and I've got just the woman to find him!"

27

The Head of Engineering, Kaci Lynch, stood over Gerald Banks' shoulder and ran her pencil along the blueprint of the *Hydra*. They were standing by a drafting table in the corner of Bank's office. Lynch was slender and attractive, but her crew had quickly learned that behind the good looks hid the exacting demeanor of an obsessive taskmaster. "The floor of the catwalk..."

"Oceanwalk." Banks corrected her.

"Right. The floor of the *Oceanwalk* is four inches thick and made from the same cantilevered glass as the Grand Canyon's Skywalk. It can hold one hundred pounds of weight per square foot and withstand one hundred mile per hour winds. It's probably the sturdiest component of the *Hydra*," she admitted. "There's an embedded LED lighting system that illuminates the path at night, but it's not so bright as to obscure the passenger's view of the ocean below. It should be pretty spectacular."

"And frightening, I would guess." Banks added.

Lynch smiled. "Only if you're afraid of heights and speed."

"Some might find it disorienting."

"That could be," the engineer conceded. "It's never been done before."

"That's exactly why Mason wants it," Banks acknowledged. "With every news outlet attending this launch, the *Hydra* needs to impress."

Lynch stood up and tossed her pencil onto the diagram. "I just wish we weren't so rushed. Mr. Mason is really cutting this close. I could use an extra two weeks."

"You have four days." Banks said, brusquely.

The engineer rubbed her lips as she walked around the table. "I'm dealing with a South Korean installation crew from Doosan International that barely understands English. We've been pointing and grunting at each other for over a month now while we're waiting for the last panel to arrive. It should be here tomorrow. That means the port walkway won't be finished until the morning of the launch, so you might want to warn Mr. Mason to keep the foot traffic to a minimum, or at least mostly on the starboard side. We'll test it, of course, but simulations and the real-world unpredictability of the ocean are two very different scenarios."

Banks shook his head. "I'll never convince Mason of that. He is committed to making sure the *Hydra* receives rave reviews. You need both sides properly secured and examined. The Oceanwalks are the crown jewels of this ship, and Mason won't settle for anything less than the full realization of his dream."

Lynch was just about to say something when she heard a slight buzzing coming from across the office. "Is that your phone?" She asked.

Banks patted his pocket. "Not mine, my phone's right…" Then it dawned on him. "I'm sorry, Kaci," he apologized. "That *is* my phone. I've got to take that call. Are we done here?"

Lynch rolled up the blueprint and carried it under her arm to the door. "If there are any problems, I'll let you know."

"Nothing less than perfection is acceptable," Banks said, walking quickly toward his desk. "This launch has to go off without a hitch."

Lynch nodded. "Gotcha, boss."

There was only one drawer in Gerald Banks' desk that he locked with a key. It was the same drawer that contained the vibrating burner phone that had rung just a handful of times before. Banks fumbled with the key as the old flip phone inside continued to rattle. Opening the phone, he greeted the caller.

"I figured I'd be hearing from you sooner rather than later," Banks said.

"I appreciate you keeping the phone charged," said the caller.

Banks looked at the old phone and pondered all of the technology that had been introduced into the communications industry since this model had been manufactured. "It's been in my desk for over ten years. I'm surprised it still works."

"You won't need it much longer," the voice confessed. "It's almost time."

"So this is what you've been waiting for?" Banks asked. "The launching of the *Hydra*?"

"Not just that," the voice insisted. "It's about to reach a boiling point. All of the players are starting to come together."

"Spoken like someone who's been doing their research."

The voice over the phone was solemn. "That's what I do, remember?"

"So, you want to be added to the guest list?" Banks asked.

"That's why I'm calling. Just use the name I gave you last time."

"Okay, I've got that," Banks confirmed, looking at the name he had taped to the back of the phone. "But why now? Why in such a public place?"

"It's got to be now, Gerald. I've been watching from the sidelines for far too long. You've been incredibly generous to stay quiet this long. I know you have your own agenda, but I think our alliance has worked out well for the both of us."

Banks gazed out his window at a formation of small birds headed east over the Saint John's River. "I wouldn't exactly call it an alliance," he disputed. "That implies that we have a common enemy."

"We don't?" The caller questioned.

"Perhaps we do, but our motives couldn't be more different."

The caller sounded in complete control of the conversation. "I know what you want Gerald, and I think I've been more than obliging with the intelligence that I've provided to you. You'll have to admit that my circumstances give me access to information and evidence that you would never have been privy to otherwise."

"I understand that."

"Well then, our goal is the same, even if our intentions are different. You want Mason's empire, while my incentive is far less material than that."

"Okay," Banks said. "So is there anything else besides putting your name on the guest list?"

"Just a word to the wise, Gerald, you've fallen in with some very dangerous people at the One Eleven Club."

"How did you..." Banks started to ask.

"I'm always watching, Gerald." The voice warned. "Just be careful." Then the line went dead.

28

Matt Walker sat in the kitchen and stared across the breakfast table at his grandfather. The early morning sun streamed in through the window as the smell of freshly brewed coffee filled the air. The tiled floor was covered with black scuff marks from his grandfather's work boots. It would be next Thursday before the maid would be here to clean them away.

It had been two days since Barbara Walker passed peacefully in her sleep, but the old man refused to show any outward signs of grief. The funeral had been a simple grave-side affair with just Matthew and himself, but he couldn't shake off the feeling that his son Franklin was also there, mourning the loss. Twelve years had passed since his murder, but the wounds were forever raw.

After the burial, friends of the family had come and gone from the house, bringing trays of food and sharing their memories of his wife. He would listen and nod cordially, but rarely spoke to any of the well-wishers. The light of his life was gone, and he had locked all the doors and drawn all the windows. There was nothing left but darkness and half his soul—the unworthy half.

Dave Walker sat with an aimless glaze in his eyes. He sipped some coffee but didn't taste it. The eggs Matt had scrambled for him sat untouched on the plate next to a piece of stiff wheat toast.

Matt reached across the table and touched his grandfather's hand to comfort him. The old man pulled his hand away as though it had been burned with a hot iron. "Don't you trace me, boy. Don't you dare and do it! I don't want any of that mumbo-jumbo in my house! It might have been okay with your grandmother, but I won't put up with any of that crap."

Matt stood up and scraped his grandfather's uneaten eggs into the sink. He didn't have to hear to know what his grandfather thought of him. The old man thought he was a freak of nature, and the less contact they had, the better they would get along. His grandson was just someone who ate his hard-earned food and couldn't keep him company as his wife had. He had never bothered to learn his grandson's hand talking…that was his wife's choice. He didn't have the time to learn all those wild gestures, nor the inclination to. She coddled the boy ever since she discovered what he was capable of. Never did an honest lick of work in his life, always afraid to touch anything. How was the boy supposed to contribute to the family when he could flip out without a moment's notice? Living with the boy was like having an electric generator hooked up to your stomach. The tension was palpable, and now he had no one to run interference for him. How he missed his soul mate.

Dave Walker was entitled to his feelings, but he never gave Matt the opportunity to help. Matt had traced his grandfather's life many times before and never tired of it. It was usually while the old man was sleeping in his recliner and was unaware of Matt's curiosity.

Touching his grandfather's shoulder was like traveling through time. He could see his father through his grandfather's eyes, as a young boy growing up on the east side of New York. It always brought a lump to his throat to see his father the way his grandfather remembered him. It was far better than the way he had last seen him and his mother.

His grandfather pushed himself away from the table and stood beside Matt at the sink and began drying the dishes as Matt washed them. It was the only thing that they ever did together. In his best speech, Matt asked, "Do you want to come to the game with me and Simone's family tomorrow?" The old man wasn't even courteous enough to turn and face Matt when he spoke. Matt thought he said, "I didn't know they had a deaf and dumb section at the stadium."

But that couldn't be, not even his grandfather was that cruel.

Matt grabbed his grandfather's arm, spun him around and asked him to repeat what he said. He had read it right. "You are a bitter old man," Matt screamed. "What did I ever do to you, except survive? I miss Grandma too, don't ever forget that! You can be ashamed of me all you want, but just remember one thing...I'll always love you, even if you hate me!" He said, as he threw down the sponge and stormed out of the kitchen.

Dave Walker hands began to shake as he leaned against the sink. He tried to stop them from trembling, but it was a growing symptom that soon engulfed his whole body. He refused to let the boy see him cry; he had to be strong. He'd promised his wife on her deathbed that he would be. He was too old to learn how to talk the boy's language. His wife had learned, but he was too busy earning a living back then. Now it seemed he had a more significant disability than his grandson. Life just wasn't the same without her. In the seclusion of his empty kitchen, Dave Walker finally broke down and wept.

Matt was halfway down the hall to his bedroom when he decided that enough was enough. This had to end now if the two of them were going to share the same roof. He turned around and fumed back into the kitchen. "Come on you old fart," he shouted. "You're coming to the baseball game with us whether you want to or not! You don't have a monopoly on anger and regret, and neither of us can get through this alone!"

His grandfather turned to him and wiped his eyes with the dish-towel. "Do you know who you sounded like when you said that?"

The two of them met in the center of the kitchen and embraced for the first time that Matt could remember. "Be ready at noon tomorrow," Matt instructed using both his voice and signing.

"Whoa Matt," his grandfather said. "I hate baseball. Please, I have things that need to be done around the house tomorrow. I'll be fine, really. You go with your friend's family."

Matt could tell his grandfather was looking for any excuse not to go. "You're not coming with us because my friend's deaf too, right?"

"That has nothing to do with it."

"It shouldn't God damn it! Her family can all hear, and you will have plenty of people to talk to. It would be good for you to get out and have a good time."

His grandfather shook his head. "Not this time, Matt. Maybe we can all go out for dinner after the game, okay?"

Matt pulled away. "What, and go to your favorite Italian restaurant, the really dark one? I hate that place! Can't we go somewhere that's well lit so I can actually read your lips? Is it the sound of my voice? Am I losing my tone, or are you embarrassed to be seen with me?"

His grandfather didn't answer; he just looked down at the floor. Matt reached over and lifted the old man's chin until their noses were only inches apart. "One of these days, I am going to walk out that front door and never come back and do you know what will happen to you then? Nothing, that's what, absolutely nothing! You won't feel a bit of difference because you think you're already alone." Matt paused for a second to collect himself and make sure his words would come out clearly before turning and leaving his grandfather standing by himself. "This is all on you, Grandpa. Grandma would be so unhappy right now. This is all on you."

This time there would be no turning back.

29

Even though he was up in his bedroom, Matt could feel the vibration of the front door slam as his grandfather left the house. From his window, he watched the white pickup truck back out of the driveway and head east toward Baymeadows Road.

Matt was becoming used to this. His grandmother was always the mediator, and now, with her gone, his grandfather was unchecked—and worse than that, unhinged. He would be back soon enough, with a case of Budweiser and a carton of smokes. The old man had quit over two years ago at his grandmother's insistence, but now he didn't care anymore.

Matt dialed Simone's number on his laptop and waited for the video to load. As he watched the dotted icon simulate ringing, he wondered what deaf people did before Skype and Facetime. It looked like she wasn't home, so Matt went into his messenger app and typed out the latest episode between him and his grandfather. He knew she would read it on her phone wherever she was and would respond back as soon as she could.

He was finishing the last sentence when the lamp on the desk began to flash on and off. That meant that someone was at the front door. His grandmother had the notification system installed years ago to make the house more user-friendly for someone who couldn't hear. She was a great woman, and he would miss her dearly. Matt looked out the window and saw an unfamiliar late model Mustang convertible parked in the driveway. As he bounded down the stairs, he wished his grandfather was home because communicating with strangers was never easy.

Lauren King stood on the porch and rechecked the address. She wasn't good with directions, but this is where the car's GPS brought her, and the numbers seemed to match. Even though there was no car in the driveway, King pressed the button repeatedly. She was just about to turn away when she heard footsteps inside, and the door began to open.

"Hello," she greeted the young man standing behind the screen door. "My name is Detective Lauren King from the J.P.D.." She pulled out her badge and held it next to her face for identification purposes. "I'm looking for Matthew Walker. Are you Matthew?"

Matt was having a very tough time reading her lips, so he held up his hand for her to stop and stepped out to join her on the porch. "I'm Matt Walker," he said to the best of his ability, "you are a policeman?"

Lauren immediately identified the deaf speech and nodded with understanding. "Can you read my lips?" She asked, inexplicably stretching out each word.

"Not if you speak like that," Matt replied, mimicking her slow pronunciation. "I'm Matt Walker. Am I in some kind of trouble?" He asked.

Lauren didn't know a lick of sign language and now regretted never having taken the course in high school or college. Add one more thing to her "to do" list. "No, no," she said, shaking her head. "I'm just here to ask you some questions if you don't mind. If you are too busy now, I can come back. I understand it's not every day the police show up."

Matt held out his hand and waited for her to hand over her identification and badge. It looked like the real thing, although he wouldn't know the difference if it was a fake. He examined it carefully and looked up at Lauren. "Detective King. Hmmm… that's very cool. Would you like to come in?"

Matt held open the door and let the Detective inside. She was pretty hot for a cop. Lauren walked into the living room and smiled at all the family photos that adorned the walls. The house was very cozy and warm. "Are your grandparents home?" She asked, not realizing that she was a few feet away from the young man and facing away from him. Matt walked up and tapped her on the shoulder. "I can't read your lips if you don't face me. Any chance you know sign language?"

Lauren shook her head. "I'm so sorry. I didn't realize. If you would feel more comfortable with an interpreter, I can make a phone call and have one here fairly quickly."

"No," Matt waggled his finger. "As long as you face me, I can do a pretty good job of reading your lips. It's much easier for me since you're wearing lipstick. It helps accentuate your mouth."

Lauren nodded. "That makes sense. I've learned something new already."

"Would you like something to drink," Matt asked and signed at the same time out of habit. "Iced tea or some water?"

"No, I'm fine," Lauren replied with a wave of her hands. "Are your grandparents home? I know you're over eighteen, but it would probably be better if one of them were here while I spoke with you."

Matt walked over and picked up one of the pictures of his grandmother and grandfather. "My grandmother just passed away a few days ago. My grandfather isn't taking it very well, and he went out for a while. Tell me what you want to know, and let me decide whether he needs to be here or not. If he does, I'll give you his cell phone number."

Lauren pointed to a lovely cushioned couch. His grandmother had exceptional taste in upholstery. "May I sit down?"

"Oh I'm sorry," Matt apologized. "That was so rude of me. Of course, make yourself comfortable. I'll sit over here in this chair so I can face you."

Lauren sat down and pulled out her notepad from her jacket pocket and crossed her legs. "Do you mind if I take notes?"

Matt shrugged and smiled. "I don't care, but you still haven't told me what this is all about. How do you know I'm going to say anything noteworthy?"

Lauren laughed. "Are you sure you don't want to wait for your grandfather to return?"

"It's fine that we talk. He's just been …" Matt didn't finish the sentence, but the remorseful pause that followed transcended any language barrier.

Lauren felt a lump in her throat. "Matt, I would like to talk to you about the night you were assaulted."

Matt sat back in his chair, completely caught by surprise. "You mean the night my parents were murdered."

Lauren nodded. "Is that okay?"

Matt didn't realize that he had begun to rock back and forth in the chair, but the detective noticed.

"Why now? Why after all this time are you asking me about that night? You're the first person from the police, any police, to ask me about that night. Why?"

Lauren leaned forward. She wanted Matt to understand every word she said. "No one has ever questioned you about that night? No one from Miami P.D. has ever spoken to you, not anyone?"

Matt shook his head. "I was seven years old, and they presumed I had brain damage. Then we moved. It was a long time ago, so why are you asking me now?" There was anger brewing in his tone. "Why all of a sudden is a detective from the City of Jacksonville, sitting in my living room trying to dredge up my memories from the worst night of my life?"

Trying to diffuse his resentment, Lauren smiled kindly. "If that iced tea is still available, I think I wouldn't mind a glass."

Matt stood up and walked quickly into the kitchen and returned with a large plastic cup filled with her drink. Lauren took a small sip even though she wasn't thirsty and placed the glass on an end table. "Delicious. Home brewed, I can tell."

Matt looked at her suspiciously. "So glad you like it. Now can we get back to business?"

Lauren wrote one word on her notepad: 'smart.' "Is it okay if I call you Matt?"

"'Matt' is fine with me. Do I need to call you 'detective'?"

She held out her hand. "No, you can call me Lauren if you want."

He never reached out to accept her hand. It was as if he didn't want to touch her on purpose. Instead, he spelled out her name with his fingers and watched as she copied his gestures. Then Matt formed his hand into a 'C" shape and put it over his heart where a badge would be worn. "Cop," he said.

Lauren did the same. "Cop. Very neat, I'm learning a new language. Thank you."

Matt nodded.

"Matt, the reason I am here today, is because I was hoping you might remember something about that night."

Matt shook his head. "I'll ask you again, why now? Why has no one ever come to me until now?"

Lauren pouted. "I can't answer for anyone else. But I'm here now, and I'm asking."

Matt stared into her eyes almost like he was looking right through her and reached out toward her. "Give me your hand."

"Why?"

"Just give me your hand."

Lauren hesitated. "Okay."

The detective felt like she had been electrocuted. Not the Old Smokey electric chair type of voltage, but enough to make the hair on her arms and the back of her neck take notice.

Matt's eyes rolled up into his head, and he began to tremble. The tremors only lasted a few seconds until Lauren yanked her hand back. "What the hell was that?"

"You are very good at your job, but in your eyes, others resent you at work for rising too far too fast. You are very close to a heavy, bearded man and his family, but you don't communicate with any of your own family. You dress in masculine clothes to fit in, but if you had your way, you would wear leggings and a workout top. You love music, but you can't dance, although you spent hours as a teenager in front of a mirror practicing dance steps. You had a dog, but you really wanted a pot-bellied pig. The scar on your stomach is from an emergency appendectomy that you had right before joining the force. You've never shot your gun except at target practice. You don't even like guns."

"STOP!" Lauren screamed. "How do you know all of this?"

Matt leaned forward until he was mere inches from Lauren's face. "Someone should have asked me about that night before now!"

Lauren hadn't noticed that her notepad had fallen to the floor. "I don't understand…"

Matt leaned back in his chair. "Not brain damage, brain enhancement. And if you tell anyone about this, first, they'll think you're crazy, and second, I'll deny it."

"How is this possible?" She stammered.

Matt tapped the side of his head. "The Lord giveth and the Lord taketh away. I just don't know which is which yet."

Lauren put her hand over her mouth which Matt immediately asked her to move. "You're a clairvoyant? A mind reader? There's no such thing. How did you know all of that stuff about me? I've never met you until fifteen minutes ago. What you did is…I'm speechless, I don't understand."

"Yeah, I know. It's pretty freaky. It started a few years ago. I've been to a few doctors, but I won't do it when they ask me to. I don't want to be used as a guinea pig in some government lab. I've read enough Stephen King books to know what happens when they find out what you can do."

"So why did you show me?" Lauren asked.

Matt shrugged. "I don't know. I'm a pretty good judge of people, and I trust you. I think you want to find the man that killed my parents and that means a lot to me. If I can use what I've been given to help find the truth, then I was given this power for a good reason."

"So how exactly does it work?"

"I call it 'tracing,' for lack of a better name. It actually has a scientific name, psychometry. I looked it up."

Lauren picked her notepad off the floor and Matt grabbed it out of her hand and tossed it on the coffee table. "No notes," he warned her.

She pulled out her phone. "Do you mind if I Google the word?"

"Don't bother," Matt said. "I've memorized it. 'The ability or art of divining information about people or events associated with an object solely by touching or being near to it.' In my case, I have to touch it."

Lauren thought for a moment. "So you can see into an object or person's past, but not the future. So you're not like a fortune teller or a medium."

Matt squirmed a bit in his chair. "I don't know what I am. I just know things."

Lauren looked astonished. "That's amazing. If I hadn't seen it with my own eyes...."

"So now you are a member of a very exclusive club, and I expect it to stay that way. Remember, you can't prove what I can do."

"I understand, I'm just in shock still. Do you realize how many unsolved murders you could crack just by touching the murder object?"

"Don't you think I've considered that? Do you know what would happen if people knew what I can do? I would be dead in a week. Don't you watch the news? The world is going crazy!"

"But you could help so many people," Lauren cut in.

Matt began wringing his hands. "There is no way I could ever go public with this. Now, if you want to know what I remember about that night, I'll be glad to tell you, but otherwise please don't ask me for more than that. I don't know if what I'm seeing is the actual past or just a person's personal version of their past. Think about it, there's a huge difference. I've given myself migraines considering the possibilities and the problems. I'm telling you, it's a curse and not a blessing."

Lauren could feel the goosebumps on her skin. "You have a God-given power, Matt. My mind is going a mile a minute just thinking about all the great things you could do with your life. I understand your hesitancy, and I swear I'll never try to change your mind, but I just don't want you to dismiss all of your options yet. You're still young, and your point of view might change as you grow older. I'm not saying wiser, just older. Just don't put up the shutters on all the windows quite yet, okay?"

Matt shrugged. "I don't know what that means, but okay."

Lauren picked up her pad again. "So tell me what you remember about that night."

Matt recounted the events of November 30th, 2005 to the best of his recollection, which happened to be amazingly accurate. It would have been a truly horrifying night for a person of any age, but for a seven-year-old to go through the trauma of those fifteen minutes almost brought Lauren to tears. "So you remember his face?"

'I'll never forget it," Matt said with conviction.

Lauren flipped her notepad closed. "What if I got you a sketch artist, or had you look through mug shots?"

Matt chuckled. "Who, besides you, would trust the memory of a seven-year-old from twelve years ago, who was nearly beaten to death with a baseball bat? Be serious, detective."

Lauren was about to do something she never did. She was going to trust a man on the first date. This was a big step for her. "Matt, the main reason I'm here is that there has been another murder very similar to your parents. Through fragments of forensic evidence left at the crime scene, we believe our victim was also viciously attacked with a baseball bat. We also have a few more facts that might link the two cases. Would you mind if I call someone else over to ask you some questions? It's the heavy, bearded man you mentioned before.

His name is Toby, and he's an expert in forensics. A great guy."

"Like a father to you," Matt added.

Lauren suddenly felt like she had experienced open heart surgery. "Yes, but please don't tell him that."

Matt smiled. "Sure. I think I'd like to meet him."

Lauren pressed Toby's contact key on her phone. "While I give him directions, would you mind putting some more ice into my tea?"

Matt took the glass. "If he's still got the beard, I'm going to have a tough time reading his lips," he said, heading for the kitchen.

Lauren began tapping her foot impatiently. "Come on Toby, hurry up and answer the damned phone!"

The phone picked up on the fifth ring. "Hey there Kiddo, I was going to call you soon. I spoke with Ensign Hale's commanding officer, and I may have a lead for you. How are you doing on the Beckworth case?"

Lauren didn't know why she was whispering, but she was. "Stop talking, Toby. I need you to come to the address that I'm about to text you right away."

"Are you okay?" Toby asked, not trying to hide his concern. "What's the problem?"

Lauren screamed and whispered at the same time. "Just get here fast, Toby."

"Okay, I'm leaving right now."

"Oh, and Toby…"

"What?"

"Bring the gas mask!"

30

Waiting for Toby's arrival, Lauren sipped her tea alone in the living room after Matt excused himself to go upstairs and have a video chat with a friend. From his guarded demeanor and her phenomenal investigative prowess, she surmised he was calling a girl. She could only imagine what that conversation would be about. There was no doubt in her mind that he was talking to someone he trusted. She wondered how many people he had let in on his secret and she asked herself what she would do if she had been granted such an extraordinary gift.

There had to be a downside to having such an ability, she thought, but wouldn't the good she could accomplish far outweigh the bad? She suddenly felt tremendous empathy for Matt, knowing full well this was a complex burden he carried on his young shoulders every day of his life. Would she give up her sense of hearing to gain this exceptional power? Matt was never offered that choice. There was no doubt that life had a cruel sense of equilibrium. Would a cello virtuoso choose not to play music? Would an artist refuse to paint? Not likely, but Matthew Walker hadn't yet realized that he was in much the same situation. He was a one of a kind that needed to mature into and develop the power he had been granted. It would take more than her inspirational pep talk to convince the young man that he held more answers than questions—and that's why she made the decision to involve Toby.

Lauren had never brought up Peter Mason to Matt. The teen was probably too young at the time to even care who his father worked for. She had done her research and learned that Mason had paid for all of Matt's medical care after the assault. One Brownie point for the millionaire, she mused. He was generous to a fault. What a humanitarian.

The sound of a car pulling into the gravel-covered driveway interrupted the detective's train of thought. She was glad that Toby was willing to help her out. He would probably have the teen trusting him within seconds, but she wasn't sure whether someone who had dedicated his life to science would believe or even fathom what he was about to witness. She was about to stand and answer the door when she heard a key turn in the lock. An older man stepped through the entrance and juggling two bags of groceries closed the door behind him. When he turned, he was more than startled to see the detective standing in the middle of his living room.

"Who the hell are you?" He demanded.

Lauren reached into her pocket and pulled out her credentials. "I'm sorry to have startled you, Mr. Walker. I'm detective King from the Jacksonville Police Department."

The old man set the bags of groceries down on the counter that separated the kitchen from the living room. "Startled is too understated." He muttered. "I saw the car in the driveway, but I thought it might belong to a friend of my grandson. I guess I was just optimistic. The kid doesn't have any friends."

It felt like the temperature had dropped thirty degrees inside the house since the old man had shuffled in. The hostility in the air was palpable. "I've been having a lovely conversation with your grandson, Matt."

"A conversation?" He asked over his shoulder, as he opened up the refrigerator and began stocking the groceries. "You speak his language?"

"Your grandson is quite adept at reading lips. We've had no problems communicating."

"What do you want with him? He do something wrong?"

Lauren shook her head. "No, not at all. The Jacksonville P.D.

is working on a recent case, and in the process, we noticed a few similarities between our current case and your son's death in Miami back in two thousand and five."

The old man noticeably stiffened up with a jar of pickles in his hand. "The boy doesn't know nothing about that night. He won't be able to help you. I'm sorry you wasted your time coming out here."

The detective took a few steps towards the kitchen. "On the contrary, Mr. Walker. Your grandson seems to remember quite a lot from that night."

David Walker slowly turned with the pickle jar still in his hand and closed the refrigerator with his elbow. He walked over to the counter and placed the jar down and feigned a smile. "I'm really sorry, detective, but whatever Matthew has told you isn't worth a hill of beans. The boy's skull was crushed, and he suffered irreparable brain damage. I wouldn't put much credibility in anything he says. The boy is prone to flights of fancy. Ever since his grandmother passed away, he's been acting out and craving attention. That's why I thought he had done something wrong. Now if you don't mind, I would kindly ask you to leave us alone."

The lights throughout the house began blinking.

"Sure, let's throw a party!" The old man grunted in exasperation.

"I'm really sorry for this intrusion, Mr. Walker, but I've also asked one of my colleagues to join us. He should be here any minute now."

"I don't think that my grandson is going to be of any use to you. You can see what's happened to him. He was an energetic, joyful child, with a wonderful life ahead of him. Now he's stuck in a world of silence. He has no future."

Lauren looked at the old man incredulously. "You don't actually believe that, do you?"

Walker looked at her sternly. "I can't even hold a normal conversation with my grandson, detective, and I'm too old to learn a new language now. While I was out trying to keep bread on our table, my wife took care raising the boy. Now that she's gone, the boy and

I have nothing much in common."

Lauren put her hand on her heart. "Mr. Walker, forgive me for being so direct," she apologized, "but Matt seems to be an exceptional young man. I'm willing to bet he can accomplish anything he sets his mind to. If anything, his hearing loss might motivate him even more. You need to give him a chance. He might just surprise you."

The elder Walker's hands clenched in and out of fists. "You just met my grandson, detective. You don't know the first thing about him. Excuse *me* for being so direct, but you need to leave us the hell alone."

Lauren shook her head. "This is technically a police investigation, and your grandson is of consenting age, but if you would rather we speak with him off of your premises that can be arranged."

Matt Walker came bounding down the stairs as the lights in the living room continued to blink. He waved his grandfather away and went to answer the front door. The blinking lights signaled that someone was pressing the doorbell.

Matthew opened the door and greeted Toby with a firm handshake. "I'm Matt," he said, in the distorted English that made his grandfather look down at the floor in shame.

The teen took a step back in surprise as Toby began to sign to him. "My name is Toby Bilston," he signed, spelling out his name one letter at a time.

"You know sign language?" Matt signed excitedly.

"I'm no expert," Toby replied back, "but my son wanted to learn how to sign, so we took a few classes together at Flagler College. It was a good father and son bonding moment."

Matt reached out and patted Toby on the shoulder. "Please come in."

It was pleasantly cool in the house, but as usual, Toby was sweating through his shirt. The handle of the leather satchel he carried was stained dark from the moisture of his palm. The doctor was a walking poster boy for climate change. He pulled out his handkerchief before walking over and shaking David Walker's hand. "Hello…Toby Bilston, head of the JPD forensics department."

The old man grudgingly accepted Toby's greeting. "Expecting anyone else?" He asked sarcastically.

Toby wiped his beard and scalp. "I don't think so. Are we detective?"

Lauren shook her head. "Just the four of us."

David Walker waved to get his grandson's attention. "You okay with all of this?"

Matt nodded affirmatively.

The old man stood face to face with his grandson and spoke patronizingly slow. "You want me to stay? I think I should stay."

Matt shook his head. "I'll be fine. You've had a long day. Go upstairs and rest and I will take care of dinner."

The elder Walker nodded as he headed for the stairs forgetting the lone pickle jar still sitting on the counter. He paused and looked directly back at his grandson. "If you need me, you know where I'll be."

Matt nodded. "No worries grandpa. I'll be fine."

The old man climbed the stairs and two out of the three people that remained downstairs, heard a door slam shut. One was acutely aware of the vibration.

"He's always been a tough guy, but ever since my grandma passed away unexpectedly, he hasn't been the same. I think he's given up." Matthew signed, and Toby interpreted as best as he could for Lauren.

"How long were they married?" Lauren asked.

Matt made a d-shape with his right hand next to his temple then moved it in a circle and changed it into a y-shape and pushed it away from his face.

"Forever and ever," Toby translated for Lauren.

Toby took a seat on the couch, placed his bag by his feet and patted the seat for Lauren to join him. Matthew sat across from them.

The first thing Toby noticed was that the soft table that separated them had a sheet of thin glass covering it. Between the glass and the wood was filled with old family photos. Toby studied the pictures like a time capsule. There were black and white pictures of family that easily dated back fifty years or more. This was a treasure trove of Walker history, and Toby studied each picture meticulously to glean as much as he could about this family's background. Toby tapped on one image in particular, a family photo taken by a swimming pool. He recognized the beach behind the family. Miami Beach. "Is this you?" Toby signed, tapping on a grinning four-year-old peeking out from behind a young woman's leg.

"That's me," Matthew spoke.

"Your mother?"

Matthew leaned over and began to identify the people in the picture. "My father, mother, grandma, grandpa and some friends of my parents."

Toby brushed his finger across the photo. "So this is your family, and these are the family friends?"

"Yes. Mr. and Mrs. Jannick and their daughter, Hope. Mr. Jannick worked with my father, and our families were very close. I still chat with Hope from time to time."

Toby looked up. "Mr. Jannick worked with your father at Mason Cruise Lines?"

Matt nodded. "He still works for Mr. Mason. I think he's still got a pretty important position, but I don't know for sure. I haven't seen them since I moved to Jacksonville."

Toby moved his finger to another photo, and Lauren leaned in close. "This is your parent's wedding photograph?"

Matthew sat back in his chair and stared into the kitchen. He remained silent. When he turned back to the policemen, Lauren was looking right at him. "They made a beautiful couple."

Matt frowned. "This table was something that my grandma used to keep her memories alive. Personally, I think setting a can of Pepsi down on my parent's wedding photo seems pretty rude. I never said it to her though. It worked for her, so that's all that mattered."

Toby signed to Matt. "So what do you remember about your mother and father?"

"This isn't going to turn into a shrink session, is it?" Matt signed furiously. "I don't want my head examined. You may not like what you find."

Toby shook his head, as Lauren placed her hand on his knee and squeezed gently. "I'm not that kind of doctor, Matt. I was just asking to learn more about you. Detective King said you might be able to help us with a case we're working on, and I just wanted to learn more about your background. I am sorry if I trespassed. That was not my intention."

Matt reached out his hand to Toby which the Doctor assumed was a gesture of forgiveness. He couldn't have been more wrong. Before Lauren could reach out and prevent the contact, Toby could feel the energy pulse up his arm and fill his entire being. Matt locked eyes with the Doctor and noticeably stiffened in his chair. The warmth flowed through his hand and into Toby Bilston, returning with a flood of images from Toby's past. Matt's breathing nearly stopped while Toby appeared to be panting and straining to catch his breath. Lauren tried to break the bond, but she didn't have the strength. It felt like the two hands had mutated into a single limb.

Less than a minute had passed when Matt finally released his grip.

"What the hell was that?" Toby said, falling limply backward on the couch and massaging his hand. "What did you just do to me?"

Matt sat back in his chair and looked at Lauren. "He is a good man, a family man. He loves his wife and children."

Lauren nodded slowly. "I said, you can trust him."

Toby leaned forward. "Hello? I'm sitting right here! Pretty large guy. Hard to miss."

Matt's focus slowly swiveled toward Toby. He looked almost robotic the way his head methodically pivoted. "Your son is the center of your life. That's good. He cherishes the time you spend together."

"How do you know my son?" Toby signed.

"I don't know him," Matt paused. "I know you."

Toby looked at Lauren who smiled slightly. "Would one of you please tell me what the hell is going on here?"

Matt spoke quickly in the purest voice he could muster. "You were born and raised in Florida. Bullied as a child because of your size. You had a fight in a playground and came home bruised and covered in dirt. You wouldn't let your mother go to the school to complain. Your father taught you how to defend yourself. You've never used the skills he taught you. You decided your brain was more powerful than your fists. You grew a hard shell, a sharp sense of humor to protect you from the humiliation. You laughed it off. It kept you focused on what matters the most to you. Perseverance. The ability to keep going until you find what you are looking for. People must earn your trust; it is not something you give away freely. Your parents live together in an assisted living facility. You visit them often. You still go to them for advice. There is a male nurse there that you trust very much. You slip him cash on the side to look after them."

Toby stood up forcefully. "Enough! I don't know what Detective King has told you about me, but this stops now!"

Lauren reached up and pulled on Toby's arm for him to sit back down. "I haven't told him a thing about you, Toby. I swear to God."

Toby's bottom lip was noticeably quivering. "There is no way in hell that you know all that just from grabbing my hand. That's impossible. Is this a prank, Lauren?"

The detective shook her head.

Matt finger-spelled the word "psychometry." "Do you know what this is?"

Toby sat silently for a long moment, letting the absurdity of what had just transpired sink in. Outside of snake-oil salesmen and a world filled with con-artists bilking millions of believers by pretending to read Tarot cards and coffee grinds, the reality of someone who actually possessed some sort of supernatural ability was beyond the realm of his scientific belief.

Lauren broke the silence. "He's the real deal, Toby. Matt did the same thing to me. He knows everything about my past just by touching me. I know it's crazy, but the blow to his head as a child might have flipped some switch in his brain that gives him this extraordinary skill."

Toby rubbed his hands through his salt and peppered beard. He tried to shake off the feeling that the walls of the room were closing in on him. "Do you realize that what you're suggesting goes against every scientific principle that I was ever taught and practiced?"

Lauren took Toby's hand. "If you don't trust Matt then trust me. Do you see any neon signs on the front of the house advertising for psychic readings? He's not in this for the money. Only a handful of people know he has this ability."

Toby looked at Lauren and then signed to Matthew. "Then why us?"

Matt answered without a moment's hesitation. "You're going to find the man that killed my parents."

Toby's eyes narrowed. "And you know this?" He signed.

"I believe it." Matt signed back.

31

Gerald Banks tapped his foot impatiently, waiting for the elevator to carry him up to the twentieth floor. He jabbed at the already-lit button as though that would make the lift ascend faster. Banks checked his wristwatch and noted that even though the offices weren't closed yet, Peter Mason might have left already. He had dialed his brother-in-law's extension and his cell phone, but both attempts had gone directly to voicemail. This news had immediate ramifications, and there was no way he'd leave it on an answering system.

Banks stepped out of the elevator before the doors had opened entirely. It was a minute walk to the corner office, but he made it in a quarter of that time. The lights were still on in the outer reception area, but the secretary's desk was vacant. Without bothering to knock, Banks burst through the doors to find Mason leaned back in his chair with his eyes closed. "Peter, we need to talk." Banks urged.

Mason's eyes slowly opened as he brought himself forward. It was apparent that he was not happy with the sudden intrusion. A loud thump came from beneath the desk as his secretary emerged with her long brown hair in a tangled mess. As she rose to her feet, she adjusted her clothing and grinned bashfully at Banks, who just shook his head. "For God's sake, Peter. In your office?"

Mason reached under the desk and zipped up his trousers. "Take the rest of the day, Bunny. We'll finish this discussion tomorrow."

The secretary maneuvered around Banks, who was unaware that he was blocking the exit. "Thank you, Mr. Mason. Have a good rest of your day."

The look on Bank's face was worth a million dollars. "Bunny?"

Mason shrugged from behind his desk. "What do you want from me? She takes great dictation."

Bank's head slumped. "You act like a sixteen-year-old, do you know that?"

Mason looked quizzical. "I'm not quite sure of what reaction you're looking for Gerald, offended or flattered? For the sake of your job, let's go with flattered. So then I guess I should say thank you, and you're much too kind."

"I'm here because you've got a serious problem, Peter."

Mason nodded. "I know, right? I was so close! But you didn't need to show up, I could have handled it on my own."

Banks shook his head. "Okay, that's disgusting on so many levels, but I'm talking about something just a bit more important."

Mason leaned forward. "I'd bet you a month's salary that what I was doing was more important to me."

Bank's walked around one of the two leather-bound desk chairs and took a seat. "I think I'll take that bet…Hitchcock is dead."

In the second it took to inhale a single breath, Mason's demeanor and facial color changed. He blanched. "What do you mean, Hitchcock's dead? I just spoke with him on the phone like three hours ago."

"Well, you might have been one of the last people to talk to him then, because right now he's lying on a slab in the city morgue."

Mason gritted his teeth. "Don't mess with me, Gerald. If this is your idea of a practical joke, I'm not laughing."

The sunlight filtering in from the late afternoon sky suddenly turned the room oppressive as a blockade of clouds floated across the city. The atmosphere in the office was just as cheerless.

"It was a hit and run."

Mason was stupefied. "Hit and run? How does that happen? Why would hit someone and then just keep driving?"

Banks gazed out at the city; suddenly, it looked colder and more indifferent than ever. "Hitchcock was getting his mail when a car either swerved or lost control and hit him. His wife heard the scream, but by the time she reached him on the front lawn, the car was gone. He died in her arms."

Mason rested his head in his hand. "Oh my God! This is a freaking mess now."

"I know."

"Make sure his family is taken care of. Whatever they need."

Banks nodded in agreement. "Of course. No question."

Mason looked like a man who was literally lost. He stared around the office blindly as though it was his first time being there. Slowly, his eyes fixed on a picture mounted on the far wall. He had taken the photo himself and had it duplicated for nearly every office. He remembered the day he had snapped it, flying above the *Hydra* in the company helicopter, looking down on the graceful ship as Ken Hitchcock maneuvered her on a trial run from the Port of Miami to Andros Island in the Bahamas. Hitchcock had made the round trip in record time that day, and confirmed that his dream of Hydrofoil travel in a ship this large was not only feasible but, more importantly, profitable. No one knew the *Hydra* the way Ken Hitchcock did.

"So I've got less than a week to find someone to helm the *Hydra* for the maiden voyage," Mason lamented. "That's impossible."

Banks crossed his legs and ran his finger along the seam of his trousers. "I've been giving it some thought since I heard the news."

Mason leaned forward his teeth were clenched as he spoke. "I am not piloting the *Hydra*. Get that idea out of your head. There are going to be dignitaries onboard from all over the world who represent future ports necessary for our expansion. I can't be on the bridge and schmoozing clients at the same time. We're screwed."

"I wasn't even considering you on the bridge."

Mason rubbed his forehead. Headaches were uncommon to him, but his head was really starting to pound. "Not one of our Class C captains can pilot the *Hydra*. She is five times the size and three times the speed of our shuttles. It's comparing apples to oranges."

Banks waited patiently as his brother-in-law struggled with his alternatives. He would speak up when the time was right.

Mason reached over to his computer keyboard and tapped a few keys. Within a few seconds, a list of his qualified crew members appeared in alphabetical order. He clicked a few more keys and their years of experience were also displayed. Who among them had the expertise to for him to entrust the *Hydra* to? He scrolled slowly down the list until he reached the H's. Ken Hitchcock had not only been with the line since its beginning, but he was also always more than just an employee. He was loyal, incredibly intelligent, and had shown his composure under pressure on more than one occasion during the *Hydra's* trial runs. Anything Mason or the sea could throw at him was handled with an unruffled poise that was scarce nowadays. He drew in a heavy sigh. "We might be able to pull Bill Norvath off of the Siren of the Sea and train him in the basics."

Banks shrugged. "It's a huge difference between a one hundred thirty mile Nassau-to-Freeport ferry trip and a thousand mile Jacksonville-to-Bermuda run with the fanbines at full throttle."

Mason looked up from the monitor. "Gerald, if you can't say something constructive, would you at least ditch the negativity for a few minutes? This trip cannot be rescheduled. It needs to be fast, and it needs to be safe. The ramifications of a postponement—or even worse, a cancellation—would spread far beyond just the cruise line. It could taint our reputation with the city and quite possibly our negotiations on the ballpark project. Ken Hitchcock's loss is not only a personal tragedy, but everything that we have riding on this trip has become a real hot mess." He grumbled. "How did we let this happen? Why were we so short-sighted? We needed to plan for every contingency, and we blew it."

Gerald Banks frowned, but inside he felt entirely different. Somewhere deep inside his soul, he was taking a morbid satisfaction in Peter Mason's suffering. Suddenly, Banks was aware of a chink in the great man's armor, and he had to nibble on his tongue to keep from smirking. "I might have a solution if you want to hear me out," he announced.

Mason had gone back to staring at his list of possible candidates for the sudden vacancy. "You think there's someone on this list that's qualified to Captain the *Hydra*? Do you know something that I don't?"

"Not something…someone."

Mason looked up. "I'm listening."

Banks said the name slowly, savoring both of its syllables. "Roy Sowell."

Mason's head tipped from side to side as he considered the revelation. Sowell was experienced. He was used to commanding a more powerful ship. He was ailing, but this wasn't a permanent position. Maybe his brother-in-law wasn't such a waste of space after all. "Hmm," he contemplated aloud as he rubbed his chin. "The world thinks he's dead."

Banks smiled. "We've already set him up with a new identity. We can fly him back here, get him a haircut, forge some credentials and a badge. Not a problem. I think we just need to make sure he stays on the bridge so that no one sees him."

Mason pursed his lips. "Some of the guests will want a tour of the bridge."

Banks never hesitated. "Tell them no one is allowed until it meets final OSHA and TSA regulation compliance."

"Do you think Sowell would agree to it?"

Banks nodded. "I do. For two reasons. First: money. We'll pay him whatever he asks, although I don't think money means that much to him anymore."

"And second?"

"I think he wants to see this through. He committed treason because of the way the military treated him. Helping to steal the laser was his way of evening the score. We gave him a new identity and covered all his tracks. For all intents and purposes, Captain Roy Sowell is lying on the bottom of the Atlantic with the rest of his crew."

Mason frowned. "You should have seen him when his ship went down; he went berserk."

"You did what you needed to." Mason drew in a deep breath. "What did he expect we would do, leave his crew to identify us? You know I was this close to killing him on the bridge that night." He said, separating his fingers a bit.

"But you didn't."

"I figured his cancer would kill him soon enough; plus, I got the impression that he might have taken out an insurance policy."

"You think so?"

Mason nodded. "I think Captain Sowell is a very resourceful man. The first thing I noticed was that he never unholstered his sidearm when he stepped onto the bridge of the *Hydra* that night like I might have. I got the feeling he had secreted away some piece of incriminating evidence for just that possibility."

"It almost sounds like you admire him."

"I do admire him. Sowell's a smart cookie. He was always a step ahead of me, and that's not easy."

Gerald Banks stood up. "So you want me to track him down?"

Mason nodded. "Absolutely. The future of Mason Cruise Lines might depend on it. Offer him whatever he wants. Do whatever it takes."

"And we'll be able to get him up to speed on time?"

Mason swiveled in his chair and stared out the panoramic window at downtown Jacksonville. The sky was still overcast, but now it didn't seem so forbidding. "I'll train him myself."

Banks turned to leave. "I'll make sure he's here tomorrow, incognito."

"Gerald," Mason called out. "You did well."

Banks basked in the rare victory as he exited the office.

32

Toby looked up at the ceiling as the light rain began to ping off the house's concrete roof tiles.

"What's wrong?" Matt signed.

Toby wiggled his fingers downward. "It's starting to rain."

Matt looked toward the front window. "One of the sounds I miss the most," he said aloud. "But this is Florida, you can set your watch by the afternoon rain."

Lauren placed her hand on Toby's wrist. "Did you bring the item I asked you for?"

Toby patted the briefcase lying at his feet. "Reluctantly....I don't usually like to mess with the chain of custody when it comes to possible evidence," he replied, "but since this is government property received from a source that is technically unlinked to our case as of now, I brought it. Now I can understand why you asked for it, but I'd be lying if I didn't say that this idea was ludicrous."

Lauren patted his arm. "Thank you for trusting me. I don't know if Matt can tell us anything, but I figured it was worth a shot."

Matt had been sitting across the coffee table from them trying to read their lips. The detective was no problem, but the doctor's beard was making the interpreting difficult. He comprehended the chain of custody part, but the rest was lost on him. "Could you please face me when you speak?" he signed to Toby. "I am having trouble reading your lips because of the beard."

Toby circled his fist over his heart. "Sorry."

"What is this evidence you've brought with you?"

Toby looked at Lauren and then across at the teenager. He couldn't believe he was actually considering doing this. It went against every scientific principle he had ever learned. What was next for his resume, an alien autopsy?

Suddenly, Matt began to sign with determination on his face. Toby tried to interpret for Lauren the best he could. "Look, I understand your doubt. You don't know me. For all you know, I could be a mental case. If I were in your position, I probably wouldn't trust me either. Whatever I can tell you, whether you believe me or not, this is not my choice. I can't control this thing anymore," Matt growled gutturally. "It grows stronger every year. I never asked for it, I don't like it, I don't want it. And who knows, I might wake up tomorrow, and it could be gone."

Toby leaned back on the couch and tried to cross his legs but to no avail.

Matt leaned forward and made sure he had complete eye contact with the Doctor. "But why not give me a chance while I still have it?" He pleaded. "If what I can tell you can help track down my parents' killer, then maybe I can start thinking of this thing as a gift instead of a curse. If whatever I trace means nothing, then we can shake hands and move on. Either way, you've got to give me the chance to try. I've kept this thing a secret for so long; there might actually be some cosmic reason to why I have it. If what I tell you is useless, then at least I've had the chance to brush up on my signing skills with some new friends. I don't have that opportunity too often."

The room filled with shadows as the sky continued to darken, and the rain grew stronger. Water poured off the roof obscuring the front window's view of the street outside. This storm was stronger than the passing showers Floridians were accustomed to during this time of year. The living room grew noticeably cooler as well, making Toby feel much more comfortable as his perpetual sweat began to evaporate. He was just about to reach into his briefcase when the lights in the house began to flicker, and the front doorbell started to chime.

"That must be Simone," Matt signed. "I invited her over."

David Walker came halfway down the stairs. "Who's at the door?"

"It's just Simone, grandpa. I asked her to come over," Matt answered, as he walked toward the door. "Everything is fine. Do you want to join us?"

The elder Walker just grumbled under his breath and turned back up the stairs. "None of this can lead to anything good." He complained.

Simone Chase was shaking out her umbrella on the front porch when Matt opened the door. He waved her in and took her raincoat into the kitchen and draped it over the sink to dry.

Toby and Lauren smiled politely at Simone while she waited for Matt to return and introduce her. Matt spelled her name one letter at a time so Toby could translate for Lauren.

"This is my friend Simone. I called her over so she could verify that what I'm telling you is the truth."

The beautiful young woman walked over to the table and shook Toby and Lauren's hands. Lauren thought she looked like an Egyptian princess. Toby smiled at Matt and winked slyly.

"It's a pleasure to meet you," Toby signed. He tried to stand, but the cozy couch had sucked him in. "I apologize for not getting up, but I think I'm too heavy for this sofa."

Simone looked at Matt and smiled. She was thrilled that the Doctor knew sign language. She suddenly felt more at ease. "I hope you don't mind that Matt called me. He told me that you might not understand this thing he can do. To be honest, I'm amazed he told you about it. Matt must really trust you. The few of us who know are like a secret society sworn to secrecy, but if I hadn't witnessed it myself, I never would have believed it. It freaked me out the first time it happened, but I guarantee what he can do is real."

Toby still looked skeptical, but that was nearly always his facial expression.

"Is it alright if I sit?' Simone asked. "I don't want to interfere with your police work."

"No, no," Toby tapped his fingers, "please join us. Detective King doesn't sign, so if you don't mind, I will interpret for her the best I can, but please sign slower."

Simone sat down across from Lauren and shook her head. "Of course. I'm really only here to support Matthew. If there is something that you don't want me to know, please feel free to ask me to leave. I don't want to get in the way of your investigation. I just know that Matt told me he is very excited that someone is finally looking into his parents' case."

Toby translated for Lauren the best he could, but it was obvious he was missing a few words he was unfamiliar with.

Lauren asked Toby to sign for her. "Miss Singh…"

"Simone." She spelled.

Lauren jotted the name on her notepad. "Okay…Simone. I hope we have not misled Matt. We are not primarily here to investigate the death of his parents. We are working on another more recent case that has a few similarities to their murder. Please relay to Matt that we are not here to get his hopes up, but if the two incidents are related somehow, then that would be icing on the cake."

Simone looked at Lauren curiously. The metaphor made no sense to her. She shrugged her shoulders at Toby.

"It would be terrific," he signed.

Simone nodded her understanding.

"So what is this piece of evidence you want me to look at?" Matt asked.

Toby begrudgingly nodded, and let Lauren reach down into his briefcase. Her hand came out holding an opaque yellow and black neoprene bag. The material looked thick, not like an ordinary storage bag you would find on a supermarket shelf.

"It looks official," Matt said.

"It's a Coast Guard issued flotation device, but what's inside is not military grade."

Matt leaned forward with his hand outstretched. "So do you want me to trace the bag, or what's inside?"

Toby looked at Lauren. "Can you do both?"

Matt turned to Simone. "What do you think?"

Her face revealed faith in him. "You'll never know until you try," she signed.

Toby placed the bag on the coffee table where it sat for nearly a minute. Matt just stared at it, as though touching it might burn him. One at a time, he glanced at each of the people sitting around the table. "I'm not used to an audience," he admitted.

"Are you going to be alright?" Toby signed.

Matt nodded. "Let's do this," he said aloud and signed to Simone.

Matt picked up the bag, and the shockwave was instantaneous. The trembling started in his hands and worked its way up his torso until his head began to quiver and his eyes rolled upward. "It's so dark," he stammered to no one in particular. His eyes closed and he was transported into blackness. He was suddenly finding it hard to breathe.

"What is he saying?" Simone demanded from Toby.

Toby signed back. "Dark...hard to breathe."

"Underwater." Matt moaned.

Toby looked over at Lauren. "Holy fuck!" was all he could manage to say.

Matt began clawing at the bag like a blind man trying to get to its contents. "There is light. Floating on the surface now," he announced. "What is inside this?"

Lauren reached over and pried the bag loose from Matt's tenacious grip. She slid open the plastic zipper lock and handed the container back. Matt reached inside, and the convulsing began all over again, this time with even more intensity. He never looked at the gas mask, but he moved it around in his hands, feeling every nuance of the different surfaces. Glass, plastic, metal and leather, each material combining to create a single image in his mind. "This is very old but seldom used. The parts are shipped in from various parts of the country, but I can see it being assembled at a plant in Columbus, Ohio."

Toby gulped audibly since he had been watching Matt like a hawk the entire time, and saw that he had never looked down at the mask. Toby knew from his initial examination that there was a tiny manufacturing stamp on the inside of the right plastic goggle that read, "Mfg. Columbus, Ohio". It was stamped into the dark plastic and was barely noticeable unless you actually looked for it.

"This mask has only been used twice, by two different people," Matt continued. "The first time is very vague to me. It is put on and taken off very quickly. Maybe someone is just trying it on during the manufacturing process...testing the fit. I can't make out a face."

Lauren was writing as fast as she could. This was freaking crazy.

Simone was staring at Toby as he interpreted the best he could, but he was so transfixed on Matt, that there were gaping pauses in his translation.

"Someone else has it now, trying the mask on. Come on, get lucky for once," Matt implored to his imperceptible tour guide. "Yes! He is checking the fit in a small mirror. I can't make out the face through the mask, but the uniform shirt is beige with royal blue epaulets on both shoulders. Four gold bars and a gold shield. A pin on his chest has a silver eagle holding a shield."

"Captain's insignias...royal blue...4 bars and a shield...Coast Guard," Toby whispered to Lauren. "Okay, now my mind has officially been blown."

"I don't know what this means," Matt sounded suddenly confused. "All I can see is white...vapor...like a thick cloud or maybe fog that's swirling all around."

Lauren shook her writing hand to relieve a cramp. She was already on her third page of notes, nearly transcribing Matt's monologue word for word.

Toby couldn't help but ask. "Can you make out a ship in the fog? What type? What size?" But clearly, there would be no response from

Matt. He was somewhere else. A place only he had been invited to.

"The vapor is thinning out, but now there is only darkness. The mask is tumbling slowly, maybe falling, slowly downward. Time passes. Not for long though; hours, maybe days, I can't tell. Someone else touches the mask, but the impression I'm getting is that it's very dark. I sense cold too, but I don't know why. This is something new. I've never experienced the sensation of temperature change before."

Lauren looked up from her notes to see Toby staring across at the teenager wide-eyed and slack-jawed.

"The mask is in the bag, and now... it's out of the bag and warmer too. Someone else is holding it. Not the same person who was wearing it. The officer who wore it was much older. This person doesn't put it on, but the feeling I get is that the hands are definitely younger, stronger, and male."

"Probably Petty Officer Simms," Toby whispered out of the corner of his mouth.

Lauren jotted it down with a question mark.

Matt rocked quietly back and forth in his chair. His breathing was normalizing. He seemed to be calming down. It was another long moment before he spoke. "Doctor Bilston is the last to handle it before I did. I shook his hand. I can tell it's him," Matt smiled.

The teenager took one more deep breath and let his head relax. He reached out and took hold of Simone's hand. "How did I do?" He signed to her.

Not knowing exactly what the police were looking for, she shrugged. "Ask them," she gestured across the table.

Toby strained to lean forward but eventually built up enough momentum to shift his weight. He took the mask from Matt and secured it back in the water-tight pouch. He signed slowly, his hands were visibly trembling. "Detective King will tell you from experience that I am not caught speechless very often, but I've got to say that if I hadn't witnessed this in person, I would have never believed it. Whatever this thing is you have, it is extraordinary. I fully realize why you would want your anonymity, but do you have the slightest understanding of the thousands of cold cases you could help solve? All the closure you could give to inconsolable families? All of the fugitives you could help bring to justice?"

Matt's eyes were narrow and his glare palpable. "Was I wrong to trust you, Dr. Bilston?"

Toby shook his head as Lauren closed her notepad and slipped it back into her coat pocket. "Of course you can trust me, Matthew. Why would I tell anyone? How could I tell anyone?" Toby signed. "Nothing you've told us here can be used in a court of law. As far as the law is concerned, all of this is pure conjecture. It's mumbo-jumbo... a magic trick. Did you expect me to walk you into a courtroom to testify dressed like a swami with a turban and cape? It would have the same effect on a jury. There is no way to prove your visions are the truth."

Matt frowned. "So you don't believe me then?"

Toby reached across the table and patted the teen's knee. "Are you kidding me? Hell yes, I believe you! Whatever this power is you've been granted is a miracle not to be squandered or regarded indifferently. Everything you said only confirms what the detective and I have begun to piece together. Can I use your revelation as actual proof or evidence? Absolutely not. But taken at their face value, I've got to tell you, I don't know about detective King, but I almost peed in my pants."

Simone giggled. "I know the feeling. Spooky, right?"

Toby nodded and signed back to her. "Perfect description...scary."

"So what now?" Matt signed and spoke. "Does this guy wearing the gas mask have something to do with the death of my parents?"

Lauren clicked her pen closed and slipped it into the same pocket as her notepad. She spoke succinctly so that Toby could interpret. "All I can tell you since this is an ongoing investigation is that we seem to have two and now perhaps three cases that parallel each other. The death of your parents is chronologically the oldest and, therefore, the coldest, but their similarities are too obvious to dismiss as mere coincidences. Like Doctor Bilston said, there is nothing you've revealed today that we can use as definitive proof, but it has gone a long way to reassure us that we are on the right track. Personally," she admitted, "I would never hesitate to consult with you again on some of my cases…if you would allow me to."

Simone was grinning as she squeezed Matt's hand gently.

Matt nodded his approval.

"Perhaps the three of us could get together sometime, and you could teach me some signs. It's a beautiful language, and I don't want Doctor Bilston to think he's special."

Matt looked at Simone, and they both nodded. Simone signed, "We would like that."

Lauren and Toby stood up, Lauren about a minute faster than her mentor. "That's great," she said, once Toby had regained his equilibrium and could sign for her. "Perhaps until we meet again we could stay in touch by texting?"

Simone tugged on Matt's sleeve and turned her back to Lauren and Toby. Matt turned so he could read her proposal and shrugged. "Whatever you want. I like them too. Ask her," he signed back.

Simone turned to Lauren and signed slowly so that Toby wouldn't miss a word. "Would you be interested in going with us to the big exhibition baseball game on Saturday? We have an extra ticket since Matt's father doesn't want to go. The seats aren't great, but we would love for you to join us. It would be your first immersion into our world."

Lauren looked at Toby. She spoke between her teeth. "This is Peter Mason's event?"

Toby eyed the detective perceptively and winked.

Lauren turned back to the teens. "You know what? I would love to go to the ballgame with you. If you give me the ticket, I can meet you there. I might miss a few innings, but as soon as my shift ends, I'll be there. I've never been to a professional baseball game."

Simone looked at Toby and signed. "We would love you to join us too, but we only have one ticket to spare."

"That's very nice of you," Toby signed. "I'm not into most sports, but suddenly I find myself very interested in going to this game. I think I can use some of my police connections to acquire a pair of seats for my son Ben and I. He'll need special accommodations for his wheelchair. Maybe we can all meet up for a hot dog between innings…my treat. I'll stay in touch with Detective King."

Simone raised her opened palms into the air, signing "awesome."

Toby took the neoprene bag and slid it back into his briefcase. Outside the rain was starting to subside.

"Say goodbye to your grandfather for us," Lauren said, opening the front door.

Toby looked back at Matt who had his arm around his girlfriend and smiled. "I hope to see you at the ballpark," he signed. "I'm sure it will be a game to remember."

Take me out to the ball game,
Take me out with the crowd;
Buy me some peanuts and Cracker Jack,
I don't care if I never get back.
Let me root, root, root for the home team,
If they don't win, it's a shame.
For it's one, two, three strikes, you're out,
at the old ball game.

-**Norworth and Von Tilzer, 1908**

33

It was ideal weather in which to play a baseball game. The hometown Jacksonville Jumbo Shrimp were facing off against the draftees of Peter Mason's yet unnamed team. Today was to be the day of the big reveal, and the fans were eager with anticipation. A slew of names had been proposed from the logical to the absurd, but in less than an hour, the City of Jacksonville would finally learn the identity of their new franchise.

A front that had stalled over the largest city in Florida had now moved out over the Atlantic, bringing clear skies and pleasant Fall temperatures. The smell of freshly roasted peanuts and hot popcorn filled the air for blocks around The Baseball Grounds of Jacksonville. Vendors filled the streets, hawking their pennants and buttons. A banner, painted in the Jumbo Shrimps' red, white and blue colors, stretched across the front of the ballpark welcoming the fans to a new era in Major League Baseball for the city. Some children carried pennants, showing the minor leagues' team logo, while others carried blank white pennants given away as a promotional stunt for the nameless new franchise.

The ballpark was alive with the sounds, smells, and pageantry of America's greatest pastime. The atmosphere harkened back to a bygone era when any person, regardless of age, was filled with the excitement of a child. Fans had been gathering outside the box office since early in the morning to buy the remaining five hundred tickets that were still available for sale.

The Baseball Grounds of Jacksonville was built with six thousand stadium-style chairs that could accommodate more than eleven thousand fans, the highest capacity in all of Double-A baseball. First opened in two thousand and three with a throwback brick facade, it replaced the nearly sixty-year-old Wolfson Park as part of the Better Jacksonville Plan.

The Baseball Grounds featured twelve modern luxury skyboxes, four skydecks for panoramic viewing, and a state-of-the-art video scoreboard in left field. Some of the park's unique features were a kid's playground, and the "knuckle," a distinctive 9-foot-high mound for casual seating at the left field corner. Whether Peter Mason would demolish the facility as part of his new park's construction was still in question. Ardent fans were hoping it would remain and continue to function as a minor league park for the new expansion team's farm system, but most modern ballparks were being developed as city centers that included nearby shopping and trendy eateries that would make the baseball experience take on more of an all-inclusive community feel.

The parking lots had filled in the three hours before game time, and fans had to pay as much as twenty dollars to park within walking distance of the stadium. The local residents near the ballpark were making money hand over fist allowing cars to park on their property for twenty dollars a pop. The minor league Jacksonville Jumbo Shrimp had never stirred up this much interest. Major League Baseball along with the thriving Jaguars football team would revitalize the neighborhood year-round, and boost the city's status as a tourist destination. Peter Mason was being treated like a knight in shining armor who could do no wrong.

A few short minutes after the box office windows opened, the exhibition game was sold out. People had to resort to splitting up their groups, but gladly did for the opportunity to get inside. It would be another hour before the gates would open, but outside the walls, a variety of local bands took to temporary stages celebrating the event. Local food trucks lined the streets, creating international dishes that filled the air with tempting aromas drawing in hungry fans.

People of all ages gathered at the entrances, listening to the public address system announce the statistics for the players the unnamed team had recruited. When all was in readiness and the gates were finally opened to the public, the fans swarmed the entrances, receiving free programs as each of their tickets were scanned and the contents of any bags and purses were checked for contraband.

Peter Mason looked down at the crowd from high up in his skybox and waved appreciatively to the fans as they filed in. He was succeeding where others had tried and failed. He was bringing the city back together again. Mason knew the way this crowd felt about him. He felt invincible.

Eight blocks from the ballpark, Simone's father was arguing with a homeowner over the price of parking on his front lawn. The man, who spoke very little English (but knew the words *ten dollars* very well) motioned for him to either pull in or move on. The cars on the lawn were packed in so tightly that everyone had to unload in the street. The man who owned the house was trying to fill every square inch of his property with automobiles. Everyone in the car except Matt and Simone could hear the noise from half a mile away, but even they could feel the anticipation and excitement in the air.

Everyone wore broad smiles as they made their way to the ballpark. Simone's father had said that the seats were way out in right field, but no one cared. As long as they were inside, it was good enough for them. They crossed through backyards making sure they didn't trample bushes and flowerbeds like others fans had done before them. A few residents of the neighborhood were shooing away the unwanted intruders from their yards. Their lawns were littered with beer cans and empty fried chicken buckets, and they were tired of cleaning up the mess. Every silver lining had its cloud.

What was once considered a run-down part of town had been rejuvenated and was alive with energy. When Matt and the entourage finally came face to face with the ballpark, they all stood silently in awe. Most could hear the pipe organ music coming from inside, but

Matt and Simone felt the vibrations and were delighted to take it all in with their eyes. The colors and smells flooded their senses with beautiful sensations. Matt had to buy a hat. He ran across the street to a street vendor that had set up shop beneath a pop-up beach shelter. He urged Simone to follow him, signing to her asking if she wanted a hat, but she shook her head. Matt bought her a matching one anyway. He put the change back into his pocket and reached for the binoculars that Simone had been holding for him. Slipping the glasses over the brim of his cap, he tucked the strap into the collar of the green army jacket his grandfather had given him. Simone smiled as she put on her hat. It was the little things that Matt always did that made her feel so content. She only asked for friendship, but Matt gave her so much more. She slipped her arm through his as they ran back across the busy street to rejoin her family.

By now everyone was equipped with either a hat, pennant, or button. Sound didn't seem to matter here; they all shared the universal sense of excitement. Simone's younger brother had his hat tilted to the side and strutted around like he owned the city. Her little sister didn't want to wear anything red, white, or blue since she was wearing green and yellow, so she put her button in her purse. She was the fashionista of the family. Even Simone's father had bought himself a hat and pin for his wife, who'd chosen to skip the game and spend the day shopping instead.

Each held his or her own ticket as they pushed their way through the silver turnstiles. Matt studied the ballpark diagram on the wall and quickly realized they still had a long walk to their seats. An usher who saw Simone signing was kind enough to point the way to their section. As they plodded up the inclined walkway towards their reserved seating, light filtered through the tunnel leading out to the field. Matt tried to look out onto the field whenever he passed an opening, but they were usually too full of fans blocking his view.

It was an arduous climb to the seats, which were on the top deck and about as far out into right as you could get. His seat was on the aisle right next to the railing. The right field foul pole was so close he could almost reach out and touch it. Matt smiled at the excitement he was witnessing, and he wished his grandfather had reconsidered joining them. It would have been nice to have him here, but even more than that, there were so many fathers and sons enjoying the day together that it made Matt take a deep breath and struggle not to dwell on the opportunity he had lost.

***

Across the field, Toby Bilston wheeled his son Benjamin out of the tunnel and into a designated handicapped section. Thank goodness for elevators. They were so high above the field, Benjamin was almost afraid to look over the railing. Even at this height, the aroma of the freshly cut outfield grass filled his nostrils. "Nice seats," Ben said sarcastically as Toby locked the brakes on his son's chair and stepped around him.

"What do you want for free? This is what you get for twenty years on the force." Toby mused as he unwrapped the aluminum foil from a hot dog for his son.

"You know dad," Benjamin complained, as he took a bite. "I'm used to mom's cooking, but these hot dogs are actually worse! I never would have believed it."

Toby smirked as he watched his son down his food. "I wouldn't say anything to her," he advised. "It's one of her few flaws."

His son acknowledged that truth with a slightly twitching nod.

Toby remained standing at the rail and looked down over at the crowd. He couldn't believe how many people could fit into the redesigned ballpark. When he used to work in the lab, Toby would duck out every once in a while to watch the Jumbo Shrimp play if it was a slow afternoon. If the team drew a crowd of two thousand fans, it was a big day for them. Now everyone was wearing the team colors; the ballpark was an ocean of red, white and blue. He stared at the big screen in left field as the minor league players took batting practice.

The new team wouldn't take the field until the ballpark filled to capacity. The secrecy surrounding their name and colors had been tenacious, but today was supposed to be the big reveal. The uniforms were rumored to be something special. Speculation around the name had gone from the bizarre to the boring. Toby put his money on something nautical, since Mason owned a cruise line.

Toby turned his focus to the V.I.P. boxes above them. He caught a glimpse of Peter Mason and some of his associates sitting next to the Mayor.

"Isn't this place something?" Ben asked. "I've never seen this much enthusiasm, even at a Jaguars' game."

"Well, the Jaguars haven't had much to celebrate until they made it to the final round of the playoffs," Toby added as he squeezed into his chair. "Damn! They could have spent some more money on these seats. These things are not for the derriere-challenged." Toby complained.

Benjamin's finger trembled as he pointed to the outfield walls. "What do you think those companies paid for those advertisements?" He asked, focusing on the banner for a local bank.

Toby squirmed in a failing attempt to get comfortable, which would be impossible until he shed seventy-five pounds. "I haven't got a clue, but they have probably been up there for years, and this will be the first time they ever pay off. There must be twenty thousand people here today."

***

Next to the right-field foul pole, Matt Walker looked to his left at the seats above him as he was handed a bag of roasted peanuts from Simone. Most of the men sitting around them had removed their shirts, trying to get a tan. Their pale beer bellies pointed up to the cloudless sky. They were crazy, he thought. The weather was still too cool for that.

Sitting in the last seat of the row, Matt was able to lean to his right and see over the railing. It was a sheer drop to the field below. Matt hadn't realized how high up they were, and began to feel queasy. He hated heights. It wasn't fearful enough to be considered a phobia, but it really bothered him. They were nearly one hundred feet up and probably four hundred feet from home plate. If he hadn't brought his binoculars, he never would have been able to see the players.

Simone's family took turns borrowing the glasses from him, but he didn't mind. Matt handed the glasses to her brother who was signing to him. Everyone in her family knew sign language. Simone was extremely fortunate to have such an understanding clan. Seeing their camaraderie made Matt feel even more estranged.

Matt studied the fans sitting around them. No one seemed to notice that they were all signing. It quelled his regrets about his grandfather not being here. The old man would have been embarrassed when they all started to sign. It was better that he wasn't here, Matt thought. He reached for Simone's arm to read her watch. It was almost time for the new team to take the field.

34

The skyboxes had been completely renovated for today's game. Rarely used for the minor league games, they were occasionally rented out to large groups for rock concerts or local events that the ballpark hosted. Peter Mason and his entourage of employees and invited guests mingled with each other in the suite above home plate. The Commissioner of Major League Baseball drank Mason's expensive champagne while munching on bacon wrapped scallops and shaking hands with total strangers. He was a politician in every sense of the word as he pointed down to the fans and smiled. The Commissioner patted strangers on the back as though he'd known them for a lifetime and waved obliviously to the crowd who taunted and cheered him at the same time.

The mood inside Mason's suite was excited, but anxious at the same time. Everything was riding on today's turnout, and the impression the new team would leave with the fans—and especially the sports journalists from around the country—would determine the team's fate.

Three suites away, the mood was less than ecstatic. Nick Coltello sat solemnly in the front row of the skybox and watched the crowd file in. Jaime Diaz acted as his ambassador at the back of the suite, greeting the friends Coltello had persuaded to attend. Not many cared if they were there or not; most were diehard Yankees fans and couldn't have cared less about a team named after a half-woman half-fish. Nicky the Knife had asked them to be there, and that was an invitation one didn't usually turn down.

Nicky had a curvaceous blond sitting on his left and a stunning redhead on his right. He didn't even know their names. It didn't matter. All he cared about was how the day turned out, and so far, he had nothing to be hopeful for. He had considered every option for how he could ruin this game, but he drew the line at terrorism. With one sharpshooter on a rooftop he could have taken Mason out at his own premiere, but as flawed as they were, he did have scruples. The last thing he wanted was to have the Feds turning the city into a sideshow—not to mention the press that would never leave. Jimmy had convinced him that it was just too risky. Florida was becoming known as the "Gunshine State," and it made him nervous. Today, he would just sit back and watch. If this thing turned out to be a success, he still had one more chance to put an end to Mason's dream of building a new ballpark on the land his crew had been using as a cemetery for nearly twenty years.

Jimmy had procured for them an exclusive pair of invitations on the maiden voyage of Mason's new ship in a few nights from now, and a plan B was already in the works. One way or another, on land or at sea, he would put an end to Mason's stupid pipe-dream once and for all and stop the construction of the new ballpark.

The public address system crackled to life, playing the familiar theme to 2001: A Space Odyssey. As the music built up to its ultimate crescendo, the giant screen in left-center field burst to life, revealing the best-kept secret in the City of Jacksonville. Peter Mason stood up in his skybox waiting for the feedback from the crowd. What he anticipated and what he received were two entirely different reactions.

In the press box, the unveiling was met with uncertainty and confusion.

"What the hell is a Jengu?" One of the reporters asked aloud, as he stared at the new logo.

"That name has got to go," another writer announced.

In the stands, nearly twenty-one thousand fans found themselves compelled to pull out their cell phones and Google the definition of

Jengu. The answer the internet supplied was a water spirit from West African mythology. The new logo was a blue and aqua mermaid holding a trident. It was a name that Peter Mason had researched himself. He liked the idea of the alliteration that the Jacksonville Jaguars used, and believed the logo and mascot of a mermaid would initially look peaceful, but the trident she wielded would symbolize she wasn't to be taken lightly.

Mason turned and looked at Gerald Banks who remained sitting. The rest of his invited guests sipped nervously from their champagne flutes and averted their gazes, afraid that Mason might turn his anger toward them. "What don't they get?" he asked, with his back to the field.

"Maybe they were expecting a tie-in to the football team like they did in Chicago with the Bears and Cubs. What about a jackal?" Banks suggested, keeping the alliteration intact.

"A jackal?" Mason barked. "A feral jungle animal?"

Banks was feeling an odd sense of satisfaction in his brother-in-law's distress. "I'm just saying…"

Outside of the skybox, the ear-splitting screams of discontent were rising. Peter Mason turned and waved to the crowd shamelessly. What else could go wrong?

***

In the locker room, the Jacksonville Jengu were making their final preparations for their debut. The team was made up of a blend of players from other Major League teams who were on the bubble with their own franchises and needed to make a good showing or risk being sent down to the minor leagues.

Manager Jack Wolinski was rolling his trademark cigar in his fingers as he gave the team their pep talk. Pacing around the locker room like a squatty preacher, he reminded the players that even though this was only an exhibition game, it would be a hell of a lot better if they won. He made it clear that the hometown Jumbo Shrimp were playing with an experienced lineup and had a chip on their shoulders to prove that they could play on the same field as their higher-paid rivals. Wolinski warned every player that the future of professional baseball in the city of Jacksonville was at stake today, and it was up to each of them to show their worth. For some of the players, it would be their last opportunity to play in front of a crowd this large.

Wolinski pinned the opening line up on a corkboard next to the locker room exit. He asked the players for a moment of silence before they went out for batting and fielding practice. The room went quiet for almost a minute until Wolinski picked up the phone and called up to the press box. The Jengu were ready to take the field. All the players in the locker room crowded around the starting line up to see who got the nod. They all bumped and jostled for position to see the list. Everyone, except one man.

He was the batting coach. He made sure the red velvet-lined case was standing upright inside his locker and gently closed the door shut, clicking the lock to secure the contents. He never looked up as the team let out a unified roar as they headed out onto the field for the first time ever. He was older, grayer, but still had the same rock-steady concentration and determination.

Anthony Magnetti grabbed a canvas bag full of baseballs, rested his trusted bat Sweet Amy on his shoulder, and confidently followed the team onto the diamond.

35

It all happened in the blink of an eye, and the swing of a bat. Matt had just taken the binoculars back from Simone's little brother when the crowd around him began to stir. He didn't see it coming, but everyone around him suddenly stood up. The wind had shifted direction, and now the flags in center field were blowing directly toward him. He watched as if in slow motion, as the surrounding crowd began clawing the air with outstretched hands. In a fraction of a second, he saw it flying toward him. A ball was hit deep to right field, but the wind was hooking it foul. There were a group of outfielders taking their turn at catching the practice balls, and they all turned in unison to watch it leave the park.

All the spectators along the railing were lunging out at it, trying to be the lucky one to take home a free souvenir. Matt, as if by reflex, reached out too.

It was an instinctive motion; he knew he didn't stand a chance with everyone else flailing and grabbing for the ball. Suddenly, there was a stinging sensation in the palm of his hand. He drew his arm in and held the baseball firmly in his hand. Simone tugged on his arm with excitement. He hadn't even tried, but he'd caught it anyway. Matt felt Simone's father patting him on the back as he wrapped his fingers around the ball to protect it. Matt didn't mean to trace it, but it was out of his control. The twitching turned into a trembling, and then his eyes rolled back into his head. He lost all sight of the stadium as his eyes blinked shut. Simone immediately realized what was happening and she pushed back the fans that had crowded around to see the baseball or congratulate the teen on his barehanded catch.

Matt slumped back into his chair, the wooden slats creaking under the sudden pressure. Simone wrapped her arm around him. She didn't know how long it was going to last, but she wanted to be there when he snapped out of it.

These experiences were growing more intense, but they were still unexpected and random in their occurrence. More of his senses were becoming involved as the smells of the ballpark were replaced with the natural odor of a countryside landscape that was entirely unfamiliar. Matt felt like an omnipresent spectator flying over a herd of cows grazing on a hillside, in an emerald green pasture. It was hotter here; he could almost feel the oppressive heat as the sun baked the earth. It was like being there without actually being there. He got the distinct impression that he was not only traveling over the terrain but also moving forward through time as the greenery gave way to a more somber scene and sensations.

The cattle were being led to slaughter, and he could hear the tormented sounds as the animals were being gutted. Their hides were left hanging in the sun to dry. He wanted to avert his eyes, but the skins were everywhere. He watched as one particular hide, the hide that would eventually become the ball in his hand, was being cut and sewn. He was aware that most major league baseballs were assembled in Haiti, which explained the extreme temperature. He could feel the perspiration collecting on his forehead even though it was 65 degrees in the stadium. He watched as one particular woman toiled tirelessly, stitching the hide around the cork center by hand. She was only one of the hundreds of women working in a factory that would have probably been condemned in any other country. Beads of sweat rolled down the arms of the woman who was creating the ball he was holding. When she completed her masterpiece, the woman put the ball delicately into a cardboard box, sealed it, and everything went dark. It was pitch black for the next few moments, but Matt could smell the unmistakable scent of salty sea air.

At the very far reaches of his mind, he thought he heard the crashing of waves against the hull of a ship. It led him to believe that ball was being transported by freighter. The next time he was able to see anything, the ball was being dumped into the darkness of a canvas sack with a few dozen others.

Another few seconds passed, and Matt became aware of Simone wiping the moisture from his face. Instinctively, he felt like the trace was coming to an end.

Like driving out of a tunnel, the sunlight was blinding as he now viewed the stadium from an entirely different perspective. He was down on the grass, looking out towards center field. He was on the ground beside the batting circle. He could see a player's foot right next to him. The smell of the ballpark once again filled his nostrils. He was back, but not in the present. Not quite yet. It was batting practice, Matt thought. This should be pretty interesting, taking a ride on the back of a baseball as it rocketed through the air. He watched as the ball next to him got picked up and hit toward the shortstop. It was his turn next, and he wondered if he would feel any pain when the ball was hit.

The next vision he saw would be etched into his mind forever. In a sensation that was new to him: everything became tinted in a red hue, as though an alarm was going off. He half expected to hear an audible alarm, but there was none. The color was pulsing as the hitter began juggling the ball to perfect his timing. As if some power greater than his was imposing its influence, his perspective changed once again, now focusing in on the batter's face. It was a face he could never forget. It was older and more weathered, the mustache a bit greyer, but it was still him! He would always remember the face of the man that killed his father and mother! The ball was tossed up one last time as the bat met cowhide and the ball sailed errantly into Matt's hand.

Matt jumped out of his seat screaming, with the baseball clenched in a death grip. Simone was trying to calm him down, but he was no longer aware she even existed. He started spinning and gesturing wildly in his seat, not knowing where to go, or what to do first. Matt wanted to get help, to tell someone, but everyone around him backed away as though he was having a seizure. Nearby onlookers brushed his hands away as he grabbed for help. Simone hung onto him as Matt lashed out at anyone who came near him. He felt helpless; he had to do something himself. Now that he had found the man who murdered his parents, he could never let him get away!

Peter Mason looked out over the crowd and was happy to see that everyone seemed to be focused on the players and no longer obsessing over the team name. That would have to be dealt with during the post-game press conference. He wasn't sure how, but he had nine innings to figure it out.

It was turning into a perfect day for baseball. Out of the corner of his eye, he caught a disturbance in the right-field bleachers but paid little attention to it. He was sure the staff would take care of it. He picked up the telephone and was told that security had already dispatched someone to handle the trouble. The game hadn't even started, and someone was probably drunk already. Strike two.

Matt could see the private security guards coming down the aisle for him. They were wearing bright yellow shirts and stood out like sunflowers in the crowd. He pushed Simone out of the way and grabbed the program lying on his seat. If he couldn't get to the killer, at least he could find out his identity from the roster. Simone's father tried to grab Matt as he wrestled past him. With strength that came from out of nowhere, Matt pushed him over the back of his seat.

It was like running an obstacle course. Everyone was reaching out to stop him, but Matt's physical strength was now coming from an untapped source. He punched, and squirmed, and at one point crawled on his hands and knees to get away from the guards who were trying to restrain him.

He was beginning to draw more attention than anything that was happening on the diamond. It was a wave that moved through the stands as all heads turned to the right field bleachers. The crowd cheered Matt on with each narrow escape he made from the guards. They booed the security people every time the guards closed in on him. Running down the last aisle along the fence, Matt finally came to the railing. He was cornered. It was thirty feet to the stands below; he would never survive the jump. More guards had been called, and they were surrounding him. He looked down at the fans looking up at him. He could tell they were yelling at him to jump. A few cleared out from under him, just in case he went through with it.

Matt had his back to the railing, and with nowhere to run, the guards were moving in cautiously. They were yelling at him to calm down. It was times like this that he found it fortunate not to be able to hear. He could have absolute concentration, without any distractions. He moved up a few steps and looked over the railing to his right. He was almost back in his original seat. He looked over the Simone who was crying hysterically in her father's arms. One of the guards saw him look away, and dove for him.

In that same split second, Matt spun over the railing with baseball in hand and wrapped his arms around the foul pole like it was a long-lost friend. The crowd went crazy applauding the young escape artist. Another guard reached over the railing, missing Matt by mere inches as the teen corkscrewed down the pole. Pulling out his walkie-talkie, the guard called for additional help.

The crowd cheered Matt on as he ran along the home team's bullpen. Pitchers who had been busy warming up were now raising their gloves in the air to root him on. Four more guards came out of a nearby tunnel to join the pursuit.

The fans had been enjoying the spectacle until Matt ran out on the field. Now, the intruder was an interruption, and the tide of emotion began to turn against him. The cheering quickly turned to booing, but Matt couldn't tell the difference, nor did he care. He had his sights set on the man now sitting in the Jengu's dugout, and nothing was going to stop him.

***

In his skybox, Peter Mason found himself trying to maintain his composure and make light of the commotion on the field. He managed to joke that the teenager was probably the only person in the crowd that liked the team's name. His guests chuckled uneasily.

Mason casually waved his finger summoning Gerald Banks to join him at the window. "Make this go away," he whispered. Banks nodded and exited the suite.

Four luxury suites away, Nicholas Coltello found it all very amusing. Anything that threw a monkey-wrench into the festivities and made Peter Mason look bad was alright with him. He was yelling for the kid to run like he was watching a horse race.

Anthony Magnetti just sat in the dugout making small talk with the third base coach, totally unaware that he was the catalyst of this entire incident. Once Matt was on the field, every guard that was available took to the grass. It was like watching an old episode of Benny Hill. Twenty guards were chasing after a screaming teenager around the infield and then into the outfield. Even the sound technician got into the act and pulled up Benny Hill's theme song; "Yakety-Sax" and began blasting it onto the field.

The players moved out of the way, not wanting to get hurt. The crowd would cheer every time a guard would fall over or trip chasing the teenager. Exhausted, Matt didn't know how much longer he could keep running. He wasn't getting any closer to the dugout; in fact, they were chasing him into the outfield.

Matt could see the players standing at the railing of the Jengu's dugout; they were all pointing and laughing at him. Tears began to stream down his face as his legs began to buckle. There was no one to help him. He had found the man that had killed his family, but there was nothing he could do about it. With his lungs feeling like they were going to burst and his chest heaving, Matt finally collapsed in center-field. Within seconds, his hands were cuffed behind his back, and he was being carried off. He looked to his right toward the Jengu's dugout. The killer was wiping off his cleats and heading back into the locker room.

The crowd was standing and screaming as they hauled Matt away. He looked up into the right-field bleachers, but he couldn't make out Simone or anyone in her family. He wouldn't have blamed her if she had left.

As he was escorted to a waiting patrol car, someone reached in and put Matt's cap back on his head. He didn't see who it was and hadn't even noticed that it had fallen off during the scuffle. The media followed him down the tunnel snapping his picture as he was put into the back seat of the cruiser. He would make the front page of tomorrow's sports section.

Matt turned his head and gazed out the rear window of the patrol car as the ballpark grew smaller in the distance. Beyond the group of photographers, a lone figure stood outlined by the sunlight. He thought it might be the same good Samaritan who replaced his hat, but that really wasn't important. God had given him this power for a reason, he thought. Now Matt knew its purpose. He would not rest until he brought his parents' murderer to justice.

36

It was a rarity whenever Toby Bilston found himself speechless. Sitting next to his son Benjamin, he stared dumbfounded at the video screen in left-center field. The frantic saxophone music was blaring over the stadium's sound system, and the crowd was enjoying every moment of the chaos playing itself out beyond the clay diamond.

Benjamin's body began to noticeably shudder as he tried to make sense out of what he was seeing. In his precise way of looking at the world, he was expecting to see a baseball game, and this wasn't supposed to be part of the experience. He knew the crowd would stand for the national anthem, he understood that, but this was not right. He had overcome his fear of the sounds produced by fireworks and had primed himself just in case there might be some. His father had tried to reassure him that whatever happened, he would be right there by his side and that always made him feel safe.

Toby dropped his handful of peanuts and covered his mouth with his hand. This couldn't be happening. No way was Matthew Walker out on the field running from a troop of security guards. He recognized him immediately when the camera zoomed in on the panicked teen. What the hell was he doing?

"What is that kid doing out there, dad?" Benjamin asked. "Was this supposed to happen? You didn't tell me anything about this."

Toby put his hand on his son's shoulder to calm him down, even though it was he who needed the reassuring. "I don't know, son. Nothing to worry about. Just a kid trying to get attention."

Benjamin's face turned sad. "Everyone is starting to yell at him. Are they mad at him?"

Toby pulled his cell phone out of his pocket and dialed Lauren King's number. "No, they're not mad at him, son. He's just acting very stupid." He replied, overemphasizing the last two words of his sentence.

Toby listened as the phone rang, sticking a finger in his free ear to block out the sound of the crowd. *Don't go to voicemail, dammit!*

Lauren picked up on the fifth ring. "Toby where are you?"

"Where are you?" He asked.

"I'm at the stadium. I just got here."

Toby was still having a hard time over the crowd noise. "Can you meet me at the entrance to section two-thirty-eight?"

"You're at the ballgame?"

Toby stood up and walked behind his son's wheelchair and unlocked the brakes. "I'm here with Ben. You need to meet me now."

Lauren was standing at the entrance to section three-forty-two one deck above and the last section in right field. "I promised Matthew Walker I would join him and his girlfriend's family. Let me just tell them I'm here first."

"No time," Toby barked into the phone. "Matt Walker isn't there."

Lauren looked at the phone quizzically. "How do you know they're not here?"

"Now, Detective," and the phone call ended.

Toby leaned over his son's shoulder and spoke into his ear. "Lauren is here, Benjamin. Do you want to go and say hello to her?" He asked, playing on the boy's adolescent crush.

Benjamin's face lit up. If it was a choice between seeing Lauren or sitting through all of this sensory overload, the decision was evident as he began to excitedly pat the padded arms of his chair.

"I'll take that as a yes," Toby said, as he backed his son away from the railing.

37

Lauren just had to take one quick look at the field and the crowd before she met Toby. She checked her ticket stub to confirm that she was in the right place and headed up the tunnel and into the bright sunlight. The noise grew louder as Lauren walked up the ramp but the afternoon sun was so intense it nearly blinded her. She accidentally bumped into a man who was heading in the opposite direction with his family. He was protecting his daughter while the girl sobbed hysterically with her face buried in his chest. For an instant, she thought to ask if everything was alright, but they moved past her quickly and vanished into the crowd still bustling about on the third level.

The game was just getting underway, and Lauren chastised herself for being late and missing the opening festivities. She took another look at her ticket and matched the numbers with the row and seat where she expected to see Matt and his girlfriend's family. She thought it would be impolite if she didn't at least introduce herself before excusing herself to meet up with Toby.

Something wasn't right. Lauren checked the section, row and seat numbers on her stub for a third time, noting the correct section number posted on the railing at the end of the tunnel. She appeared to be in the right place, but something was off. The six seats in the front row were empty. She walked down the steps and stared down the row. "Excuse me," she asked a young woman who appeared to be wearing all the makeup she owned. "I'm supposed to meet some friends here. Have you seen anyone in those seats?" She pointed.

The woman flipped her lustrous black hair over her shoulder and placed the five-dollar beer she was drinking on the floor next to her seat. She was wearing a Chicago Cubs t-shirt and had a Cubs logo painted on her left cheek just below her eye. "You mean the crazy family?"

"Excuse me?" Lauren asked, confused.

The woman shrugged her head toward the tunnel. "The rest of them just left the normal way."

Lauren assumed the half empty glass on the ground couldn't have been the woman's first or even eighth beer. "I don't understand. What do you mean the normal way?"

"The deaf people," she said, mimicking inappropriately with her fingers. "They just left."

The girl's boyfriend stood up much to the outrage of the fans whose view was suddenly blocked. He had a yellow "P" painted on his cheek representing the Pittsburgh Pirates. Lauren wondered how they would ever make it as a couple. "Come on, lady! The game's about to start. You just missed them. If you hurry, you can probably still catch them outside."

"Down in front!" Someone hollered from the bleachers above them.

Lauren looked out at the field and back at the empty seats. The last thing she wanted was to cause a commotion. "Thank you," she said, appreciatively.

In less than five minutes Lauren had met up with Toby and his son. She bent over and gave Benjamin a gentle peck on his cheek. The teen smiled and blushed. "I didn't know you were coming to the game," she said.

"I thought Benjamin might enjoy it," Toby replied, as he ran his hand through his son's hair. "And then all hell broke loose."

"What happened?"

"Matt Walker is what happened."

Lauren was more baffled than ever. "I was just up at their seats, and they weren't there. Someone told me that they had all left."

Toby began to roll his son toward the elevator. "You're not going to believe it."

"Tell me," Lauren begged, as she flanked Benjamin.

"I'm sitting with Ben and watching the team's take fielding practice before the game and the next thing I know, a guy is sliding down the right-field foul pole and running out onto the diamond. The crowd is going crazy, and they're showing him on the big screen trying to outrun the security team. "

"You're kidding me. What does it have to do with Matt Walker though?"

Toby stopped pushing momentarily. "Really? How did you ever earn a gold shield?"

Lauren grimaced. "You've lost me."

Toby sarcastically spoke slower. "It *was* Matt Walker!"

" Who was?"

Toby suddenly felt like Lou Costello. "The guy on the field! Matt Walker was the one on the field running from security."

Lauren shook her head. "No. It couldn't be. You must have been mistaken. Why would Matt Walker run out onto the field?"

"Well, I doubt he was doing it to raise deaf awareness."

Benjamin giggled. "That's funny, dad."

"That might explain why his girlfriend and her family left the ballpark," Lauren added.

It was between innings as they continued on toward the elevator. The mezzanine was filling up with fans who were taking bathroom breaks and loading up on refreshments. Toby weaved his son slowly through the crowd. "Normally, I wouldn't have thought twice about this, but after what I witnessed yesterday in his living room, you've got to figure something must have set him off."

They reached the elevator and waited. "A unit probably took Matt to our station. East Bay Street is the closest precinct to the ballpark," Toby said. "I want you to head over there and make sure they don't enter him into the system. I have to take Benjamin home, and then

I'll meet you there."

Lauren took hold of the handles of the wheelchair. "Let me drive Benjamin home. You understand sign language and can pull more strings than I can. I'll catch up with you at the station as soon as possible."

The door to the elevator opened, and Lauren pushed Benjamin inside as Toby reached over and pressed the button for the ground floor. "This is gonna take an awful lot of bullshitting," he said, taking in a heavy sigh.

"And you're just the guy to do it," Lauren smirked, as the door slid closed.

38

Captain Roy Sowell waited impatiently in the backseat of Peter Mason's limousine parked across the street from the ballpark. He had just finished reading the file they'd left for him when he looked out through the darkly tinted side window as a teenage boy in a pea green army jacket was hustled into a waiting police car. Pulling out his Swiss Army knife, Sowell cleaned his nails as the cruiser pulled away. Wondering what the boy had done to get arrested drew his attention away from what he was doing, and the knife dug deeply under his index finger's nail. He sucked at the bitter red liquid until the bleeding stopped.

Although the windows were rolled up and the air conditioner was running, Sowell could hear the thunder of ovation coming from inside the ballpark. Leaning forward, he turned on the television and poured himself two fingers of single malt from the fully equipped bar. It burned Sowell's throat. The cancer was spreading, and now he could feel it in his esophagus. When it reached his voice box and vocal cords, he would no longer have the ability to speak. He had considered learning sign language, but why? He had nothing of importance left to say.

A vendor who had been selling buttons next to the car walked over and pressed his face up against the window to see inside. The man was unshaven and grubby in his appearance. Sowell reached over and rolled down the window immediately smelling alcohol on the man's breath. "Can I help you?"

The old man jumped back, his Jengu's cap almost falling off his head. "Jeez Louise, you scared me, mister. I couldn't tell if anyone was inside." He said poking his face inside the limo. "My god, you've got all the comforts of home in there."

Sowell began to feel a little self-conscious. "Is there something you wanted?"

"Sorry friend, I just wanted to see inside, that's all."

"Well, now you've seen it. So beat it before I call a cop!"

"Well, up yours, pal!" The vendor stammered as he stumbled away.

The car gave Sowell the feeling of living in a cocoon as he rolled the window back up. It was a feeling Peter Mason must have felt every day of his life. "No dirt under his nails," Sowell muttered.

Pouring another drink, he looked at his watch; the game should be underway already. How much longer did he have to sit here? At first he was curious when Mason reached out to him, but now he was feeling like a second-class citizen. He had been getting ready to leave for Andros island to live out his days in the surfside house he had bought with the blood money Mason had paid him. No matter how peaceful his exile, no matter how blue the sky, or green the ocean, Sowell still spent every waking hour in self-inflicted darkness. The guilt ate away at him faster than his cancer ever could. The disease was his penance and the beach house the irony. Don't anyone ever tell you that there is no higher power; Sowell knew there was, and it was one sadistic son of a bitch.

The basketball playoffs were on the television, so he pointed the remote and shut it off. Watching sports bothered him lately; all the athletes were too healthy and filled with vitality. Seeing teams work together reminded him of the comradery of his old crew—now lifeless, bloated corpses serving as fish food at the bottom of the ocean. The thought of them made him reach for his third refill.

The limo door opened and sunlight and the smell of hot dogs and popcorn flooded into the car. While they could never calm the Captain's relentless anguish, they did offer a temporary distraction. Gerald Banks climbed in across from Sowell and sat down. He was grinning like he had just found out his best friend's secret.

"Why did you bring me here?" Sowell asked. "Our business is finished."

Banks unbuttoned his jacket and loosened the knot in his tie. "Things change."

Sowell shook his head. "Not as far as I'm concerned. I did what I had to, and now I'm done."

Banks sat back and studied the Captain for a few seconds. He had the leathery skin of someone who either smoked too much or spent too much time in the sun. His hair was full but nearly white. He had the look of someone who was ill but tried not to show it. "We need you to pilot the *Hydra*. Are you up to it?"

Sowell looked into his empty glass. "Did you not hear me? I'm retired."

Banks drummed his fingers on his knee. "You put a down payment on a place on

Andros Island. I can have that mortgage paid off before I leave this limo."

Sowell's eyes narrowed. "How do you do that?"

"Do what? Pay off your house?"

"No. Play God with someone's life? How do you do that?"

Banks shrugged. "I'm not playing God, Captain. I just made you a very generous offer, that's all."

Sowell could feel his teeth clenching. "Because of your boss, I will die a traitor to the country I pledged to serve and protect. I have to live with that. I have to live with the memories of that horrific night when your boss personally killed my crew. And he's got the balls to ask me for more? I wouldn't piss on Peter Mason if he were on fire!"

"Just one last favor," Banks said, reaching for a glass and the bottle of whiskey. "Then you can live out your life as a rich man, sipping boat drinks and searching for sand dollars."

The two men sat across from one another trying to sum the other up. "Why should I?" Sowell asked.

"Because we need you."

"So I have a choice?"

Banks stared into his glass wishing he had some ice. "Yes, you have a choice. Live out whatever time you have left in the peaceful seclusion of your Caribbean island, or await your execution for treason in Guantanamo Bay. You decide."

"You know that proposition works both ways, right?" Sowell suggested.

Banks yawned. It had been a long morning. "Captain, you thought you had disappeared. Using very little of our extensive resources, we found you in a matter of hours. You are the only living witness who isn't on Peter Mason's payroll. Do I really need to draw you a picture? If we had wanted you gone, you'd be gone."

The Captain let out a reluctant sigh and looked outside at the entrance to the ballpark. "Am I to assume that the game is a success?"

"Are you serious? The crowd is larger than Mason ever anticipated. It couldn't be better."

Sowell reached over and poured himself another shot of whiskey. "What happened to that kid they were taking away a little while ago?"

Banks shrugged indifferently. "I don't know. Some teenager goes crazy in the stands and then bolts out onto the field. Security caught him and took him away. Mason won't press any charges. He'll just let the kid simmer for a while. He doesn't want the negative publicity."

Sowell rubbed his eyes, they were red and puffy.

"When was the last time you had a good night's sleep?" Banks asked.

Sowell rolled his head from side to side. It felt like his neck was a mess of twisted cables. "It's been awhile. I can't stop thinking about my crew. I keep seeing their faces."

Banks swirled the amber liquid in his glass. "If Mason had told you what he was planning, he knew that you would have never agreed to it. Was it humane? Of course not. Was it necessary? Unfortunately, it was. We needed the military to believe that their technology was destroyed, not stolen."

Sowell braced himself for another swallow of the burning liquor. "I'm no better than the Las Vegas shooter or any other mass murderer. I don't know how Mason can live with himself, but I know my crew will never stop haunting me."

Banks turned the television back on and lowered the sound. "You armed forces guys are all alike. I've never quite understood the whole military mindset. The chain of command mentality. No one thinks for themselves in the service. No one ever questions authority. You're all trained to follow orders, or else the entire system breaks down. If Peter Mason were your commanding officer, and he ordered you to scuttle that ship, you'd do it without batting an eyelash. But because he was a civilian, you feel guilt-ridden. Why is that? I've never quite been able to grasp that concept. How can you guys take out an entire village in some bum-fucked middle-eastern country, and then hold a press conference preaching that the end justified the means?" Banks wondered, sitting the glass down on his armrest. "The only difference I can see is this time is that you were paid better."

The Captain could feel his anger boiling within him. "Killing your own troops is not the same thing as engaging the enemy, Banks. You'd know that if you had ever manned a post. No matter how the Coast Guard treated me, I would never have agreed with the idea if I'd known Mason's full intentions. I couldn't care less about the stolen technology. Today it's a laser, tomorrow it'll be something bigger and more lethal."

Gerald Banks studied Sowell for a long moment. "You want to know something, Captain?" He said as he spun the ice in the glass. "It was my idea to bring you back into this, and now I'm second-guessing myself. I'm not so sure you can be trusted."

Sowell gave back the same malevolent stare he was receiving. "Don't threaten me, Banks. How is it that you don't understand the concept of chain of command? Mason barks and you jump. You're just a grunt wearing an imported suit instead of a uniform. He shits and you wipe his ass. He needs me, but you're just a minion. No one can learn to command the *Hydra* in two days except me, and he damn well knows it. I've read the newspaper. I know your Captain is dead. That's the only reason you brought me back into this. You're not the only one who's done his research."

"Don't flatter yourself," Banks growled. "The ship can practically run itself on auto-pilot."

Sowell laughed. "I can steer that hydrofoil through a garden hose, and you know it. You've seen my record. No auto-pilot can do that. Mason wants the transfer to take place without any of his guests the wiser, and I'm the only living person who can make that happen in three days. Not only does your boss want the perfect alibi, but he also wants a smooth ride to Bermuda and back with the Governor and all the hoity-toity dignitaries onboard. Without me at the helm, his crown jewel and the laser will never leave Jaxport!"

Banks reached over and poured twice as much whiskey into his glass. "Okay Captain, I'll admit it. We need you."

Sowell opened up his pocketknife and began rolling it between his fingers like a magician with a silver dollar. Banks watched him, mystified. "I'll do it, Gerald, but your boss and I have to come to a mutual understanding," Sowell said, never masking the condescension in his tone. "I'm the best at what I do. Mason informed me of his scheme for unloading the laser right after he killed my crew. He also showed me the basics of how the *Hydra* runs. He plans on docking the *Hydra* inside a modified supertanker while at sea. A hydrofoil that rides above the water has that capability. He wants it to happen in the middle of dinner without anyone even flinching during their prime rib. While everyone is finishing up their baked Alaska, they won't have an inkling that they've been moored inside another ship. I can have us in and out in less than twenty minutes. Unloading the technology in Bermuda was never going to happen. The local customs service would be all over it."

Banks smiled every time he heard the plan. It was brilliant. "Twenty minutes? Are you sure about that, Captain? Docking at sea is far more difficult than docking on land."

Sowell rechecked his watch. "You just make sure the tanker is on time and at the right coordinates, and I'll handle the rest." He put his glass down on his knee and leaned across to Banks. "I just have one last thing for you to tell your boss."

"Enlighten me," Banks said.

Sowell leaned forward menacingly. "Make no mistake, Gerry. I let you find me. Otherwise, you'd still be looking. If you think that I would ever agree to this arrangement without having my own insurance policy, then you would be seriously underestimating me."

Banks eyes narrowed. "Do tell."

"I just want you to tell Peter Mason that after this weekend, I want to live out what little time I have left without anymore outside distractions. I understand that there is a special place in hell for men like me, but I want to get there of my own accord, and he needs to know that I've taken certain measures to ensure that happens."

Banks smirked.

"Tell your boss that should some wayward automobile drive up on my front lawn or any other unforeseeable twist of fate befall me, then certain incriminating pieces of evidence will make it into the hands of the appropriate U.S. government officials. My quality of life may be deteriorating, but I choose to leave this earth on my own terms."

Banks squirmed a bit in his seat. Roy Sowell's fate had already been determined long before this face to face. The *Hydra*'s Captain, Ken Hitchcock, had been sacrificed as an excuse to track down Roy Sowell. He was surprised at how easy it had been to find him, but now the Captain was proving to be more problematic than cooperative. Banks hated that he always had to clean up his brother-in-law's mistakes. Peter Mason was too spineless to do what needed to be done. He should have killed Sowell on the bridge of the *Hydra* that night and dumped him overboard along with his crew. Nice and neat. Now, as usual, it was up to Banks to get his hands dirty. Insurance or no insurance, bluff or no bluff, after this weekend, Sowell had to die.

Banks held out his hand to Sowell as he opened the limo door. "You have my word on it."

The Captain sat in silent contemplation as the limo pulled away from the curb. He stared out the window and carefully considered his options. The thought of the young boy in the green army jacket that Peter Mason had carted off to jail was still nagging at him. Why should a young man committing a harmless prank have to be taught such a severe lesson? Many members of the *Intrepid's* crew hadn't been much older than that boy. Who gave Peter Mason and Gerald Banks the dominion over so many innocent lives?

Because of that kid in the green army jacket, for the first time in nearly a week, the Captain found himself at peace. A smile creased his face.

39

"He won't say a word to us," Detective Marcos Soto said, looking at Matt Walker through the two-way glass.

"I don't even know why he's here," his partner Moses Green admitted. "The kid ran onto the field before a baseball game. Big fucking deal. Why are we wasting our time? Peter Mason isn't even pressing charges."

Soto shrugged to his partner. "Peter Mason asked the Chief of D's to have the kid cool his jets in here for a while, and that's what we're going to do. Trust me, no one hates babysitting more than I do."

Green shook his head. "He's disrespectful…not even talking to us."

"Have you tried sign language?" Came a voice from down the hallway.

Both detectives turned in unison to see Toby Bilston frowning at them.

"We didn't see you standing there Dr. Bilston," Santos admitted. "Is he deaf?"

"Well, that would explain a lot," Moses added.

Toby moved into the light. "Yes, the boy is deaf."

"We didn't…"

I'm releasing you from your duty, Detectives," Toby commanded. "I'll take it from here."

"Are you sure, Doctor? The Chief of Detectives personally asked us…"

"Tell the Chief of D's to go fuck himself," Toby said casually. "I know the kid personally. I'll vouch for him."

The Detectives were well aware of Toby's reputation and trusted his judgment. "He's all yours, Doc," Green said, as he held open the exit for his partner.

"Good luck," Santos added.

Toby stared through the window at Matt Walker for a good three minutes trying to decide how he would handle the teenager. Matt was facing the glass probably aware that someone was watching him. He sat expressionless with his hands clasped together. His hair was unkempt, and his baseball cap was sitting on the table in front of him.

Toby entered the interrogation room and smiled at Matt. The teen's dour expression never wavered. "How are you?" Toby signed.

Matt never looked in Toby's direction.

Toby grabbed the only other chair in the room, and the dragged it over, groaning as he sat down across from the boy. "These seats are so uncomfortable," he signed. "I heard they do it on purpose."

Matt blinked slowly and then clasped his hands behind his back. A gesture Toby interpreted as him not wanting to speak.

"Okay, then let me talk," Toby signed. "Pretty crazy day I've had. I'm sitting at the ballgame minding my own business, having one of those great father-son bonding moments, and then guess what? I look out at the video screen in left-center field and guess who's up there making an ass of himself?"

Matt remained expressionless and unresponsive.

"What the hell were you thinking, Matt?" Toby signed furiously.

The room went quiet as they both considered the consequences of their situation. Finally, Toby broke the silence by slamming his hand down on the desk. Matt may not have heard the sound, but he definitely felt the vibration. The two-way glass shuddered in its frame. "Did you know that your girlfriend and her family are waiting for you outside in the squad room? She seems pretty upset. Do you want me to bring her in here?"

Matt's head turned robotically in Toby's direction, but there was still no outward sign of emotion.

"I realize that we just met yesterday, but I thought we trusted each other," Toby signed. "I thought we were friends. Am I wrong about that?" Toby asked with a questioning facial expression. "You trusted me enough to share your amazing gift. Why won't you talk to me? I just want to help you."

"What gift?" Matt signed defiantly, as he looked toward the window. "I don't know what you're talking about."

Toby turned and looked over his shoulder. "You think someone is out there watching us?" Toby chuckled. "Trust me, kid, your secret is safe. No one here thinks you're that important."

Matt remained stone-faced staring distrustfully at the two-way window behind Toby.

"Maybe I need to bring your girlfriend in here," Toby signed. "Maybe she can give me some answers."

Matt's opened hand came down on the table like a clap of thunder. Toby actually flinched. "Okay, fine. Your girlfriend stays outside… for now. But you've got to talk to me, Matt," Toby signed. "What set you off at the ballgame?"

The door to the interrogation room opened, and Lauren King walked in. "What the hell is going on in here? Are you trying to break our furniture, Matthew?"

Matt watched her take a seat on the edge of the table. Toby made an effort to stand, but the detective put her hand on his shoulder to stop him. "I'm fine. Relax."

"How's Benjamin?" Toby asked.

Lauren smiled. "Terrific as always. I dropped him off, and Harriet sends her love. You both raised an amazing kid."

Toby smiled. "Doing the best we can."

The detective shimmied herself into a more comfortable position on the table. "You should be proud."

Toby nodded. "Thank you."

Lauren looked at Matt to make sure that he was looking at her mouth and understanding her. "How are you?"

He continued to be wary.

The detective unbuttoned the denim jacket that was restricting her movements. "I've got a funny story to tell you both. Not hysterical, but funny ironic." She crossed her legs. "So I go to the big ballgame today because a really nice young guy offered me a ticket. Truthfully, I wouldn't know a baseball from a golf ball, but because he seemed so nice, I agreed to go. So when I get to the seats where we're supposed to meet, he's a no-show! Can you believe it? I put a desk-load of murder cases on hold for this guy, and he stands me up! The nerve of this guy!"

Toby could tell that Lauren's satirical charm was softening Matt's demeanor. Good cop, fat cop. It seemed to be working.

"Believe me," the detective continued. "I've been dumped before, so I've learned not to take it personally," she admitted, "but this time I honestly felt a little disappointed."

Matt frowned slightly.

The detective held up her palms. "Wait, wait…I haven't even told you the best part of my story yet. I have to back up a bit." She leaned in toward Matt making sure their eye contact was rock-solid. "As I'm walking up the tunnel to the seats, this family is walking past me in the opposite direction, which I thought was really weird because the game was just about to start. But then I noticed that the beautiful young woman in her father's arms is crying her eyes out. I mean the faucets are going full blast, and there's nothing her dad can do to console her. She looked devastated, like life had just run over her dog. I wanted to ask her if she was okay, but by the time I turned around, the family had disappeared down the tunnel."

Matt's eyes began to glisten with moisture.

Lauren smiled. "Hold on, I'm not done yet. Here's the kicker. When I show up to the station just now, who should I run into?" She paused for effect. "You guessed it! The same family! I mean, what are the odds? And the girl still hasn't stopped sobbing! How is that even possible? It's been over an hour and a half, and she's still crying out there! I don't know how she isn't dehydrated yet!"

Matt's arms burst forward with expression. "Enough!" he screamed gutturally.

Toby thought all the oxygen had been sucked out of the room. He made a mental note to warn any future spouse of Lauren King's about her cross-examining skills. The student had become the master.

"What do you want from me?" Matt said in his best pronunciation. "Either lock me up or let me go. I know my rights."

Toby waved to get Matt's attention. "Are you planning on lawyering up, Bugsy?"

"What...who?" Matt asked.

Toby shook his head. "You're free to go anytime you want. Peter Mason isn't pressing charges against you. You picked a good day to pop his party balloon."

"So I can go then?" Matt asked, putting on his cap.

The detective shook her head. "Not until you sign some release papers and I'm not giving you a pen until you tell us what made you run out onto the field today. "

Matt looked at her. "I thought it would be fun. . . a stupid prank."

"Trying to raise deaf awareness, were you?" Toby spoke and signed.

"It was just a spur of the moment thing," Matt said, belligerently.

The detective crossed her legs. "It sure doesn't look like your girlfriend thinks you did it on a whim."

Matt's head drooped. "Leave Simone and her family out of this. They weren't involved."

Toby scratched at his beard. "Simone...what a beautiful name. Its origin comes from the French. The meaning of Simone is 'to be heard.'"

"How the hell do you know that?" Lauren asked, turning to her mentor.

Toby grinned. "I am a veritable font of obscure trivia, my dear."

"Oh yeah? A font?"

Toby shrugged. "A font; it's the abbreviated form of the word fountain, as in a source from which knowledge springs."

Lauren laughed under her breath. "You're not a font of anything."

Toby quickly conceded the debate. "Okay, I also watch a lot of Jeopardy with the kids. I'll take Etymology for one thousand, Alex."

The detective rolled her eyes and turned her attention back to the other youngster in the room. "Tell us the truth, Matt, and you can walk out of here in five minutes. Simone needs you. This had something to do with your tracing ability, am I right?"

Matt rested his chin in his hands and let out an exasperated sigh. "You swear there's no one out there?"

"I promised you there wasn't," Toby insisted. "You need to start trusting people, Matt. Especially us. We want to help you. Whatever you tell us stays between the three of us."

Matt pouted. "Yes, I admit it. I had another one of my episodes."

Toby leaned forward. "Tell us what happened."

Matt began rubbing his fingers along the brim of his cap as he spoke. His voice had the usual deaf intonation but was still understandable. "I do trust the two of you, but no one else can know what I am about to tell you. They'll lock me up and study me like some newly discovered species. My grandmother tried to have me tested, and I faked every minute of it. I don't want people to think I'm some kind of circus freak. I get enough of that in my daily life without this curse."

"Why do you think you're a freak?" Toby signed.

Matt looked up at the lone light fixture hanging from the ceiling. "I see the way people look at me when I use my hands to talk. If I use my voice, they look at me like I'm retarded."

Lauren reached out and touched his arm. "I'm sure you're just overreacting."

"I don't talk, and I don't sign unless I'm with Simone or my grandfather. It's just easier for me that way."

"Seriously?" Toby signed, unable to hide his irritation. "If you're here looking for a pity party then you've picked the wrong people, kid. Detective King can testify that my son's life is a thousand times more difficult than both yours and ours combined." Toby's bottom lip trembled. "We could all learn an important lesson from my son Benjamin. He lives each day like it's his last because it just might be." Toby fumed. "You just need to suck it up, play the hand you're given, and count your blessings."

The room went quiet except for the hum of the central air conditioning cycling on.

"I'll tell you what really happened," Matt said, suddenly feeling ashamed.

The detective smiled assuringly at the teenager. "You're amongst friends here, Matthew."

Matt took a deep breath to gain his composure. "So we get to our seats, and I ended up having another one of my episodes."

Toby leaned closer to the table. "You need to elaborate. We have no idea how your ability works."

"I don't either," Matt admitted. "So Simone's father comes back to the seats with all the food; drinks, peanuts, and hot dogs. Just about every kind of food they sold there. He must have thought we hadn't eaten in a week."

Lauren nodded.

"He's passing the food down the row," Matt continued, "and he decides he'll be funny, and he tosses me a hot dog instead of handing it to me. It slips out of the wrapper, the bun falls to the ground, and here comes this naked weenie flying in my direction."

Toby looked at Lauren who returned his gaze.

"I don't know when this thing is going to happen," Matt admitted. "I don't have any control over it. I pluck the hot dog out of mid-air and the next thing I know, I'm tracing it. I become completely disoriented. Have you ever seen how a hot dog is made, or ever wondered where the meat comes from? Everything they tell you is a lie. It's disgusting. They're made from ass and cheek meat ground up guts and bone."

Toby and the detective both winced.

Matt drummed his fingers feverishly on the table as he recounted his story. "So, I see all of these disgusting images and the next thing I know, I'm being handcuffed out in centerfield. I have no idea how I got there, and I'm exhausted like I had just run a marathon."

Toby ran his fingers across his lips thoughtfully. "So what you're telling us, is that this ridiculous chain of events was started by you grabbing hold of your weiner?"

Lauren placed her hand over her mouth, but she still thought she peed a little bit.

Matt drew an X over his heart. "Yes…yes, it was."

Toby grabbed a folded detention form out of his jacket pocket and handed Matt a pen. "Sign at the bottom, and I'll fill out the rest of it."

Matt looked back and forth at the two police officers. "So I can go now?"

"Just get out of here and take care of your girlfriend." Toby gestured.

Matt did as he was told and placed the pen on top of his signature. "I'm really sorry for all of the attitude, but I can't let anyone find out about this thing. I just wish I could learn to control it. You don't know how much I appreciate both of you keeping this our little secret."

"We're going to talk again, Mr. Walker." Toby signed. "Count on it."

Matt stood up and looked around the room. "This place is so intimidating. It's a lot scarier than how they portray it on television. Thank you again for letting me go." He said, strolling toward the door.

"Don't thank us," Lauren said. "Thank Peter Mason. He's the one who's letting you off."

A devious grin crossed Matt's lips as he held the door open to leave. "Don't worry about that," he assured them. "I plan on thanking Mr. Mason personally."

Toby and Lauren sat for an extra few minutes before either of them said a word. They knew that Matt might be watching through the glass to see their reactions.

Finally, Lauren King decided enough time had passed. She covered her mouth as she spoke. "What do you think?"

Toby made sure his back was to the window. "I don't believe a single syllable."

40

Matt burst through the glass doors of the police station and out into the crisp evening air. He inhaled deeply; proud that he had kept his secret safe. Matt trusted Detective King and Doctor Bilston and knew they were smart enough to see through his story, but the information traced from the baseball was far too valuable to share. If it was his destiny to bring his parent's killer to justice, then he didn't want the police interfering. More than ever, Matt believed that his curse might actually be a gift. It was reparation bestowed upon him as some sort of karmic tit for tat, and now his part of that deal needed to be fulfilled.

Simone and her father followed close behind knowing that Matt wouldn't be giving them any explanations for his behavior at the game. Simone knew what triggered him, but refrained from saying anything to her family. She understood that when Matt was ready, and they were alone, he would confide in her. At least she hoped he would.

As they walked into the parking lot, Simone's father reached out and tapped Matt on the shoulder and began to sign to him angrily. When he asked Matt how he had been released so fast without any consequences, Matt looked surprised. "You didn't pay my fine?"

Simone's father shook his head. "Not me. It was three thousand dollars. Of course, I would have gladly paid it, but they told me it was already taken care of."

"That's weird. Who would have paid for me?" Matt signed.

"I guess you must have a guardian angel." Simone's father replied, by touching his shoulders and pivoting out his hands to mimic a pair of wings.

Matt leaned against the family van and waited for the doors to unlock. Simone's younger brother Donny was waiting in the car with strict instructions not to open the doors for anyone. Even though Matt tapped on the window and pointed to the lock, the little boy remained resolute and obeyed his father's instructions.

Simone's brother had never been to a police station, much less this close to someone who had actually been arrested. It made the drive back home uncomfortable.

Matt gazed out at the passing traffic on the expressway and contemplated what his next move would be. Every once in awhile, he would look over at Donny, who would be gawking at him as if he expected Matt to do something else nefarious.

The lights of downtown Jacksonville were beginning to blink on, and reflected across the inky blackness of the Saint John's River. Matt watched the northern flowing water shimmer like multicolored diamonds, and wondered who he could confide in besides Simone. Who else did he trust enough to tell about the baseball? Simone would want to know, that was a given. He would confide in her back at the house. Matt wondered how much time the detective and doctor would give him before they came knocking on his door again. Not very much, he presumed.

As the car turned south on Interstate ninety-five, Matt looked to the west. The sky was draped in hot pink gauze, and the sun was a bright orange disk half-submerged over the horizon. The drive seemed endless as the headlights of the oncoming cars came to life. The ballpark was far behind them, like the day's events, solemnly retreating into the darkening sky. He thought of how quiet it must be inside the ballpark now, with only the cleaning crews at work. Should he gamble sneaking back to the ballpark later to see if there was anything else in the locker room he could trace? The more he thought about it, the riskier it seemed. The last thing he wanted was to get arrested again. Doctor Bilston and Detective King would never trust him again.

Matt could feel a sudden rush of adrenaline coursing through his body. He finally had a sense of purpose to his life. The trail of his parents' killer had been revealed. Now it was up to him to follow the breadcrumbs. Matt reached into his jacket pocket and touched the baseball. The sensation it relayed was still there and as vivid as ever. Looking over at Simone's' little brother, the kid was busily thumbing through the team program from this afternoon. Matt felt his back pocket and realized he had probably lost his copy sometime during the chase on the field. He signed to Donny asking if he could borrow the magazine for a minute. Reluctantly, the boy handed it over. Matt thanked him and opened the magazine, but reading the print in the light from passing cars was difficult. He flipped through the pages looking for the team roster. It didn't take him long to find the face that was haunting him. He turned past an advertisement for a local car dealer and there he was, set alphabetically amongst the younger faces on the page, listed as the batting coach. Anthony Magnetti— Matt finally had a name. How ironic that he was the batting coach. Ironic, or calculated? It was the perfect cover to use when traveling from city to city. The killer's picture smiled up at Matt from the wrinkled pages of the Jengu's program. It was a confident smile, a smile Matt planned to erase.

Fifteen minutes later, the van turned a corner and Matt knew that they had reached his street. The trees that lined the block were bathed in the misty glow of the street lights. Simone's father pulled into the driveway and looked in the rearview mirror at Matt. He turned and signed to him. "Do you want me to come in?"

Matt shook his head from side to side as he opened the car door. He walked up to Simone's window and stuck his head inside. Her father continued to sign to him. "I'm not going to tell your grandfather what happened today because the police let you go. You should be honest with him and say something."

Matt leaned past Simone and shook her father's hand. He

didn't sign; he spoke the words "thank you." Tapping Simone on her shoulder, Matt signed to her below the door where her father couldn't see. "Can you come back over tonight?" She didn't want to sign her response, so she just winked at him. "Give me two hours," he continued to sign where only Simone could see. Walking around the front of the car, he waved to the rest of the family through the windshield. Simone wasn't sure of how she was going to get out, but she knew that whatever Matt wanted, it had to be significant.

Walking up the porch steps, Matt waved a last time to Simone and her family. Unlocking the front door, he entered the house to find the living room empty. It was business as usual. His grandfather was probably upstairs asleep with the television on. Matt walked into the kitchen and grabbed a bottle of flavored water from the refrigerator. He looked at the label as he took a long slug from the bottle, wishing he'd had more of those electrolytes when he ran out onto the field.

The clock on the kitchen wall read eight thirty-five. If Simone could slip away from her house, he figured she would probably be back by ten. Tossing the empty bottle into the recycle bin in the corner, Matt was startled when he turned to see his grandfather standing at the kitchen entrance.

"Grandpa, I thought you were sleeping."

"I heard you come it," replied the old man. "I wanted to find out how it went at the ballgame."

"You scared me," Matt admitted. "You need to flicker the light switch to let me know you're there."

His grandfather opened the refrigerator and removed a bottle of apple ale. He never took his eyes off of Matt the entire time. "You seem jumpy. What's the matter?"

"It's been a long day, I'm tired," Matt said. "How was your day?"

The old man pulled a chair away from the kitchen table and straddled it backward. "Interesting."

Matt leaned against the sink. "How so?"

Dave Walker took a long pull from his drink. "Not every day my grandson makes the six o'clock news."

All the color drained out of Matt's face. "It was on the news?"

His grandfather was stone-faced. "Imagine my surprise."

"Grandpa I…"

"Sit down," the old man said calmly, as he slid another chair with his foot in Matt's direction.

"I can explain," Matt admitted, as he sat down.

"I don't need any explanation," his grandfather said. "Besides, you can't explain the unexplainable, am I right?"

Matt nodded.

"Are you alright?"

Matt nodded again. "Yes, grandpa, I'm okay."

There was a long silence before Matt's grandfather spoke. "Do you want to talk about it?"

Matt shook his head. "Probably be better if I didn't. I know your intentions are good, grandpa, but I think this is something I have to figure out for myself."

Dave Walker stared at the half-empty bottle of apple ale. "Would you talk if it was your grandmother sitting here instead of me?"

Matt looked across the table, and for the first time, he saw a desperate sadness in his grandfather's eyes. He reached out and took the old man's hand. Over thirty years of memories and experiences flashed through Matt's head. So much laughter and so many tears, a lifetime of emotions almost too intense for anyone to bare passed in mere seconds. There was the love of a lifetime and her passing, the loss of a son, the burden of all of his choices right or wrong…then emptiness. All that remained was a void as dark as the deepest hole. Dave Walker was lost in the darkness with a climb so severe that it would be insurmountable without someone else's help.

"Don't talk like that, Grandpa. This has nothing to do with missing Grandma. I wish she were here every day, but I'm so glad that you're here for me."

The old man gently removed his hand from Matt's grip.

"I really want to tell you what happened today, but if I involve you, it could get complicated."

"Complicated? How so?"

"Criminally," Matt said, reluctantly.

The old man raised an eyebrow as he leaned forward against the back of his chair. "Like misdemeanor, criminally?"

Matt looked down at the kitchen table uncomfortably. "I'm guessing more of the felony type."

Dave Walker sat silently while his grandson waited for some kind of response. WWBD—what would Barbara do? It was the same question that he found himself asking daily. How would she deal with a mistake on a credit card bill? How would she handle the neighbor who trespassed into their backyard to steal mangoes? "What have you gotten yourself into?" He asked.

"Do you really want to know?" Matt asked.

His grandfather's lips wiggled back and forth as he deliberated. "I think I do."

A small smile creased Matt's face. "What you don't know, you can't be held responsible for," Matt warned.

Dave Walker leaned forward. "I've been an observer in your life for far too long. I think it's time I get involved."

Matt got up and hugged his grandfather so hard, the old man's chair rocked on its front legs. "Thank you, Grandpa," he whispered in the old man's ear, "I could really use your help."

It felt awkward for a second, but Dave Walker found undeniable contentment in wrapping his arms around his grandson's torso. There was a bond that felt so familiar, and one he regretted not realizing until now.

Matt spent the next half hour recounting the day's events. There were times where the old man covered his mouth in shock, but more often than not just listened in disbelief. He knew that his grandson *believed* what he saw, but there was nothing that could stand up in a court of law.

Dealing with the supernatural wasn't new to Dave Walker; his wife Barbara was always reading his mind and finishing his sentences. He chalked it up to being soul-mates, but never questioned if it could be more than that. Was it genetic? Did it skip generations like the twins gene? One thing for sure: Matt was convinced that he had found the fugitive that had escaped justice for over a dozen years. But was this a ride the elder Walker wanted to get on, or should he nip this in the bud before his grandson jeopardized his future? WWBD? The answer came to him in his wife's soft voice whispering prophetically in his ear.

"Let's get the bastard that killed my family," the old man growled. "What do you need from me?"

Matt was taken aback by his grandfather's language. A sense of determination came over the old man like Matt had never witnessed before. "Are you sure, grandpa? A lot of people would think I'm crazy."

His grandfather's eyes narrowed. "Sometimes crazy is good. What do you need?"

Matt patted the back of his grandfather's hand and smiled proudly. There was a renewed sense of determination and zest for life in his grandfather's demeanor. "I think I have a plan."

The old man rubbed his hands together excitedly. "Tell me."

Matt tapped his finger on the table. "The first thing I need you to do for me is to call Hope. I'm not sure she'll talk to me."

"Hope Jannick? Why? Why aren't you dealing with the police?"

Matt stood up and began pacing. "I confided in the two officers that were here the other day because they are working the case from another angle. They told me they were investigating another murder that has a lot in common with the way mom and dad were killed."

"You mean the baseball bat? You've never told anyone about that."

Matt was thinking about his time in the interrogation room. "One of the cops is a forensics expert, and the woman detective is very sharp."

Dave Walker's eyes tracked his grandson as he walked the kitchen floor. "A baseball bat doesn't seem like your everyday choice of weapon."

Matt paused to pick up a dish towel and began to twist it nervously in his hands. "I don't believe that mom and dad were the only people this man has murdered. I could sense that he's not retired from killing either. It's what he does. Baseball is just his cover."

"That's ironic."

"Not ironic, it's ingenious," Matt added. "And like I said, the fact that the last body was found only a few weeks ago leads me to think that he's still killing."

His grandfather looked at him quizzically. "So why Hope Jannick? How long has it been since you've seen or talked to her? I'm not an expert on women, but didn't you dump her when you started seeing Simone? What makes you think that she wants anything to do with you?"

Matt shrugged. "Actually, we parted on pretty good terms. While she had absolutely no problem with my deafness, I think deep down she had decided that we were moving in two different directions. We just grew further apart as we developed our own circle of friends."

Dave Walker took the last swig from his bottle of apple ale. "So, other than complicating your love life, how can Hope help you?"

Matt sat back down at the table and tossed the dishtowel onto the counter. "Her father still works for Mason Cruise Lines, just like dad used to."

"And?"

"And I want her to get me onboard one of their ships."

"Why?"

"Because Saturday night Peter Mason is hosting a celebration to drum up support for his new baseball franchise, and the party is taking place aboard his newest ship, the *Hydra*. I need Hope to get me a job on that ship. I don't care if it's washing dishes or busing tables, I just need to be onboard."

"Again, why?" His grandfather asked.

"The *Hydra* will be buzzing with celebrities and dignitaries, including the players and staff from his baseball team. The man who killed mom and dad will probably be one of the invited guests!"

Dave Walker couldn't hide his concern. "And what are you gonna do if he's on the ship, confront him? Take him down single-handedly? This isn't some action movie, Matthew. Real life doesn't work like that, and the choices we make have consequences. I'd like revenge as much as you would, but I'll be damned if I'm going to risk losing another member of my family to that psychopath."

Matt drew in a deep breath. "I've thought about that, grandpa, but I'm living proof that he makes mistakes."

"No offense, but you'd never hear him coming!" The old man argued.

Matt nodded. "I realize that. That's why I'm bringing Simone with me."

"What?" His grandfather exclaimed. "She can't hear either! She barely reads lips! Why would you involve her in this?"

Matt's attitude never wavered. "I trust her, Grandpa. She'll have my back."

Dave Walker held up his hands in opposition. "That is the worst idea in the history of bad ideas, and there is no way in hell that I'm going to let you drag that beautiful young woman on this cockamamie adventure of yours! Uh-uh," he said, shaking his finger, "that's not going to happen!"

"I haven't even asked her yet."

"Then don't."

Matt sat in silence mulling over his grandfather's concerns. "I'm leaving that decision up to Simone. The police know I lied to them. If they're as smart as I think they are, then they're already piecing together the evidence they've found. I'm the one that can connect the dots for them, but they can't make an arrest based on a vision.

They're going to need hard evidence, and right now my insight has given me the advantage. I need to get onto that ship."

The old man scratched at the stubble on his face. "And you think Hope Jannick will come through for you? Have you even talked to her since you started going out with Simone?"

Matt winced. "No, it's been awhile, but I think she'll help us," he said, trying to sound confident. "I'd be there for her if she ever needed me, and she knows it."

Dave Walker crossed his arms over his chest. "You've got a lot to learn about women, kid."

"Please, grandpa, just call her for me."

The old man leaned forward. "No. You're going to call her. You need to ask her yourself."

Matt put his elbows on the table and rested his head in his hands. "You're right," he admitted. "I need to talk to her."

"And there's no way I can talk you out of this?" His grandfather asked.

Matt didn't answer.

"And you're going to do this no matter what I say, aren't you?"

Matt nodded. "Yes, sir. I am."

Dave Walker frowned in defeat. This was no longer a floundering teenager he was looking at. This was a determined young man. "You are definitely your father's son."

Matt managed a slight smile.

The old man put his pinky to his mouth and his thumb to his ear. "Telephone" was one of the very few words in sign language he had ever bothered to learn. "Here's the deal, take it or leave it."

Matt concentrated on his grandfather's mouth as he spoke. "You're going to Skype Hope Jannick right now. If she can get you onboard lawfully, then I'll let you go. Your grandmother would kill me for doing this, but come first thing Sunday morning, we're skipping church services, and you're going to tell the police everything you know, understood?"

Matt was certain that Hope would come through for him. Well, almost certain. Well, maybe seventy percent. "You've got a deal," he agreed, shaking his grandfather's hand. Seventy percent would have to do for now.

41

It was still early for a weeknight, and the pulsating bass rhythms inside the One Eleven Club hadn't started to pound yet. The dreadlocked D.J. was still unpacking his equipment and checking over his evening's playlist. Across the dance floor, nine bartenders at three separate bars were carefully slicing lemons and other citrus fruits for the mad rush of patrons expected in the next two hours when the club doors finally opened. Everything appeared to be running smoothly at one of the most popular nightspots in downtown Jacksonville. But in the executive office at the rear of the club, it was anything but business as usual.

Jaime Diaz sat in a plush red leather armchair with his legs crossed, sipping a malt whiskey and watching the ESPN app on his phone. The office was quiet except for the sound of running water coming from the bathroom across the room. Nicholas Coltello was always washing his hands, almost to the point of germaphobia. A weird affectation, considering how often they were drenched in other people's blood.

Nicky came out of the bathroom drying his hands on a paper towel. He balled the sheet into a small wad and threw it at the trash can next to his desk. He missed his target by nearly two feet. "Not even close," Diaz commented.

"Must be a draft in here," Coltello countered as he walked around his desk and sat down.

"Must have been a pretty strong draft to miss that badly," Diaz admitted. "Category one hurricane at least."

Coltello leaned back in his chair and began cracking his knuckles one at a time. The sound was annoying, so Diaz turned up his phone's volume to drown it out.

"Anything on the sports channels?" Coltello asked.

Diaz took a sip from his glass. One of the perks of his job was being able to afford the smoothest whiskey. It went down like a royal flush. "It's been mentioned here or there, but I haven't seen any highlights yet. It seems like they're treating it as a non-story."

Nicky paused at his forefinger. "Are you watching national or local?"

"ESPN."

Coltello looked at his watch. "We'll probably have to wait until eleven for local news. Too late for the early news."

Diaz nodded. "You're probably right. Didn't get back in time for the six o'clock sports."

Coltello tapped his fingertips together. "What did you think about today?"

Diaz shrugged. "I don't know. It seemed like a success."

"What about that kid running out onto the field before the game?" Coltello chuckled. "That was hysterical."

"Kid was just being a kid," Diaz mused.

"So you think it was enough to put the deal over the top?"

Diaz turned off the sports app and slipped his phone into his jacket. "I don't know what the Commissioner of Baseball is thinking. The other owners will still have to vote on it anyway."

Coltello shook his head. "We can't let it get that far. There is no way in hell I'll let them break ground on the concrete field. I've lost track of how many we've buried there."

"We?" Diaz asked.

"We!" Coltello corroborated. "If this stadium breaks ground, we're all fucked."

Diaz uncrossed his legs and set his glass down on a nearby table. "We tried to stop it in the city council, and our key vote was killed."

Coltello bristled. "I know that bastard Mason was behind that. If we could prove he had something to do with it..."

"The cops are all over it," Diaz interrupted. "You can't kill a city commissioner and not expect a full investigation. If Mason was behind it, then whoever he hired is a pro. Maybe I can check it out from that angle."

Coltello waggled his finger. "Make some calls. See what you can find out."

Diaz picked a piece of lint off his trouser leg. "I can ask around, but if the cops had any leads, they would have made an arrest already. I can check out a few of my contacts."

"Then we need a plan B," Coltello said, rising to his feet and moving around to the front of his desk. "I want to meet with Mason face to face. Maybe I can use my lavish sense of style and my abundance of panache to make him see the error of his ways."

Diaz winced. "Did you just use the words 'abundance' and 'panache' in the same sentence?"

"I am not an animal!" Coltello declared, mimicking the famous 'Elephant Man' quote.

"Why would Mason take a meeting with you?" Diaz asked, looking up suspiciously at his boss.

"I'm not going to ask for a meeting, Jimmy. I don't ask for meetings. People just see me."

Diaz rolled his eyes. "This is the real world, Nicky. You can't bully your way into Peter Mason's office. You have to be discreet and stay under the radar. There's too much at stake."

Nicky the Knife stood quietly for a moment while he considered his options. "Then I'll have to meet him in public...like a chance meeting that's really not."

Diaz needed another drink...fast. "I don't understand what you're suggesting."

"Simple," Coltello said, leaning on the edge of his desk. "I want you to call Gerald Banks and get us two invitations for Mason's party Saturday night. Tell Banks that this is not a request, but a demand."

"On the *Hydra*?"

Coltello shrugged. "Why not? It's the perfect place! Hundreds of people will be getting snockered. We'll get to mingle with the hoi-polloi! It's as public as you can get. Just get us on that boat, and I'll make sure I get a few minutes of quality time with Peter Mason."

Diaz looked skeptical. "And you think you can change Mason's mind in a few minutes?"

"And you don't?" Coltello smiled, slyly.

Diaz frowned. "I don't know, Nicky. You're gonna have to leave your hammer home."

42

The lights inside the Walker house flashed on and off each time Simone Goodman pressed the front doorbell.

"Are you expecting someone?" Matt's grandfather asked.

Matt stood up from the table and headed out of the kitchen. "I asked Simone to come over. I haven't told her anything yet. She deserves an explanation, and I want to be honest with her."

Dave Walker caught his grandson by the wrist. "It's almost ten o'clock. Do you really want to involve Simone in all this?"

The lights continued to flicker. "Please, grandpa, you've got to trust me on this. Simone understands me better than anyone. I really care about her, and I don't want to keep any secrets."

"But you're still going to call Hope Jannick?" "I'm going upstairs to Skype with her as soon as I let Simone in."

The old man looked confused. "So you're planning on talking to your ex-girlfriend with your new girlfriend sitting in the same room?"

Matt never thought twice about it. "Sure. Why not?"

"You realize that you're making a video call, right? So, you don't care if Hope sees Simone?"

"Hope knows all about Simone," Matt assured his grandfather. "She's fine with it. We've both moved on."

Dave Walker scratched his forehead. "Really? I've never been more confused. Things sure have changed since I was dating your grandmother. She would have kicked my butt."

"I'm sure she would have," Matt concurred, with a sympathetic smile. "But don't worry, Grandpa. I know what I'm doing."

Dave Walker released his grandson's wrist. He could hear Barb's voice whispering to him, telling him to have faith in the boy. "Okay, kiddo. Good luck. Just let me know what Hope says."

Matt sprinted across the living room and opened the front door. "I'm sorry," he signed by circling a fist over his heart. "I was talking to my grandfather. I didn't mean to make you wait so long. Come in," he signed, holding the front door open. As Simone walked past him, Matt swatted away a bunch of pesky gnats that were drawn to the porch light. He took in a deep breath as she entered the house. She smelled great.

Simone had changed her clothes and showered. She was wearing gray sweatpants with the word "juicy" written in large pink letters down her left leg. She wore a light pink V-neck tee shirt that fell comfortably over her curves. Her long black hair, dark eyes, and olive skin accentuated her middle-eastern appearance, even though her genealogy was pure French Canadian.

"Is your grandfather here?" she signed, as she stepped into the living room.

Matt chuckled. "Where else would he be?"

Simone laughed too. "Have you talked to him?"

Matt's hands moved gracefully as he signed. "I told him everything, and now I want to tell you."

Simone tried not to blush, but it didn't work. "I'm glad," she signed back.

"I have to warn you," Matt gestured. "If you don't want to get involved, I would fully understand, but I have to see this thing through. I would just appreciate you keeping what I tell you just between us."

Simon took a step back. "You're scaring me a little."

Matt moved forward and hugged her reassuringly. "I don't mean to," he signed. "It's just that I have to see this thing through, no matter what happens."

"Then tell me everything," Simon signed, never breaking eye

contact with Matt. "Let me decide."

The couple took a seat on the couch and Matt began to reveal his story. He signed steadily, only interrupted once when his grandfather walked into the room, waved to them, and headed up the stairs to his bedroom. Simone sat engrossed by what Matt was telling her. The room was eerily quiet, except for the slapping of hands and the guttural sounds Matt tended to make when he signed. Usually he would speak aloud as he signed, but Simone's hearing was beyond saving, even with the latest cochlear implant technology. She had been tested many times, but was never a candidate for the procedure. The problem was not a hearing loss, but a physical birth defect in both her inner ears.

When he finished, Matt studied Simone's face to see if he could glean her reaction.

"You're positive this is the same man?" she signed.

"Positive." Matt signed confidently.

Simone's mouth wiggled back and forth as she reminded herself that everything she had just been told was based on something unexplainable. "Sneaking back into the locker room would have been really dangerous. I'm glad you changed your mind. To be honest, I'm not sure about the boat part either. Maybe you should just leave this to the police."

"Even if these two policemen believe what I tell them, they can't raid the *Hydra* based on my visions."

Simone couldn't hide her concern. She hated to state the obvious, but maybe it was time for Matt to have a reality check. "And if Magnetti is on the ship, what are you going to do when you find him?"

"I don't know." Matt signed.

Simone frowned. "That's not much of a plan."

"That's all I have for now. I don't even know if Hope can get me onboard."

"You mean us, right?" She said, forcefully emphasizing the word "us."

Matt put his hand on her cheek. "You don't have to come with me. I can do this alone."

Simone looked worried, but she wasn't afraid, knowing that they would be together. "Of course I'm going with you," she signed. "I just have to figure out what I'm going to tell my father."

Matt stood and held out his hand to help Simone up from the couch. "None of this will matter unless Hope can get us on the *Hydra.*"

Simone looked down at the floor. "Do you want me to wait down here while you call her?"

"Of course not," Matt signed, as he lifted her chin to make eye contact. "I want you sitting right next to me."

Simone grinned delightedly and signed, "Cool."

43

"Well, hello stranger," Hope Jannick said from the laptop's monitor. "I thought you had forgotten all about me. It's such a coincidence that you called, I'm going to be in Jacksonville this weekend."

Matt waved into the camera above the screen. "I'm sorry," he apologized. "Everything has been a bit crazy around here since my grandmother passed away."

Hope circled her fist on her chest. She had made an effort to take sign language classes her last two years of high school, but didn't have much use for it lately. "I'm sorry for your loss. How are you and your grandfather holding up?" She spoke slowly, knowing that the video call could get choppy at times, and peppered the occasional sign that she could still remember into the conversation .

"We're doing okay, I guess," Matt said. "It's been tougher on my grandfather. He's really depressed. As much as they nagged and fought, they were still soul mates."

Hope nodded. "How long were they married?"

Matt tilted his head back trying to do the math. "Just about fifty years, I guess."

"Wow," Hope acknowledged. "That's incredible. My folks are going on thirty years, and I thought that was a lot."

"How are your mom and dad?" Matt asked.

Hope shrugged. "Same old, same old. Mom hangs out at the country club, and dad's still a workaholic. I don't see them that often since I moved into the dorms."

Matt studied Hope's face. There had to be Scandinavian in her heritage because of her soft blue eyes and the yellow blond hair she wore in a quickly fashioned bun perched crookedly on the top of her head. "College treating you okay?"

"Ask me what you want to ask me, Matthew."

Matt didn't understand her question. He asked her to repeat herself, slower this time.

"Don't you want to know if I am seeing anyone?" She questioned.

Matt shifted to his left and gently pulled Simone into the frame. It was times like this that he was thankful that Simone wasn't very adept at lip-reading. "You remember Simone, don't you?" He spoke and signed so everyone would understand.

Simone waved at the screen, and Hope half-heartedly waved back. "You guys look so cute together," Hope said, with a soft grin. "That's terrific. I'm so happy for you both."

Matt interpreted for Simone who signed at the screen. "Simone says you look great. College becomes you."

Hope moved her fingers away from her mouth. "Thank you."

Simone waved again and slid back out of the frame.

"She's so cute," Hope said. "I'm really happy for you."

Matt smiled. "Is the University of Miami treating you well? Have you decided on a major yet?"

"It's still a little early to make a final decision, but I'll probably end up in business school and carry on the Jannick tradition. Probably finance or accounting. I don't know."

Matt nodded. "Is there a reason you're living in the dorms? Your parents are still living in Coral Gables, right?"

Hope paused. "I just wanted to get off on my own. I know the University is practically in my backyard, but I just needed to spread my wings. My parents were fine with the idea. I still see them a few times a week."

Matt took a quick glance over at Simone who was preoccupied thumbing through the books in his bookcase. "So have you been seeing anyone?"

Hope looked surprised. "Is Simone still there?"

"Yes, she's still here, but we can speak freely. It's okay. She doesn't read lips that well, and more importantly, she trusts me."

"I'm really happy for you Matthew. I know your life has had so many ups and downs. I wish you only the best, you know that."

Matt nodded.

"I've been focusing on my classes," Hope added. "So I really haven't found the time to socialize. I still hang out with my friends from Gables High. The ones that are still around."

"It seems like you're doing what you want to do. I'm proud of you, and even though we don't talk that much, I just want you to know that if you ever need me, I'll always be there."

Hope nodded. "The same for you, Matthew," she said. "You'll always have a special place in my heart."

"I know," Matt said.

Hope's eyes narrowed. "As much as I like seeing you, I have the feeling that you weren't just calling to catch up."

"I did have a favor to ask of you."

Hope turned away from the screen for a second. "Sorry, my roommate just came in."

Matt saw someone pass behind Hope and then vanish out of the frame. "College life seems so hectic."

"I'm still getting used to sharing a bathroom."

"Priorities," Matt replied.

"That's so true. So, what can I do for you?" Hope asked.

"I know this is going to sound really bizarre, but does your father have any clout with personnel or hiring for the cruise line?"

"Are you looking for a job?"

Matt tipped his head back and forth. "Kind of. More temporary work."

"Such as?"

"I was wondering if your father could get Simone and me a job on the *Hydra* Saturday night. We would do anything, bus tables, wash dishes, whatever..."

Hope looked shocked. "Are you serious?"

"Dead serious," Matt said. "Do you think it's possible?"

"That's so random," Hope confessed. "The reason I'm coming to Jacksonville this weekend is that my father is taking my mom and me on the *Hydra*'s maiden voyage!"

Matt wasn't sure how to react. "Well, this is awkward."

Hope shook her head. "Very awkward. I don't even want to ask him about jobs for you. Having you working on the ship would be too weird."

Matt frowned. "I understand. I just really wanted to be on that trip."

"Is it money? " Hope asked. "If you need some cash, I can help you out."

Matt would never tell Hope about his real intentions. Plausible deniability. The less she knew, the better. "Don't worry about it, Hope. I didn't mean to put you in an embarrassing position."

"So you're sure it's not the money?" she asked.

"Positive. I just thought it would be exciting to be onboard with all the celebrities. This kind of shindig doesn't happen that often in Jacksonville."

Hope smiled. "Well, if you really want to go that badly, then I guess I'll just have to make it happen."

"Excuse me?"

"Matt, if you want to be on the *Hydra*, then you'll be on the *Hydra*. But you sure won't be cleaning dishes."

"What are you saying?"

"What I'm saying is, there is no way my father would let you work on the ship. You're like one of our family. Our fathers were best friends. I'm sure my folks would jump at the chance to see you. Don't worry about a thing. Leave it to me. I'm positive my father can swing two more invitations."

"Are you kidding me?" Matt said excitedly.

"Of course not," Hope confirmed. "It's going to be pretty formal though. I had to buy a new dress. Do you both have something nice to wear?"

"I'll make sure we do," Matt said.

"Then I look forward to seeing you both on Saturday night," Hope added. "I wasn't that excited about going, but now that I'll get to see you in person, it will be like old times. A night to remember."

Matt turned to Simone who was looking through a book on Hurricane Andrew. He gave her a thumbs up, and she smiled back. He returned to the screen and thanked Hope one more time.

"See you Saturday night," she said. "I'll text you the information."

As he said goodbye and signed off the app, Matt's mind was already grinding away. If this power he had been granted was meant to lead him to this exact place and time, then Saturday night would be just as Hope described it…a night to remember.

44

Petty Officer Simms sat in the Forensics Lab outer office with a manila envelope resting on his thighs. He checked his watch to confirm that he was five minutes early. Simms tapped his foot anxiously, wondering what Dr. Bilston and Detective King had uncovered over the last week. He hoped that the evidence he'd brought would confirm their conclusions and not prove worthless.

The door opened again, and Detective Lauren King confidently entered the outer office. She was wearing a pair of white New Balance running shoes, blue jeans, and a plain white collared shirt. Her navy blue jacket was unbuttoned and exposed the handgun and badge clipped to her belt. "Petty Officer Simms, so glad to see you again," she said holding out her hand. "You're right on time."

Simms placed the folder under his arm and stood, chivalrously taking her hand. "Punctuality is next to honor," he said.

"Really?" She asked. "I thought it might be next to 'punctuate' or maybe 'punctuation.'"

"Funny and beautiful." Simms complimented her.

Lauren waved her hand in front of her face. "Why Petty Office Simms, I do believe you are giving me the vapors," she feigned, in her best southern accent.

"Why don't you two get a room?" Toby asked, standing in the doorway to his office. "Wow Detective, I don't know if I've ever seen you blush!"

Lauren King cleared her throat. "The Petty Officer and I were just..."

"I don't care," Toby interrupted. "Nice to see you again, Petty Officer."

Simms shook Toby's hand. "Same here," he said. "I sure hope we can help each other."

Toby held open the door to his office. "Come in and let's talk."

The doctor walked behind his desk and pointed at two leather chairs for his colleagues to take a seat. "I've got to say, Officer Simms, I'm really amazed at the job the government is doing keeping this entire incident quiet. I haven't heard anything, and it's been over a week."

Simms waited for Lauren to sit and then took the seat next to her. "I don't even think the families have been notified yet," he admitted. "The last thing they want is to have it known that a piece of secret tech has been stolen. They're probably working on a cover story as we speak."

"Understandable," Lauren interjected, "but I feel for the families of the crew. I'm sure they think their loved ones are still alive. They can't be left in the dark too much longer."

"And that's when all hell will break loose," Toby added. "We need to do our part to get answers for those families."

Simms shifted uncomfortably in his chair. "The military has its priorities. The danger of this technology falling into the wrong hands far outweighs any loss of life, as insensitive as that may sound."

Toby shook his head sadly. "You're not insensitive, Petty Officer. You're pragmatic and honest."

"Thank you for your understanding," Simms acknowledged, "but please, call me Scott."

"Are you sure?" Toby asked. "You've earned that recognition."

"I appreciate that, but I prefer Scott whenever possible."

Toby looked to Lauren who concurred. "Scott it is, then. So what do you have for us?"

"Oh, you want me to go first?" Simms asked.

"First?" Toby wondered aloud. "I'm a bit confused. We're not at liberty to discuss information about an ongoing investigation with you. We'll be more than happy to listen to whatever you have to tell us, but unless the circumstances should drastically change, we have to treat the military probes and ours as two independent investigations."

Simms slipped the manila envelope between his leg and the arm of the chair. "Oh, I'm sorry for the misunderstanding. I thought we were kind of working quid pro quo."

Toby smiled and waved his hands. "Hell, I'm just messing with you, Scott. I'm just trying to lighten the mood now that we're on a first name basis. Of course we're sharing information."

Lauren couldn't hide her disapproval. Toby had conned her too. "You're a horse's ass, Toby. Why do you screw with people like that?"

The doctor shrugged. "I don't smoke. I don't take drugs. Except for the occasional beer, being a horse's ass is my only vice."

Lauren put her hand on Simm's shoulder. "I apologize for the doctor's warped sense of humor. It's an acquired taste."

"For the most sophisticated palate," Toby added, wiggling his eyebrows.

Simms was accustomed to the Coast Guard's strict adherence to protocol and decorum. This casual banter would take some getting used to. "No problem, Detective," he said, "I'm in the military. I'm used to inedible chow."

"Direct hit," Toby exclaimed, leaning back in his chair, and holding his hand over his heart. "Well played, Scott."

Lauren rolled her eyes. "Can we please get serious here? It looks like Scott has brought something to show us."

Toby leaned forward as Simms opened the envelope. "I have satellite images of the night that the Truman sank."

Lauren stood up for a better view as Simms spread out the handful of images on Toby's desk.

"I was told that the satellites were shut down during the mission," Toby said.

Simms nodded. "All the military and recon satellites were, but not the NOAA weather birds. This is hurricane season, don't forget."

"How did you get your hands on NOAA Intel?" Toby asked.

"It's not what you know..." Simms said.

Toby looked up at Lauren and smiled. "I like this guy."

Lauren looked puzzled. "What are you two looking at? I don't see anything but a bunch of random cloud formations."

The lines of latitude and longitude were superimposed onto the images. Toby ran his fingers down one of the latitude lines. "Where are we supposed to be looking?" He asked.

"The last coordinates were approximately twenty-nine degrees north and seventy-six degrees west."

"That's nearly sixty square miles of surface area."

Simms nodded. "Correct. That's the scale of each of these images."

Lauren leaned closer. "I still don't understand why we're staring at a bunch of clouds."

Simms flipped through the pictures until he got to one near the bottom of the stack. "While it's true that we can't see the Truman—or any ship, for that matter—using a weather satellite, we *can* make out all forms of water vapor."

Lauren turned her head toward the Petty Officer. "And being able to see all these clouds tells us what?"

Simms laid out four pictures that were in chronological order taken five minutes apart, and computer-enhanced for clarity. "Notice this triangular-shaped anomaly right here?" he said, pointing to a specific spot on the first picture. "I had my contact at NOAA run a combination of Doppler and infrared scans on these last few images. I had him zoom in on the last coordinates we had on the Truman. The Doppler radar enhances the pictures with shades of color that run from green, which tells us there is very little water vapor, to deep shades of red, where the air is very moist and dense. The infrared is used to measure cloud height using temperature. My guy says that this concentrated triangular cloud formation, which wasn't visible in the previous images, extends from sea level upward to nearly one hundred meters. That's far too low for ordinary atmospheric conditions."

"Like a heavy fog." Toby surmised.

Simms tapped his finger on the cloud. "That's what I thought too, but when they ran the density analysis on it, it showed that this formation was relatively heavy, meaning it was made up of more than just water vapor. This cloud is not something that naturally develops in our atmosphere."

"Not fog?" Lauren asked.

Simms shook his head. "My man at NOAA says it has to be man-made; he has no explanation for it otherwise. And look at this picture here," he added, pointing at the last image. "This is about twenty minutes later."

"It's practically gone," Lauren said.

"Evaporated." Toby corrected her.

Simms waggled his finger. "Not evaporated," he revealed. "Settled more likely. NOAA seems to think this is some kind of gas mixture that eventually sank to the surface and dissolved in the ocean. If we had a way to view any phosphorescence in the water, NOAA believes we would have found a lime-colored stain over this same area. Unfortunately, the satellite can't show that."

Toby rubbed his beard. "Nice work, Petty...I mean, Scott. Can I assume your friend at NOAA will keep a lid on this?"

Simms stood up. "We're old mates. I bought him a six-pack and we called it even."

"My kind of guy," Toby grinned.

But Simms still wasn't satisfied. "If this cloud mass or fog or whatever it is is a synthetic toxin, I still can't figure out the delivery system for a spread like this."

"There had to be another ship out there," Toby concluded. "Just look at the differences between these first two pictures. It looks like the cloud is emanating from a specific point and spreading outward. That's why we get this widening v-shape dispersion."

Lauren took one of the pictures and held it up close. "So if there is another ship out here, then it's located right where this cloud fans out from."

Toby and Lauren looked up at each other in unison. "Fans!" they both blurted out. It was as if they were suddenly sharing one brain. "It would have to be a ship that could approach quickly and quietly, with a huge set of fans capable of releasing a debilitating payload and then dissipating it just as fast." Toby acknowledged.

"That would incapacitate everyone on the Truman," Lauren added.

Simms rapped his knuckles on the desk. "Not everyone. Not if you were prepared with the proper gas mask!"

Toby sat down in his chair and leaned back deep in thought. Lauren and the Petty Officer stared at him as if waiting for advice from Buddha himself. "Does your wardrobe consist of more than just uniforms?" He asked Simms.

"I only have my service uniforms and my dress whites," Simms replied.

Toby intertwined his fingers and rested his hands on his portly abdomen. "I'm gonna need you to go out and buy yourself a nice suit and all the trimmings by Saturday night. I don't want you dressed in your livery. We need to blend in. I'll clear your leave with Admiral Baer. Just bring me the receipt, and I'll get my department to pay for it. Just keep it reasonable."

Toby then turned his attention to Lauren. "And I want you to look especially gorgeous, doll face. I know you've got something fancy to wear, but make sure it's accommodating enough that it allows you to be fully-equipped should the occasion arise."

Lauren nodded her understanding.

"What is this all about?" Simms asked. "Why are we getting dressed up? Where are we going?"

Toby loosened the knot in his tie and tried to sound sincere. "Have you ever schmoozed with the rich and famous, Scott? They're a hoot."

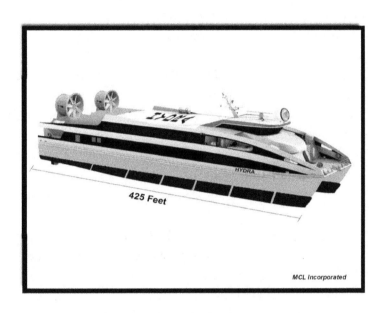

425 Feet

HYDRA

MCL Incorporated

THE HYDRA

THE ULTIMATE IN SPEED...
THE ULTIMATE IN COMFORT.*

* Model rendered prior to the addition of the glass Oceanwalk

Hydra noun

Hy·dra | \ ˈhī-drə \

Definition of *hydra*

Noun, plural hydras, hydrae

1   : Classical Mythology. A water serpent with nine heads, each of which, if cut off, grew back as two.

2   : A persistent or many-sided problem that presents new obstacles as soon as one aspect is solved.

45

Jaxport Cruise Terminal
Saturday, 3:00 P.M.

A sleek white cruise ship named *The Spirit of the Seas* pulled away from its berth at the lone passenger terminal along the banks of the Saint John's River. The vessel would traverse the river for nearly twenty miles before reaching the Atlantic Ocean. From there, it was seven relaxing days of fun and sun in the Western Caribbean for its nearly three thousand passengers and crew.

Passengers stood at the railing waving down to dockworkers and anyone else that would return the gesture. Times had certainly changed. Gone were the days of friends and families being able to cheer "bon voyage" from the pier. Security on the water was nearly as tight as it was in the air. Nowadays, if you were fortunate enough, you got a kiss and a hug in front of the terminal with the Port Authority Police urging you to move on. There was no animus intended, they were just doing their job, keeping the unloading process to a minimum and the traffic moving efficiently. Weekdays, the terminal was like a ghost town; but on Fridays and Saturdays, when the majority of ships usually arrived and departed, the scene was a madhouse.

Once the *Spirit of the Seas* cleared its berth, the entire peninsula of the seaport became visible to its passengers. Many of them who cruised often were used to seeing an empty plot of land to the Northeast of the terminal, but now something was different. Many of the passengers began walking toward the stern of the ship to get a better view of the unusual structure that now occupied that undeveloped acreage.

It was greater in size than a football field, resembling an arch-roofed Quonset hut, but it looked temporary, not built from corrugated metal. The skin was some type of synthetic fabric, white in color, stretched over an enormous frame. The edifice was windowless and bore no logo or other identifiable markings. It appeared to be protecting something inside from the elements—or perhaps from prying eyes.

There was plenty of activity surrounding the structure, with hard-hatted workers and executive types milling about the area. Four massive cranes supported taut cables that pierced the roof of the structure. Whatever the building housed was an enigma. Passengers aboard the *Spirit of the Seas* pointed at it and speculated about the building's contents. It wasn't tall enough to accommodate a commercial cruise ship, but the travelers agreed that it was far too large for any private vessel they had ever seen. No one seemed aware of or made the connection to the hangar's remarkable tenant.

As the distance from shore increased, the terminal and the unique structure became nothing more than unintelligible details on the horizon. The passengers quickly turned their attention elsewhere and began preparing for their mandatory muster station safety drill.

***

Peter Mason was livid as he stomped his foot down onto the newly installed glass Oceanwalk. "This panel feels loose, and there are less than four hours until we get underway! What are we going to do about this?"

Kaci Lynch had out her notepad and added it to the list of her bosses' concerns. "The installation crew from Doosan are already on a flight back to South Korea, but I can assure you that every bolt and seam were x-rayed and approved by the state inspectors."

"Then why does this feel unstable to me? Even with the fanbines at half thrust, these four inches of glass are the only thing that separates our passengers from the boiling water seventy feet beneath them."

Lynch knelt down and ran her fingers along the seams in question. "There has to be a bit of elasticity for expansion and contraction of the joints. This walkway isn't one solid piece of glass, Mr. Mason. It's made up of over twenty separate panels that were built to flex with the stress that a moving ship can produce." The head engineer stood up and paced slowly along the walkway, some sixty feet off the ground. "Nothing like this has ever been attempted on a sea-going vessel before. The Skywalk overlooking the Grand Canyon is a stationary structure built to handle its own set of issues, such as extreme wind gusts rising up the wall of the Canyon, but this walkway must deal with many more variables. She's been tested, inspected, poked and prodded, but if it convinces you more, I'm telling you unequivocally that I wouldn't hesitate to let my children walk on it. I trust it that much."

Mason leaned against the stainless steel handrail that ran along the inside of the glass tunnel. "Well then, why don't we put your money where your mouth is?" he said, bluntly.

"Excuse me?" Lynch questioned.

"Bring your entire family tonight," Mason said, making it sound almost like an order. "Consider this a special invitation. We'll let your kids be the first to experience the Oceanwalk at sea! Who knows, they might even make the front page of the newspaper!"

The pen fell out of Lynch's hand and clattered to rest on the transparent deck. "Are you serious?"

"Like a heart attack," Mason responded. "The press will eat it up."

46

Gerald Banks stared up at the bow of the *Hydra*. The ship was a marvel of marine engineering, suspended ten feet above the ground by four thick cables. Once her fourteen lift pods were inflated, and the fanbines beneath the *Hydra* spun to life, she would support herself on a ten-foot cushion of air, no longer needing the assistance of the cranes.

A temporary ramp had been installed on the port side of the ship so that crates of food and supplies could be loaded by forklift into the *Hydra*'s hold. On her trial runs, the *Hydra* had run lean, but tonight she would be decked out in all her glory, a shining accomplishment for all other cruise lines to envy. Once the *Hydra* was authorized for her bi-weekly cruises, the ship would only be hoisted into dry dock for routine inspections and maintenance. This was the only way the fanbine technology beneath the hull could be accessed safely.

There were no more sounds of drills and hammers grinding and banging on metal. The time for that had long passed. This ship was a white-plated beast, mean, sleek, and just begging to be freed. The crew was in the last-minute processes of feeding her belly, and soon her shackles would be released. With her crisp angles and bright trim, she looked like she should pounce into the channel rather than float majestically out on a cushion of hot air.

Banks strolled to the right side of the ship and looked up to see his brother-in-law in what seemed like a serious discussion with the Head of Engineering. They were on the Oceanwalk, which from below was an eerie sight to behold. They were standing outside of the ship suspended in midair, the bottoms of their shoes clearly visible. What a coup this would be for the company.

Mason didn't look pleased. Backs waved to get their attention for nearly a minute before he was noticed. Bank's phone rang immediately.

"Everything okay?" Banks asked.

"Meet me in the Siren's Lounge," Mason insisted. "It's quiet there, we can talk in private."

Banks signaled his acknowledgment and headed for the loading ramp. Five minutes later, he was sitting in a secluded booth in the back of the Siren's Lounge. Across the room, there was a small well-lit stage filled with musical instruments and a video screen for karaoke. Five booths lined each wall and fifteen tables dotted the lounge. One long bar with an aquarium base filled the remaining wall space. A variety of colorful saltwater fish swam lazily amongst the coral and marine plant life. The shelves behind the bar were being stocked by three bartenders with domestic and exotic liquors, while two more stood in front of the bar, cutting various citrus fruit into slices for the garnishes.

Peter Mason entered the lounge at a brisk pace and slid into the booth. "Tell me about Sowell." He said, under his breath.

Banks could plainly tell the crew was out of earshot, but he kept his voice down anyway. "He's been on the bridge for three hours already. We made him up to match the picture on his credentials, and he's already settling into the Captain's chair."

"And our imposter?"

"You mean my Uncle Morty?"

"Uncle Morty? You mean, Morty Poe?"

Banks nodded. "You wanted someone who looked like an experienced sea captain. The first person that came to mind was Morty. You've got to admit he fits the part. He's got the white beard and broad shoulders. He's perfect."

Mason took a paper cocktail napkin off the table and wiped his forehead. He was quiet for what seemed like minutes. "Morty Poe used to smuggle bales of weed with my father."

"Exactly! He knows the ocean, and he knows boats," Banks argued.

Mason tapped his finger angrily on the table. "Not this boat, he doesn't!"

Banks leaned back and spread his arms along the back of the booth. "He 's the spitting image of Captain John Smith. We always said that."

Mason crumpled up the napkin and tossed it in Bank's direction. "John Smith sailed the Titanic into a fucking iceberg, Gerry!"

Banks held up his hands. "You need to take a breath. I told you I would handle this. I sent Morty the manuals two weeks ago. He'll be able to bullshit his way through any questions the guests throw at him. I've quizzed him personally. When you introduce him to the crowd, he'll charm them like a cobra."

"I swear to God, Gerald. He can't screw this up."

"Relax Pete. He's making more tonight then he would in a year tending bar at the Paradise Shack in the Keys. All of his credentials are impeccable. Tonight he's Captain Oskar Karlsson by way of Oslo. No one will suspect a thing. You need to take a deep breath, or you'll give yourself a stroke before the most important night of your life!"

Mason checked his watch nervously. "I don't have to remind you of what a fiasco the ballgame turned out to be. The media was vicious."

"So you'll change the team's goddamned name," Banks suggested.

"You can't just *change* the name," Mason said, indignantly. "You have to get the approval from the Commissioner of Baseball and all the other owners. You have to do a trademark search and file copyrights. Not to mention all the money we've already spent on branding and merchandising."

"Perhaps more should have been spent on researching the name," Banks muttered.

"What's that?" Mason asked.

"I was just saying that the name was a bit obscure for a sport's franchise. Maybe if you had asked a few more people for their input..."

"What's done is done," Mason said curtly, avoiding any personal responsibility. "If tonight's trip doesn't go as planned, the franchise, our fleet—our company—could hit a reef and never right itself."

"Once a pirate..." Banks chuckled.

Mason stood up and leaned over the table. His eyes burned with intensity. "The company needs this influx of cash to survive, Gerald. You need to make sure everything goes on schedule while I'm wining and dining the crowd."

Banks' eyes darted around the lounge and then met Mason's stare confidently. "Sowell can handle this. Uncle Morty can handle this. I can handle this."

Mason stood erect, unaware that his hands had clenched into fists. "We only have one shot at this tonight. If it all goes tits up, we're all going down."

Gerald Banks watched his brother-in-law turn to leave the lounge. He couldn't let him walk away without getting in the last word. "I told you, Pete," he called out. "Everything is copacetic. Tonight you're going to get everything you deserve!"

47

The sun had just set over the city of Jacksonville, and the sky was evolving from vivid shades of pink and orange into the intrusive darkness of night. In the distance, the city skyline was blinking to life. It was a moonless night, as expected, and both the Saint John's River and the Atlantic Ocean were working in partnership by remaining calm and smooth. The wind was light out of the south, and the course was plotted and locked in. This was the *Hydra's* moment, and she was purring as softly as a newborn kitten.

The white material that covered the structure had purposely been backlit by half a dozen portable stanchions of high-powered floodlights that created a silhouette of the ship visible to the arriving invitees. As expensive cars and limousines were directed to park in the adjacent lot, a line of celebrity passengers and dignitaries were already walking the red carpet that had been rolled out along the pier.

Three hundred invited guests, a third of the ship's actual capacity, were captivated by the sleek shape and enormity of the giant shadow only a few hundred yards away. There was something about seeing the dark form of a ship on dry land that made everything seem surreal.

As the guests mingled excitedly on the pier, the local—and a few of the national—cable news networks were conducting interviews and photographing the event. While there was almost no sound emanating from the vessel, everyone could feel the reverberation of the ground beneath their feet. This is what made the *Hydra* different from her predecessors: her technology was so refined that she operated with virtually no sound, except for whatever was created by the three lounge bands and the excitement of happy passengers.

Toby Bilston, Lauren King, and Petty Officer Scott Simms did not arrive in a limousine. Instead, they pulled into the parking lot in a JPD patrol car driven by a uniformed sergeant who shook his head in disbelief at the craziness of the event. The detective and seaman were in the backseat, while the doctor rode shotgun. Not out of choice, but out of necessity. Toby could barely function in a dress suit that felt four sizes too small. In the back of his head, he kept thinking of the late comedian Chris Farley singing "Fat man in a little coat."

"Do you want me to actually park?" The sergeant asked.

Toby loosened the knot in the tie that Harriett had picked out for him. It had been less than an hour, and it already felt like he was being choked by a python. "Just leave us off over there," he said, pointing to an isolated area away from the rest of the cars. "We don't want to be seen stepping out of a cruiser. Just let us out here and go. No lights, no siren…nothing that would draw attention."

"Got it," the sergeant said, braking where he had been told. "Looks like a tough assignment for the three of you. How'd you swing a free cruise?"

Toby opened his door and struggled to lift himself out of the vehicle; the night air was so moist that he double checked behind his ear to make sure his seasickness patch hadn't slipped down his neck. "It's a dirty job, but someone's gotta do it, sergeant," he quipped. "Thanks for the ride."

Simms opened his door and rushed around the rear of the cruiser to assist Lauren out of her door. She looked elegant in a long silver gown that discreetly covered the handgun strapped to her inner thigh. A slit up the side of the dress gave her the mobility she hoped she wouldn't need.

Simms had shopped well. The dark suit he wore made him look inconspicuous enough to blend in with the crowd of high society, but handsome enough to make Lauren glad to be on his arm. Not a bad deal for less than his two hundred dollar budget.

The unlikely trio began walking toward the rear of the gathering throng of guests. Every few feet Toby needed to blot his forehead with his handkerchief. If he didn't get into the air-conditioning soon, he swore he'd be able to swim aboard. They had walked halfway across the parking lot when Toby's phone suddenly vibrated in his pocket. When he checked the number, he immediately recognized that the call was coming from a burner phone.

"Everything okay, Toby?" Lauren asked.

Toby motioned with his hand. "You two go ahead and get in line. I'll catch up with you."

"Are you sure?" Simms asked.

"Yeah, just got to take this call. Don't want to be talking police business in the crowd. Go ahead. I'll be right there."

Now that Toby was alone, he flipped open the phone but said nothing.

"Is this Doctor Toby Bilston?" asked the deep male voice.

"Who is this?"

"Not important."

"How did you get my private number?"

"Also not important."

Toby looked at the phone angrily. "Well, something better be important, pal, because I'm melting like a sweat-scented candle here, and I'm about to hang up."

"I've seen that you're a compassionate man," the caller stated.

Toby shook his head in frustration. "But one who is growing less sympathetic the more you talk in circles. I really need to know who you are and how you got access to this number."

Even though there was a gentle breeze blowing in off the river, perspiration was running down Toby's scalp in rivulets.

"You're probably going to need more than one hanky," the voice revealed.

Toby instantaneously spun around and scanned the parking lot and the crowd gathering on the pier. "Where are you?"

"Don't waste your time. You look like you don't have much energy to spare. I want you to listen to what I have to say."

"Who the fuck is this?" Toby demanded to know.

"We'll meet soon enough, Doctor, but for now, just pay attention."

"Fuck you. I'm hanging up."

"No, you won't."

"Watch me," Toby snarled, and snapped his phone shut.

Limousines were backed up bumper to bumper to Toby's left. In the distance, he thought he could just make out the sounds of music coming from the direction of the hangar, but the melody wasn't anything he recognized. The chances of a band playing a song that Toby actually knew were astronomical. He was slipping the phone back into his pocket when it vibrated again. Same number.

Toby stared at the phone as it continued to ring. He knew that call would go to voicemail, so he waited. A few seconds later, the phone began to vibrate again. "Stubborn son of a bitch," Toby muttered.

"I'm not playing games with you. I have a boat to catch." Toby fumed into the phone.

"This is no game, Doctor," the voice insisted. "Your reputation for deciphering the tiniest piece of evidence is well documented, but tonight you're absolutely out of your element. You and your colleagues have no clue of what you've stumbled onto, or what's at stake."

"Oh yeah? Then why don't you enlighten me?" Toby acquiesced. "You've got two minutes."

The caller never wavered. "I'll need ten, but I promise it will only seem like two."

48

Lauren King and Scott Simms were standing toward the back of the crowd when they were approached by a local newscaster and her cameraman. When the bright light above the camera hit their faces, and the newscaster didn't recognize them, she immediately ran her finger across her throat and ordered the cameraman to kill the light. Without the hint of an apology, the newscaster pushed her way further into the crowd.

"It sucks not being famous," Simms admitted.

The detective nodded. "Personally, I'm glad she took off. If the guys in my squad saw me dressed like this, I'd never heard the end of it."

A helicopter floated overhead, shining its searchlight on the river to keep the channel clear of curious pleasure boats.

"This is some big to-do for the launching of a ship," Simms commented loudly, to be heard over the noise of the helicopter blades.

"Supposedly, it's not just any ship," the detective admitted. "It's said to be the first of its kind."

Simms smiled politely, as he held up his finger. "First of all, 'it' is a 'she.' Don't ask me why, but even ships named after famous men are always referred to as 'she.'"

Lauren nodded. "Because they're a thing of beauty," she shouted.

"You could be right. I've never thought about it much."

"And second?" The detective asked.

Simms held up two fingers. "Secondly, hydrofoil technology has been around for years, so this concept of a vessel that travels above the water is nothing new. While I'll admit that there was never one built on this scale, smaller versions have been in use as ferries at various ports around the world. They're sometimes referred to as 'puddle jumpers' because they're used exclusively for short commutes."

Lauren put her hand on the Petty Officer's shoulder. "Wow! Intelligent and good looking! How lucky am I?"

The harsh bright lights seemed to amplify the P.O.'s blushing cheeks. "I wonder what's keeping the Doctor?" He said, checking his watch.

Suddenly, all of the lights in the parking lot and surrounding vicinity blinked off, leaving the crowd in near-total darkness. The only illumination came from the enormous white structure in the distance and a few headlights from late arrivals still hunting down a parking space.

It was precisely eight o'clock, and the front side of the hangar facing the river fell noiselessly to the ground like a silken bedsheet. At least a dozen workers scrambled to remove the pile of material, much like the grounds crew would do at a ballpark if it started raining.

The light from the police helicopter changed its focus to the sleek twin bows of the massive catamaran that was emerging like a butterfly from its cocoon. Standing alone at the front railing, a dwarfed Peter Mason waved to the admiring crowd. The *Hydra* glided slowly out of her hangar on a cushion of air. It was like witnessing the birth of something never seen before.

As the bridge of the ship revealed herself to the crowd, Mason turned and pointed up toward the single spotlight mounted high above the control room. The light flashed on with an intensity that seemed to raise the ambient temperature of the entire vicinity. The invited dignitaries and celebrities all cheered as the *Hydra* introduced herself by floating majestically across fifty yards of pavement and out over the river. Once in her natural habitat, she turned gracefully to port by pivoting one of the two fans on her aft section, and sidled up to the pier where a portable gangway was waiting to be attached to grant the passengers access.

Petty Officer Simms didn't realize it, but his mouth was hanging open. He had done his research on her, but to see the *Hydra* close up, he was genuinely in awe of how colossal she actually was! To get a ship of this size to ride ten feet above the surface of the water was nothing short of an act of God. The fans below her hull had to be whipping the water into a boiling froth. Just how much lift those blades were supplying to raise such a vast ship out of the water had to be mind-boggling. The *Hydra* was easily twice the size of any Coast Guard cutter he had ever served on, but the one feature that struck him the most was how quiet she actually ran. The casual observer wouldn't pay much attention to it, but his trained ears could drown out the cacophony of the crowd, and he was amazed at the silence. No vessel on the open ocean would ever hear her coming.

Simms looked over at the detective who was equally speechless. "This might be the most amazing feat of marine engineering I've ever witnessed," he announced. "Anyone can turn a skyscraper on its side and make it float, but Peter Mason has made one fly!"

"Incredible," was all Lauren King could utter.

As if awakening from a dream, Simms shook his head trying his best to focus on the real reason they were here, but the miracle of personally witnessing something he never thought possible was making it difficult for him to concentrate.

"How much do you think she cost?" Lauren asked.

"Who cares?" Simms replied. "She's worth every penny."

As the gangway was brought into position, the fourteen pontoons supporting the *Hydra*'s twin hulls began to deflate, lowering the ship in the water for easier boarding. The media would compare the unique sight to the landing of a UFO.

The terminal lights blinked back to life as Simms and King were jockeying for position in the sprawling crowd. Without warning, they both felt a hand on their shoulder. The detective was the first to react, instinctively grabbing the wrist and spinning around to confront the perpetrator. "Toby!" she yelled, "Don't ever sneak up on me like that!"

The doctor pulled his hand free and began rubbing his wrist. "Duly noted!"

"Are you alright?" Simms asked. "You look ashen."

Lauren nodded. "He's right, Toby. You look really pale, and I don't think it's because of the lighting. Are you feeling okay?"

"I'm sorry, but I need to leave."

Lauren placed her hand on the doctor's cheek. His face was clammy, but that wasn't necessarily abnormal. "Do you need to sit down?"

"I feel fine, but I can't stay. You'll have to board without me."

"Is anything wrong?" Lauren persisted. "Is it Benjamin? Has something happened to Benjamin?"

Toby shook his head to the contrary. "Ben is fine. This isn't a family emergency. Something has come up, and they need me back at my lab. They're sending another car."

Lauren put her hands on her hips defiantly. "We're not getting on that ship without you. That's not we discussed."

Bilston rubbed his handkerchief across his salt and peppered beard. The linen cloth was already saturated and did little to stop the torrent of moisture. "You two need to do your jobs and stop whining."

"I'm not whining," the detective protested.

"You're whining." Toby scolded her. "You both need to be aboard that boat. "

"Ship." Simms corrected him.

"Whatever," Toby glared at him. "You know your way around a *ship* better than Detective King does. Use the commotion as a distraction. See if you can find anything that would confirm your theory."

"I don't like this at all, Toby. There's something you're not telling us. " Lauren complained.

The doctor turned toward her. "What? Suddenly you can't handle undercover work?"

"I never said that."

"Look, Lauren, you need to see if you can charm your way into talking to Mason or one of his cronies and try to broach the topic of Commissioner Beckworth's death."

She looked skeptical. "Something like that doesn't just come up in casual conversation."

Toby smiled at her in that fatherly way that made her feel safe. "Just do what you do best, but you need to stay sharp because I've just noticed that there's been an extra wild card thrown into the deck."

The Petty Officer leaned in. "What kind of wild card?"

"Look over your shoulder at two o'clock. Wearing the blue sports coat and escorting the young woman in the white dress. "

Simms scanned the crowd that was still milling about patiently waiting for the gangway to be secured. "They're practically all wearing white dresses!" He complained.

Toby jabbed out his chin. "Standing beneath the light pole, signing to each other."

"Matthew Walker is here," Lauren said. "I'll be damned."

"Who's Matthew Walker?" Simms asked.

The pieces were falling into place. This was an omen that they were on the right track. Lauren smiled at Toby who nodded his head. Each could tell what the other was thinking. Using his extraordinary ability, Matthew Walker *had* learned something at the ballgame. Something important enough to compel him to be here.

"Are you sure you want to leave?" Lauren asked.

"Stay on him, but maintain your distance. Keep him safe."

Petty Officer Simms waved his hand between the two co-workers who seemed joined at the brain. "Would one of you please tell me who this Matthew Walker is?"

A car pulled into the parking lot and flashed its headlights. "That's my ride," Toby said, as he turned to leave.

"Who is Matthew Walker?" Simms called after him.

Lauren King slid her arm formally through the Petty Officer's arm. As the couple strolled past a gaggle of clicking cameras, she began swaying her hips in a manner that was entirely foreign to her. "Matthew Walker is not a wild card," she whispered into Simm's ear, looking seductive for the paparazzi. "He's the ace up our sleeve."

49

As the gala crowd began to stroll up the gangway, one limousine in particular remained occupied in the parking lot with its engine running. Nick Coltello and Jimmy Diaz sat across from one another sipping bourbon while they waited for the mob to thin out.

"You feel okay, Nicky?" Diaz asked.

"Sure," Coltello assured his most trusted confidant. "Don't I look alright?"

Diaz peered out the side window at the ship that seemed to block out the entire horizon. "Well, the doctor upped your dosages and added that new anxiety drug to your daily regiment; I just want to make sure you're not feeling any weird side effects. Sometimes when you introduce something new into your system, you can be a little off your game."

Nicky the Knife held up his glass. "It's nice to know you're looking out for me. I'm sure the instructions on most of those drugs suggest you take them with generous amounts of alcohol."

Diaz placed his glass into the holder built into the black leather armrest. "Point well taken."

Perhaps it was the interaction of the new drugs and bourbon, but Nicholas Coltello suddenly felt introspective. "I think I might have a problem with my temper," he said thoughtfully.

"Excuse me? Did you say something?" Diaz asked.

Nicky's head tipped back, and he stared up at the oval-shaped overhead lamp fixture. "Why an oval and not a circle or a square?" He wondered aloud.

Diaz leaned forward and placed his hand on his bosses' knee.

"Are you sure you're up to this tonight, Nicky? Maybe we should go back to the club."

Coltello's head snapped back into the upright position. "You think I squeezed myself into this monkey suit so that I could sit around my office? Just look at the size of that fucking boat out there! I want a piece of that fucking action!"

Diaz rubbed his fingers across lips that had suddenly gone bone dry. He didn't need a weatherman to tell him that there was a storm looming on the horizon, and by the psychotic glaze covering his employer's eyes, it was probably going to be a category five.

"Come on," Coltello ordered, with a noticeable slurring of his words. "Let's get going. It looks like most of the rainbow coalition are already on the boat."

Diaz slid forward in his seat and took his bosses' face by the chin. "Look at me, Nicky. Let me see your eyes."

Coltello batted his hand away. "What the fuck, J.D., you one of them?"

"You can't be talking like that, Nicky," Diaz replied. "I just want to make sure you don't do anything stupid tonight."

Coltello swatted a nonexistent hair off his face. "Stupid? You're stupid."

"Goddamnit, Nicky," Diaz objected. "How much have you had to drink tonight?"

Coltello's face grew flushed. "None of your fucking business. Now, are we getting on that boat, or are we just gonna sit here and have another one of your bullshit anger management sessions?"

"Nicky, there are going to be hundreds of important people on this ship…"

"None more than me," Coltello interrupted, waggling his finger.

"We can debate that point later, but for now let's ignore the shipping magnate, the Congressmen, the celebrities, and the flying cruise ship, and assume you are the person everyone has come here to see."

Nicky the Knife straightened his bow tie. "You're damned skippy."

Diaz could feel the pressure growing behind his eyes. *If there was a God in heaven, he prayed that this was the onset of something that would take him quickly.* "Nicky, why are we here tonight?"

Coltello never skipped a beat. "To kill Peter Mason."

It would have to be something quick, like getting hit by lightning. A drug overdose or carbon monoxide poisoning would take much too long. If Diaz wanted this torture to stop, he would have to pop the front hood and suck on one of the battery terminals. "No, Nicky, we're not here to kill anyone. We're here to negotiate, not to threaten."

Nicky tipped his head from side to side. "Talk, talk, talk, blah, blah, blah."

"I'm serious, Nicky. Local cops and the Feds are crawling all over that ship. You're not packing any weapons are you?"

Coltello twisted his index finger in the air. "I don't need any fucking weapons, I can kill him with a plastic spoon."

Diaz looked over at the electric cigarette lighter and wondered if the socket had enough voltage to do the trick. *Maybe if he wetted his finger first.* "No spoons, no forks, and especially no knives, Nicky! This is your first meeting with the man. I need you to be on your best behavior. And if nothing comes of our conversation, then…"

"…then I bust a beer bottle and stab him in the carotid."

"Jesus, Nicky. Who the hell raised you, Hannibal Lecter?"

"Talking is overrated, J.D.!" Coltello growled as he emptied his last sip of bourbon. "I didn't get where I am today by kissing other people's asses, and I've got an entire field full of corpses who wanted to *negotiate* with me to prove it."

"Nicky, this man wants to dig up that field. You understand that, right?"

"And that's why he needs to die."

Diaz shook his head. "No, that's why we need to convince him to move the location of his ballpark, so that you're not indicted on fifty some odd counts of first-degree murder and put down like a rabid animal."

Coltello leaned forward, and his whole demeanor seemed to change. "You really care about me, don't you J.D.?"

"What?"

"I don't have many people I can count on to have my back, J.D. You're probably my only true friend."

This crazy train had entirely jumped the tracks. Whatever concoction of psychopharmaceuticals was wreaking havoc in Nick Coltello's system, they were obviously munching away on his brain cells. "I've always got your back, Nicky. You know that."

Coltello's smile seemed abnormally exaggerated, like the Joker in the Batman comics. "I do."

"Maybe we should just call it a night," Diaz suggested. "I can set up a one on one with Mason some other time."

Nicky the Knife shook his fists jubilantly. "And miss the party of the year? Are you fucking crazy?"

Diaz could feel the bile burning its way up his esophagus. "I'm not so sure…"

But it was too late. Nicholas Coltello was halfway out the door and screaming hysterically. "Would you look at that fucking boat! It's fucking beautiful. I want one!"

Jimmy Diaz sat silently for a moment and prayed. *Perhaps in his divine wisdom, God had a plan. Albeit not a very coherent one, but a plan none the less. Maybe it was all supposed to end this way. Perhaps Nicky the Knife was destined to accidentally tumble overboard tonight, or give up the ghost in a hail of gunfire this evening.* A slight grin creased Jimmy Diaz's lips. *Would that be such a bad thing?*

50

Matt and Simone stood under one of the streetlights lining the pier so each could see what the other was signing. When the *Hydra* made her debut, and all the lights went out, Simone panicked and pulled Matt close to her, feeling that her only form of communication had been cut off. They held each other close, with the beam of the helicopter's searchlight illuminating them briefly. Ten minutes later, when the *Hydra* was tied to her berth, the lights returned and Simone released her grip.

"You didn't have to let go," Matt signed. "I like it when you hold me close."

"I don't like the dark," Simone gestured back. "Sometimes I sleep with a nightlight on."

"Thanks for the warning," Matt replied.

Although their relationship had reached the point where intimacy might play a part, Simone was always reticent to take that next step. Even though she felt more for Matt than she ever thought possible, something held her back. It wasn't physical, but emotional. She had this nagging fear of the dark and the sense of isolation it created for her. She knew it was childish, but she imagined the moment would be awkward. She found it hard to comprehend that finally being with Matt would be just as amazing in total silence. She slipped her arms back around him and squeezed him tightly.

Matt checked his watch one more time. Hope Jannick was late. They were standing at the correct meeting spot, but half the crowd was already boarded, and they still had no credentials.

As the invited guests crossed the gangway, Matt studied each of them carefully, keeping an eye out for the one person that mattered the most. He had been keeping a watchful eye on the entire crowd, but there was still no sign of anyone involved with the baseball team. He considered that they may have boarded ahead of time, but he wouldn't know for sure if he wasn't granted access.

On the aft deck of the *Hydra*, below the pair of huge fans that steered the vessel, a calypso band, steel drums and all, was performing Bob Marley's "Three Little Birds," which had everyone who was shuffling up the gangway swaying in time with the iconic reggae song. Little did the crowd know how significant the late Jamaican's lyrics would turn out to be:

"Don't worry about a thing,
'Cause every little thing gonna be all right."

Matt could feel the rhythmic beat resonate in his head, while Simone could feel the vibrations, but could not decipher the sound. It looked like everyone was having a good time, since her appreciation was strictly visual.

Hope Jannick was fighting against the tide of the crowd. Her blond hair was braided down her back and whipped from side to side as she weaved her way toward their designated rendezvous spot. The fact that her shimmering black gown was ankle length and restricted her movement wasn't helping the situation at all.

When she finally reached the couple, she was waving their badges and lanyards above her head in victory. "Matt, over here!" she called out once she was in earshot. When he never reacted, she thoughtlessly remembered that her words were literally falling on deaf ears. It wasn't until she crossed into the circle of light they were standing in before they noticed her.

Matt held out both his hands to greet his old friend. "Hope! You look terrific! The computer screen doesn't do you justice!"

Hope smiled as her aquamarine eyes sparkled in the light. "And look at you! You've grown so tall and handsome! Your speech is still excellent!"

Matt shook his head. "You don't have to say that. I know it's going downhill fast."

"No," Hope disagreed. "Trust me. It's still very good!"

Matt slapped himself in the forehead in an exaggerated movement. Exaggeration was an essential component of communication for the deaf. It conveyed the importance of a feeling or a statement. "I'm so rude. You've never met Simone in person! Hope Jannick," he said and signed, "this is Simone Goodman."

The two young women shook hands politely.

"You are so beautiful," Hope said, as she pointed as Simone and gathered her fingers in front of own face."

Simone smiled and repeated the gestures back.

"When did you learn to sign?" Matt asked warily.

"You would be proud of me," Hope signed. "I took two classes in high school for college credit. It's considered a foreign language."

"That's so great!" Simone signed.

"So why didn't you ever sign to me when we spoke online?" Matt asked and interpreted.

Hope shrugged. "I was embarrassed. I thought I would make a mistake."

Simone shook her head. "No, you are very good at it."

"Maybe," Hope said, alternating her palms up and down. "Just enough to get by."

Matt translated the last part for Simone.

"Are those our boarding passes?"

Hope mimed being a ditzy blond and handed over the laminated badges and lanyards. "Stupid me. Of course. Here they are."

Matt handed one to Simone who examined it before placing it around her neck. "You don't know how much this means to me, Hope. I owe you one, big time."

Hope looked at Simone and then back at Matt. "This is such a small thing. I'm glad I was able to do it. If you should happen to come across my father onboard, it's him you should really thank.

He remembers you well and misses your parents. I'm sure he would love to see the grown man you've become."

Simone rested her head against Matt's shoulder as he interpreted Hope's heartfelt sentiments.

"I would love to see him. It's been so long, I hope I recognize him."

Hope signed. "That shouldn't be a problem. I'll be standing right next to him. He's my date tonight."

"Your mother isn't here?"

"No, my grandmother isn't doing well, so she wanted to be with her."

Matt frowned. "I am so sorry to hear that. Tell them both I wish them well. I still remember your mother's pistachio cake. It was so good."

Hope smiled. "She's still making them. I'll see if I can't box one up and ship it to you."

Matt rubbed his stomach. "That would be so yummy." He signed turning to Simone. "Her mother makes this amazing pistachio cake that is actually green! It's so good!"

Simone licked her lips.

Then Hope turned serious. "So, do you want to tell me the *real* reason you wanted to be here tonight?"

Matt looked at Simone and then back to Hope. "It's probably a better idea if I didn't."

Hope frowned. "You two aren't radicalized or something and planning on taking everyone hostage, right?"

Matt was appalled. "Are you serious? You're kidding, right?"

"It happens all too often nowadays," Hope worried. "Especially in Florida. First with the nightclub massacre in Orlando and then the high school shooting in Parkland."

"And you think I'm capable of something like that?"

Hope immediately regretted her remark. "I'm sorry. Forget I said anything. My father has been obsessed with the security surrounding this ship, and his anxiety has probably rubbed off on me. I didn't mean to insinuate anything by it. It was stupid. I'm an idiot."

"Do you want the badges back?"

Hope's eyes began to tear up. "Can we just rewind this conversation back two minutes? I don't even know why I brought up those terrible things. Tonight we should be celebrating. You have to forgive me. Please!"

Matt reached out and took Hope's hand. "Don't be sorry. No one should ever forget what happened to those people. I understand we've grown apart and don't talk often enough, but I'm still the same guy who raced you to lunch every day when we were kids back at Whitehall Academy."

Hope squeezed his hand. "I know you are. It just makes me sad that we've taken different roads."

Matt lifted her chin. "The great thing about roads is that they intersect all the time."

She smiled. "So we're good?"

"We'll always be good."

"Will you save me a dance?"

"Of course I will."

Hope turned to Simone. "It was so nice to finally meet you in person. You're a fortunate girl. Take care of this guy. He's very special," she signed.

Simone signed back. "More than you will ever know."

51

Just as the gangway was about to be removed, two late arrivals scurried up the ramp. One flashed a badge; the other remained silent, but from his demeanor, the security guards assumed he was also with law enforcement.

On the second of four decks, the attendees had been ushered into the main dining room. Thirty-five formally set tables surrounded a brightly lit black marble dance floor. At the back of the room, a ten-piece orchestra made their last-minute adjustments on a stage bathed in multi-colored lighting. The carpeting was a muted maroon with a subtle beige pattern that was pleasing to the eye. A lone microphone stand bided its time as the privileged guests retrieved their place cards and settled into their assigned seats.

The two late arrivals never made it to the dining room; their interest lay elsewhere. Only one would have had a seat reserved for them anyway.

Waiters in formal attire came around the room pouring imported champagne into the delicate flutes that adorned each place setting. Many took their seats immediately; others mingled with people they knew or had always wanted to meet. The crowd ranged from athletes to scholars, bankers to politicians; almost every component on the spectrum of the elite had been invited. It was a Noah's Ark of the rich and famous.

Peter Mason took the stage at precisely eight forty-five. His hair had been pulled back into a ponytail and bound by a simple orange rubber band. True to his roots, he looked particularly uncomfortable in his tuxedo. If he lived in a perfect world, this cruise would have been held on a Sunday afternoon, with everyone wearing Hawaiian shirts and bikinis out on deck, sipping boat drinks and getting baked. But his world was far from perfect.

"Ladies and gentlemen, if you could all take your seats for a few minutes," he said, after tapping the microphone to test the volume. "I would really appreciate it if you could all find your seats."

Mason smiled genially and returned a few waves and catcalls while his guests settled in.

"Good evening, everyone; I'm your host, Peter Mason."

The room burst into applause.

Mason bowed his head and accepted their admiration appreciatively. "Welcome aboard a ship unlike any other you've ever traveled on…the Mason Cruise Line's crown jewel: the *Hydra*!"

People stood and applauded while Mason bathed in their recognition. "Thank you very much. You are all too kind. If I could have your undivided attention," he continued as a large screen slowly descended from the ceiling behind him. "There is a short but mandatory video we must show that describes the *Hydra*'s safety and lifeboat procedures. It is a requirement that this video is viewed by every passenger, so I ask that you pay close attention to this important information, and then we'll be able to start the evening's festivities."

The video played for seven minutes, explaining how to evacuate the ship in an orderly fashion and where each of the six lifeboats was located. Each guest's place card had a number in the upper right corner which identified which of the boats they were to report to should an emergency evacuation become necessary. Each of the lifeboats could handle eighty passengers, so there was more than enough space should the unlikely happen.

When the presentation was over, the screen retracted into the ceiling, and Peter Mason once again took center stage. He made a quick adjustment to raise the microphone to his mouth. "The *Hydra* is a marvel of marine engineering and technology. At four hundred twenty-five feet stem to stern, she is the world's largest vessel using hydrofoil technology." He paused to consider his words, which were improvised despite his staff's opposition. "The *Hydra* has taken the basic principles of lift and propulsion and amplified them a thousandfold. We've added an aerodynamic design and made comfort and safety our top priorities."

The room filled with applause again.

"Now, I'm going to ask that you all remain very quiet and still for the next two minutes so that you may experience the wonder that is '*The Hydra*.'"

Just over three hundred formally-attired guests fell still, but seconds later, all grasped their seats as the sensation of lift became suddenly apparent. It felt like the entire room was rising in an elevator. Passengers lucky enough to have seats near the windows could see the pier silently fall away as the ship rose unnaturally out of the river. The fourteen independent pontoons inflated in less than two minutes, and the *Hydra* suddenly sat eleven feet higher in the water.

Peter Mason checked his watch, and when two minutes had passed, he began to speak again. "How was that folks? Pretty amazing wasn't it?"

The crowd cheered wildly.

Mason motioned for those who stood to take their seats. "Thank you. Thank you. But to quote Al Jolson, 'You ain't seen nothing yet!'"

The guests laughed with nervous excitement. This was like nothing any of them had ever experienced. It was almost surreal.

"The *Hydra*'s hull is between ten and twelve feet above the water line right now. Fourteen independent pontoons have just inflated beneath us. You may wonder, why fourteen instead of one on each side? The reason our engineers designed these pontoons separately is for your safety and comfort. They spent months considering every possible scenario, and have built in an exclusive backup system should one be breached or deflate unexpectedly. Should one of these pontoons be compromised, it will be automatically ejected, and another will inflate and replace it. I'm sure you would agree that we would be in a heck of a situation if we only had one large pontoon on each side and had a problem. Traveling at the speeds we are capable of, the *Hydra* would end up in a barrel roll that wouldn't end up well for any of us."

The guests began looking nervously at each other.

Mason held up his hands. "Folks, not to worry! I assure you that the *Hydra* was built for safety first as well as comfort and speed. Once we are underway, you will understand how safe and exhilarating traveling on the *Hydra* can be."

Gerald Banks who was standing in the back of the room put his head in his hands. *That's why you're supposed to stick to the script, moron!*

"In a few moments, Captain Oskar Karrlson will be unleashing the *Hydra's* full capabilities by starting up our patented fanbine technology. You will hear nothing, but once again feel the sensation of lift as this nearly three thousand ton ship is lifted out of the water like the mythological creature she is named after."

The room fell suspiciously quiet.

"I know it sounds impossible, but that is what skeptics think about any great achievement in history, and I assure you, tonight, we will be making history."

A few of the guests clapped, while most of the others downed the rest of their champagne in one giant gulp.

"Later on during dinner," Mason continued, "I've asked Captain Karrlson to join us here to answer any questions you may have about the *Hydra* herself. But before that, we'll be offering a guided tour of a few of the more than one hundred luxurious cabins and twenty opulent suites the *Hydra* has to offer her passengers on future trips. I do want to apologize in advance, but some areas of the *Hydra* will be restricted for guests tonight, including the control room and the cargo hold, but you should be able to see enough to appreciate that the *Hydra* is far and away the most phenomenal ship on the..."

Once again, the ship began to rise, only this time a slight vibration could be felt beneath the passengers' feet. Through the starboard windows, the colorfully lit skyline of Jacksonville sank as if in quicksand. Seconds later, the vibration stopped, and the guests could feel the ship beginning to turn. It wasn't the slow calculating turn that cruise passengers were used to, but more of a pivoting while in place. The bow of the ship was simply spinning on an imaginary axis and changing its heading from west to east.

"Amazing, isn't it?" Mason proclaimed. "It's like riding on a cloud. The *Hydra* no longer has any draft—she is completely out of the water!"

The crowd cheered and applauded wildly. He had won them back.

"Once we reach the mouth of the Atlantic Ocean, Captain Karrlson will open her up and show you what she's capable of. Where an average cruise ship would travel the thousand mile trip to King's Wharf Bermuda in two days, we should arrive just in time to see the sunrise tomorrow."

The room filled with "Oohs" and "Aahs."

"For those of you who have prearranged with us to remain in Bermuda for a visit, rest assured that your luggage will be waiting for you at your hotel. The rest of you will be flown back early tomorrow at no expense on two jets I've chartered for your convenience. The *Hydra* will remain in King's Wharf for a few days while our staff confirms that she performed as expected." Mason tapped his forehead. "I almost forgot. For those of you daring enough, I invite you wholeheartedly to experience the most spectacular walk you will ever take. The concept of the Oceanwalk was always a dream of mine, but I'm here to tell you that dreams do come true, and if you're brave enough, I encourage you to give it a try. Feel what it's like to have the ocean racing forty feet beneath you with nothing between you and the water but four inches of glass! Just a warning," Mason smiled. "Once you step off, there's no turning back!"

Mason could hear the mumbling from his guests as they argued if they were up to the dare. People were actually taking bets and challenging each other to give it a try. While some seemed up to the test, others shook their heads defiantly against it.

This was what it was all about for Peter Mason. He would have loved the same enthusiasm from the crowd at the ballpark, but that was a miscalculation that would easily be fixed once the cargo was unloaded and the payment wired into his account. By the time they arrived in Bermuda, he would have more than enough to build his new ballpark, and maybe a hockey arena to boot.

"Whatever you choose to do," he announced, "We will be rounding you all up in about two hours to enjoy a sumptuous dinner created by our outstanding culinary staff. There will only be one seating, so we will be shutting down the tours while the food is being served. At that time, Captain Karrlson and I will be coming by each of your tables to see how you're enjoying yourselves and to answer any questions you might have about the *Hydra*."

The crowd gave Peter Mason his second standing ovation of the evening. He blew kisses and waved to his adoring audience All of the critics who had written and badmouthed him about being the son of a hippie drug trafficker who was handed everything and achieved nothing on his own, well, they could all go straight to hell. Tonight that all ended.

52

The bridge of the *Hydra* was like nothing Roy Sowell had commanded before. The technology was so advanced, he had no doubt that
the ship could have been outfitted to run itself. Gone was the traditional wheel that had long since been replaced on modern vessels by
buttons, dials, and throttle levers. It was an eerie juxtaposition to sit
in the captain's chair and be reactive instead of proactive. All Sowell
seemed to be doing was authorizing orders instead of commanding
them. Times were changing. Time was passing him by.

Every bulkhead was covered with screens that monitored every
facet of the *Hydra*'s environment. To Sowell's left, monitors displayed
engineering and mechanical information. To his right, weather and
sea conditions were continually updating through uplinks to NOAA
atmospheric and ocean monitoring satellites.

Through the panoramic windows, Sowell watched the day turn
into night. He had been onboard for almost six hours and had never
left the bridge. An elegant dinner had been delivered, consisting
of a twenty-ounce ribeye, baked potato, and five thick spears of
asparagus. They, along with a hefty slice of Godiva chocolate layer
cake, remained untouched on a shelf in the back of the cabin.
The hot food had long grown cold, and the dessert was no longer
palatable to him.

Spread before him were nearly two dozen screens, manned by
two Mason employees whom Sowell had recently learned had no
naval experience whatsoever. They were technicians trained on the
equipment that guided and steered the ship along with every other
aspect of the ship's operation. Three people; that's all it took to run

the *Hydra*, and Sowell was beginning to believe that the chair he sat in was only there to appease any passengers who might tour the bridge on future trips.

The technicians appeared to have their tasks divided evenly. The tall one on the left, who had introduced himself as Hassan, was a wiry fellow of East Indian origin who wore thick Buddy Holly glasses and carried a computer tablet that Sowell hadn't seen him put down since he arrived. Manning the right side of the console was a shorter, more affable technician who had introduced himself as Jean-Baptiste. His accent was thick with Carribean flair, and he tended to smile a lot more than Hassan did.

"Captain," Hassan said, "All systems are functioning normally, and we have word from below that all guests are onboard and the gangway has been secured, sir."

Hassan stared at Sowell expectantly. "All systems are in the green and ready to go, sir."

Sowell turned his attention to Jean-Baptiste. "How's the weather?"

"Zero chance of precipitation, Captain, seas are one to three feet near the Gulf Stream, and wind is out of the southeast at eight."

Sowell grasped the arms of his chair. "Let's take her out nice and smooth, then. We don't want to rattle their champagne glasses. Ten percent on the bottom and five percent on the thrusters. Let's raise her slowly and give them all a thrill."

"Yes, sir," Hassan replied. "We have inflated all fourteen pods to ninety percent capacity, and the pressure is holding steady across the board. It looks good."

Sowell nodded. "Once we reach the ocean, I want the pods fully inflated and the bottom to fifty-five percent and the thrusters at thirty. I want to see how she handles with the extra ballast before I open her up. Carrying passengers is a completely different ballgame. We need to keep this ride smooth, boys. Don't want the celebs bouncing around the ballroom."

Jean-Baptiste smiled. "Understood sir, we'll keep her trimmed and level."

The Saint John's river weaved its way eastward with subtle bends and turns to its geography. As this moderate speed, it would take twenty minutes to reach the mouth of the Atlantic, and then the audition would begin in earnest. While the surface of the river was calm and confined by land on both sides, the open ocean was always erratic, and even the most sophisticated equipment could not predict its temperament.

"What kind of traffic do we have on the surface between Bermuda and us?"

Hassan walked over to the wall of monitors on the port side and put his finger up to the screen. "Some small pleasure craft close to shore, and it looks like some heavier tonnage heading south out of Norfolk, most likely navy ships. Four of them."

"Are they in formation?"

Hassan shook his head. "Negative, Captain. Two are heading southeast, one northeast, and one is hugging the coastline north. There is some commercial traffic, but it's very far out. Nothing to worry about."

"And what about the *Dobrinski*? What is her position?"

"She is holding steady at thirty-one degrees north and seventy degrees west. That's about halfway to Bermuda. She's been there for a few hours now."

Sowell leaned forward in his chair. "Don't let her remain stationary. She'll arouse suspicion. Make sure she keeps moving until we get closer."

"I'll let her know, Sir."

There were fewer lights along the shore as the river twisted out to the Atlantic.

"We're passing Sisters Creek, Captain," Jean-Baptiste announced. "She's running smooth and level, and everything is still in the green. The passengers shouldn't be able to hear or feel a thing."

"That's what it's all about!" Sowell sang.

The two technicians looked at each other.

"The Hokey-Pokey...that's what it's all about. Come on guys, you've never moved your left foot in, and moved your left foot out?"

Hassan and Jean-Baptiste shrugged naively.

Sowell put his head in his hands. "How is that possible?" He muttered.

The technicians turned back to the monitors in front of them. "Passing Sherman Point, Captain. Heading into the Mayport Cut."

Sowell scratched his head, and his fingers came away with a lock of thin gray hair caught between them. "I don't need to be informed of every course correction you make. Just keep her steady."

"Yes, sir."

Sowell studied the stray strands of hair in his hand. They were dried out and brittle. "Pull up the perimeter cameras on screens one through three. I want to see if we still have an escort."

The camera located on the stern of the ship revealed a yacht filled with reporters and cameramen still trailing behind, while the port side camera showed an orange Coast Guard Zodiac, complete with a machine gunner standing on the bow. That was the standard operating procedure for the Coast Guard since September eleventh. They would tag alongside until the *Hydra* reached the Atlantic safely.

Sowell lifted himself slowly out of his chair and walked over to the waste receptacle built into the starboard bulkhead. He pushed open the cover and let his hair fall into the plastic bag.

"Are you alright, Captain?" Jean-Baptiste asked.

Sowell turned and nodded. "Sure. What makes you think I'm not?"

"Well, you didn't eat your dinner, and you're looking a bit peaked."

Sowell shuffled over and stood next to the technician. "Thank you for your concern, Mr. Jean-Baptiste. But I would appreciate it if..." The words caught in his throat as he began to cough uncontrollably.

Jean-Baptiste and Hassan each grabbed one of his arms as Sowell bent over in convulsions. Hassan reached into his pocket and pulled out a handkerchief and handed it to the Captain who stood slowly to catch his breath.

"Wow, that was intense," Sowell admitted, as he wiped his lips.

"Are you *sure* you're alright, Captain?" Jean-Baptiste asked again.

Sowell tried to stand up straight but his eyes were still tearing, and his equilibrium was off. The two technicians carefully led him back to his chair.

Hassan and Jean-Baptiste stood wide-eyed as Sowell regained some stability.

"Why are you two staring at me like that? I said I was fine. I just choked a bit, that's all. No big deal."

The technicians continued to watch him skeptically.

"What's the matter with you two? Haven't you ever seen a person have a coughing jag before?"

In unison, they pointed timidly at the handkerchief...

It was drenched in blood.

53

As the *Hydra* headed out to sea, the tours of the ship began. Employees dressed in tuxedoes and gowns and sporting name tags escorted guest around the unrestricted sections of the boat. The brave ones were anxious to experience the thrill of the Oceanwalk. Many did it on a dare, while others had no compunction about stepping over the water churning below their feet. A perimeter of docking lights located just above the inflatable pods illuminated the dark blue waves so that even during a moonless night like tonight, the passengers could sense the exhilaration. The passengers were guided one at a time on both sides of the ship, but when the waiting lines grew too long and impatient, the escorts reluctantly allowed handfuls of guests to make the walk simultaneously. Some posed for pictures, while others moved at a speedy clip just to be able to claim that they had completed the disorienting expedition.

In the dining room, many guests chose to sit and sip champagne and sample the hors-d'oeuvres being offered from table to table. Lauren King and Scott Simms were two of the crowd that decided to remain. Looking over the lip of her water glass, the detective scanned the room guardedly. The first passengers to draw her attention were Nicholas "Nicky the Knife" Coltello and his enforcer Jimmy Diaz. She wondered what a pair of low-life bottom-feeders would be doing at such a first-class event. They stood at a port side window talking to another man wearing a tuxedo. Lauren didn't recognize the third man, but got the impression he was a Mason employee from the way he appeared to be pointing out some of the boat's features to the mob boss and his lackey.

Across the room, Matt and Simone stayed seated as well, having met an older couple who knew sign language but had both chosen to have cochlear implants at a younger age to help them hear.

Simone was full of questions, skeptical about the couple's motives. She felt that "fitting in" was their priority, and boosting their communication skills was much less important to them. Many deaf people felt betrayed by this technology, believing that deafness wasn't some sort of disease or disability, but a way of life, like a person's religion or culture. It wasn't anything to be ashamed of any more than it was to be embarrassed by your race or gender. How many people would choose to change one of those traits if the technology were available? Not many, Simone believed.

They politely discussed the topic, with Matt interrupting every so often, feeling much like a referee at a wrestling match. He was part of both of these worlds, and he understood the commitment each side felt. Simone wasn't happy that Matt didn't defend her views, but she knew why he could empathize with both opinions.

Simone continued to ask questions about the implant procedure and whether the couple thought it had actually enhanced their lives, but Matt's attention was suddenly drawn elsewhere. The baseball team had entered the dining room and had taken their seats at an oversized table just to the right of the stage. The players were members of the Jacksonville Jumbo Shrimp, and none of the Major Leauge players were in attendance. The young pitchers, catchers, and fielders were of no consequence to Matt; his focus was on only one person sitting at the table.

Anthony Magnetti put his arm around the player sitting on his left and laughed heartily at a joke he had just told. Instead of champagne, an ordinary can of domestic light beer rested before him. Matt watched his parents' murderer survey the room, taking in all of the pomp and circumstance and appearing to look bored to death by it all. When their eyes finally met, Matt noticed Magnetti's head tip from side to side, perhaps in recognition, but more likely with just a fleeting sense of déjà vu.

Matt also spotted someone else he never expected to see. The detective was here, talking to a man he didn't recognize. Her husband or boyfriend perhaps? Was it a coincidence that she just happened to be here, or was she following them? In a way, he was glad to see her, but at the same time, he wondered what her motives were. Matt figured that if she was here, then the Doctor couldn't be far behind. He scanned the room but didn't see him, guessing he was probably on one of the tours. Matt decided to focus on one problem at a time

A small orchestra was playing traditional songs from Benny Goodman to Benny and the Jets. A smattering of couples danced on the parqueted floor, but most people were involved in personal conversations centering on the latest celebrity gossip and trends in the country's economy.

From an entrance on the starboard side of the dining room, Peter Mason entered with the Captain of the *Hydra* decked out in full dress uniform, including an oak-leafed peaked cap to reinforce his sense of importance.

Scott Simms wiped the corner of his mouth with his linen napkin and excused himself from the table.

"Where are you going?" Lauren asked, grabbing his arm.

"I want to talk to the Captain."

The detective stood up. "You're not going anywhere without me."

Simms pulled out her chair. "Suit yourself. Just let me do all the talking. You're on my ocean now."

Lauren noticed a sudden determination in Simm's demeanor. She was used to playing second fiddle to Toby whenever he picked up a scent, but seeing the same resolve in the Petty Officer took her by surprise.

The Captain stood alongside Peter Mason greeting a long line of guests who had quit their dancing and conversing to meet them. Simms and King patiently waited their turn as hands were shaken and superfluous questions were asked and gladly answered.

Captain Oskar Karrlson greeted each passenger with a vigorous handshake or kiss to both cheeks. He was, for the lack of a better description, jolly-looking. Santa Claus in dress whites with epaulets and enough fruit salad covering his chest to melt down and make another anchor. Peter Mason made sure that the line kept moving, reminding the guests that the Captain had a ship to run.

Karrlson gazed at Lauren's flowing red hair and took half a step back. "My dear," he sighed in a thick Nordic accent, "you are just radiant. You are a fortunate man," he added, barely giving Simms a glance. "What is your name, my dear?"

"Lauren King, Captain. Detective Lauren King of the Jacksonville Police Department."

Peter Mason's head turned like it was on a swivel. Simms hung his head, knowing full well that the detective had received the reaction she was hoping for.

"Detective," Mason interrupted, holding out his hand. "It's terrific that law enforcement is represented here tonight. I invited the Sheriff, but it seems that he had a prior engagement. I'm so glad that someone from your department could make it. I have the utmost respect and admiration for the job you and your fellow officers do. I wish I could have invited every first responder to take this inaugural trip. I think I should create a special discount for those who serve the Jacksonville community so selflessly."

Lauren smiled. "That sounds like a great idea. I'm sure my fellow officers will take full advantage of your generosity."

"I will make a mental note of it.

The detective took Peter Mason's hand. "I will hold you to your word. The last thing you want is to lie to the police."

Mason laughed, but the humor was cut off in his throat when he realized that Detective Lauren King appeared to be deadly serious. He made a slight bow and turned his attention to Scott Simms, who quickly shook his hand and nudged the detective to move on.

"What the hell was that all about?" Simms grumbled as they

crossed the dance floor. "I told you to keep a muzzle on it while I did all the talking."

"The Captain gave me a compliment, what was I supposed to do?"

"Well, I appreciate you keeping Mason occupied."

Once they reached their table, Lauren allowed the Petty Officer to pull out her chair for her. "So what did you find out from the Captain?"

Simms bent forward and whispered into her ear. "I want you to stay here while I check something out, because if that guy is running this ship, then I'm a monkey's uncle!"

54

Matt couldn't take his eyes off the table across the dining room. As Simone continued to converse with the older couple about the pros and cons of auditory technology, she slowly realized that Matt's attention was divided. This was beyond rude to her, since he was missing large parts of the conversation that Simone needed to be interpreted. She jabbed him with an elbow, and he quickly apologized to her and the others for his inattentiveness.

Simone used the best speech she could muster and thanked the couple for their insights. It was apparent that they felt strongly about wanting to fit in, but Simone was adamant in her beliefs.

Matt took Simone's arm and looked her straight in the eyes. What he wanted to say was important. "Stay here," he signed emphatically. "I don't want you coming with me."

"Where?" She asked.

"I'm going to get an autograph."

Simone turned her head to see where Matt was now staring. "Bullshit," she signed, using both hands. "Don't you dare go over there!"

"I really just want to touch him, put my hand on his shoulder. I want to see if anything comes through."

Simone took Matt's hand and squeezed it to the point where she knew it would start to hurt. "You can't trace the man in front of all these people! Do you know what you look like when it happens? They're going to think you're having a seizure! You can't do it!"

Matt looked at his girlfriend's concerned face, and then across the dining room to the table of ball players. He felt like his head was a compass needle, and his parents' killer was due north. "Then I won't engage him, I'll just ask for an autograph. That's all, no conversation. Do you have a pen with you?"

Simone frowned. "You know I always carry a pad of paper and a pen to communicate."

"Let me borrow it. If he uses the pen, I might be able to get something from it."

Simone reached into her clutch bag and took out the pad of paper and a pen. She held them up in the air just out of Matt's reach. "I'm going with you."

Matt shook his head stubbornly. "No, I want you to stay here."

A smile came over Simone's face. "No fucking way," she said, using her voice.

The couple across the table were noticeably shocked by the unusual outburst and quickly turned away, pretending to be occupied with their own conversation.

Simone waved the paper and pen in front of Matt's face. "I go where you go," she signed. "If you think you can tell me what to do, then this relationship is built on a huge misconception. Don't ever try to give me an order again!"

Matt's face softened. Simon Goodman was not a young woman to be messed with. She was drawing a line in the sand that Matt understood was more like a line etched into stone. "Fine, you can come with me, but please don't say anything."

Simone's eyes narrowed. "You just want me to look pretty?"

"That's not what I meant."

"So, I don't look pretty?"

Matt grabbed the paper and pen out of her hand. "Stop it. Now you're just being a pain in the ass!"

Simone smiled and took Matt's hand as they excused themselves from the other guests at their table.

"Excuse me," Matt said, as he approached the table of ball players. "Could I get a couple of autographs?" He was standing right beside

Anthony Magnetti, but he looked around the table at everyone but the batting coach. "I've lived in Jacksonville for most of my life, and I'm a big fan."

Magnetti turned his head and eyed them both. "That's an unusual accent you've got."

For the first time in over ten years, Matt Walker was face to face with the man that had tried to kill him. "I lost my hearing as a child; I apologize for my poor speech."

Seven other players had chosen to stay at the table instead of taking one of the ship tours. Most sat in stunned silence as their long-time assistant coach made an insensitive fool of himself.

"Please," Magnetti begged, holding up his hands in surrender, "I didn't realize that you couldn't hear. I'm very sorry; can you read my lips?"

"Yes, sir."

"What's your name?"

Matt paused. "Matt."

"Just Matt? No last name?"

Matt placed his hand on the coach's shoulder ignoring the last question. "Don't worry about the miscommunication, it happens all the time. My girlfriend Simone is deaf as well."

Magnetti stood and took Simone's hand courteously. "Very nice to meet you; I'm Anthony Magnetti, the Jumbo Shrimps' batting coach. But please, you can call me Tony."

Matt interpreted for her. "She doesn't read lips as well as I do. She's never been able to hear."

The coach waved his hands in a mad display of nonsensical gestures. "That's very interesting; so you sign for her?"

Matt nodded. "Whenever possible."

"So, Matt, can I ask you how you lost your hearing or is that frowned upon? I've never really had any interaction with deaf people other than seeing them from a distance."

Matt continued to interpret his conversation for Simone. When he translated the coach's question, she tugged on his arm to warn him.

Matt smiled. "Childhood accident. Wrong place at the wrong time."

Magnetti looked curious. "Okay, I've clearly overstepped a boundary. I apologize." He said, glancing around the table at his ballplayers. "Do I look as stupid as I feel?" He asked them.

They all nodded affirmatively.

Matt was quickly disappointed that the only sensation he was picking up was from the sports coat the killer was wearing. Magnetti had extended his hand, but Matt continued to interpret instead. If Simone hadn't reminded him about the likely physical effects of the trace, Matt would have shaken the killer's hand without a second thought. That's why he was glad she was there. He needed someone to be his guardian angel.

Magnetti took the paper and pen from Simone and inscribed it with a nearly illegible signature. He passed the sheet around the table, and each player added their name to the souvenir. Some wrote a line or two, and one player even drew the "I Love You" hand sign below his name. When it had entirely circled the table, Magnetti handed it to Simone.

"You know," the coach said, studying Matt's face. "I saw the two of you across the room before, and I thought you looked familiar. Have we ever met before?"

Matt interpreted what Magnetti was saying, and Simone surreptitiously kicked Matt with her heel. He tried not to flinch, but she caught him square on his ankle bone. Matt scratched his head. "I don't think so," he said, quickly changing the subject. "Have you always been a batting coach?"

Magnetti picked the pen off the table and waggled it in front of him. "I played some college ball, then traveled a bit with a few minor league teams, but yeah, I guess my life has been mostly about baseball. Swinging a bat has always just come naturally to me. Can you play any sports?"

Simone read the translation, and Matt could tell that she was holding her frustration in check. "You're aware that just because I can't hear doesn't mean that I can't throw and catch, right?"

"I didn't mean to imply…"

Matt snapped back with the facts. "The football huddle was invented at Gallaudet University so that the opposing team couldn't see what play was being signed by the deaf quarterback."

"I never knew that," Magnetti said, suddenly feeling very self-conscious.

"And the hand signs used between a pitcher and catcher and those gestures your manager and coaches use to signal your players on the field…you can credit the deaf for those too."

The players around the table nodded with admiration at the teenager who was taking their coach to task. It wasn't something that happened very often.

Magnetti looked around the table and nodded to each of his players. "Isn't that interesting, guys? You learn something new every day!"

Simone smiled.

"Well, thank you all for the autographs. We appreciate you being so nice."

The players at the table waved politely.

Magnetti continued to look at Matt suspiciously. "Are you sure we haven't met before? I can't shake this feeling that we've crossed paths somewhere?"

Matt shrugged. "I don't think so."

The coach held his chin thoughtfully. It was like trying to grasp for something that was just beyond his reach. "Do you look like your father? Maybe I know him, and that's why you seem so familiar."

"My father passed away when I was young."

Magnetti frowned. "That's always tough on a kid. My dad is almost ninety now, and he can still do the New York Times crossword puzzle. Crazy, huh?"

"The world works in mysterious ways," Matt said wistfully. "I miss my father every day."

The coach reached out his hand, but Simone pulled Matt away.

"I never caught your full name, kid. Maybe I can leave some tickets at the ballpark for you and your girlfriend."

Simone squeezed Matt's upper arm like she was testing a melon for ripeness. This conversation was going to leave him black and blue if he persisted.

Matt and Simone turned to leave when Magnetti put his paw on Matt's chest. "Your last name, kid? For the tickets?"

Simone looked at Matt with the same look one would give a dog that was about to pee on the rug. Her eyes screamed, "Don't you do it!".

But it had been over ten years since Matt needed to pee this badly. "The name is Walker, Matt Walker."

55

As the small orchestra played its version of Barry Manilow's "Copa Cabana," Nick Coltello, Jimmy Diaz, and Gerald Banks stood at a window and watched the ocean waves seemingly fly by.

"Damn, we are really moving!" Coltello commented. "This fucker is fast!"

Banks looked around the dining room, not really wanted to be spotted conversing with the mobster and his enforcer. "We're only running at sixty percent of our top speed right now," Banks said, rubbing a smudge off the window with one of the napkins from a nearby table. "The Captain won't open her up until we're well out to sea. You won't feel the difference though. We're riding on the same cushion of air regardless of our velocity."

Nicky the Knife gave Diaz a nudge with his shoulder. "You hear that, J.D.? We're flying over the water! Can you freakin' believe it? I never heard of such a thing! This is gonna be some successful venture for Peter Mason!"

Diaz nodded as the continued to stare down at the illuminated water around the hull of the ship. If he craned his head upward, he could look up one level and watch the feet of passengers making their way across the starboard-side glass walkway. That wasn't something Diaz had any interest in attempting. When he escaped from Cuba with his family thirty two years ago, he swore it would be the last time he was on a boat. The *Hydra* was far from the derelict tub he and fifteen other refugees had made it to Florida on, but he still hated being on the water. Besides, saying "no" to Nicky was far more dangerous than crossing the Florida Straits in the middle of the night.

"So, when do we get to meet the man of the hour?" Nicky asked.

Banks looked at his watch. "I can get you ten minutes right now. He's in his stateroom getting ready for dinner. He's going over the list of VIP's he wants to acknowledge."

Coltello sounded personally offended. "You hear that Jimmy? He's thanking all of his VIP's! I wonder what it takes to become a very important person in Peter Mason's world? Money? Influence? I got those things too."

Diaz turned away from the miserable memories in the window and smiled at his boss. "You've got them in spades, boss. Just don't forget why we came here. You need to concentrate on solving the problem. Don't let petty little things sidetrack you. No one cares what Peter Mason thinks." He held up two fingers to his eyes. "Focus."

Coltello nodded his head toward Diaz so Banks could see. "He's always looking after me. Loyal like a pit bull. That's way more important than money *or* influence. If you've got loyalty," he said, pointing at Banks, "then the world is your oyster! Remember, Nicholas Coltello told you that."

Banks led his two guests toward the stern of the ship. They stepped between two tall yellow cones with the words "restricted to guests" stamped on them in bold black letters. Walking past them made Nicky feel special.

There was nautical artwork hanging on the walls. Pictures of various vessels throughout history filled the spaces between cabins. All of the rooms had single-hung doors except for the stateroom at the end of the corridor. Double-doors differentiated the owner's stateroom from all of the rest. Banks rapped on the door and waited for a reply.

"Come in."

Banks held open the door for his guests and then followed them in and closed it.

"Mr. Mason, I'd like to introduce you to Nicholas Coltello and his associate Jimmy Diaz. They were hoping to have a few minutes of your time, and I thought it important that you heard what they had to say."

Mason had switched into a white jacket, but his bow tie was undone. He held out his hand to greet the two men and showed them to a nearby couch. On the table in front of the sofa sat an ice bucket, some short glasses, and an ancient bottle of Scotch. "Can I offer you gentlemen a drink?"

Nicky took a seat, but Jimmy Diaz preferred to stand behind the sofa with his hands clasped in front of him. It made him look like a bodyguard.

Nicky waved off the offer. "No thanks, we're good. It looks like excellent Scotch though.

Mason and Banks took seats across from Coltello. Mason poured himself a minimal amount from the bottle and smiled as he sniffed the liquor's bouquet. "You don't know what you're missing."

"Maybe another time," Nicky said.

Mason crossed his legs and brushed a piece of lint off his knee before turning to Banks. "Fill me in, Gerald. What can I do for these gentlemen?"

"Uh, you can start off by talking directly to me," Nicky intervened. "I'm sitting right here." He looked over at Banks. "You can go now, Gerald. You've done your job. Tell the guests that Mr. Mason is going to be a little while."

If Peter Mason had any idea of who was sitting across from him, his demeanor didn't show it. "Stay where you are, Gerald," he demanded. You don't take orders from this man!"

Nicky rubbed his finger under his collar while Diaz remained silent. "My name is Coltello, Nicholas Coltello. Damn, I always wanted to say it like that!"

Banks stood up. "The passengers are getting antsy, Pete." He walked over to the door and glanced back at his brother-in-law. There was a look of betrayal on Mason's face. "I'll tell them you're not feeling well."

Before Mason could argue, Banks was gone. Mason studied Nicky over the edge of his glass. "I apologize for being rude, Mr. Coltello. I didn't mean any insult by not speaking to you directly. You have to understand that I am new to the North Florida area, and I'm still getting my bearings. Miami is my hometown, and I still have a lot of new faces to learn. Again, I apologize. Now, what is it that you do?"

Diaz saw the flinch, so he put his hand on Nicky's shoulder to keep him from flying off the sofa. "I'm the owner of the one-eleven nightclub across the street from your downtown offices. They call it the Three Aces."

Mason took a small sip. "I get it; that's clever."

Diaz held firm, but it was getting more difficult by the second.

Nicky could feel his toes curling up in his shoes. He knew better than to make fists with his hands, but no one could see his feet. "Clever is what we were aiming for."

Mason looked at his watch. "Well, it's always a privilege to meet with local businessmen from the area. I look forward to one day stopping by your establishment and checking out the local *scene* as it were. Thank you for coming by to introduce yourself. I hope you enjoy the rest of the trip. The *Hydra* is hopefully the first of many ships which should, in turn, help the local businesses thrive, including your nightclub." Mason stood up and placed his empty glass on the table. "Now if you gentlemen will excuse me, I have a lot of other excited guests out there."

Nicky the Knife's head rose in union with Peter Mason. "Sit the fuck back down, you arrogant piece of shit!"

"Excuse me?"

"You heard me," Nicky snarled pointing to the chair across from him. "You'd better sit down before I stand up, motherfucker!"

Diaz made a quick scan of the cabin to make sure there were no hammers present. Only five minutes had passed, and already any chance of negotiation had failed. Nicky might have set a new record.

Peter Mason remained standing, but his whole manner seemed to change, like a cloud's shadow passing over the moon. Gone was the gracious host who minutes earlier appeared so sophisticated and naïve. Now the gloves were off, and his shoulders seemed to broaden as the smile vanished from his face. "You come into my stateroom, on my ship, on the most important evening in my company's history, and you bark at me like some junkyard dog? Who the hell do you think you're talking to? If tonight were any other night, I'd be using what's left of you for chum!"

Diaz still had a hand on Nicky's shoulder, and he could feel the muscles tense beneath the fabric of his jacket. What was intended to be a peaceful discussion had deteriorated into a clash of titans. Diaz was smart enough to understand that this was enemy territory from the get-go and that Nicky was at a distinct disadvantage, but the mobster was too irrational to realize it.

"Let's take it down a notch, shall we?" Diaz implored.

Nicky crossed his legs on the couch and ran his fingers down the seam of his trousers. "Fine. Let's discuss this like two businessmen. We need to work some things out before you build your new ballpark."

Mason adjusted the cuffs of his shirt and straightened the lapels of his jacket. "Businessmen? High praise from a gun-runner, drug peddler, extortionist, pimp, and murderer. Have I left anything out, Nicky?"

Coltello grinned. "Are you talking about you or me?"

Mason took a seat on the arm of a plush chair. "Do you think I would move a majority of my company to a new city without doing my due-diligence first?" He leaned forward to emphasize his words. "My family has been dealing with people like you since before your mother started breathing heavy. I know everything there is to know about you."

Nicky took a deep breath. "Well, some of your *due-diligence* is wrong, because I ain't no pimp."

Mason smiled. "Still not enough to get you an 'A-plus' rating from the Better Business Bureau."

"I sleep very well at night," Nicky admitted proudly.

Mason clasped his hands. "That's probably from all the clonazepam."

In another few seconds, Jimmy Diaz wouldn't be able to maintain his grip on Nicky. What were to happen after that would be anyone's guess, but Diaz prayed there was extra carpeting somewhere in the cargo hold.

Nicky the Knife's head bobbed up and down. He did that whenever he was thinking. "You know, Pete. Can I call you Pete?"

Mason shook his head. "No, you can't."

"Well Pete," Nicky continued, unflustered. "I'm not really here for a social call. I realize that I'm running over my allotted time, but I didn't come here to be no fucking welcome wagon for you."

Peter Mason blinked slowly. Nicholas Coltello was always on his to-do list, but it was looking like Nicky the Knife was going to have to be dealt with sooner rather than later. "I assumed that, Nicky. You would have been a mediocre choice on the City of Jacksonville's behalf."

Nicky pushed Jimmy Diaz's hand off his shoulder and stood up. Peter Mason stood as well. There was very little difference in height, but that's where all the similarities ended. Nicky had clawed his way up from the street, while Peter Mason's claim to fame was as a beneficiary.

The atmosphere inside the large cabin had suddenly become claustrophobic.

Mason was the first to break the standoff. "What is it that you want from me, Nicky?"

Nicky's request came across without the slightest hint of reservation and bore the full weight of an ultimatum. "You need to change the location of your new ballpark. It doesn't work for me."

"It doesn't *work* for you?" Mason said, curiously. "I'm sorry. I wasn't aware that you had been appointed the City Manager. Did I miss the referendum?"

"Disrespect me all you want, Mason, but I'm here to tell you that your stadium is not going to be built on the site by the river. Find somewhere else. I'll even help you finance a new location."

Mason looked at his watch. Dinner would be served soon, and he needed everyone to be in the dining room while the transfer was being made. "That's very generous of you, Nicky, but I have my heart set on the area by the river. The city commission is ready to approve the sale of the land, and, in less than two years time, professional baseball will have a new home in the City of Jacksonville."

Nicky shook his head. "Not by the river."

Mason walked over to a mirror and began knotting his bowtie. "I'm afraid the decision's already been made. The commission has already agreed to put the issue on the November ballot. Our polls tell us it will pass by a large margin."

Nicky the Knife stepped up behind Mason at the mirror, and his reflection grinned malevolently. "Well, if there's nothing I can do to change your mind, then at least let me give you a hand with that tie."

In a blur of speed, Coltello reached around Mason's neck and grabbed both ends of the tie and pulled the length of silk taut. Mason reached up to his collar, but the garrot was already digging into his windpipe. Nicky the Knife lifted his left knee and place it squarely on Mason's back for leverage.

"Nicky!" Diaz yelled. "Not like this!"

Nicky's teeth were gnashing, and his face was nearly as red as his victim's. "He had to go! Might as well be now!"

Mason was flailing behind his back, but Nicky had done this before and knew how to exert the most pressure. "Sorry Pete," Nicky grunted, as he choked out Mason's life, "but I never really cared much for baseball. Takes too long."

56

"Holy crap!" Magnetti screamed as he slammed his hand down on the table, sending his beer can toppling to the floor. "I don't fucking believe it!"

A young first baseman named Ortega was startled by the sudden outburst. "What's the matter, Coach? Everything okay?" He asked, in a thick Dominican accent. "You knocked your beer off the table!"

"I can't freakin' believe it! Son of a bitch!"

Ortega reached down and retrieved the half-empty can of brew. "Jesus, Coach! You scared the shit out of me? What did you do that for?"

Magnetti tipped his head back and stared at the ceiling deep in thought. The first baseman glanced around the table and shrugged at his teammates. "You want a fresh beer, Coach? You look like you just seen a ghost or something!"

The batting coach pushed his chair away from the table and stood up. "Excuse me, guys. I've got to talk to someone."

"I think they're serving dinner soon, Coach," Ortega said. "You want to tell me what you want to eat?"

Magnetti didn't answer his player as he turned to cross the room.

Simone was the first to spot the coach heading in their direction. She squeezed Matt's knee under the table like it was a tension ball. Matt winced in pain. "What was that for? He signed indignantly.

Simone jabbed her chin toward the dance floor. Matt locked eyes with the man that had killed his parents a decade ago. Simone continued to squeeze Matt's leg so hard that he literally had to peel her fingers away beneath the linen tablecloth.

"Matthew," the Coach said as a way of reintroduction, "I knew that I remembered you from somewhere. It's been driving me crazy!"

Matt translated for Simone, her eyes growing larger with each hand gesture.

"Do you mind if I sit down?"

Matt wordlessly held out his hand toward the chair next to him. Magnetti sat down and smiled at the older couple sitting across the table. "How are you folks doing tonight?

They nodded happily. "Some terrific ship Mason's got here, am I right?

"Yes, it's beautiful," the older woman testified.

"Have you taken the tour yet?"

"Not yet."

Matt continued to interpret for Simone, but she missed half of what he was telling her since she had her eyes fixed on the uninvited guest.

"I heard they're going to be serving dinner soon. If you want to see the rest of the ship, you should probably take one of the tours before they start bringing out the food. You should try stepping out on the Oceanwalk. I was scared at first, but it's pretty exhilarating once you're out there."

The old woman put her hand on her chest. "I don't think I could. I get queasy pushing a grocery cart."

Magnetti looked at her husband, but now there was more curtness in his tone. "How about you, old-timer? Have you got the stomach for it?"

The elderly man threw his napkin down on the table and grabbed his wife by the arm. "Why I never…"

"Yeah, you probably haven't," Magnetti sniped. "Why don't you take the old bitch for a spin on the dance floor?"

"You are either very drunk, sir, or very rude!" The elderly woman groused. "Either way, I won't be insulted by the likes of you!"

"Yeah, whatever. Break a leg."

Simone's bottom lip began to tremble as Matt's hands formed the words so fast, she could barely keep up. Even in silence, the look on the killer's face spoke volumes.

"So," Magnetti said, turning his attention back to Matt and his date, "Now that we've got a bit of privacy, we can talk."

Matt formed the words for Simone.

"Are you translating everything I'm saying to her?" he said, pointing to Simone.

Matt nodded.

"That's awesome. I don't know how you do that."

Instead of repeating what Magnetti had said verbatim, Matt signed, *"You see the woman with the red hair sitting at the table around the far corner of the dance floor? I want you to excuse yourself and get her over here. She doesn't sign. Get her now!"*.

Magnetti stood gentlemanly as Simone pushed away from the table. "Something you said?" He asked.

Matt shook his head. "She's going to the bar to bring me a drink. Do you want something?"

Magnetti smiled at Simone and mimicked popping open the top to a beer.

Matt looked at her with his eyes wide. "Stop by the bar and bring back a beer for him and something for me."

"But you don't drink," she signed.

"I told him you were going to the bar. Go!"

Simone excused herself and walked away. Leaving Matt alone with his parent's murderer was the last thing she wanted to do.

Magnetti watched her walk away. "Beautiful girl! So exotic looking! You're a lucky guy! In my line of work, it's hard to find anyone for more than one night, if you know what I mean. Family life is fine for some people, but I'm always on the move, so it's tough."

Matt looked at his fingernails, but he was really just double-checking to make sure that his hands weren't shaking. "What can I do for you, Tony?"

Magnetti grinned at the young man's sudden informality. Once a gutsy kid, always a gutsy kid. "It's funny. I've been sitting over there at my table, wracking my brain trying to figure out where I know you from. Your face looked so damned familiar to me."

Matt swallowed hard.

"Then I figured it out. Now I know why I recognized you…"

"Matthew!" Lauren King interrupted. "I thought that was you! How are you? It's been too long!"

Anthony Magnetti gnawed on his bottom lip as he stood up and held out his hand. "Well, hello there! I'm Tony, and you are?"

Lauren swayed past him and put her hands on Matt's shoulders almost protectively. Matt turned his head so he could read the detective's lips. "Lauren King, I'm an old friend of Matt and his family. And how do you know Matthew, Tony? I overheard you say you recognized him. So am I to assume that you've met before?"

Magnetti held out a chair so Lauren could join them. "I was just saying to young Matthew here that I thought I recognized him, but I couldn't place his face. It was driving me crazy. You see, he came over to my table for an autograph before, and I had the strangest feeling that we had met before."

Lauren put her elbows on the table and rested her chin on the back of her hands. "An autograph? Are you famous, Tony?"

Magnetti shook his head. "Not really. I'm just a coach for the team Peter Mason is putting together if his stadium deal goes through. We get fans asking for autographs all the time."

Lauren nodded dimwittedly. "I know nothing about football. Brutal game."

Magnetti half-smiled. "It's baseball actually. I coach baseball."

The detective fluttered her eyes. "And just what does a baseball coach do?"

Magnetti shrugged. If she hadn't been so hot, he would have dismissed her as he did the geriatrics. "A little of this, a little of that. I'm the batting coach actually."

Lauren sighed and brushed her hair away from her face unimpressed. "So you teach those players over there how to swing the bat?"

Magnetti looked perturbed. "That's it in a nutshell, I guess."

"Hmmm…" she replied distastefully, placing one hand on Matt's shoulder.

"And what does an attractive woman like you do, if I may ask?" Magnetti inquired.

Lauren smirked. "A little of this, a little of that."

"Ahh…"

Lauren turned her attention to Matt. "You're looking so well, Matt. How is your grandfather doing? It's been months since we've spoken."

Matt wasn't sure what she was up to or what exactly Simone had told her. "Okay," he managed.

The detective looked back at the batting coach. "Matt's grandfather is an amazing man. Have you ever met him?"

Magnetti shook his head. "No, I haven't. I just met Matt a few minutes ago."

"His grandfather raised Matthew since he was a child." She covered the side of her mouth so Matt couldn't read her lips. "His parent's were murdered in their sleep. Such a tragedy," she chagrined.

"That is tragic," Magnetti repeated.

Lauren pretended that the subject was too much for her and she shook it off with a wave of her hand. "So, you said you recognized Matt. From where? He's deaf you know."

The batting coach cringed a little at how ditzy this woman was. It's always brains or beauty. Why are the ones he meets never both? "Yes, I'm very aware Matt can't hear, but he seems to read lips very well."

Lauren rubbed Matt's shoulder. "Yes, it's one of Matt's varied talents."

Now Magnetti understood. But how did a kid with only four of his senses hook up with the two hottest women on the boat? It wasn't fair.

"So where did you think you knew Matthew from?"

"I'm not sure, but I came over here to ask him."

The detective turned Matt's face toward her. "Tony says, he knows you from somewhere. Do you recognize him?" Her eyes never blinked. It was a one-man lineup, and she was waiting for an acknowledgment from the only witness.

Matt shook his head slowly. "I just met him."

Magnetti interrupted. "He wouldn't know me. I think I know who he is though. I might be mistaken, but I think he's the kid who ran out onto the ball field the other day. Am I right?"

Matt could feel his pulse pounding in his temples. He felt like he was sitting between a shark and a bigger shark, he just didn't know which one was which. He nodded his head.

The killer banged his open hand on the table. Neither Matt or Lauren flinched, but for entirely different reasons. "I knew it!" he announced excitedly. "I told my guys that I knew him from somewhere, but I wasn't sure. Then it came to me! You were the kid on the field. Damn, son, what were you thinking?"

Matt was about to make something up when Simone returned to the table with a beer for Magnetti and a ginger ale for him.

The batting coach took the bottle and held it up in appreciation. "Well, if two's company, and three's a crowd, then four is an orgy. So good evening ladies, I think I'm going to get back to my team now, but Matt, " he said, standing to leave. "I promise we'll finish our conversation before I leave this ship tonight. I don't like leaving loose ends."

Matt didn't interpret what Magnetti said, but Simone didn't need a translator. She could feel his menace from where she stood. Simone bent over and wrapped her arms around Matt's neck from behind. She leaned in and kissed him on the cheek, then looked at Lauren. Simone needed to be understood, so she actually spoke the words aloud in the best voice she could muster. "It's him."

The detective smiled back reassuringly. "I know."

57

Two bells rang, and throughout the ship, a man's voice came over the public address system asking all guests to return to the dining room. The tours had ground to a halt, and the passengers were all guided back to their tables by employees in white tuxedoes or long, black gowns. Almost every seat was filled.

Ten minutes later, two more bells sounded as the room filled with subdued laughter and idle chatter and the lights began to dim. The orchestra finished their version of Kool and the Gang's "Celebration," and put down their instruments. A lone spotlight lit the stage, but the guests were surprised by the sudden change of hosts.

"Good evening, ladies and gentlemen; let me take a moment to introduce myself to those here tonight that may not know me. I'm Gerald Banks of the Mason Cruise Line Corporation, and I would like to officially welcome you to the maiden voyage of the luxury hydrofoil slash cruise ship, *The Hydra*."

A round of applause, hoots, and whistles filled the room.

Gerald Banks took a half-bow. "Thank you all very much. That long description, like the name of Peter Mason's new baseball team, is a work in progress."

The passengers laughed and moaned at Peter Mason's expense.

"Too soon?" Banks asked.

The crowd was delighted by the host's honesty. The name given to the ball club had been soundly repudiated throughout the city and all over the media.

Banks pointed across the room. "Well, if any of you have suggestions, I'll be leaving a box by the back entrance, and you can drop some names in as you disembark. Just please, keep them family-friendly."

The guests continued to laugh.

"So, are you all enjoying the trip so far?" He called out.

The response was a rousing affirmation.

"That's terrific! For those of you who are wondering just who I am, and why Pete is not officially welcoming you, let me answer the second question first. Pete's been fighting off a stomach bug for the last week or so, and it's finally won the battle. So he's resting in his cabin, but he wanted me to assure all of you that he'll be just fine, and there is nothing he would wish more in this world than to be standing in front of you live."

A round of sorrowful groans and murmurs permeated the room.

Banks held up his hands to settle the crowd. "Pete's stateroom is not that far from here, and I'll bet that if we all gave him a rousing round of applause and cheered really loud, he would probably hear it and know how much we care about him!"

The guests all jumped to their feet and began clapping and hooting and hollering.

Banks put the microphone under his armpit and joined in the applause. "Thank you all so much, I'm sure Pete heard that! As a matter of fact, I think most of Bermuda would have heard that!"

Out of the corner of his eye, Banks saw Nicholas Coltello and Jimmy Diaz returning to their table. They avoided eye-contact and just took their seats like all the rest of the passengers.

"Uh, so to answer the second question from before, I am the Chief Financial Officer of the Mason Cruise Line. Some may call me a bean-counter, or an overpaid accountant," he said, jovially. "But my most important title is Peter Mason's brother-in-law if that answers any of your questions about how I got to where I am today!"

The guests laughed, and Nicky the Knife flagged down a waiter to get himself another drink.

Banks had no idea how he was keeping everyone so entertained after just being witness to a cold-blooded murder. It felt like he was having an out-of-body experience. He tried not to think about what they had done with the corpse, but there was a vast ocean outside, filled with ravenous marine predators.

"While you are enjoying your dinners prepared by one of the most prominent Northeastern Florida chefs, Chef Justin Bonner, we will be performing a series of simulations on the *Hydra*'s propulsion and engineering systems. I can assure you that everything is running better than we could have ever hoped for, but we want to try out these basic maneuvers to see how our ship handles during food service. The Captain has assured me that not one drop of wine will spill nor one dinner roll...roll," he chuckled.

Banks placed the microphone back into its stand and put his hands in his pockets. He was worried someone might spot them trembling.

"We will also be testing out our severe weather protocols, which means our windows will shutter automatically for a few minutes. This is to test the integrity of our watertight seals and the stability of the recently added Oceanwalk, which some of you were daring enough to experience tonight. Not to worry! I can tell from the headcount that the Oceanwalk is perfectly safe."

The guests giggled nervously. One of them yelled out, "seemed a little wobbly to me!"

Banks turned to the heckler. "Bartender, cut him off, he seems a little wobbly to me!"

Everyone laughed, and Banks took a step back from the microphone stand. He was worried that if he touched the metal rod with his sweaty hands, he would probably electrocute himself.

"So, to wrap it up, you might feel the ship slow down, hover in place for a few minutes, then reverse direction; finally, Captain Karrlson will increase the *Hydra*'s forward speed and resume our course to King's Wharf, Bermuda. I apologize for any inconvenience, but I'm sure you will be so enraptured with the cuisine that you'll be oblivious to any changes in the *Hydra*'s movement. Thank you all for being a part of this momentous evening, and on behalf of Peter Mason and the entire Mason Cruise Line family, enjoy your food, drink all you want, and by all means, dance the night away to our incredible house band, Nia Rohan and The Legacy!"

Banks stepped off the stage and waved as Nia Rohan began singing "Shut Up and Dance." Waiters poured out of the kitchen carrying menus and baskets of rolls and butter for each table. The women at each table were given menus first, and the men last. Another set of waiters filled water glasses and handed each guest their linen napkin. If someone was wearing black, they knew enough to give that guest a black napkin so no lint would show on their clothing. Everything was done first-class.

Even though she had taken a temporary seat with Matt and Simone, Lauren King had noticed Nicholas Coltello and Jimmy Diaz's vanishing act before dinner. Perhaps a restroom pitstop, perhaps not. Maybe it was the fact that the man they had been speaking so intensely with fifteen minutes earlier had suddenly become the master of ceremonies. That was the way her mind operated; if she thought the worst, then she'd never be disappointed. But what bothered her more than Nicky the Knife's tardiness or the unexpected change of hosts was the fact that Petty Officer Simms had never returned.

58

As Scott Simms wormed his way toward the bridge, Captain Roy Sowell was going over the docking procedures with Hassan and Jean-Baptiste. He re-read the dossier that had been provided about the *Dobrinski*. She was a recommissioned supertanker of the VLCC class, which stood for Very Large Crude Container. With dimensions of over one thousand feet in length and nearly two hundred and fifty feet wide, four ships the size of the *Hydra* could comfortably fit inside her massive cargo hold.

For the past four weeks, the *Dobrinski* had been anchored off the coast of Morocco while her interior was retrofitted to make room for the *Hydra*. She was so large that when she was at full capacity, she had to remain at sea to unload her oil because no port in the world was deep enough to accommodate her.

Usually, the supertanker would have a draft of well over sixty feet, but with her cargo hold stripped down to the hull, she would be riding much higher in the water. She had two massive twin screws with redundant propulsion and maneuvering should the occasion warrant it. In layman's terms, Sowell surmised, she was one quick beast.

The *Dobrinski*'s stern was equipped with a loading ramp that could be lowered enough that the *Hydra* would effortlessly glide inside. If all went as planned, the *Hydra*'s cargo would be unloaded in less than five minutes, and the two ships would go their separate ways.

Sowell closed the file and rested it on his lap. He took off his readers and rubbed the bridge of his nose. His head was pounding as the consequences of his actions played through his mind. He imagined the devil sitting on one of his shoulders and an angel on the other. He wasn't a religious man, but nonetheless, they were screaming in his ears, tearing his soul in two.

It wasn't about the technology; if he had been worried about a satellite-killing laser falling into the wrong country's hands, he could have gone below and torn out the damned circuitry himself. If the United States had one of these things, then rest assured the other guys did too. Stealing and selling this technology would be nothing more than an ampersand in the history book of warfare.

No, this was payback for the way he had been treated. Plain and simple. This was about the money. It was about the ability to take care of his family when his country would not. This was the logic that the devil had persuaded him with.

The angel was just as relentless. He kept seeing the faces of his crew flash before his eyes. He mourned each and every one of them. He had no idea that they were going to die, but he had made a pact with the living devil, and this internal slideshow was his penance.

"Captain," Hassan called out, "The *Dobrinski* is two nautical miles out."

"Slow her down to one-fifth and check to see that we're buttoned up downstairs. We want to be in and out in as fast as possible. Is the crew ready to unload?"

Jean-Baptiste spoke into his headset. "They're ready on your signal, Captain."

"Slow and steady then. Let's make this as smooth as possible."

One deck below, Simms had his back to the bulkhead and was making his way cautiously toward the bow. He had already been reminded by at least three crewmembers that dinner was being served and the rest of the ship was off limits until the meal service was finished. He graciously thanked each steward and asked for directions back to the dining room, which he totally ignored.

With his back to the wall, he was surprised at how smooth the

Hydra actually ran. The Coast Guard might well consider using this hydrofoil technology when building any new ships. There was an elevator at the far end of the passageway with guest suites lining each side. The walls continued the theme of nautical art that he had seen elsewhere on the ship. Moving past depictions of the German Battleship *Bismark* mounted alongside the U.S.S. *Constitution* made him take pause and question the interior decorator's allegiances.

He was halfway down the long corridor when he heard a cabin door open and then slam shut. He could make out two male voices heading his way. He ducked into the doorway of the nearest cabin and squatted low against the wall. Two men walked by in a hurry, undoubtedly late for dinner. Simms wasn't paying attention to their conversation, but one of the two was dropping "F" bombs like they were a dime a dozen.

The bridge was one deck above where he stood. He sprinted the rest of the hallway, continually looking over his shoulder to see if anyone was following him. When he reached the elevator, he pressed the "up" button, but the light didn't come on. He tapped it over and over, but there was no response. There was a slot running the length of the control panel which he now surmised was activated by a key card. This was a dead end, but there had to be another access to the bridge. There was never only one exit from a control room. Somewhere there had to be another way in, one that didn't require an elevator; an escape route in case the ship had to be abandoned in case of an emergency. He just had to find it.

"Five hundred yards and closing, Captain," Hassan called out.

Sowell got up from his chair and walked to the window. "Leave the spotlight off, we can do this with the light from inside the tanker. Are we all secure below?"

"Yes, sir," Jean-Baptiste affirmed. "The guests are in the middle of dinner and have been told what to expect."

Sowell nodded. "Okay then, slow her down to a hover and let the *Dobrinski* know we're coming in. Alert the crew in our cargo hold that time is of the essence."

Once the *Hydra* was within one hundred yards of the supertanker, the horizon disappeared and was replaced with a towering red steel wall. In ten foot high white lettering, the name *Dobrinski* was painted on the stern, along with her country of registration.

Jean-Baptiste spoke into his headset and two rows of parallel lights, like lines of longitude, came to life on the tanker's stern. Slowly and deliberately, the loading ramp began to descend like a drawbridge, and the lights inside the supertanker's cargo hold came into view. Once the door was level with the water, Sowell watched half a dozen of the *Dobrinski's* crewmembers attach flotation buoys to the end of the ramp. When the floats were secured, the ramp splashed into the water, and a crewman on the top of the door signaled the thumbs up.

Sowell grabbed a handrail that ran the length of the control panel. "Let's make her as tall as she can get, gentlemen. We want to keep the incline to a minimum. We don't want some Sunday sailor downstairs to question what's going on. Increase our forward speed to one-fifth and keep it there. We don't want to rattle any dishes."

With the precision of a surgical scalpel, the *Hydra* slipped into the rear of the supertanker and slowed to a hover once she was in position. The velocity of the bottom fanbines was gradually slowed until the ship settled onto her inflatable pods. Sowell pressed a button on his watch. "The clock is running. Five minutes and we're out of here, finished or not."

Inside the cargo hold of the *Dobrinski*, a series of cranes crisscrossed the ceiling. Used generally for loading and moving shipping containers weighing tens of thousands of pounds each, the crane positioned above the *Hydra's* cargo hatch had no problem removing an eight hundred pound wooden crate.

When the task was completed, the *Hydra's* hatch was sealed, the bottom fanbines were increased in speed, and the two fans on the stern were thrown into reverse.

Sowell checked his watch. There were forty-five seconds to spare. Easy-peasy. "We're all secure?"

"Yes sir," Hassan replied. "The cargo hatch shows green and locked."

The Captain returned to his seat. "Then bring her to the same height and speed we used going in, boys. When we're half a mile out, we'll crank her up to full speed and put this leviathan in our rearview mirror."

Hassan and Jean-Baptiste smiled at each other from different sides of the front control panel.

"Yes, sir, one half-mile, sir."

"Yes sir, full speed, sir!"

The *Hydra* glided effortlessly in reverse and backed out of the supertanker. As soon as she had cleared the ramp, the *Dobrinski's* flotation buoys were removed and the loading ramp began to rise and seal. It looked like a giant mouth closing after a satisfying meal.

"The *Dobrinski* is underway, Captain," Jean-Baptiste called out. "She's heading east at five knots, and her speed is increasing."

Sowell took a sip of water, and let the liquid soothe his raw throat. He had pulled it off, and now his family would never want for anything. "Okay, gentlemen," he said, between coughs, "next stop, King's Wharf, Bermuda. Let's see if we can make it in record time!"

59

"So why don't you arrest him?" Simone signed, furiously.

Matt rolled his eyes as he interpreted for his girlfriend. He knew what the detective's answer was going to be even before she said anything.

"There is nothing I would rather do more, Simone, but it's not that easy."

Simone pushed her place setting toward the middle of the table and continued to sign with anger in her gestures. "He killed Matt's parents! Matt knows it, and I know it. Why is it so difficult for you to believe him?"

Matt blew out an exasperated breath as he turned to Simone. As he signed to her, he spoke softly so Lauren would understand. "The fact that I was able to use this crazy thing to find him isn't exactly irrefutable evidence that the police can use. There is no solid proof."

"But he threatened you!"

Lauren held out her arm to interrupt the conversation. "All he said was he wanted to continue his conversation with Matt later and that he hated loose ends. Even though you know, and Matt knows, and I know what that implies, it wasn't a direct threat."

Simone shook her head in frustration. "He knows who Matt is now. He's the loose end!"

Matt put his arm around Simone and pulled her close. He kissed the side of her face to calm her down.

Lauren looked over her shoulder at Magnetti, who was staring back at them. She leaned in to whisper, even though the band was playing so loud it wouldn't have mattered even if Matt and Simone could hear. "Everything you say is correct, Simone. I do think he recognized Matt and now he realizes he's left a witness. There is no statute of limitations on murder, so I would be lying to you if I said I didn't believe that Matt was in danger. I just don't think that Magnetti is stupid enough to attempt something on a crowded boat out in the middle of the ocean." She reached out and took Simone's hand. "I need you to calm down. I know it won't be easy, but the more suspicious you behave, the more concerned Magnetti will become. Eat your dinner," the detective instructed, as she moved the place setting back into position, "and try not to look over there. Let me handle this."

Matt nodded. "She's right," he signed to Simone, "I trust her."

"I'm scared."

Matt kissed her cheek again. "I know, but everything will be alright."

The detective stood up. "I want you to come with me, Matt."

Simone grabbed his arm as he stood up.

Matt rubbed her arm and released it. "The room is full of people, Simone. Nothing is going to happen here. We have to act like everything is normal."

"Where is she taking you?"

The detective smiled warmly. "I just want to introduce him to a few people, and then he'll be right back. Five minutes tops."

"Order the chicken for me," Matt signed. "And the shrimp cocktail."

Simone looked up at him mystified. "Seriously?" She signed.

"Order the steak for yourself, and we can share the dinners."

Simone rapped her knuckles on the table. "He wants me to order dinner!"

Matt moved to his right to regain her line of sight. "No, I want you to act normal. I'll be right back, I promise."

The detective smiled down at Simone, but the gesture was not reciprocated.

"Where are we going?" Matt asked.

Lauren turned her head toward Matt as they walked around the edge of the dance floor. "There are two people I want you to meet."

"By meet you mean…"

The detective nodded. "Exactly. Just see if you get any impressions from them."

Nicholas Coltello and Jimmy Diaz were buried in a secretive discussion. When the waiter came to get their dinner choices, Coltello waved her away.

"Hello, Nicky," Lauren said, walking up to the table with Matt at her side. "Not eating tonight?"

Coltello stood up as any gallant gentleman would. "Detective King. How nice to see you again. I thought that was you over there, but I've never seen you all dolled up. You clean up nice!"

Lauren grinned. "How long has it been, Nicky?"

Coltello shrugged. "I don't know, Detective. A few months, maybe? I'm trying to cut pork out of my diet."

"Nicky, Nicky, Nicky," Lauren sighed. "You can try to dress up a turd, but it'll always smell like one."

Coltello's fist clenched, which was Jimmy Diaz's signal to interrupt the exchange. "Did you just sashay over here to insult Mr. Coltello, Detective King? Or is there some other reason you have to ruin this nice evening for us?"

"Oh, I'm sorry," she apologized, putting her hand on her chest. "I just wanted to introduce you to someone. A friend of mine, Matthew Walker."

Nicky the Knife shook his head. "Kinda young for you, ain't he, Detective?"

"No, no, you've got it all wrong. Matthew is working as a kind of consultant to the department, and I wanted him to introduce him to the underbelly of our city firsthand."

Jimmy Diaz chimed in. "There's no need for that kind of talk, Detective. Everyone is here to have a good time and share in Peter Mason's good fortune. Why don't we try to table our animosity for tonight? Would you like to dance?"

The band had taken a break for dinner, but Lionel Ritchie's "Truly" was playing through the speakers on the stage. The Detective looked at Matt. "Why don't you introduce yourself to Mr. Coltello while I dance with Mr. Diaz."

Jimmy Diaz took Lauren by the hand and escorted her to the dancefloor. She tried to maintain her space, but Diaz pulled her close.

"Have a seat," Nicky told Matt. "Do I know you from somewhere? You look kinda familiar."

Matt assumed Coltello had been at the ballgame too. "Sorry, but I don't think so."

"What the hell is the matter with your voice?"

Matt held the letter "D" up to his ear. "I'm deaf. I'm reading your lips. I'm sorry if you're not understanding me."

"Holy shit," Nicky exclaimed. "I'll be damned. And you're reading my lips right now?"

Matt nodded.

"And if I turn my head like this?"

"Excuse me?"

Nicky laughed. "That's fucking hysterical!"

"I don't know what you're saying if you turn your face from me."

"The J.P.D must really be scraping the bottom of the barrel if they're hiring retards now. Wait till this news gets around!"

Matt had dealt with it all before, but there had to be a reason why the Detective had left him alone with this ignorant asshole. There had to be something she wanted him to find out. "Excuse me, Mr. Coltello," Matt said, courteously. "My ears can't hear, much in the same way that your brain can't think. It's just the cross we both have to bare."

It was apparent from the vacant look on Nicky's face that he wasn't sure if he had just been insulted or not. "No hard feelings, kid. You're just the first deaf person I ever met, " Nicky admitted, as he held out his hand to shake in a gesture of seldom felt empathy.

The minute flesh touched flesh, Matt began to convulse. His eyes rolled back into his head, and the connection was unyielding. Nicky Coltello's felt like his hand was caught in a vise. Something was happening that he didn't like. He tried to pry the kid's hand loose, but it only made the kid tighten his grip with more resolve. He was reaching for his serrated dinner knife when Jimmy Diaz, the Detective, and Simone Goldman came running across the dance floor.

"This fucking kid won't let go of my hand!" Nicky howled. "What the fuck is going on? What's he doing to me?"

Simone stepped in and cupped Matt's face in her hands. She put her cheek next to his and could feel that he was cold and clammy. She ran her hands through his hair as the Detective, and Jimmy Diaz looked on helplessly. Matt's grip suddenly sprang open.

Nicky stood up and backed away from the table. "What the hell is wrong with that kid? Get him away from me!"

Diaz looked at Lauren suspiciously. He wasn't sure what was going on, but he was determined to find out.

Matt's breathing began to slow, and he sat up slowly in the chair with his head bent over. "I'm sorry," Matt apologized between deep breaths. "I'm prone to seizures. I'm taking medication, but I never know what will trigger one."

Simone was on one knee and was wiping his forehead with a napkin she had dipped in a water glass.

When Coltello realized his outburst had gathered the attention of most of the passengers, he held up his hands. "Nothing to see here, people. The kid is okay. Go back to your food."

Lauren helped Simone get Matt to his feet, and each of them took him by an arm.

"What the hell happened?" Diaz asked Nicky.

Coltello straightened his tie and sat back down. "Fuck if I know. Just keep that freak away from me."

Jimmy Diaz watched as the Detective, and the other two walked at a snail's pace across the room. Anthony Magnetti had put down his knife and fork and was watching too.

Matt turned his head to the Detective.

"Is that what normally happens?" She asked. "Why didn't you warn me?"

The trio made it back to the table, and Matt slumped exhaustedly in his chair. "Why didn't I warn you?" He asked, sarcastically. "Do you have any idea of the crazy shit that guy has done in his life?" Matt signed and spoke softly.

"I know exactly what he does," the Detective answered.

Matt shook his head slowly to the contrary. "Well, I'll bet you don't know that he just strangled Peter Mason, and I know where the body is!"

60

"Is everything okay over here?" Hope Jannick asked, walking up to the table. "What happened to you over there?"

"Nothing," Matt answered. "Just a bit of motion sickness, I guess."

Matt's long-time friend looked surprised. "Motion sickness? It doesn't even feel like we're moving!"

Matt shrugged. "Thanks for checking up on me, but with our hearing loss, sometimes our inner ears can throw off our equilibriums. Simone said she was feeling a bit queasy too."

Hope looked over at Simone who rubbed her stomach in agreement.

"Well, I hope it passes. I don't want you telling anyone that you got seasick on this trip. Everyone enjoying themselves and having a smooth ride means a lot to my dad's company."

Matt zippered his lips. "Not a word. I promise."

Hope smiled. "Well, enjoy the rest of the trip. The food is going to be something else!"

"I'm sure it will be," Matt said. "I'm not sure if I have much of an appetite though."

"Just give it a taste, and tell me what you think, okay?"

Matt nodded to Hope as she walked away. "Will do."

Now that the obligatory chit-chat was out of the way, the Detective pointed to her own mouth. "Make sure you understand what I am asking you! You saw Nicholas Coltello strangle Peter Mason?"

Matt emphatically nodded. "He was standing behind Mason, and I could see his reflection in a mirror. Mason was fussing with his bowtie, and that guy over there came up from behind and strangled Mason with his own bowtie!"

Simone slapped Matt on the arm because he had stopped signing. "Sign!" she motioned, fiercely.

Matt turned to her. "I don't want to get you involved," he signed.

Simone scowled at him. "I'm already involved. Tell me, now!"

Matt summarized for her what he had seen, but he fingerspelled out the word "choked" because the gesture was so visual.

Lauren King waved her hand in front of Matt's face to get his attention. "You're telling me that you actually saw Nicholas Coltello strangle Peter Mason?"

"Yes," Matt said, positively.

"Was there anyone else there?"

"I could only see through his eyes," Matt whispered and made a stabbing motion with the letter "K," his new sign language name for Nicky the Knife.

The Detective rubbed her hand over her mouth trying to assess her situation. She was in the middle of the ocean, sitting across a dance floor from two possible murderers, both accused by a teenager who saw it all in a hallucination. The cherry on the sundae was that Peter Mason, the missing puzzle piece in this crazy jigsaw, might now be dead according to her psychic! Yeah, that was her predicament pretty much in a nutshell. Where was Toby Bilston when she needed him? The only thing that was bringing her comfort right now was the feel of the revolver strapped to her thigh.

The Detective didn't speak but rather mouthed her words so that Matt would understand without anyone else the wiser. "I know you believe you saw Peter Mason killed, but I just can't go on this sixth sense of yours. I want with every ounce of my being to…"

Matt looked disappointed in her as he continued to whisper and sign for Simone. "First of all, it's my fifth sense, remember? You think I'm crazy? You think that I'm making all of this up? Why?"

Lauren hung her head. "I didn't…"

Matt lifted her chin. "I don't know what you're saying when you look down at the table! I was able to trace your past! How did I do that?"

Simone jumped angrily to Matt's defense. "If Matthew says he saw something, then he saw it!"

Matt smiled and rubbed his hand on Simone's back. "If the Detective doesn't want to believe me, then there's nothing I can do to convince her."

"Bullshit," Simone signed. "Show her the body!"

Matt stared at his girlfriend for a second and smiled before turning to the Detective.

"What did she say? She's mad at me, right?"

Matt leaned over and whispered in Lauren's ear. "You want proof? I can show you the body!"

The Detective sat upright and without realizing it, began to tap her feet nervously on the carpet. What if Peter Mason was dead? What could she do? How would she handle this in the middle of the Atlantic Ocean? These were international waters! Did that even matter?

"Show me," she mouthed.

All three of them stood up, but Matt wasn't having any of it. "You can't come, Simone," he signed.

"Like hell I can't!" she signed back.

He moved in close to her and started signing with smaller gestures to make sure that no one else could see what he was saying. It wasn't necessary, but just instinctual. "Those men are watching our every move. If we all leave together, it might look suspicious. Please stay here, for me."

Simone chewed on her upper lip. "I'm frightened!"

Matt held her hand. "The Detective knows what she's doing. I trust her. Please eat something, and I'll be back in a few minutes. I promise."

Simone crossed her arms on the table and looked past Matt to the Detective. "If anything happens to him," Matt translated.

Lauren hitched up her dress far enough so they both could see her weapon. "He'll be fine."

Matt and the Detective stood up, but not before Simone kissed him harder than she had ever done before. "She knows that showing us her gun doesn't make me feel any better, right?"

"Relax sweetheart," Matt signed by wiggling his thumbs over his heart. "We're just going to check out a dead body on a flying boat. What could possibly go wrong?"

61

Anthony Magnetti was the first to spot Matthew Walker and the redhead exiting the dining room together. He wondered where they were going, and why the girlfriend would be left behind. Something didn't feel right.

Two tables away, Nicholas Coltello watched the kid and the cop leave the dining room together. His deranged brain was assuming the worst as he tried to guess what they were up to, and why the girlfriend had stayed behind. Every scenario his twisted mind could imagine stunk like week-old scungilli.

"Tell me what you saw," Lauren asked Matt, as they headed out of the dining room.

Matt was walking a few steps ahead of her and had his head turned to read her lips. "They were definitely in a cabin. I saw a bed and sofa in the room."

The Detective slowed down. "There are over one hundred cabins on this ship! We can't search them all."

Matt stopped walking. "Peter Mason wouldn't be in a passenger cabin; wouldn't he have his own suite?"

Lauren waggled her finger. "I like the way you think. You might make a good cop someday."

Matt rolled his eyes. "Yeah, like they'd ever let a deaf person carry a gun."

"There's a lot more to police work than just shooting people! I've never had to fire my weapon ever in the line of duty! If your ability were something that you could actually learn to control, do you realize what an asset you could be to law enforcement?"

"Nah," Matt said, with a wave of his hand. "I'm in no hurry to make this thing public. I'd end up in a laboratory somewhere with wires sticking out of my head. No thanks."

"You are so wrong."

Matt shook his head mournfully. "No, I'm not, and you know it. My grandmother thought the way you do and had me tested. I won't live my life like that."

The Detective held up her hands in submission. "Okay, we don't have to talk about it now, but please don't rule it out."

Matt pointed to a floor plan of the *Hydra* that hung framed on the wall. "All the suites are one deck up. It shows a staircase down this hallway, and then we hang a right."

"I'm following you," Lauren proposed. "Lead the way."

Matt ran his finger along the diagram and took off down the passageway. When they reached mid-ship, he turned right and found the grand staircase. There wasn't anything really *grand* about it, except perhaps the brass handrails and the giant piece of abstract art that was mounted on the rear wall of each landing. This one was a mixture of swirls and squares with a myriad of colored splotches all over the canvas. Forget police work, Matt thought. All he needed was a few cans of paint, some brushes, and an agitated monkey to make a great living.

They reached the third deck, and Matt stopped in his tracks.

"What's the matter?"

"None of this looks familiar."

"Really?"

Matt made the stabbing gesture again to signify Nicky the Knife. "He didn't touch anything in the hallway. I don't know which suite he was in."

There were two directions they could go. The Detective walked over to the port side passageway and looked in both directions, and then walked past Matt to the starboard side passageway. "His suite is this way," she said, pointing to starboard.

"How do you know that?"

The Detective winked. "There's only one suite with double doors at the end of the corridor. I'm guessing it's like the ship's Presidential Suite. If I were Peter Mason, that's the one I would stay in."

The Detective held her arm out straight. "Stay behind me. If you see something or someone, get my attention; otherwise, stay close."

Matt nodded as they made their way cautiously down the passageway to the lone cabin that had double doors. Ten feet from the door, Lauren stopped short. She turned to Matt and put her finger over her lips for him to remain still.

He looked at her quizzically. She pointed to her right ear and mouthed the words, "I hear something."

"From inside?" Matt silently mouthed back.

Lauren nodded affirmatively, and reached down between her legs and drew the gun from its holster. She motioned for Matt to stay put. With her back pressed against the bulkhead, Lauren inched her way toward the door. Matt was looking back and forth, between watching the Detective and keeping vigil for her.

There was definitely movement in the suite. No one was speaking, but things were being moved around inside.

Ever so cautiously, Lauren reached out and grabbed the doorknob, which was of the lever variety, with her left hand. She held her gun at the ready in her right. To her surprise, even though the door needed a key card for entry, it was unlocked. The Detective gently pushed the lever on the left door downward staying behind the right door for added protection. When she turned the knob, the sound inside abruptly stopped.

She looked back at Matt and motioned for him to get down. He followed her instructions and lowered himself into a squat.

The Detective drew in a deep breath and slowly opened the door. She stayed low until the door was opened wide enough for her to enter. She peeked her head inside quickly and pulled it back out. The cabin was completely dark except for the sliver of light that poured in from the opened doorway. Even though it was ten o'clock at night, the window shades might have been drawn shut. If there was someone inside, they knew she was coming. No one had fired at her or had made a run for it, so that was one point for the home team.

While still outside, she stood up slowly and began counting down from three to herself. On three, she burst into the room with her gun outstretched and took a low shooting stance, which she found really difficult to do in an evening gown. Her weapon moved left and then back to the right, scanning into the darkness, across into the path of light, and then back into the shade on the other side of the suite. She knew someone had to be here. She had heard them moving around. Her heart was pounding like Seabiscuit's coming down the home stretch, and she wasn't even sure if she was breathing. She took one more step into the room and then she felt it. It was the one thing that every cop feared the most. There was the muzzle of a gun pressed up against the back of her head.

62

The Petty Officer made his way back to the middle of the ship where he remembered seeing a map of the *Hydra*'s floorplans. The diagram showed the locations of the cabins, common areas, exits, elevators, and central staircase, but it lacked directions to the bridge. He understood that there were safety precautions behind that practice. Usually, only invited guests would be allowed to visit the control room, and they would probably be escorted up by elevator.

Even though the *Hydra* was an extraordinary vessel, she was probably built like every other ship, which meant an exterior access to the bridge. There had to be a ladder outside. Simms put his finger on the map where the exit closest to the bridge was located. He sprinted down the passageway, made a left at the intersection, and continued running forward toward the bow.

When Simms reached the glass doors, he was surprised that the floor sensors didn't automatically open the exit. There was a bright red decal emblazoned on both doors cautioning passengers of the danger:

"WARNING!"

OUTER DOORS AUTOMATICALLY LOCK AT CRUISING SPEED.

RISK OF HIGH WINDS AND DANGEROUS CONDITIONS ON DECK.

IN CASE OF EMERGENCY, DOORS MAY BE OPENED BY PRESSING THE RED OVERRIDE BUTTON LOCATED NEXT TO THE EXIT.

Simms debated the advice in his head for about three seconds before pressing the red button. The force of the wind was staggering. He had never had the misfortune of being on an airliner when the cabin decompressed, but he imagined that this was what it must have felt like.

While it didn't lift Simms him off his feet, the wind still hit him like a ton of bricks. He never realized how fast the ship was actually moving! Compared to a Coast Guard cutter running at full speed, this was like standing on top of a bullet train! If drug runners ever got hold of one of these ships, no naval vessel would ever be able to stop them. Peter Mason could make a killing building them for the military. Armed and equipped with stealth capabilities, a ship like this could usher in a new era of warfare.

Simm's brand new suit was soaked in seconds. His jacket was flapping like a sail during a hurricane, so one arm at a time, he slipped out of it. He tried to toss the coat inside, but the wind grabbed it, and he watched it blow overboard into the darkness. He wondered if the police department would make him pay for it himself.

Simm's inexpensive loafers, with their smooth soles, couldn't gain traction on the wet deck. He was fighting to keep the automatic door from closing on his fists while at the same time trying to slide off his shoes. One at a time, they cartwheeled down the deck toward the stern. On the bulkhead to his left was a teakwood handrail running the length of the ship. With his upper body struggling to keep his grip, he lifted his left leg and slipped his foot between the railing and the outer bulkhead. If his shoes were terrible, his nylon socks were worse. One he thought his foot was secure enough, he let the doors slide shut. He managed to grab the handrail and stayed poised like a ballerina for more than a minute while he caught his breath.

Once Simms managed to remove his socks, his footing became more stable. He was soaked to the bone, hanging on to the railing by his left arm. He had braved hurricanes both large and small while carrying out search and rescue missions, but no one was ever allowed out on deck during a storm unless it was absolutely necessary. These conditions validated that rule.

What amazed Simms the most was that it was a crystal clear night. He could see that the ocean was calm, but the *Hydra* was traveling so fast she was literally creating her own squalls. The Petty Officer wasn't sure if she was running at top speed, but he had never experienced anything like this before.

The ladder Simms needed was straight ahead. He would have to pull himself forward along the railing for at least another fifty feet and then ascend the metal stairs fully exposed to the wind and stinging ocean spray. What a delightful evening this was turning out to be!

It took the Petty Officer ten minutes to cover the distance, with his necktie slapping him in the face every other step. Once he reached the stairs, Simms tore off the tie and let the wind take it. He kept his head down as he climbed the stairs. Each metal step had perforations for traction, but he almost lost his footing twice.

When the Petty Officer reached the landing, he held on for dear life and tried to regain his composure. The hatch to the bridge opened with a lever, but Simms knew it would be locked from the inside. He looked up and saw a security camera pointed down at the landing. If first impressions were lasting impressions, then he was screwed. He pounded on the hatch. A red light blinked on above the camera. Simms wiped the water out of his eyes and stared up at the lens. The lever moved, and the door opened.

"Petty Officer Scott Simms of the Cutter *Intrepid*, as I live and breathe," Roy Sowell declared, swiveling to see the waterlogged trespasser. "They sent you? I have to admit, I didn't see that coming."

Simms looked over at the two other technicians manning the bridge. They were both pointing handguns in his direction. Sowell looked almost unrecognizable. He was gaunt, patches of his hair were missing, and his face bore dark spots that were the third telltale sign of a degenerative illness.

"Put your weapons away!" Sowell commanded. "The Petty Officer isn't a threat. "Hassan, get the poor man a towel, he's dripping like a coffee brewer."

Simms took the towel he was handed and began to dry himself down. "I knew it. I told them you were still alive, but no one would believe me."

"Ah," Sowell smiled. "I'm in the presence of a budding detective. I'm curious, what gave me away?"

The Petty Officer gazed around the control room in awe that not one piece of equipment looked vaguely familiar. "The gasmask."

"Hmm…they recovered the gasmask. Stupid of me to have tossed it overboard."

Simms began to stroll slowly around the bridge, examining each monitor and control panel. "My Captain and a fellow officer were killed retrieving that mask."

Sowell sighed regretfully. "I heard about it on the news. I was very close with Rich Fitzpatrick; he was a good man, and he loved the service. I never had the honor of meeting C.P.O. Parker though."

"And what about your own crew? Are you as remorseful about their deaths?"

"I can assure you, Petty Officer, that a second doesn't go by that I don't mourn the brave men and women that served under my command."

Simms stood still. "So what is this all about then? Explain it to me so that I can understand exactly what would turn a dedicated American soldier into a traitor and a murderer."

Sowell leaned back in his seat. "If you'd like, I could place my hand on the bible and honestly testify that I am neither of those things."

"I don't think I'd bring God into this conversation if I were you, Captain."

Sowell laughed under his breath. "God has already sentenced me to a quick and painful death, Mr. Simms."

"Divine retribution?" The Petty Officer suggested.

Sowell tried to sit up straight, but the advanced atrophy in his spine denied him. "I understand that if our roles were reversed, I would probably feel the same anger and revulsion you're feeling for me right now. I can see it in your eyes and hear it in your voice, but you couldn't be more wrong. I am not sitting in this chair fearing God, Mr. Simms. I am sitting in this chair as his avenging angel."

63

"**BANG!** You're dead!"

The Detective turned slowly, not wanting to make any sudden moves. "Toby, you son of a bitch! I thought I was going to die!" She berated the Doctor.

"With this?" He asked, wiggling his index finger in her face.

Lauren lowered her gun, and her left hand came up open palmed and struck the Doctor squarely across his face. Not even his beard could cushion the force of the blow.

"Okay, I probably deserved that," he said, rubbing his face. "But in my own defense, you could have been anybody. I didn't know it was you until you stepped into the light."

The Detective holstered her weapon and drew in a deep sigh of relief. "I could have shot you, Toby!"

The Doctor smiled. "Not if my finger got you first!"

"Seriously, Toby! Stop making jokes! I could have actually shot you!"

Bilston reached out and took her hand. "Relax, take a deep breath. We're both fine."

Then it occurred to the Detective. "What are you doing here, Toby? I thought you were going back to the station? How did you get back on the ship?"

"Three questions?" The Doctor asked. "That's it?"

Lauren looked genuinely perplexed. It was a feeling, as a Detective, she hated more than Brussel sprouts. "No, I've got about a million more, but you can start with the basics."

Matt Walker stuck his head into the doorway. "Detective King, is everything alright?"

Toby stared at the teen and then glared at the Detective. "What is he doing here?"

Lauren waved Matt inside and gestured for him to close the door and hit the light switch. The opulence of Mason's suite was on a caliber with any five-star hotel anywhere in the world. It was four times more spacious than an average passenger's cabin and was decorated with only the most expensive furnishings and décor.

"He told me that Peter Mason was dead."

Toby looked at Matt. "Like a confession?"

"Is Mason dead?" The Detective asked.

The doctor shrugged his head toward an adjacent room. "Check out the bathroom, but don't touch anything."

The bathroom was nearly the size of the Detective's downtown apartment. Gold faucets, Italian marble, and a tub that any Roman would have been jealous of...except for the dead body lying in it.

Peter Mason's face was contorted in a painful death mask. There were visible ligature marks around his neck and contusions to both sides of his face. If Matthew was right, Nicky the Knife not only strangled Peter Mason but also decided to take out his aggression on his face. Lauren walked out of the bathroom and nodded. "He's dead alright."

"The body was moved into the tub. I'm guessing to hide it until it could be disposed of later. No one would leave Mason there to be found." The Doctor surmised.

Lauren stood in front of the full-length mirror which Matt had told her about in his vision. She could visualize Coltello pulling the tie taut around Mason's throat. "Mason's C.F.O. told the crowd in the dining room that Mason was feeling under the weather. Talk about an understatement."

"So you think he has something to do with this?"

The Detective shook off her hallucination. "Could be another piece of the puzzle," she said, turning her attention back to the conversation.

Toby turned to Matt and began signing. "You didn't come here knowing anything about Peter Mason. What are you doing here?"

"The man that killed my father is on this ship," Matt signed angrily.

The Doctor pointed a thick finger at Matt. "Why didn't you come to us with this information about your father? Why did you take matters into your own hands?"

"I found out by catching a foul ball! Who would have believed me? Either of you?" Matt irately signed back.

The Doctor pointed toward the bathroom. "Is it the same man that killed Peter Mason?"

Matt was a bit disconcerted that the Doctor wasn't as troubled about his father's case as he was about the dead body in the bathroom. He tapped his thumb and first two fingers together. "No, not the same man."

"So now you're telling me, there are two killers on this ship?"

Matt signed furiously. "Peter Mason was murdered and I told the Detective where she could find his body. I was just trying to help."

"Please don't leave me out of this conversation, Toby," Lauren interjected. "I want to know what you're saying to him."

"I want to know how he knew that Mason was dead."

"He says he saw it," she answered.

"So he was a witness."

Lauren twisted her mouth. "In a manner of speaking."

Toby's chin dropped to his chest. "Oh no," he groaned. "Not another vision."

Matt patted the Doctor on the arm to get his attention. "I know what I saw!" He said, aloud.

Lauren walked over and stood next to Matt. "When he first told me that Mason was dead, I didn't believe him. He insisted I follow him, and he led me here."

Toby signed as he spoke. "He saw the murder in his mind? I thought he had to touch something to have one of his visions?"

Matt's hands slapped at the air. "I did touch something. I touched the killer's hand!"

The Doctor massaged his throbbing temples. "So tell me, who strangled Peter Mason?"

Matt made the stabbing gesture.

"What the hell, does that mean?" Toby asked, mimicking the gesture. "I don't know what you're trying to say! Is that even a sign?"

"Nicholas Coltello killed him," Lauren jumped in.

Toby was stunned, and his sudden change of expression showed it. "You're telling me that Nicky the Knife is on this boat?"

The Detective nodded. "Sitting in the dining room with Jimmy Diaz as we speak."

Toby continued to sign as he ranted aloud. "Did I miss the part of the invitation that said, 'if you're a cold-blooded murderer, please join us for an evening of fun and excitement aboard the *Hydra*'? How many killers are running around this damned boat?"

Lauren knew Toby's off-handed effort at humor was just his way of hiding his anger. "Two that I know of," she answered.

The Doctor looked at Matt curiously. "So you just sashayed up to one of the most notorious mobsters in Florida, and just like that, said glad to meet you?"

"I introduced him," Lauren admitted.

Toby's puffed out his cheeks. "Of course you did. Why wouldn't you?"

"He was acting suspiciously, and I wanted to know if Matt could see what he was up to."

Toby needed an entire bottle of Tylenol, and quickly. "I realize that I'm just a Doctor and I never went through the police academy, but when exactly did they teach you to involve innocent civilians in your investigations?"

Lauren put her hands on her hips. "Matt jumped at the chance, as long as I agreed to check out the man he believes killed his father."

Toby took a deep breath to ward off what he was sure to be an impending stroke. "I just want to get all my facts straight," he said, feigning composure for everyone's sake. "So you, a decorated Police Detective, decided to introduce our young friend here to Nicholas Coltello, mob boss, in the hopes that he would fall into one of his trances and unlock Nicky's crime vault for you? How am I doing so far?"

Lauren stared down at her high heels.

Toby continued to sign, but his gestures were growing grander, and full of flourish and exaggeration. "And lo and behold, our young visionary sees Nicky choking Peter Mason to death. That about sum it up?"

Matt shook his head. "And then he put his body in the bathtub."

Toby smiled at him. "Of course, how silly of me! Then he put his body in the bathtub!"

Matt was defiant. "I was right, wasn't I?"

The Doctor glared at the Detective. "What does Nicky the Knife have to do with Peter Mason? Why would he kill him?"

Matt got Toby's attention and placed the letter "D" next to his ear. "I can't hear, remember? I don't know what they were talking about."

Lauren stepped in between Toby and Matt. "Hold up a second, before you come off all high and mighty, Doctor Bilston, we explained why we're here, but what are *you* doing here? How did you know that Peter Mason was dead?"

Toby stood quietly for a long moment and then signed to Matt calmly. "The Detective and I have to discuss police business. I need you to go back to the dining room and wait for us. Don't go anywhere near Nicholas Coltello, or the man you think killed your father. Do not interact with either of them. Do you understand me?"

Lauren agreed with Toby. "Do what the Doctor says, Matt. Let us handle it from here. I promise we'll finally bring you some closure. You did good, really good."

Matt suddenly felt excluded, but it wasn't a new emotion for him. "I need to check on Simone anyway," he signed, belligerently. "I don't want to leave her alone for too long."

Lauren waited for Matt to close the door before she went into full rampage mode. She began backing Toby up by poking him in the chest as she reamed him out. "Now are you going to tell me what's really going on here, or do I have to pound it out of you?"

The Doctor put up his hands in submission. "Okay, okay! Do you want the full story," he asked, "or the Reader's Digest version?"

64

"How do you consider yourself an avenging angel if you allowed your entire crew of the Truman to perish without mercy?" Simms growled. "That's just cowardice and greed."

Sowell swiveled in his chair. "Hassan, where is the *Dobrinski* now?"

The technician moved to another monitor that was tracking the supertanker. "Heading is eight-six-oh degrees at fourteen knots, Captain. She's picking up speed."

"Thank you, Hassan. Keep me informed of her course and speed."

"Yes, sir."

Sowell turned his attention back to the Petty Officer who was standing with the towel draped over his shoulders. "I didn't mean to interrupt you, Mr. Simms. Please continue."

Simms walked over to check out the radar that showed a large blip just off its center.

"What is going on here?" He asked.

The Captain drew in a painful breath as he crossed his legs. "You called me a coward and accused me of treason for monetary gain. Since it seems like you are ready to convict me, I'd like you to finish making your case."

"You knew what was going to happen to your crew."

"Absolutely not!"

"The original captain of this ship was killed so that you could take his place."

Sowell shook his head. "A misdirection so that I could take his place. Captain Hitchcock is alive and well and enjoying a much-needed vacation in Europe with his entire family."

"You knew that Peter Mason was stealing the technology to be sold to a foreign government to infuse capital into his overextended company."

"Well, I didn't know his exact rationale, but that sounds as plausible as any other."

Simms was shivering, but he never let on. "I can understand Mason's motivations, as heinous as they were, but what about you? Why did you go along with his scheme?"

"Mr. Hassan, the speed and bearing of the *Dobrinski*, please."

"Holding steady at eight-six-oh degrees and she's up to sixteen knots," the technician called out. "She's twelve miles due east of our current location."

"Very good, Hassan. Thank you."

Simms looked over the technician's shoulder and then turned back to Sowell. "Why are you tracking an oil tanker?"

The Captain wiped the corner of his mouth with his handkerchief. "You asked me about my motivation...look at me. What do you see? Do I look like the picture of health to you?"

"I'm sorry, but no."

Sowell cringed. "Have you ever had to deal with our country's Veteran's Administration? I will be long gone before any doctor from the V.A. even knows I exist. Do you have any idea what a private oncologist charges these days? I would use up every cent I have only to prolong the inevitable. Where does that leave my family? If that justifies your motivation of greed, Mr. Simms, then I'm guilty as charged."

"Captain," Hassan called out. "We have eight, no, nine contacts closing in on the *Dobrinski*'s location."

Simms looked at Sowell who had a satisfied smile on his face. "That would be the cavalry. Keep me posted, Hassan."

"What cavalry?" Simms asked. "What the hell is going on here?"

The Captain reached into a pocket on the side of his chair and pulled out a plastic bottle of water and took a long swig. "I have done a lot of things that I am not proud of, Mr. Simms, but treason is not one of them."

Simms stared at the radar and watched as the distance closed between all the targets on the screen.

"What you're seeing is the United States Navy out of Norfolk closing in one the supertanker *Dobrinski*. As you might guess, she is not heavy with crude, but she does contain a crate that our government would like to have back."

The smaller targets were encircling the larger blip on the screen.

"The minute Peter Mason scuttled my ship and killed my crew, all deals were off as far as I was concerned. Any man that values his own ambitions over human life will eventually have to pay the piper."

To say the Petty Office was confused would be an understatement. Suddenly, up was down and black was white. He rubbed his forehead trying to get his thoughts in line. "So this entire evening was a ruse to catch Peter Mason in the act of treason?"

The Captain took another sip of water. His throat felt so parched lately. "There is so much going on here, Mr. Simms, I can't begin to explain it to you. This ship really is a mythological creature with many heads."

"And you orchestrated this whole thing?" Simms asked.

Sowell chuckled. "You give me too much credit. You and I are nothing but pawns in a much larger game."

"So who is running this show?" The Petty Officer asked.

Roy Sowell felt a sharp twinge in his side in a spot where he never had one before. He smiled through the pain. "*That*, Mr. Simms is the million dollar question you should be asking yourself."

65

The Doctor and Detective headed down the central staircase to the dining room level. Lauren was holding up the hem of her skirt with one hand and was swearing aloud that if she ever got married, she would be wearing pants. Toby was two steps behind her huffing, puffing and miserable. It wasn't the gallons of perspiration he was losing that bothered him so much as the fact that someone must have just washed down the handrails, because they felt all wet to him.

"Why are these rails so wet?" He complained.

"Even your palms are sweating, Toby" the detective explained. "Harriett needs to buy you a treadmill or a gym membership!"

They reached the landing and turned for one more flight of steps.

"She's suggested that," the Doctor admitted.

"And?"

"What do you mean, 'and'? Can't you tell that I've been pumping iron? For the last three years, when I'm not dissecting cadavers, I'm working as a stunt double for The Rock! Would you please slow down?"

The Detective reached the dining level and let her mentor catch his breath. "Seriously, Toby. What would Benjamin do if something happened to you?"

Toby was bent over with his hands on his knees. "I notice you didn't say, 'Harriett.' You think she'd find someone that fast?"

Lauren put her hand on his shoulder. "Eat a salad every once in a while so we won't have to find out!"

Toby blew out a deep breath and nodded. "I hear you loud and clear. Now, how do you want to handle this?"

Lauren let the hem of her dress fall to its full length. "Nicky is a psychopath with a hair-trigger temper. We don't want him going off in a roomful of civilians. We need to separate him from the rest of the passengers. Divide and conquer."

Toby matted his forehead with his handkerchief. "You make it sound so easy."

Lauren put her hand on the doorway leading into the dining room. "Let's hope it goes that way!"

A flaming Baked Alaska was being prepared at each table as the dessert course was served. Lauren and Toby looked at each other as they stepped into the room. "Are you kidding me?" Toby asked under his breath. "There's like twenty-five fires burning in here!"

"Walk slowly," Lauren advised. "Let them burn out."

They spotted Matt at his table across the room talking to an elderly couple. They were both glad to see that he was safe. What they didn't notice was that Simone Goldman was missing.

Nick Coltello was sitting at his table trading stock tips with a business regulator from one of Jacksonville's largest banks. Jimmy Diaz was the first to spot the Detective returning to the table. He didn't know who was with her, but he assumed it wasn't her date. Diaz stood and held out his hand. "Detective, so glad to see you again! Here for another dance?"

"Sit down, Mr. Diaz. I need to have a few words with your employer."

Diaz did as he was told. "May I ask what this is about?"

"It's a private matter."

Diaz picked a napkin off the table and handed it to Toby. "You seem to be sweating, Mr...?"

"Doctor," Toby answered.

"Doctor? Are you with the police department as well, Doctor?"

"Bilston."

Diaz smiled at him. "Is somebody sick, Doctor Bilston?"

Lauren held up her hand to stop Toby from saying any more. "We'd like to speak with Nicky, now!"

Diaz gestured toward his boss who was still speaking with the banker. "As you can tell, he doesn't seem interested in talking to you."

Lauren shook her head. "Jimmy, we don't want to create a scene. There are too many people here. We need to talk to him. We can do this like civil human beings, or I can drag him out of here by his hair. Either way is fine with me."

Toby thought his bladder just leaked a little. He knew Lauren's reputation, but he had never witnessed this side in person. It was scary and a little arousing at the same time.

Nicky the Knife halted his investment conversation in mid-sentence. He gave no excuse or apology. His head slowly turned upward as he glanced at the Detective and then at the Doctor. "You are the biggest fucking Weeble I have ever seen! Is it really true that you wobble, but you can't fall down?"

Toby immediately got the toy reference, but it went right over Lauren's head. What did kids ever play with before smartphones?

"Don't let the body fool you, Nicky," Toby said, unabashedly. "Underneath, I've got the reflexes of a nineteen-year-old arthritic cat."

Coltello dabbed the corner of his mouth and stood up. "You're a funny guy, Doc. I like you."

Toby didn't smile. "Stop it, Nicky. You're making me feel all warm and fuzzy."

To the Doctor and Detective's disbelief, Nicky the Knife started to walk away. "I'd really like to stay and talk, but I don't think so."

Lauren looked at Toby and then at Jimmy Diaz. Was Nicky trying to make a run for it? Where did he think he was going to? They were out in the middle of the ocean! "Nicky, you need to stop," she called out, trying not to draw too much awareness to their situation.

Coltello picked up his pace and burst out through the dining room doors. Lauren turned her attention to Jimmy Diaz. "He realizes that there's nowhere to run, right?"

Diaz shrugged. "I don't know what he thinks anymore. I'm just here to have a good time and enjoy the food and music."

Toby grabbed Lauren by the arm. "You need to go after Nicky while I head for the control room to see if I can slow down this ship!"

Lauren called out to Toby as he started to walk away. "I think you're going to need a pass key to access the bridge!"

The Doctor reached into his jacket pocket and held up the required card. "Already taken care of!"

66

When Matt got back to the table, Simone was gone. He sat down for a few minutes, figuring that she might have gone to the restroom, but when she never returned, he started to get nervous.

Everyone else at the table was enthralled by the waiter as he flambeed the extravagant dessert. They clapped politely as the waiter began to portion out slices of the Baked Alaska. Matt looked around the dining room and spotted Detective King and Doctor Bilston heading to Nicholas Coltello's table. He hoped they knew what they were doing.

"Excuse me," he asked of the elderly couple with the cochlear implants, who had introduced themselves before as Eloise and Jonathan Harmon. "Have you seen my date? I doubt she would go wandering off by herself."

Eloise looked at her husband as if she were afraid to say something that might get the pretty young woman in trouble for leaving with the older man. Jonathan assured her that if he were in the same position, he would want to know. They were whispering to each other, but for someone who could read lips as well as Matt could, volume wasn't an issue.

"What don't I know?" Matt said, rising to his feet. "Where is Simone?"

Jonathan nodded at his wife, and she reluctantly spilled the beans. "Simone. That's a beautiful name for such a lovely young lady!"

Matt gritted his teeth. They were older and set in their ways just like his grandfather, but if Eloise didn't get to the point soon, he was going to flip out. "My date. Where did she go?"

"Personally, I thought he was much too old for her. Didn't I say that to you, John?"

The old man nodded.

Too old for her? His head snapped to the right, and he immediately saw that Anthony Magnetti's seat was empty and his Baked Alaska was nearly melted.

"Did she leave with an older man? Did he introduce himself as one of the guys from the baseball team?"

"Why yes!" Eloise exclaimed like Matt had just shown her a card trick. "How did you know that?"

"Do you know where they went?"

The old woman put her hand on her chest. "I didn't even see them leave. Did you see them leave, John?"

Jonathan had a rivulet of vanilla ice cream dripping down his chin. "She got up before him. He followed her."

Eloise occasionally dipped into her dessert and spoke at the same time, making it very hard for Matt to understand what she was saying. He wanted to stop her from eating, but he didn't want to cause a scene by slapping her spoon across the room.

"I don't remember that, John. Are you sure?"

The husband continued to ignore his chin. "Positive."

"Well, he seemed like a nice enough fellow. He brought over his souvenir baseball bat to show her. It must have had sentimental value, because he said he never traveled anywhere without it. He kept it in his cabin. A bit much if you ask me. How emotional can you get over a piece of wood? Did you know that Jonathan and I had our poodle Mitzi stuffed when she died? But she was a living thing and part of our family."

"Crazy old goat," the old man grunted under his breath.

"How long ago did she leave?" Matt pleaded.

Eloise looked at her husband. "Couldn't have been more than a few minutes, wouldn't you agree, Jonathan?"

Jonathan never looked up as he scraped his dish to get every last drop. "You just missed them."

There were four levels and over one hundred cabins to search. It wasn't like he could knock on every door and wait for a response. Matt would have to wait for someone to personally open the door. The search would take all night!

Matt sprinted out of the dining room and headed for the central staircase. His only choice was to start at the bottom of the *Hydra* and work his way up. He reached the second deck landing when a thought occurred to him. *If they had just left the dining room, they were probably still on the move. He wouldn't take her into a secluded cabin. It wasn't Simone he wanted. It was him! He would take her somewhere they could be seen. Somewhere in the open!*

Matt ran over to the diagram of the ship mounted on the wall and moved his finger around the picture, floor by floor, cabin by cabin, public space by…the Oceanwalk! How much more out in the open could you get? Everyone was busy in the dining room, so the walkway would be empty now!

The Oceanwalk was on the same floor as the dining room, where he had just come from! He had to go back up. He flew up the stairs two at a time, u-turning on the landing, and made the last ten steps in five long leaps. Left or right? He was a natural southpaw, so he went left.

There was an automatic sliding door that opened onto the Ocean-walk. There was a warning posted on the glass, but Matt paid no attention. He raced into the glass tunnel and stopped short. Matt's inner ear was his Achilles heel, and he knew it. Plane travel was difficult, and even long rides in a car could mess with his equilibrium. He couldn't hear a thing, but his accelerated breathing was coming in loud and clear. He reached out and pressed his hands up against the glass walls on both sides to steady himself. Beneath him, there was nothing. Just the froth of the ocean rushing by under his shoes. Even if he didn't have ear damage, this would probably be one of the most disorienting sensations a person could be subjected to. Why would anyone conceive of such a horrible experience?

The tunnel was empty ahead of him, so he slowly backed his way out of the glass passage. One step at a time, like he was walking an invisible tightrope...backwards. He could feel the sweat running down his forehead like the ice cream on Jonathan Harmon's chin. This wasn't some kind of psychological phobia, this was a real physical reaction, one that until this moment he was totally unaware he had.

He was starting to hyperventilate as the sliding glass doors slid open behind him. The rush of cold air was a welcome relief as he paced back and forth to regain his composure. Matt kept repeating to himself that he could overcome this.

Matt checked his watch. Five more minutes had passed. Precious timed wasted because he was as disabled as his grandfather believed him to be. It was time to step up to the plate and prove him wrong. He had been through far worse, and Simone was in trouble. Whatever it took, he would handle it.

The entrance to the starboard-side Oceanwalk was past the central staircase. This time, Matt paused to read the warning posted on the doors. The sentences where it mentioned disorientation and proceeding at one's own risk were something they should have considered writing in a bolder font. He would have to complain about that on the post-cruise survey.

Anthony Magnetti stood in the middle of the glass tunnel holding Simone by one hand and his baseball bat in the other. Matt stood in the open doorway, his feet refusing to step onto nothingness. Simone was clearly petrified, and with his hands trembling, he signed to her that everything would be alright now. Her expression didn't change with the news.

Magnetti waved the bat in Matt's direction, gesturing for him to come out and join them. In his mind's eye, Matt was already on top of the murderer, beating his head to a pulp with his own weapon and saving the day. The human brain could play cruel tricks on people.

Matt was sure that the moment he placed one unsteady foot onto the walkway, the predator before him would sense his weakness and strike.

The *Hydra* suddenly shuddered, and its forward speed began to decelerate rapidly. Matt grabbed onto the door frame to steady himself. The ship was coming to a stop! That off-kilter feeling didn't seem as intense anymore. In less than a minute, the *Hydra* was hovering in place above the surface of the ocean. If Matt kept his eyes focused straight ahead, and didn't look down; the dizziness was almost gone. Seventy-five percent would have to do.

The Oceanwalk was well lit along the edges of where the walls met the ceiling. There was no lighting on the floor, to minimize the glare and allow the passengers to see the water at night. Without a reflective surface, shadows were practically non-existent, making it very easy for Matt to see what Magnetti was saying.

Matt signed to Simone. "Did he hurt you?"

She shook her head, and the killer pulled her in closer.

Magnetti tapped the floor with the head of the bat as he spoke. "How are you not dead? It took me over three hours to refinish Sweet Amy after that night! You were one bad-ass little mother fucker! You even broke my nose! Yeah, I remember that night like it was yesterday. Now look at you, all grown up!"

"Why did you kill my parents?" Matt asked, inching closer. He chose not to interpret the conversation to keep Simone as calm as possible.

Magnetti tried to stop the girl from struggling in his grasp. "It wasn't personal, kid. I still can't believe you're standing here in front of me! I've got to tell you, this is a first. I have never had a survivor before you."

Matt held out his hand in front of him to try and keep Simone and the killer still. "Well, there's a first time for everything," Matt said peacefully.

Magnetti dragged Simone backward with him. "I still don't know how you tracked me down, but there's only one way this can end for you two. I need you to walk over to me very slowly," the killer ordered, motioning with the bat.

Matt did as he was told, but stopped just short of what would have been Magnetti's batter's box.

"Closer." Magetti urged.

"We're out in the ocean, how do you expect to get away with this?"

The killer motioned toward the ship with his head. "Those lifeboats have engines. I'll be out of here before the blood dries. Now, get over here, or I swear I'll break her neck!"

Simone was pulling with both hands to free herself, but his arm was like a tree trunk.

Matt didn't move.

"I killed your parents in their sleep. What makes you think I've mellowed with age?" Magnetti asked as he snapped the head of the bat against Simone's right ankle. She yelped in agony as the fragile bone shattered. Tears streamed down her face as she cried out to Matt for help.

The killer loosened his grip on the girlfriend, and she crumpled into a sobbing heap on the glass floor. Magnetti now had both hands on the bat with the grip that felt so comfortable to him. He could feel the power surging down the length of his arms, through Sweet Amy's handle all the way to her gleaming brown head. "I really don't care about the girl, kid."

Matt looked down at Simone and rubbed his fist over his heart. "I'm so sorry!"

Magnetti moved around the girlfriend. "I want you to know that I'm kicking myself over this, kid. Why didn't I hear about you still being alive? I'm feeling guilty, like I should give some of the money back."

"To Peter Mason?"

"Who else?"

"But why?"

Magnetti grew impatient. "Because he paid me! I don't ask the reasons!"

Matt wanted to sit down next to Simone and comfort her, to hold her and tell her everything was going to be okay. But it would have been a lie.

The killer circled around Matt until the girl, and the kid were both in front of him. "You want to take a run at me, kid? I busted all of the surveillance cameras out here. Give it your best shot! At least you'll go down swinging."

Simone was holding onto Matt's leg.

"Hey, I'm giving you a fighting chance to save yourself and your cutie-pie here. If you run, she dies, and you spend the rest of your life looking over your shoulder for me. It could be next week or next month, but you and I are definitely going into extra innings. Come on, whatever happened to that scrappy little slugger?"

Matt lunged at Magnetti, but the trained athlete was much too quick. He swept the bat in an arc a foot off the floor and knocked Matt off his feet. Matt was lying on his back with the killer standing over him. A flashback from his childhood sped through his thoughts. He raised himself to his elbows and began pulling himself backward toward Simone. She was reaching out for him, agony and fear making her entire body shake. She let out a guttural scream that reverberated throughout the tunnel.

Magnetti stood over the couple. "You've got balls, kid. I'll say that much for you. I thought for sure you would have run. Color me impressed!"

The killer raised the bat over his head, as Matt and Simone held each other tight and closed their eyes. The bat reached its apex and stayed there. Anthony Magnetti looked up to see a single hand wrapped around Sweet Amy's barrel. "It ends tonight," said an unfamiliar voice.

Magnetti spun around to see a figure dressed entirely in black, his face buried in the shadows of a hoodie. "Who the hell?"

Another hand grabbed hold of Sweet Amy and with a lightning-fast twisting action, pried her loose from her owner's grip. The shadowy figure held out the bat, raised a knee and brought Sweet Amy down in one swift motion, snapping her in half.

Magnetti was beside himself. He threw a quick right, but his opponent was holding the two halves of Sweet Amy like Chinese nunchucks. The larger end blocked the punch while the jagged end of what remained of the handle sliced through the air and caught Magnetti across the face. Blood sprayed out of the slice taken between his ear and mouth. The killer stumbled backward. "Who the fuck are you?" He screamed.

Matt and Simone had opened their eyes, but neither was sure what they were witnessing. Where had this person come from? How did he know they were in trouble?

Magnetti raised his fists and took up a boxing stance with his fists circling in front of him. The shadow mimicked his every move with the two sharp halves of Sweet Amy exposed. The killer punched, Sweet Amy blocked and stuck. A red stain spread across Magnetti's tuxedo cumberbund. He felt the wound with his right hand, which came away soaked in blood.

Simone was trying to get up, but with one ankle damaged she would struggle and then fall back down. Matt got to his knees and let his girlfriend use his shoulders for leverage. She managed to grab the handrail and pull herself up. Matt placed his hands on the glass wall and inched himself upward until he too could pull himself up using the railing.

Magnetti was losing blood fast, but his athletic ability was keeping him upright. He put all his effort into a left hook that was met with Sweet Amy's handle, followed by her barrel breaking every finger in his hand. He dropped to his knees holding his limp hand, his fingers flailing in different directions. His breath was coming out in gasps as the life drained from his body. "Just tell me who you are," he begged. "I've got to know."

"I want you to know," the shadow said, pulling back his cowl.

Magnetti blinked, trying to focus because what he was seeing was impossible. It was an apparition, a figment of a dying brain. "It can't be…" were Anthony Magnetti's last words, as he keeled over and bled out on the glass floor.

Simone turned to Matt who looked like all the blood had drained out of his face as well. She patted his chest to get his attention. "Matt? Do you know him?"

Matt nodded slowly; so slowly that you could barely tell his head was moving.

"Who is it?" Simone signed insistently.

Matt put his hand on his chest and then gradually raised his thumb to his forehead. "My father."

67

The first thing Lauren King did when she saw Nick Coltello bolt for the exit was to reach down and rip off her high heels. The second thing she did was to pull out the weapon from between her legs and apologize to everyone at the table. The few women sitting there were speechless; the men not so much.

"No worries, I'm a cop." She assured them.

Nicky had a good head start, but the Detective wasn't in a rush. Where could he go? It would be five more hours before they would reach dry land. Even if he somehow managed to elude her for the rest of the trip, they would seal all but one exit when they reached port.

"No one leaves this room until you hear it from someone wearing a badge," the Detective warned one of the waiters. "Spread the word!"

In her stocking feet, Lauren burst through the dining room doors and onto the main concourse. "There's nowhere to run, Nicky!" She yelled, running with her pistol out in front of her. She felt like she was competing in a potato sack race, the way her dress was binding her legs.

The Detective came upon the central stairwell. There was one deck above and two more below. The bottom level was the engineering deck, filled with lots of heavy equipment to hide behind. There would be all of that thick machine fluid and grease all over the place. She looked down at her beaded gown and decided she would search there last. *Why ruin such a beautiful dress if she didn't have to?*

Eighty percent of the cabins were vacant; only the ones for the specially invited guests had been allowed pass card access. Those suites were on the top level. If Nicky had received a key card, there was a slim chance he might head back to his room. It was a place to start.

The Detective ran up the carpeted stairs, and could feel the static electricity generated by her feet. She was almost to the top level when the *Hydra* noticeably shuddered beneath her. She grabbed onto the handrail to steady herself and almost dropped her weapon. The ship was coming to a stop. "Toby, you da' man!" She screamed victoriously.

**

On the bridge, Toby Bilston grabbed the back of the Captain's chair as the ship was thrown into idle. "Whoo," he moaned. "That's gonna upset some stomachs."

"You didn't tell me to slow her down," Sowell argued. "You told me to stop her. This ship has reverse thrusters and can do just that."

The Doctor looked over at Scott Simms, who was holding onto a console in front of him. "Not complaining, just wasn't expecting to hit the brick wall."

Sowell glanced over his shoulder. "So you're Bilston?"

Toby reached around and shook the Captain's hand. "Captain Sowell, I presume?"

The Petty Officer didn't know what to think. He had never been more confused in his entire life. "You two know each other?"

Toby shook his head. "No, just met."

"Would someone like to tell me what the hell is going on here?" Simms demanded.

"Captain," Toby asked. "Can you pull up all of your surveillance camera feeds onto a single monitor?"

Sowell looked over a Jean-Baptiste. "I don't know. Can we?"

The technician began typing. "Yes, sir. Pulling that information up over there," he said, pointing to the opposite wall of the cabin.

A single monitor split itself into over fifty separate sections. "Get over here," Toby ordered Simms. "Keep an eye out for Detective King. Tell me if you spot her."

While the Petty Officer was looking for Lauren, Toby was searching for someone else. He found Coltello on the third deck. "Where is the microphone for your public address system?" he asked the same technician. Jean-Baptiste handed the Doctor a wireless headset. "Just press the button on the earpiece."

"She's on the central staircase!" Simms shouted as he pointed at the screen. "I can't tell what deck though."

Hassan walked over and stared at the artwork on the wall behind her. "She's heading up to deck three."

"Ladies and gentlemen," Toby announced. "This is *not* your Captain. Please remain in the dining room until further notice and kindly ignore the following announcements. So glad you've joined us on Mason Cruise Lines, and we hope you enjoy the rest of your trip!"

"Did you just say that?" Simms complained.

Toby grinned like a kid who'd been caught being naughty. "Something I've always wanted to do."

The Petty Officer rolled his eyes and turned back to the screen.

"Lauren, this is Toby. We're monitoring you on the surveillance cameras. If you can hear me, wave at us."

In the third row, the fourth screen down, the Detective flapped her arms.

"She hears you!" Simms called out.

"Great!" Toby announced. "Nicky's on the third deck. Keep going and make a right when you get to the next floor."

Lauren waved her gun and bounded up the remaining stairs.

"He went right and then took a left at the hallway."

Toby watched Coltello run the length of the passageway, moving from screen to screen as he came into view of the next camera. "This is your conscience, Nicholas," Toby said smiling into the microphone. "Be a good little psychopath and stop running. There's a very well-dressed Detective hot on your trail. Please don't make this any more difficult than it has to be."

Nicky ran up to one of the cameras and stuck out his middle finger.

"I wouldn't have expected any less," Toby said, covering his mouthpiece.

"He's heading toward the front of the ship, Lauren. It looks like he's going outside."

The Doctor looked over at Hassan. "What's out there?"

The technician walked over to the screen that monitored the ship's movement. "If we were at cruising speed, he'd probably be blown overboard, but while we're hovering, he can go anywhere he wants."

"What deck are the lifeboats on?" Simms called out.

Sowell spun in his chair. "The same deck. He's heading for a lifeboat."

"Can he access a lifeboat?" Toby asked.

"Just by pressing a button," Hassan answered. "They're automatically released in case of an emergency."

"Can you cut the power to them?"

Hassan shook his head. "They are part of the evacuation protocols. We can't shut them down."

Toby pressed the button on his earpiece. "Lauren, he's gone out on deck and is heading for one of the lifeboats at the front of the ship. Make a left when you go outside. Be careful out there, the deck is soaking wet!"

"Captain," Jean-Baptiste called out, "LB3 is going over the port side."

Simms pointed to the segment of the monitor that showed the lifeboat davits extending themselves over the railing of the ship. The lifeboat the two metal arms cradled could hold up to thirty passengers. LB3 contained only one. "Here comes Lauren!" The

Petty Officer shouted. "She's slipping and sliding all over the place! She's not going to reach him in time!"

"Pull me up an external diagram of the *Hydra*," Sowell commanded. "Specifically the section where LB3 is being lowered."

Hassan tapped a few keys, and a cross-section of the bow popped up on the central monitor.

"Tell your girl to back off, Doctor Bilston."

"What?" Toby asked.

"Tell her to stop her pursuit. I've got this."

Toby and Simms gathered by the Captain's side. "Tell her!" Sowell barked.

Toby skeptically pressed the button on his earpiece. "Lauren! Stop where you are! Do not proceed. Do you understand me? Do not proceed any further!"

They watched Lauren grab onto the handrail to steady herself. Even on the small screen, she didn't look happy.

"Hassan," Sowell called out. "Once LB3 reaches thirty feet, please transfer pod control to my tablet."

"What are you up to?" Toby asked.

"Captain, you can't!" Hassan warned.

"Just do it, Hassan. Thirty feet!"

The technician hit a few more keys on his console. "Twenty feet, Captain. Transferring pod control to your station."

Sowell stared at the computer tablet attached to the right arm of his chair. "Confirm that pod number two is the one I want."

Jean-Baptiste silently stood next to Hassan. "Pod number two is confirmed, Captain. Twenty-five feet."

Toby looked across at Simms for answers but received a blank stare in return.

"Five seconds," Hassan announced. "Are you sure about this, Captain?"

Sowell pressed his boney finger against the surface of his tablet, and the *Hydra* momentarily shook. The inflatable pod adjacent to the lifeboat exploded outward and was immediately replaced by a backup. The mighty concussion ignited the gas engine on the stern of the raft, which erupted into a flaming ball of debris that hissed into the ocean and slowly burned itself out. Nicky the Knife was instantly cremated, and his ashes spread out to sea. It was a burial most would say was too good for him.

68

The Old Royal Naval Dockyard in Bermuda is also known as King's Wharf. It is home to two piers large enough to accommodate cruise ships: the King's Wharf and the Heritage Wharf. The Sunday morning sky was gray and ominous. A light drizzle was starting to fall as the mooring lines from the *Hydra* were tied up to the King's Wharf. Even the brightly painted pink, yellow, and orange buildings that were a hallmark of the island couldn't lighten the gloom. It was nearly nine in the morning, three hours past the *Hydra*'s estimated time of arrival.

It was customary for a ship's Captain to be the last to disembark, but not this morning. Roy Sowell was the first off, led down the gangway with his arms handcuffed behind his back escorted by two warrant officers from the U.S. Coast Guard Investigative Service (CGIS) and two Masters at Arms from the United States Navy. Admiral Theodore Baer stood at the end of the gangway wearing a weathered poncho. A waiting Humvee would take them to former Kindley Air Force Base, which had been converted into the Bermuda International Airport in nineteen-ninety-five. Captain Sowell would be flown by military transport back to Mayport Station in Jacksonville, which held jurisdiction over the Southern docket, including the Caribbean. He would not live long enough to face trial.

Six Bermudian paramedics boarded the *Hydra* rolling two empty gurneys ahead of them. Fifteen minutes later, they exited the ship accompanying two bodies encased in black zipped bags. The corpses would catch a ride on the same transport as Captain Sowell, but their destination would be Toby Bilston's forensics lab at the Jacksonville Police Department's Central Station.

Two hundred and eighty-six passengers would disembark the hydrofoil and enter the British customs house to be screened. The complaints from the disgruntled guests were non-stop, unlike most of the flights they would have to secure to return to Florida. The Mason Cruise Line would pick up the tab for all the trips, including many charter flights for the more affluent passengers, who refused to fly commercial. The hotel stays incurred by the guests inconvenienced by the airline schedule were also paid for by the cruise line. MCL was doing everything in its power to curb this public relations nightmare. There was no question that when the *Hydra* returned to Jaxport in two days, the media would be swarming the terminal. When the news broke of the deaths of Peter Mason and a coach from the city's triple-A baseball franchise, every news outlet, including the sports networks, wanted the exclusive story.

MCL stock would plummet more than thirty-five percent over the next week. Major League Baseball backed out of any further negotiations for a team in Jacksonville. The City Commission would vote unanimously to invalidate the MCL Ballpark and City Center projects.

Aboard the *Hydra*, the cleaning crew was busily scrubbing down the decks, except for the Oceanwalk, which was cordoned off with yellow police tape. The stewards and room attendants were stripping the linens from each of the suites and cabin—except for the Presidential Suite, which was also barricaded by yellow and black tape.

Captain Ken Hitchcock was already on a flight from Amsterdam to the island to return the *Hydra* back home. There would only be eight passengers on the return voyage; the same eight that were sitting around one of the tables in the dining room sharing a makeshift breakfast of leftover rolls and fresh fruit they were able to scrounge from the kitchen.

Simone Goodman's ankle had been worked on by one of the paramedics and she had her leg up on a second chair. Frank and

Matt Walker's cuts and bruises had been attended to as well.

"So exactly how is it that you're alive again?" Lauren asked as she tore a seeded roll in half.

Frank Walker had already explained everything to his son, but he didn't mind retelling the story for the table. He knew he would have to meet with the police eventually. He signed as he spoke, having taken classes at the University of North Florida as soon as he learned of his son's circumstances. Matt was beaming with pride watching his father interpret for him and Simone. "My wife and I had grown apart during the last year of her life. Matt was away at school, and we didn't want to upset him until we came to an agreement on the terms of our separation. We planned on talking to Matt about it on the weekend she was murdered. We had finally worked out the details, and both believed that Matt was old enough now to understand and handle the situation."

Toby wiped a crumb away from the corner of his mouth. "So obviously she was in bed with someone else the night Magnetti came calling."

"Poor schmuck," Walker said.

"You don't know who he was?" Lauren asked.

Walker shook his head. "Everyone including the police assumed it was me."

David Jannick, with his daughter Hope sitting by his side, spoke up. "We both knew Peter Mason was behind the attempt of Frank's life. It was no secret that he opposed the direction that Mason wanted to take the company. Not a single board meeting went by where they didn't end up toe to toe over Mason's vision for the company."

"So you decided to stay dead?" Petty Officer Simms asked. "What about Matt? Didn't you consider his well-being?"

Frank Walker put his arm around Matt and pulled him close before he continued to translate as he spoke. "Matt was the main reason I did it. If Mason knew I was still alive, he might have made a run at Matt again, or maybe my parents. Believe me, Matt has not been out of my sight for the last ten years. I bought a place in Jacksonville less than a mile from my parents' house to keep tabs on him."

"It was you at the baseball game, wasn't it?" Matt signed.

Walker patted the back of his son's hand. "And at your graduation, and in the back booth of your favorite pizza place." He paused for a moment. "I even hid behind a tree at your grandmother's burial service."

Matt bolted upright. "Oh no," he signed. "What about Grandpa? Grandpa is going to have a heart attack when he finds out you're still alive!"

Frank Walker frowned. "Yeah, we're going to have to think about how we're going to handle the old man."

"So how did you know about everything that Peter Mason was planning?" Toby signed and spoke.

Walker shifted his water glass on the table. "I only entrusted two people with my secret: Dave here, who kept me in the loop from his Miami office, and Gerald Banks, who is Peter Mason's brother-in-law in Jacksonville. They both agreed with my opinion of Mason's business goals and mental stability. Just the fact that I lived through an assassination attempt was all the proof they needed. I was Mason's right-hand man at the time. If I wasn't safe, then no one who worked for him, nor their families, would be safe either."

Scott Simms leaned forward in his chair. "So where did the stolen military technology fit into his scheme?"

"MCL was hemorrhaging cash under Peter Mason's management. With the expansion plans in Jacksonville, his utterly narcissistic need to build a ballpark, and own his own Major League franchise, he had to do something to raise capital. He saw an opportunity, and he took it."

"He killed fifty innocent American servicemen onboard the *Intrepid*," Simms added. "How does a person do that?"

"And don't forget about Arthur Beckworth, a sitting City Commissioner," Walker added. "Anyone who got in his way, or who he thought might be a witness, was expendable. The man was a modern day pirate, just like his father, and his father before him. I wasn't going to let him get anywhere near Matthew. Thanks to Dave, Hope, and Gerald Banks, my son has been the best-kept secret since Colonel Sander's chicken recipe."

"We'll need to talk to Banks," Lauren said.

"You should," Walker agreed. "He's been keeping meticulous records of all of Mason's shady dealings. It'll take forensic accountants years to sift through all of the files."

Toby buttered his third roll. "So, Mason hired Anthony Magnetti to do all of his personal dirty work for him?"

Walker shook his head. "Magnetti was a thug, plain and simple. He would work for whoever paid him. This whole coaching career was just a cover that allowed him to travel unnoticed around the country," he said, looking across the table at Lauren. "You might want to check the cold-case files in the cities that his teams played in. I'd be willing to bet that you'll get a few hits, pardon the pun."

"So I guess that about wraps it up," Toby announced, as he eyed his fourth roll.

The Detective disagreed. "We've got two crime scenes on this ship that you need to analyze and report on Toby. I've got interviews with the staff, and I need to get Mr. Walker's story on the record. I'm sure my superiors are going to want to further investigate the circumstances around Anthony Magnetti's death."

Matt slapped his hand on the table making the shell-shaped pat of butter fall off of Toby's knife. "But my father was just protecting us! He won't be in any trouble, will he?"

Lauren smiled as Toby interpreted for her. "I wouldn't worry too much about it. Your father's actions were certainly justifiable considering the circumstances."

Matt put his arm around his dad. It was like having all of his prayers answered.

Scott Simms snapped off a grape from the plateful of fruit at the center of the table. "I guess since we've gotten our technology back, all of those crimes in international waters will probably be handled by the State Department. I'll be out of the loop, probably reassigned to another cutter," he said, with a hint of sadness in his voice.

Lauren bit into a slice of pineapple. "If you ever decide to take off the uniform, you might have the makings of a pretty good detective," she said.

"The sea is my mistress," Simms professed.

"Did you actually just say that?" Toby said, rolling his eyes. "The boat's not even moving, but suddenly I feel queasy."

Lauren stood up and stretched. "Well, we've got a lot of work to do before we get back to Jaxport, but the first thing I want to do is to find a store on shore where I can pick up a pair of jeans! This dress is cutting off the oxygen supply to all my lady parts."

The Petty Officer was the next to stand up. "Would you mind if I tagged along? The next transport is six hours from now."

"Do you have good taste?" Lauren asked.

Simms smiled. "I'm here with you, aren't I?

Everyone at the table groaned out loud, as Toby translated.

Dave Jannick and his daughter excused themselves. "I have a few things to check on, and then we're going to spend a day or two on the island before heading back to Miami." He shook Frank Walker's hand. "Glad to have you back, buddy. We missed you."

Hope gave Matt a peck on the cheek and did the same to Simone. "I'll see you online, okay?"

Matt stood up and gave her a hug.

"Well," Toby said, tossing his napkin on the table. "I've got a lot of work ahead of me, but I think I'm going to wash up and check out how comfortable the bedding is in one of those suites. It's time for my power nap!"

Frank Walker stood up and walked around the table with his hand outstretched. "Thank you, Doctor Bilston, for all of your help.

I know it took a bit of convincing, but I knew you could be trusted. As the father of a terrific son like Benjamin, I knew you were the person I needed the most on my side."

Toby stood up and grabbed Frank Walker in a bear hug. "You take care of that boy," he said in Walker's ear. "You've got ten years to catch up on, and he's more special than you know. If you need anything, you know where to reach me."

Frank Walker returned the hug. "I might just take you up on that."

Toby pointed across the table at Matt. "You take care of that young lady," he signed. "I have a feeling we'll be working together again."

Frank Walker reached into his pocket and pulled out his cell phone. "Before you leave, Dr. Bilston, would you mind taking a picture of me and my son? I've been waiting a long time for this moment."

Toby took the phone as everyone around the table fought hard to hold back their emotions. "Yes sir, it would be my pleasure."

EPILOGUE

"I like what you've done with the place," Gerald Banks commented, as he took a seat on the sofa in the back office of the One-Eleven Club.

Jimmy Diaz laid down his pen on the purchase order he still needed to sign. "It's been two months. How long was I supposed to wait? I thought it was time to redecorate."

The walls had been painted a pale blue, and the black furniture had been replaced by lighter pieces.

"It almost feels welcoming."

Diaz leaned back. "Welcoming...that's what I was shooting for. Do you want something to drink?"

Banks declined. "No thanks. Any progress yet?"

Diaz stood up and walked around to the front of the desk. He leaned against it and crossed his arms. "There won't be any excavation. We're just covering it all up with topsoil, sod, and a bunch of trees."

"I'll bet those trees grow fast. There's lots of fertilizer in that ground."

Diaz nodded. "I appreciate you buying up the land and turning it into a public park. It was a nice touch naming the place after Commissioner Beckworth."

"It was the least I could do for him and the city," Banks admitted. "It's going to take a long time to earn our reputation back. We had to sell off half the fleet. I'm talking to the government about a hydrofoil contract for the Coast Guard to use against drug runners."

Diaz shrugged. "Drugs are a nasty business. I hope it works out for you."

"Didn't Nicky deal?"

Diaz held up his hand. "That's all behind us now."

"Glad to hear it."

"You're a shrewd businessman just like me," Diaz said. "You'll do what needs to be done to survive."

Banks laughed to himself. "First thing I did was file for divorce. I don't want anything to do with that family anymore."

Diaz nodded. "No one does."

"I'm thinking about changing the name of the company too. Might help people forget."

"What would you change it to?"

Banks shrugged. "Don't know. Got any ideas?"

Diaz pondered the question for a second. "Not really."

"How's the club business going?" Banks asked.

"The employees smile a lot more now," Diaz admitted. "No one has to walk around on eggshells anymore. Now a hammer is just a hammer."

Banks smiled. "That's terrific. So what did you want to talk to be about? I know this isn't a social call. You couldn't call me? You made me walk all the way across the street?"

"Exercise is good for you."

Banks rubbed the front of his pin-striped shirt. "That's what they say, but I wouldn't know."

Diaz uncrossed his arms and leaned back on the desk. "I've been thinking about something ever since I set foot on your ship. You've got financial problems, and my business could always be better. What do you say about a partnership?"

Banks eyes narrowed. "I'm listening."

"You look nervous all of a sudden."

Banks squirmed on the sofa. "That's because I'm nervous all of a sudden."

"You want your company to turn a profit?" Diaz asked.

"No, I think I'd rather continue on the downward spiral my company is in until I drill through to the center of the earth."

"I might have the answer," Diaz announced.

Banks looked skeptical. "Are you waiting for a drum roll?"

"Casinos."

Gerald Banks ran his finger across his lips. "That's not the worst idea I've ever heard. Cruise lines make a considerable chunk of their revenue from onboard gambling. Once a ship is three miles from shore, you're in international waters, casinos are legal."

"Who the hell needs one hundred cabins for a trip that lasts ten hours?" Diaz asked skeptically. "You renovate your ships, and I'll take care of the rest."

Banks stood up and held out his hand. "I like it. Have your lawyer drop off the papers, and once my legal team looks over the contracts, we'll talk designs."

"A drink to celebrate?" Diaz asked.

"Too early for me," Banks admitted.

Diaz held up his glass of bourbon. "Here's to pirates!" He toasted.

"Seriously?" Banks asked.

Diaz smiled. "Arrrrrrrrrr!"

AUTHOR'S NOTE

*I hope you enjoyed reading **A Trace of Revenge**.*

When I first came up with the concept for the story, I wanted it to be mainly about flawed individuals and redemption. Everyone is different. I think we should embrace those distinctions and celebrate what makes each of us unique.

We seem to be living in a time where our differences are dividing us, but if you look back throughout history, that's the way it's always been. I don't want to get too sappy, but if we can focus on what we all have in common and understand that each person's exceptionality adds to the answer, and not subtracts from it, we would all be much better off. It's just something to think about.

Okay, now I'm done.

I would love for you to subscribe to my website www.
lylehoward.com. It doesn't cost a thing, and it's where I'll
keep you updated on the latest news about my work.

If you could take a few minutes to leave an honest review
on my Amazon page, I would really appreciate it. Reviews
are what we writers live for. I read them all and take them to
heart. Here is the link:

https://www.amazon.com/s/ref=nb_sb_noss?url=search-
alias%3Daps&field-keywords=lyle+howard

Feel free to join me on Facebook @ Lyle Howard. It's always
great to make new friends, and you can see what I do with
my free time. I hope to hear from you!

As a little gift, I'm attaching the first chapter of TROUBLE IN
PARADISE. I hope you enjoy it and will read all of my other
stories as well.

Until next time.

I love you all!
LH

TROUBLE IN PARADISE

LYLE HOWARD

The Nocturne

One

23.42° North 75.50° West

60 Nautical Miles West of Andros Island, the Bahamas

Through the night vision lenses, everything was bathed in a soft green glow. The sea looked even more ominous through the specialized glasses as the white caps continued to batter the bow of the thirty-six foot Thunderboat, *Rosalita*.

"Douse the running lights," Pedro Gallinas ordered, pointing at the instrument panel. His younger brother Estaban flipped a switch, and whatever meager light there was illuminating the darkness evaporated. It was a moonless night, and most of the stars were hidden behind a low layer of clouds. An eerie shroud fell over the boat as the warm night air suddenly made all five men in the boat shiver in unison.

The *Rosalita* rolled with the sea, cutting steadily through the void, tracking the faint green target on the edge of their radar. After years of drunken sea tales of a mysterious ship that only appeared at night and vanished at first light, and fruitless searches for this ocean phantom, perhaps the mythological ship was finally going to reveal herself. "Any estimate of her size yet?" The younger brother asked, continuing to scan the pitch dark horizon through his night-vision goggles.

Pedro, who was deftly manning the throttles and wheel, shrugged his shoulders. "I won't know until we get closer. It could be anything. It could just be a freighter like every other time we thought it was her. I've switched the radar back to the five mile range, but I still have no sense of scale. The computer database is searching, so I know this isn't some glitch in the program." Pedro tapped at the radar screen with his finger in frustration. "I just don't understand why it can't identify…."

Gallinas' words were cut off in his throat as a bright green oblong shape suddenly filled half the radar screen. The colossal vessel seemed to materialize out of nowhere. She burst through the curtain of gloom, spewing seawater from her bow like a rabid dog foaming at the mouth. The nose of the ship rose nearly sixty feet out of the water and sliced through the waves like a buzz saw. The formidable *Rosalita* was dwarfed by the enormity of the fast-approaching behemoth.

It took Gallinas' quickest reflexes to slam the steering wheel hard to port and jam the throttles forward to avoid being rammed by the gargantuan ship. The three mercenaries sitting in the stern of the *Rosalita* were flung to the opposite side of the boat and clutched wildly for any sort of handhold as the speedboat nearly went vertical to avoid being cut in half.

"Hang on!" Gallinas screamed. She was immense, he thought. At least three hundred feet stem to stern and, like the *Rosalita*, swathed in dark paint. Gallinas adjusted his night-vision goggles to scrutinize the ship…

There was a helipad astern with a Bell 206 Jet Ranger helicopter secured to its deck with tie down straps. The bridge climbed another two levels from mid-ships, equipped with a full weather and navigational array. He figured this yacht had to cost in the millions, and it was undoubtedly state of the art. But Gallinas's aesthetic appreciation soon gave way to his professional cynicism. There were no running lights, no light from her portholes, not even a glimmer from the bridge. Every ship had to display running lights. It was international law. This desire for stealth concerned him more than anything else.

The *Rosalita* performed like a champion. Gallinas pulled back on the dual throttles and opened a wider distance between the two ships. Once the larger vessel was ahead of them, Gallinas swung the boat gently to port and took up a position in the middle of the larger ship's churning wake.

In the hazy green tint of Galinas's goggles, he pointed at the ship's stern and muttered aloud the single word etched in dark letters on the huge vessel's transom...

"*Nocturne.*"

Two

The three-pronged grappling hook caught on the first attempt. Manuel Salazar, the most nimble of the bandits, climbed to the bow of the *Rosalita* and tied the end of the rope to one of the forward cleats. "The rope ladder won't reach," he said, as he staggered his way back to the Gallinas brothers, swaying at the controls. "She's sitting too high in the water. I'll climb the rope and make my way down to that starboard entry hatch," he said, pointing up to the side of the Nocturne. "The ladder should be plenty long enough from there."

Galinas shifted the throttles to neutral position, allowing the *Rosalita* to be towed along by the more powerful ship.

"Give me five minutes once I get over her railing," Salazar instructed. "Be ready to go!"

The small band of mercenaries nodded as Salazar began pulling himself across the tether to the Nocturne. Once he was halfway between the two ships, the others began taking a quick inventory of their supplies. Each man was an expert in his own specific field. Victor Montoto was the ordnance expert, but as he rummaged inside his backpack, he was concerned that he didn't have enough C-4 to scuttle a ship of this size.

Diego Torres was the close arms expert. His stock of various blades was impressive, to say the least, but all the knives in the world might not fend off a crew large enough to maintain a ship of this size.

The minutes passed as the crew finished their preparations.

Pedro Gallinas tapped his watch and looked at his brother. "Seven minutes…" He whispered warily. "Salazar is better than this. It's been too long."

The younger Galinas brother jerked the slide of his pistol, loading a round into the chamber. "Give him three more minutes. It's a big ship…easy to get lost in."

Two stories above them, the side hatchway suddenly slid open. Through the portal a flashlight blinked on and off as the rope ladder cascaded down the side of the ship.

"See, Pedro?" The younger brother grinned, as he held out a fist for his brother to bump. "You worry too much."

Three

In less than two minutes, all five men were aboard, leaving the *Rosalita* tethered behind and bobbing in the *Nocturne's* wake. As the group tried to get their bearings, each man adjusted the headset they wore, equipped with a tiny L.E.D. light which surrounded them in a ten foot cone of soft white radiance.

"Where's Salazar?" Montoto softly asked, as he took up the lead. "Why isn't he here? Where would he have gone?"

Four circles of light swept the deserted and seemingly endless passageway in different directions, trying to track down their missing comrade. If the *Nocturne* was to be defined by this single hallway, then the ship appeared to have a split personality. Opulent on the exterior, but sparsely decorated within.

Estaban tapped his older brother on the shoulder. "What do you want to do, Pedro?" He whispered, while pressing the button on his headset so each of the soldiers could hear. "Do we abort? What about Salazar? Do we go after him?"

Pedro Gallinas's face was hit simultaneously with three beams of light as each soldier looked at him for the solution. He put up a hand as if to say, *hold on a minute*. "Salazar?" He called out softly into his mouthpiece. "Answer me, Salazar?" He waited. They all waited, but their earpieces sizzled with silence.

"I don't like this, Pedro," Estaban admitted. "This ship feels like death. No running lights. No signs of life. And now, Salazar's gone missing. Something is wrong here. I say we cut and run!"

Pedro Gallinas was adamant. After years of searching, he was actually standing aboard the ship that had only been whispered about after long nights of heavy intoxication. But this was no fantasy …this was real! Wood and metal, brass and fabric…he could reach out and physically touch it. This was no apparition! He had not come this far to turn back now and become one of those people who everyone would look at as if he were *loco*. He needed proof of her existence! The riches that a ship this opulent possessed were probably too extensive for the *Rosalita* to haul. They would have to be very selective of what they robbed.

"And leave Salazar behind? No, we stay," he announced, matter-of-factly. "He is onboard somewhere. We'll find him. We'll split up, and stay in touch. If one of us locates Manuel, tell him we will all rendezvous back at this spot in thirty minutes. No matter what we've found."

They all spontaneously synchronized their watches.

Pedro Gallinas' headlight illuminated each man one by one. "Listen… all of you… It is obvious that we won't be able to take everything with us, so we must be selective in our choices. Take notes on the most valuable items you find and mark their location. We will go back together and collect them once we join back up."

The interior of the *Nocturne* was as stagnant as an abandoned basement. The only audible sounds came from the outside world… the steady anger of the restless ocean through the open hatchway. Estaban Gallinas looked toward the open portal and then at the other two soldiers. They all knew what the younger brother was thinking, and somewhere in the back of their collective minds they all shared his same instinct. *Escape… now!*

"And if we run into interference?" Montoto finally asked.

Pedro Gallinas' eyes narrowed and his voice never wavered. "Then we all do what we do best!"

Four

Victor Montoto spoke with a slight stutter, which was why he chose his words carefully and used them sparingly. This was what he considered his only flaw. Of the five men set to plunder the *Nocturne*, he was the playboy of the group. Women found his silence mysterious, while men found it menacing. All but a handful of people knew that the handsome features masked behind the dark makeup belied a very sadistic temperament and a fascination from childhood with fire, explosions, and the mayhem that ensued from both.

Slowly, Montoto inched his way down an unfamiliar passageway, with the narrow beam from his headlamp revealing very little. As the circle of light swept back and forth ahead of him, the desolation of the ship really surprised him. There were no pictures adorning the bulkheads, no chairs or tables that he could see. The corridor's only remarkable feature was the crimson red carpeting that appeared to floor the entire deck.

Montoto suddenly stopped short and held his breath when he thought he saw a shadow flutter through the edge of his light. The wraith made no sound. He waited, not breathing... listening. Slowly and deliberately he shifted into a shooting stance and raised his pistol into the light at eye level. More comfortable with creating a homemade pipe bomb than firing a gun, he kept the barrel focused at the center of the beam. This would prove to be a fatal mistake.

The assailant struck from behind, wrapping one arm around Montoto's shoulders and the other across his face. Without hesitation his head was twisted in the opposite direction of his body, snapping his neck and spine. His trigger finger involuntarily twitched, sending a salvo of bullets into the empty corridor. With minimal effort and flawless efficiency, his lifeless body was whisked away into the darkness.

Five

Light from his headset glinted off the two eight inch blades Diego Torres held before him. After making his way up one deck, Torres came to a stop at the end of yet another long passageway. Doors with ornate gold handles lined each side of the corridor, reminding him of the numerous foreign palaces he had already plundered as a soldier for hire in the Far East.

Torres went wherever he was needed, but for the last three years since he had teamed up with the Gallinas Brothers, he no longer felt the inclination to wholesale his particular set of skills. His father, being a long time circus performer on the European circuit, had trained him in the fine art of wielding and throwing knives. By the time he was in his teens, the student had surpassed the master, with Diego being able to split an apple in midair from nearly fifty feet away. The circus life was not for him, though. His skills were better suited to a more adventurous and prosperous life.

Each door handle he jiggled silently failed to budge. He was halfway down the corridor when he realized something very peculiar. With the hundreds of staterooms and equipment rooms on this massive vessel, there were no signs or markings anywhere to be seen. No way to differentiate one location from another without memorization or perhaps a diagram. *Very strange.*

Suddenly... there was movement...

There... ahead on the left... behind the next door. He definitely heard something move or shift behind it. Not wanting to sheath either weapon, he decided to use his right foot to test the handle.

The beam from his headlight tightened on the lever as the heel of his boot forced down the bar. The door flew open and Diego lunged inside with both blades slashing the air in defensive figure eights. A shadow flitted through his light, followed by the most horrendous agony he had ever felt.

He looked down at his right arm only to witness that his hand was missing, severed cleanly at the wrist. Blood sprayed around the cabin as he let go of the other blade and collapsed to his knees, frantically attempting to stem the torrent pumping out of his amputated wrist.

A single scream pierced the air. *Just one.* Then there was a nauseating crunch as the final death blow was dealt, and Torres' still twitching body was whisked away into the shadows.

Six

There was no way in hell they were going their separate ways. Not after hearing the scream and the chorus of gunshots. "What do we do?" Estaban asked his older brother.

The barren passageway in which the two brothers stood smelled of salt air from the open hatch. Pedro Gallinas walked over to the portal and looked down at the *Rosalita*. She was still attached to the grappling rope and bobbed in the darkness alongside the *Nocturne*. Only twenty minutes had passed since the five soldiers had breached her, but it felt like an eternity. The decisions that he would have to make in the next few seconds would alter their lives forever.

The older Gallinas brother stepped back from the only opening that lead to freedom and drew his pistol from its holster. "We told them half an hour and we will give them half an hour."

Estaban Gallinas did not share the same sense of loyalty as his older brother. These were cutthroats, criminals, deviants each in their own fashion. He owed nothing to them. He knew damned well that if the situations were reversed, they wouldn't hesitate to abandon him. "So, what do we do for ten minutes, Pedro? Just stand here and do nothing?"

"Do you want to go look for them?" His older brother inquired, raising a skeptical eyebrow.

Estaban grimaced as he looked down at his watch. "No, we can wait."

As they paced the passageway in different directions, the lights from their headsets danced off the barren walls and deck. "Why is a ship this decadent lacking any style or furnishings?" Estaban asked, loud enough for his brother to hear.

Pedro Gallinas looked up at the ceiling, letting the beam illuminate nothing but a smooth steel surface. "This is just the gangway, Estaban. With access to the sea air, they probably don't want valuables kept where the corrosive salt air can damage them."

Estaban shook his head. "But nothing, Pedro? No paintings? No curtains? No photographs? No pottery or sculptures? Something isn't right here. You know it and I know it."

Pedro walked back to where his brother was standing tapping his right foot nervously. "So what do you want to do, little brother? Leave our men behind? Then what becomes of us? How do we ever recruit another crew if we suddenly have the reputation of being cowards?" He put his hands on his brother's shoulders. "Now get hold of yourself. It sounds like a few of them have met some resistance, but there's nothing, and I mean nothing, that these guys can't handle…"

Moving from left to right, a shadow streaked through the beam cast by Estaban's headlight. "What the hell was that? Did you see it?"

Pedro Gallinas raised his pistol and his finger to his mouth to quiet him. Both brothers went silent. Even though both brothers were sweating profusely, they felt a frosty shiver shroud them like they had both just taken the ice bucket challenge.

Again, there was a glimpse of something that stayed just beyond the reach of their lights. Pedro fired once into the darkness. The bullet sparked as it hit the steel bulkhead at the far end of the passageway striking nothing in its path.

The phantom shape was on Estaban's side now, staying hidden just beyond the edge of his headlamp. Pedro blindly shot again, barely missing his brother's head. For the second time, the bullet hit nothing but steel bulkhead.

Estaban stared at his older brother not even concerned that he had just come mere inches from having his brains blown out. "Screw the ten minutes," he said to his older brother. "You can stay if you want to, Pedro, but I'm getting the hell off this ship!"

With still no reply from anyone on his team, and much to Pedro's regret, he chose survival over fortune.

The Gallinas brothers were down the rope ladder in seconds, taking two rungs at a time. Once onboard the *Rosalita*, Pedro yelled to his brother. "Cut the line!"

Estaban didn't have to be told twice; he pulled out a blade he kept sheathed around his ankle and with one swift thrust cleanly sliced through the rope as Pedro gunned *Rosalita's* twin engines. The two men breathed a sigh of relief as their speedboat began to open the distance from the *Nocturne*.

"Are you over it now?" Estaban asked, as he shouldered past his older brother, standing at the helm. "Are you finally over your obsession with that ship? *Es el Diablo!*"

A million thoughts were racing through Pedro Gallinas's mind. The least of which was his fixation on the mysterious vessel and what he *thought* they saw. No one would ever believe them. How would he explain his missing crew? What credible excuse could he come up with for their disappearance? They were probably better off never mentioning this night again, but there would be questions. He turned the *Rosalita* southeast and headed home toward Andros Town.

The warm sea air was like a soothing elixir blowing through his hair, drying the perspiration on his forehead. The *Nocturne* was nothing more than a miniscule blip on the edge of the radar screen when his brother called out to him.

The younger Gallinas brother was hunched over a dark canvas bag lying on the deck. "Pedro, why would Montoto's backpack still be on the boat? Didn't he have it with him?"

Suddenly Pedro Gallinas's hands began shaking uncontrollably on the steering wheel. "Don't open it!" He yelled, over *Rosalita's* roaring engines. But it was too late.

Estaban Gallinas stared down at the satchel full of C-4 explosives and the digital timer that had been attached and activated. The blinking red numbers were counting down and now read... 00:01

CPSIA information can be obtained
at www.ICGtesting.com
Printed in the USA
LVHW022315210319
611507LV00007B/108